THE NEW HUGO WINNERS VOLUME II

Presented by

ISAAC ASIMOV

BAEN
BOOKS

THE NEW HUGO WINNERS, VOLUME II

This is a work of fiction. All the characters and events portrayed in this book are fictional, and any resemblance to real people or incidents is purely coincidental.

A Baen Books Original

Baen Publishing Enterprises
P.O. Box 1403
Riverdale, N.Y. 10471

ISBN: 0-671-72103-8

Cover art by Bob Eggleton

First printing, January 1992

Distributed by
SIMON & SCHUSTER
1230 Avenue of the Americas
New York, N.Y. 10020

Printed in the United States of America

Contents

Contents

Credits

INTRODUCTION

Before the year 1960, magazine science fiction could be divided into four stages, each dominated by a particular personality or personalities.

(1) *The Twenties*, which covers the ground between 1926 and 1933. The dominant personality was then Hugo Gernsback and the dominant magazine *Amazing Stories*. It was the time of the introduction of the superscience story by E. E. Smith, Ph.D., and John W. Campbell, Jr. Smith's "The Skylark of Space" was the great story of the period. It was a time, in addition, of mad scientists and giant insects and lost civilizations. It was, in fact, just right for the junior high school kid that I then was.

(2) *The Thirties*, which covers the ground between 1933 and 1938. The dominant personality was then F. Orlin Tremaine, and the dominant magazine was *Astounding Stories*. It was the time of the "thought-variant" and of such writers as Nat Schachner and Jack Williamson. Williamson's "The Legion of Space" was the great story of the period, with Weinbaum's "A Martian Odyssey" as a prelude to the future of science fiction. The accent was on daring, mind-stretching plots, and it was, in fact, just right for the teen-ager that I then was.

(3) *The Forties*, which covers the ground between 1938 and 1949. The dominant personality was then John W. Campbell, Jr., and the dominant magazine was *Astounding Science Fiction*. It was the time of scientific realism, when mad scientists and wild plots were both eschewed in favor of scientists and engineers who sounded like scientists and engineers. It was the time of such writers as Robert Heinlein, A. E. van Vogt, Arthur Clarke, and, if I may be allowed to say it, Isaac Asimov. The great

stories of the period included such items as van Vogt's "Black Destroyer", Heinlein's "Blowups Happen," and Asimov's "Nightfall," and his "Foundation" series. The time was just right for the young beginning writer that I then was.

(4) *The Fifties*, which covers the ground from 1949 to 1960. The dominant personality was H. L. Gold and the dominant magazine was *Galaxy*. It was a time when human values and social comment were added to the Campbellesque story, when Campbell himself still continued the older tradition of *Astounding* and when Anthony Boucher in the new magazine *Fantasy and Science Fiction* stressed literary values that served as a prelude to the future of science fiction. The great writers of the period were such men as Theodore Sturgeon, Fred Pohl, Clifford D. Simak, and (still) Isaac Asimov. The typical stories of the period were such stories as Alfred Bester's "The Demolished Man," Pohl's and Cyril Kornbluth's "The Space Merchants" and Asimov's "The Ugly Little Boy." The time was just right for the mature writer I then was.

But then came 1960, and something happened.

In the first place, comic magazines, picture magazines, and television had all combined to change the face of fiction. The pulp magazines with their enormous quantities of semiliterate, mass-produced adventure-oriented stories, disappeared. The slick magazines with their polished romances either disappeared or shifted largely to nonfiction. Book publishers grew less interested in fiction, too, except for sure best-sellers.

In the second place, the literary puritanism that had dominated American literature lessened and disappeared. It became possible to make use of vulgarisms in one's writing and to be as clinical as one wished about sex.

The result of these changes was that the number of ambitious young would-be writers (and their numbers did not decrease) turned to those forms of popular fiction that survived the onslaught of the visual media, and one of these was science fiction. Suddenly, there was a vast increase in the number of science fiction writers, and they brought with them the kind of fiction they would ordinarily have poured into other, more "respectable" media.

They were much more "literary" than the earlier writers had been. They indulged in stylistic experimentation, in multiple layers of meaning, in involved and abstract (and often obscure) writing. They made free use of sex, violence and vulgar language. The accent shifted away from solid science fiction in the direction of social commentary and outright fantasy. It became so large and diverse a field that there was no longer a dominating personality or magazine. Indeed, the novel, particularly in its paperback form, became far more important than all the magazines put together.

It was no longer the sort of thing that was just right for me. Beginning in 1960, I virtually retired from science fiction and involved myself almost exclusively with nonfiction of one sort or another.

In the 1980s, I returned to science fiction as a result of the anguished demands of my editors at Doubleday but I continued to write in the style of the 1960s. I was not capable of advancing beyond it. I expected the worst (in fact, I warned Doubleday in the strongest terms that I was a back number) but I didn't get it. My new books turned out to be very popular, from which I deduce that there are a number of readers as backward and as old-fashioned as I am.

Nevertheless, the fact remains that I am out of touch with post-1960 science fiction. This has made the preparation of these "Hugo Winner" volumes a peculiar problem for me.

In the first place, I often do not know the various prize-winning authors, or have been out of touch with them for a long time. For another, I am amazed at the advanced notions of the fans, who, once a year, select prize-winning stories by vote. The winners are not those I would have selected, for they are usually far too good for my aging mind, stuck as it is with the values of the 1940s and 1950s.

Therefore, I'm just going to sit back and congratulate you on having the opportunity to read this collection of fine stories.

Enjoy!

—Isaac Asimov

1986
44th World SF Convention Atlanta

24 Views of Mount Fuji, by Hokusai
by Roger Zelazny
Paladin of the Lost Hour
by Harlan Ellison
Fermi and Frost by Frederik Pohl

24 Views of Mt. Fuji, by Hokusai

by Roger Zelazny

1. *Mt. Fuji from Owari*

Kit lives, though he is buried not far from here; and I am dead, though I watch the days-end light pinking cloudstreaks above the mountain in the distance, a tree in the foreground for suitable contrast. The old barrelman is dust; his cask, too, I daresay. Kit said that he loved me and I said I loved him. We were both telling the truth. But love can mean many things. It can be an instrument of aggression or a function of disease.

My name is Mari. I do not know whether my life will fit the forms I move to meet on this pilgrimage. Nor death. Not that tidiness becomes me. So begin anywhere. Either arcing of the circle, like that vanished barrel's hoop, should lead to the same place. I have come to kill. I bear the hidden death, to cast against the secret life. Both are intolerable. I have weighed them. If I were an outsider I do not know which I would choose. But I am here, me, Mari, following the magic footsteps. Each moment is entire, though each requires its past. I do not understand causes, only sequences. And I am long weary of reality-reversal games. Things will have to grow clearer with each successive layer of my journey, and like the delicate play of light upon my magic mountain they must change. I must die a little and live a little each moment.

I begin here because we lived near here. I visited the place earlier. It is, of course, changed. I recall his hand upon my arm, his sometime smiling face, his stacks of

7

books, the cold, flat eye of his computer terminal, his hands again, positioned in meditation, his smile different then. Distant and near. His hands, upon me. The power of his programs, to crack codes, to build them. His hands. Deadly. Who would have thought he would surrender those rapid-striking weapons, delicate instruments, twisters of bodies? Or myself? Paths . . . Hands . . .

I have come back. It is all. I do not know whether it is enough.

The old barrel-maker within the hoop of his labor . . . Half-full, half-empty, half-active, half-passive . . . Shall I make a yin-yang of that famous print? Shall I let it stand for Kit and myself? Shall I view it as the great Zero? Or as infinity? Or is all of this too obvious? One of those observations best left unstated? I am not always subtle. Let it stand. Fuji stands within it. And is it not Fuji one must climb to give an accounting of one's life before God or the gods?

I have no intention of climbing Fuji and accounting for myself, to God or to anything else. Only the insecure and the uncertain require justification. I do what I must. If the deities have any questions they can come down from Fuji and ask me. Otherwise, this is the closest commerce between us. That which transcends should only be admired from afar.

Indeed. I of all people should know this. I, who have tasted transcendence. I know, too, that death is the only god who comes when you call.

Traditionally, the *henro*—the pilgrim—would dress all in white. I do not. White does not become me, and my pilgrimage is a private thing, a secret thing, for so long as I can keep it so. I wear a red blouse today and a light khaki jacket and slacks, tough leather hiking shoes; I have bound my hair; a pack on my back holds my belongings. I do carry a stick, however, partly for the purpose of support, which I require upon occasion; partly, too, as a weapon should the need arise. I am adept at its use in both these functions. A staff is also said to symbolize one's faith in a pilgrimage. Faith is beyond me. I will settle for hope.

In the pocket of my jacket is a small book containing reproductions of twenty-four of Hokusai's forty-six prints of Mt. Fuji. It was a gift, long ago. Tradition also stands against a pilgrim's traveling alone, for practical purposes of safety as well as for companionship. The spirit of Hokusai, then, is my companion, for surely it resides in the places I would visit if it resides anywhere. There is no other companion I would desire at the moment, and what is a Japanese drama without a ghost?

Having viewed this scene and thought my thoughts and felt my feelings, I have begun. I have lived a little, I have died a little. My way will not be entirely on foot. But much of it will be. There are certain things I must avoid in this journey of greetings and farewells. Simplicity is my cloak of darkness, and perhaps the walking will be good for me.

I must watch my health.

2. Mt. Fuji from a Teahouse at Yoshida

I study the print: A soft blueness to the dawn sky, Fuji to the left, seen through the teahouse window by two women; other bowed, drowsing figures like puppets on a shelf. . . .

It is not this way here, now. They are gone, like the barrel-maker—the people, the teahouse, that dawn. Only the mountain and the print remain of the moment. But that is enough.

I sit in the dining room of the hostel where I spent the night, my breakfast eaten, a pot of tea before me. There are other diners present, but none near me. I chose this table because of the window's view, which approximates that of the print. Hokusai, my silent companion, may be smiling. The weather was sufficiently clement for me to have camped again last night, but I am deadly serious in my pilgrimage to vanished scenes

in this life-death journey I have undertaken. It is partly a
matter of seeking and partly a matter of waiting. It is quite
possible that it may be cut short at any time. I hope not,
but the patterns of life have seldom corresponded to my
hopes—or, for that matter, to logic, desire, emptiness, or
any patterns of my own against which I have measured them.

All of this is not the proper attitude and occupation
for a fresh day. I will drink my tea and regard the mountain. The sky changes even as I watch. . . .

Changes . . . I must be careful on departing this place.
There are precincts to be avoided, precautions to be taken.
I have worked out all of my movements—from putting
down the cup, rising, turning, recovering my gear, walking—until I am back in the country again. I must still make
patterns, for the world is a number-line, everywhere dense.
I am taking a small chance in being here.

I am not so tired as I had thought I would be from
all yesterday's walking, and I take this as a good sign. I
have tried to keep in decent shape, despite everything.
A scroll hangs on the wall to my right depicting a tiger,
and I want this, too, for a good omen. I was born in the
Year of the Tiger, and the strength and silent movements
of the big striped cat are what I most need. I drink to you,
Shere Khan, cat who walks by himself. We must be hard
at the right time, soft at the proper moment. Timing . . .

We'd an almost telepathic bond to begin with, Kit and
I. It drew us to each other, grew stronger in our years
together. Empathy, proximity, meditation . . . Love? Then
love can be a weapon. Spin its coin and it comes up yang.

Burn bright, Shere Khan, in the jungle of the heart.
This time we are the hunter. Timing is all—and *suki*, the
opening . . .

I watch the changes of the sky until a uniform brightness is achieved, holds steady. I finish my tea. I rise and
fetch my gear, don my backpack, take up my staff. I head
for the short hall which leads to a side door.

"Madam! Madam!"

It is one of the place's employees, a small man with a
startled expression.

"Yes?"

He nods at my pack.

"You are leaving us?"

"I am."

"You have not checked out."

"I have left payment for my room in an envelope on the dresser. It says 'cashier' on it. I learned the proper amount last night."

"You must check out at the desk."

"I did not check in at the desk. I am not checking out at the desk. If you wish, I will accompany you back to the room, to show you where I left the payment."

"I am sorry, but it must be done with the cashier."

"I am sorry also, but I have left payment and I will not go to the desk."

"It is irregular. I will have to call the manager."

I sigh.

"No," I say. "I do not want that. I will go to the lobby and handle the checking out as I did the checking in."

I retrace my steps. I turn left toward the lobby.

"Your money," he says. "If you left it in the room you must get it and bring it."

I shake my head.

"I left the key, also."

I enter the lobby. I go to the chair in the corner, the one farthest from the work area. I seat myself.

The small man has followed me.

"Would you tell them at the desk that I wish to check out?" I ask him.

"Your room number . . . ?"

"Seventeen."

He bows slightly and crosses to the counter. He speaks with a woman, who glances at me several times. I cannot hear their words. Finally, he takes a key from her and departs. The woman smiles at me.

"He will bring the key and the money from your room," she says. "Have you enjoyed your stay?"

"Yes," I answer. "If it is being taken care of, I will leave now."

I begin to rise.

"Please wait," she says, "until the paperwork is done and I have given you your receipt."

"I do not want the receipt."

"I am required to give it to you."

I sit back down. I hold my staff between my knees. I clasp it with both hands. If I try to leave now she will probably call the manager. I do not wish to attract even more attention to myself. I wait. I control my breathing. I empty my mind.

After a time the man returns. He hands her the key and the envelope. She shuffles papers. She inserts a form into a machine. There is a brief stutter of keys. She withdraws the form and regards it. She counts the money in my envelope.

"You have the exact amount, Mrs. Smith. Here is your receipt."

She peels the top sheet from the bill.

There comes a peculiar feeling in the air, as if a lightning stroke had fallen here but a second ago. I rise quickly to my feet.

"Tell me," I say, "is this place a private business or part of a chain?"

I am moving forward by then, for I know the answer before she says it. The feeling is intensified, localized.

"We are a chain," she replies, looking about uneasily.

"With central bookkeeping?"

"Yes."

Behind the special place where the senses come together to describe reality I see the form of a batlike epigon taking shape beside her. She already feels its presence but does not understand. My way is *mo chih ch'u*, as the Chinese say—immediate action, without thought or hesitation—as I reach the desk, place my staff upon it at the proper angle, lean forward as if to take my receipt and nudge the staff so that it slides and falls, passing over the countertop, its small metal tip coming to rest against the housing of the computer terminal. Immediately, the overhead lights go out. The epigon collapses and dissipates.

"Power failure," I observe, raising my staff and turning away. "Good day."

I hear her calling for a boy to check the circuit box.

I make my way out of the lobby and visit a rest room, where I take a pill, just in case. Then I return to the short hall, traverse it, and depart the building. I had assumed it would happen sooner or later, so I was not unprepared. The microminiature circuitry within my staff was sufficient to the occasion, and while I would rather it had occurred later, perhaps it was good for me that it happened when it did. I feel more alive, more alert from this demonstration of danger. This feeling, this knowledge, will be of use to me.

And it did not reach me. It accomplished nothing. The basic situation is unchanged. I am happy to have benefited at so small a price.

Still, I wish to be away and into the countryside, where I am strong and the other is weak.

I walk into the fresh day, a piece of my life upon the breakfast moment's mountain.

3. Mt. Fuji from Hodogaya

I find a place of twisted pines along the Tokaido, and I halt to view Fuji through them. The travelers who pass in the first hour or so of my vigil do not look like Hokusai's, but no matter. The horse, the sedan chair, the blue garments, the big hats—faded into the past, traveling forever on the print now. Merchant or nobleman, thief or servant—I choose to look upon them as pilgrims of one sort or another, if only into, through, and out of life. My morbidity, I hasten to add, is excusable, in that I have required additional medication. I am stable now, however, and do not know whether medication or meditation is responsible for my heightened perception of the subtleties of the light. Fuji seems almost to move within my gazing.

Pilgrims . . . I am minded of the wanderings of Matsuo

Bashō, who said that all of us are travelers every minute of our lives. I recall also his reflections upon the lagoons of Matsushima and Kisagata—the former possessed of a cheerful beauty, the latter the beauty of a weeping countenance. I think upon the complexion and expressions of Fuji and I am baffled. Sorrow? Penance? Joy? Exaltation? They merge and shift. I lack the genius of Bashō to capture them all in a single character. And even he . . . I do not know. Like speaks to like, but speech must cross a gulf. Fascination always includes some lack of understanding. It is enough for this moment, to view.

Pilgrims . . . I think, too, of Chaucer as I regard the print. His travelers had a good time. They told each other dirty stories and romances and tales with morals attached. They ate and they drank and they kidded each other. Canterbury was their Fuji. They had a party along the way. The book ends before they arrive. Fitting.

I am not a humorless bitch. It may be that Fuji is really laughing at me. If so, I would like very much to join in. I really do not enjoy moods such as this, and a bit of meditation interruptus would be welcome if only the proper object would present itself. Life's soberer mysteries cannot be working at top-speed all the time. If they can take a break, I want one, too. Tomorrow, perhaps . . .

Damn! My presence must at least be suspected, or the epigon would not have come. Still, I have been very careful. A suspicion is not a certainty, and I am sure that my action was sufficiently prompt to preclude confirmation. My present location is beyond reach as well as knowledge. I have retreated into Hokusai's art.

I could have lived out the rest of my days upon Oregon's quiet coast. The place was not without its satisfactions. But I believe it was Rilke who said that life is a game we must begin playing before we have learned the rules. Do we ever? Are there really rules?

Perhaps I read too many poets.

But something that seems a rule to me requires I make this effort. Justice, duty, vengeance, defense—must I weigh each of these and assign it a percentage of that which moves me? I am here because I am here, because I am following rules—whatever they may be. My understanding is limited to sequences.

His is not. He could always make the intuitive leap. Kit was a scholar, a scientist, a poet. Such riches. I am smaller in all ways.

Kokuzo, guardian of those born in the Year of the Tiger, break this mood. I do not want it. It is not me. Let it be an irritation of old lesions, even a renewal of the demyelination. But do not let it be me. And end it soon. I am sick in my heart and my reasons are good ones. Give me the strength to detach myself from them, Catcher in the Bamboo, lord of those who wear the stripes. Take away the bleakness, gather me together, inform me with strength. Balance me.

I watch the play of light. From somewhere I hear the singing of children. After a time a gentle rain begins to fall. I don my poncho and continue to watch. I am very weary, but I want to see Fuji emerge from the fog which has risen. I sip water and a bit of brandy. Only the barest outline remains. Fuji is become a ghost mountain within a Taoist painting. I wait until the sky begins to darken. I know that the mountain will not come to me again this day, and I must find a dry place to sleep. These must be my lessons from Hodogaya: Tend to the present. Do not try to polish ideals. Have sense enough to get in out of the rain.

I stumble off through a small wood. A shed, a barn, a garage. . . . Anything that stands between me and the sky will do.

After a time I find such a place. No god addresses my dreaming.

4. Mt. Fuji from the Tamagawa

I compare the print with the reality. Not bad this time. The horse and the man are absent from the shore, but there is a small boat out on the water. Not the same sort

of boat, to be sure, and I cannot tell whether it bears
firewood, but it will suffice. I would be surprised to find
perfect congruence. The boat is moving away from me.
The pink of the dawn sky is reflected upon the water's
farther reaches and from the snow-streaks on Fuji's dark
shoulder. The boatman in the print is poling his way
outward. Charon? No, I am more cheerful today than I
was at Hodogaya. Too small a vessel for the *Narrenschiff*,
too slow for the Flying Dutchman. "La navicella." Yes.
"La navicella del mio ingegno"—"the little bark of my
wit" on which Dante hoisted sail for that second realm,
Purgatory. Fuji then . . . Perhaps so. The hells beneath,
the heavens above, Fuji between—way station, stopover,
terminal. A decent metaphor for a pilgrim who could use
a purge. Appropriate. For it contains the fire and the
earth as well as the air, as I gaze across the water. Transi-
tion, change. I am passing.

The serenity is broken and my reverie ended as a light
airplane, yellow in color, swoops out over the water from
someplace to my left. Moments later the insectlike buzzing of its single engine reaches me. It loses altitude
quickly, skimming low over the water, then turns and
traces its way back, this time swinging in above the shore-
line. As it nears the point where it will pass closest to
me, I detect a flash of reflected light within the cockpit.
A lens? If it is, it is too late to cover myself against its
questing eye. My hand dips into my breast pocket and
withdraws a small gray cylinder of my own. I flick off its
endcaps with my thumbnail as I raise it to peer through
the eyepiece. A moment to locate the target, another to
focus . . .

The pilot is a man, and as the plane banks away I
catch only his unfamiliar profile. Was that a gold earring
upon his left earlobe?

The plane is away, in the direction from which it had
come. Nor does it return.

I am shaken. Someone had flown by for the sole purpose of taking a look at me. How had he found me? And
what did he want? If he represents what I fear most,

then this is a completely different angle of attack than any I had anticipated.

I clench my hand into a fist and I curse softly. Unprepared. Is that to be the story of my entire life? Always ready for the wrong thing at the right time? Always neglecting the thing that matters most?

Like Kendra?

She is under my protection, is one of the reasons I am here. If I succeed in this enterprise, I will have fulfilled at least a part of my obligation to her. Even if she never knows, even if she never understands . . .

I push all thoughts of my daughter from my mind. If he even suspected . . .

The present. Return to the present. Do not spill energy into the past. I stand at the fourth station of my pilgrimage and someone takes my measure. At the third station an epigon tried to take form. I took extreme care in my return to Japan. I am here on false papers, traveling under an assumed name. The years have altered my appearance somewhat and I have assisted them to the extent of darkening my hair and my complexion, defying my customary preferences in clothing, altering my speech patterns, my gait, my eating habits—all of these things easier for me than most others because of the practice I've had in the past. The past . . . Again, damn it! Could it have worked against me even in this matter? Damn the past! An epigon and a possible human observer this close together. Yes, I am normally paranoid and have been for many years, for good reason. I cannot allow my knowledge of the fact to influence my judgment now, however. I must think clearly.

I see three possibilities. The first is that the flyby means nothing, that it would have occurred had anyone else been standing here—or no one. A joyride, or a search for something else.

It may be so, but my survival instinct will not permit me to accept it. I must assume that this is not the case. Therefore, someone is looking for me. This is either connected with the manifestation of the epigon or it is not.

If it is not, a large bag of live bait has just been opened at my feet and I have no idea how to begin sorting through the intertwined twistings. There are so many possibilities from my former profession, though I had considered all of these long closed off. Perhaps I should not have. Seeking there for causes seems an impossible undertaking.

The third possibility is the most frightening: that there is a connection between the epigon and the flight. If things have reached the point where both epigons and human agents can be employed, then I may well be doomed to failure. But even more than this, it will mean that the game has taken on another, awesome dimension, an aspect which I had never considered. It will mean that everyone on Earth is in far greater peril than I had assumed, that I am the only one aware of it and that my personal duel has been elevated to a struggle of global proportions. I cannot take the risk of assigning it to my paranoia now. I must assume the worst.

My eyes overflow. I know how to die. I once knew how to lose with grace and detachment. I can no longer afford this luxury. If I bore any hidden notion of yielding, I banish it now. My weapon is a frail one but I must wield it. If the gods come down from Fuji and tell me, "Daughter, it is our will that you desist," I must still continue in this to the end, though I suffer in the hells of the *Yü Li Ch'ao Chuan* forever. Never before have I realized the force of fate.

I sink slowly to my knees. For it is a god that I must vanquish.

My tears are no longer for myself.

5. Mt. Fuji from Fukagawa in Edo

Tokyo. Ginza and confusion. Traffic and pollution. Noise, color and faces, faces, faces. I once loved scenes such as this, but I have been away from cities for too long. And to return to a city such as this is overpowering, almost paralyzing.

Neither is it the old Edo of the print, and I take yet another chance in coming here, though caution rides my every move.

It is difficult to locate a bridge approachable from an angle proper to simulate the view of Fuji beneath it, in the print. The water is of the wrong color and I wrinkle my nose at the smell; this bridge is not that bridge; there are no peaceful fisher-folk here; and gone the greenery. Hokusai exhales sharply and stares as I do at Fuji-san beneath the metal span. His bridge was a graceful rainbow of wood, product of gone days.

Yet there is something to the thrust and dream of any bridge. Hart Crane could find poetry in those of this sort. "Harp and altar, of the fury fused . . ."

And Nietzsche's bridge that is humanity, stretching on toward the superhuman . . .

No. I do not like that one. Better had I never become involved with that which transcends. Let it be my *pons asinorum*.

With but a slight movement of my head I adjust the perspective. Now it seems as if Fuji supports the bridge and without his presence it will be broken like Bifrost, preventing the demons of the past from attacking our present Asgard—or perhaps the demons of the future from storming our ancient Asgard.

I move my head again. Fuji drops. The bridge remains intact. Shadow and substance.

The backfire of a truck causes me to tremble. I am only just arrived and I feel I have been here too long. Fuji seems too distant and I too exposed. I must retreat.

Is there a lesson in this or only a farewell?

A lesson, for the soul of the conflict hangs before my eyes: I will not be dragged across Nietzsche's bridge.

Come, Hokusai, *ukiyo-e* Ghost of Christmas Past, show me another scene.

6. Mt. Fuji from Kajikazawa

Misted, mystic Fuji over water. Air that comes clean to my nostrils. There is even a fisherman almost where he should be, his pose less dramatic than the original, his garments more modern, above the infinite Fourier series of waves advancing upon the shore.

On my way to this point I visited a small chapel surrounded by a stone wall. It was dedicated to Kwannon, goddess of compassion and mercy, comforter in times of danger and sorrow. I entered. I loved her when I was a girl, until I learned that she was really a man. Then I felt cheated, almost betrayed. She was Kwan Yin in China, and just as merciful, but she came there from India, where she had been a bodhisattva named Avalokitesvara, a man—"the Lord Who Looks Down with Compassion." In Tibet he is Chen-re-zi—"He of the Compassionate Eyes"—who gets incarnated regularly as the Dalai Lama. I did not trust all of this fancy footwork on his/her part, and Kwannon lost something of her enchantment for me with this smattering of history and anthropology. Yet I entered. We revisit the mental landscape of childhood in times of trouble. I stayed for a time and the child within me danced for a moment, then fell still.

I watch the fisherman above those waves, smaller versions of Hokusai's big one, which has always symbolized death for me. The little deaths rolling about him, the man hauls in a silver-sided catch. I recall a tale from the Arabian Nights, another of American Indian origin. I might also see Christian symbolism, or a Jungian archetype. But I remember that Ernest Hemingway told Bernard Berenson that the secret of his greatest book was that there was no symbolism. The sea was the sea, the old man an old man, the boy a boy, the marlin a marlin, and the sharks the same as other sharks. People empower these things themselves, groping beneath the surface, always looking for more. With me it is at least understandable. I spent my earliest years in Japan, my later childhood in the United States. There is a part of me which likes to see things through allusions and touched with mystery. And the American part never trusts anything and is always looking for the real story behind the front one.

As a whole, I would say that it is better not to trust, though lines of interpretation must be drawn at some point before the permutations of causes in which I indulge overflow my mind. I am so, nor will I abandon this quality of character which has served me well in the past. This does not invalidate Hemingway's viewpoint any more than his does mine, for no one holds a monopoly on wisdom. In my present situation, however, I believe that mine has a higher survival potential, for I am not dealing only with *things,* but of something closer to the time-honored Powers and Principalities. I wish that it were not so and that an epigon were only an artifact akin to the ball lightning Tesla studied. But there is something behind it, surely as that yellow airplane had its pilot.

The fisherman sees me and waves. It is a peculiar feeling, this sudden commerce with a point of philosophical departure. I wave back with a feeling of pleasure.

I am surprised at the readiness with which I accept this emotion. I feel it has to do with the general state of my health. All of this fresh air and hiking seems to have strengthened me. My senses are sharper, my appetite better. I have lost some weight and gained some muscle. I have not required medication for several days.

I wonder . . . ?

Is this entirely a good thing? True, I must keep up my strength. I must be ready for many things. But too much strength . . . Could that be self-defeating in terms of my overall plan? A balance, perhaps I should seek a balance—

I laugh, for the first time since I do not remember when. It is ridiculous to dwell on life and death, sickness and health this way, like a character of Thomas Mann's, when I am barely a quarter of the way into my journey. I will need all of my strength—and possibly more—along the way. Sooner or later the bill will be presented. If the timing is off, I must make my own *suki*. In the meantime, I resolve to enjoy what I have.

When I strike, it will be with my final exhalation. I know that. It is a phenomenon familiar to martial artists of many persuasions. I recall the story Eugen Herrigel told, of studying with the *kyudo* master, of drawing the bow and waiting, waiting till something signaled the release of the string. For two years he did this before his *sensei* gave him an arrow. I forget for how long it was after that that he repeated the act with the arrow. Then it all began to come together, the timeless moment of rightness would occur and the arrow would have to fly, would have to fly for the target. It was a long while before he realized that this moment would always occur at the end of an exhalation.

In art, so in life. It seems that many important things, from death to orgasm, occur at the moment of emptiness, at the point of the breath's hesitation. Perhaps all of them are but reflections of death. This is a profound realization for one such as myself, for my strength must ultimately be drawn from my weakness. It is the control, the ability to find that special moment that troubles me most. But like walking, talking, or bearing a child, I trust that something within me knows where it lies. It is too late now to attempt to build it a bridge to my consciousness. I have made my small plans. I have placed them upon a shelf in the back of my mind. I should leave them and turn to other matters.

In the meantime I drink this moment with a deep draught of salty air, telling myself that the ocean is the ocean, the fisherman is a fisherman, and Fuji is only a mountain. Slowly then, I exhale it . . .

7. Mt. Fuji from the Foot

Fire in your guts, winter tracks above like strands of ancient hair. The print is somewhat more baleful than the reality this evening. That awful red tinge does not glow above me against a horde of wild clouds. Still, I am not unmoved. It is difficult, before the ancient powers of the Ring of Fire, not to stand with some trepidation, sliding back through geological eons to times of creation and destruction when new lands were formed. The great outpourings, the bomblike flash and dazzle, the dance of the lightnings like a crown . . .

I meditate on fire and change.

Last night I slept in the precincts of a small Shingon temple, among shrubs trimmed in the shapes of dragons, pagodas, ships, and umbrellas. There were a number of pilgrims of the more conventional sort present at the temple, and the priest performed a fire service—a *goma*—for us. The fires of Fuji remind me, as it reminded me of Fuji.

The priest, a young man, sat at the altar which held the fire basin. He intoned the prayer and built the fire and I watched, completely fascinated by the ritual, as he began to feed the fire with the hundred and eight sticks of wood. These, I have been told, represent the hundred and eight illusions of the soul. While I am not familiar with the full list, I felt it possible that I could come up with a couple of new ones. No matter. He chanted, ringing bells, striking gongs and drums. I glanced at the other *henros*. I saw total absorption upon all of their faces. All but one.

Another figure had joined us, entering with total silence, and he stood in the shadows off to my right. He was dressed all in black, and the wing of a wide, upturned collar masked the lower portion of his face. He was staring at me. When our eyes met, he looked away, focusing his gaze upon the fire. After several moments I did the same.

The priest added incense, leaves, oils. The fire sizzled and spit, the flames leaped, the shadows danced. I began to tremble. There was something familiar about the man. I could not place him, but I wanted a closer look.

I edged slowly to my right during the next ten minutes,

as if angling for better views of the ceremony. Suddenly then, I turned and regarded the man again.

I caught him studying me once more, and again he looked away quickly. But the dance of the flames caught him full in the face with light this time, and the jerking of his head withdrew it from the shelter of his collar.

I was certain, in that instant's viewing, that he was the man who had piloted the small yellow plane past me last week at Tamagawa. Though he wore no gold earring there was a shadow-filled indentation in the lobe of his left ear.

But it went beyond that. Having seen him full-face I was certain that I had seen him somewhere before, years ago. I have an unusually good memory for faces, but for some reason I could not place his within its prior context. He frightened me, though, and I felt there was good reason for it.

The ceremony continued until the final stick of wood was placed in the fire and the priest completed his liturgy as it burned and died down. He turned then, silhouetted by the light, and said that it was time for any who were ailing to rub the healing smoke upon themselves if they wished.

Two of the pilgrims moved forward. Slowly, another joined them. I glanced to my right once more. The man was gone, as silently as he had come. I cast my gaze all about the temple. He was nowhere in sight. I felt a touch upon my left shoulder.

Turning, I beheld the priest, who had just struck me lightly with the three-pronged brass ritual instrument which he had used in the ceremony.

"Come," he said, "and take the smoke. You need healing of the left arm and shoulder, the left hip and foot."

"How do you know this?" I asked him.

"It was given to me to see this tonight. Come."

He indicated a place to the left of the altar and I moved to it, startled at his insight, for the places he had named had been growing progressively more numb throughout the day. I had refrained from taking my medicine, hoping that the attack would remit of its own accord.

He massaged me, rubbing the smoke from the dying fire into the places he had named, then instructing me to continue it on my own. I did so, and some on my head at the end, as is traditional.

I searched the grounds later, but my strange observer was nowhere to be found. I located a hiding place between the feet of a dragon and cast my bedroll there. My sleep was not disturbed.

I awoke before dawn to discover that full sensation had returned to all of my previously numbed areas. I was pleased that the attack had remitted without medication.

The rest of the day, as I journeyed here, to the foot of Fuji, I felt surprisingly well. Even now I am filled with unusual strength and energy, and it frightens me. What if the smoke of the fire ceremony has somehow effected a cure? I am afraid of what it could do to my plans, my resolve. I am not sure that I would know how to deal with it.

Thus, Fuji, Lord of the Hidden Fire, I have come, fit and afraid. I will camp near here tonight. In the morning I will move on. Your presence overwhelms me at this range. I will withdraw for a different, more distant perspective. If I were ever to climb you, would I cast one hundred and eight sticks into your holy furnace, I wonder? I think not. There are some illusions I do not wish to destroy.

8. Mt. Fuji from Tagonoura

I came out in a boat to look back upon the beach, the slopes, and Fuji. I am still in glowing remission. I have resigned myself to it, for now. In the meantime, the day is bright, the sea breeze cool. The boat is rocked by the small deaths, as the fisherman and his sons whom I have paid to bring me out steer it at my request to provide me with the view most approximating that of the print.

So much of the domestic architecture in this land recommends to my eye the prows of ships. A convergence of cultural evolution where the message is the medium? The sea is life? Drawing sustenance from beneath the waves we are always at sea? Or, the sea is death, it may rise to blight our lands and claim our lives at any moment? Therefore, we bear this *memento mori* even in the roofs above our heads and the walls which sustain them? Or, this is the sign of our power, over life and death?

Or none of the above. It may seem that I harbor a strong death-wish. This is incorrect. My desires are just the opposite. It may indeed be that I am using Hokusai's prints as a kind of Rorschach for self-discovery, but it is death-fascination rather than death-wish that informs my mind. I believe that this is understandable in one suffering a terminal condition with a very short term to it.

Enough of that for now. It was meant only as a drawing of my blade to examine its edge for keenness. I find that my weapon is still in order and I resheathe it.

Blue-gray Fuji, salted with snow, long angle of repose to my left . . . I never seem to look upon the same mountain twice. You change as much as I myself, yet you remain what you are. Which means that there is hope for me.

I lower my eyes to where we share this quality with the sea, vast living data-net. Like yet unlike, you have fought that sea as I—

Birds. Let me listen and watch them for a time, the air-riders who dip and feed.

I watch the men work with the nets. It is relaxing to behold their nimble movements. After a time, I doze.

Sleeping, I dream, and dreaming I behold the god Kokuzo. It can be no other, for when he draws his blade which flashes like the sun and points it at me, he speaks his name. He repeats it over and over as I tremble before him, but something is wrong. I know that he is telling me something other than his identity. I reach for but cannot grasp the meaning. Then he moves the point of his blade, indicating something beyond me. I turn my head. I behold the man in black—the pilot, the watcher at the *goma*. He is studying me, just as he was that night. What does he seek in my face?

I am awakened by a violent rocking of the boat as we strike a rougher sea. I catch hold of the gunwale beside which I sit. A quick survey of my surroundings shows me that we are in no danger, and I turn my eyes to Fuji. Is he laughing at me? Or is it the chuckle of Hokusai, who squats on his hams beside me tracing naughty pictures in the moisture of the boat's bottom with a long, withered finger?

If a mystery cannot be solved, it must be saved. Later, then. I will return to the message when my mind has moved into a new position.

Soon, another load of fish is being hauled aboard to add to the pungency of this voyage. Wriggle howsoever they will they do not escape the net. I think of Kendra and wonder how she is holding up. I hope that her anger with me has abated. I trust that she has not escaped her imprisonment. I left her in the care of acquaintances at a primitive, isolated commune in the Southwest. I do not like the place, nor am I overfond of its residents. Yet they owe me several large favors—intentionally bestowed against these times—and they will keep her there until certain things come to pass. I see her delicate features, fawn eyes, and silken hair. A bright, graceful girl, used to some luxuries, fond of long soaks and frequent showers, crisp garments. She is probably mud-spattered or dusty at the moment, from slopping hogs, weeding, planting vegetables or harvesting them, or any of a number of basic chores. Perhaps it will be good for her character. She ought to get something from the experience other than preservation from a possibly terrible fate.

Time passes. I take my lunch.

Later, I muse upon Fuji, Kokuzo, and my fears. Are dreams but the tranced mind's theater of fears and desires, or do they sometimes truly reflect unconsidered aspects of reality, perhaps to give warning? To reflect . . .

It is said that the perfect mind reflects. The *shintai* in its ark in its shrine is the thing truly sacred to the god— a small mirror—not the images. The sea reflects the sky, in fullness of cloud or blue emptiness. Hamlet-like, one can work many interpretations of the odd, but only one should have a clear outline. I hold the dream in my mind once more, absent all querying. Something is moving . . .

No. I almost had it. But I reached too soon. My mirror is shattered.

Staring shoreward, the matter of synchronicity occurs. There is a new grouping of people. I withdraw my small spy-scope and take its measure, already knowing what I will regard.

Again, he wears black. He is speaking with two men upon the beach. One of the men gestures out across the water, toward us. The distance is too great to make out features clearly, but I know that it is the same man. But now it is not fear that I know. A slow anger begins to burn within my *hara*. I would return to shore and confront him. He is only one man. I will deal with him now. I cannot afford any more of the unknown than that for which I have already provided. He must be met properly, dismissed or accounted for.

I call to the captain to take me ashore immediately. He grumbles. The fishing is good, the day still young. I offer him more money. Reluctantly, he agrees. He calls orders to his sons to put the boat about and head in.

I stand in the bow. Let him have a good look. I send my anger on ahead. The sword is as sacred an object as the mirror.

As Fuji grows before me the man glances in our direction, hands something to the others, then turns and ambles away. No! There is no way to hasten our progress, and at this rate he will be gone before I reach land. I curse. I want immediate satisfaction, not extension of mystery.

And the men with whom he was speaking . . . Their hands go to their pockets, they laugh, then walk off in another direction. Drifters. Did he pay them for what-

ever information they gave him? So it would seem. And
are they heading now for some tavern to drink up the
price of my peace of mind? I call out after them but the
wind whips my words away. They, too, will be gone by
the time I arrive.

And this is true. When I finally stand upon the beach,
the only familiar face is that of my mountain, gleaming
like a carbuncle in sun's slanting rays.

I dig my nails into my palms but my arms do not
become wings.

9. Mt. Fuji from Naborito

I am fond of this print: the torii of a Shinto shrine are
visible above the sea at low tide, and people dig clams
amid the sunken ruins. Fuji of course is visible through
the torii. Were it a Christian church beneath the waves
puns involving the Clam of God would be running
through my mind. Geography saves, however.

And reality differs entirely. I cannot locate the place.
I am in the area and Fuji properly situated, but the torii
must be long gone and I have no way of knowing whether
there is a sunken temple out there.

I am seated on a hillside looking across the water and
I am suddenly not just tired but exhausted. I have come
far and fast these past several days, and it seems that my
exertions have all caught up with me. I will sit here and
watch the sea and the sky. At least my shadow, the man
in black, has been nowhere visible since the beach at
Tagonoura. A young cat chases a moth at the foot of my
hill, leaping into the air, white-gloved paws flashing. The
moth gains altitude, escapes in a gust of wind. The cat
sits for several moments, big eyes staring after it.

I make my way to a declivity I had spotted earlier,
where I might be free of the wind. There I lay my pack
and cast my bedroll, my poncho beneath it. After removing my shoes I get inside quickly. I seem to have taken
a bit of a chill and my limbs are very heavy. I would

have been willing to pay to sleep indoors tonight but I am too tired to seek shelter.

I lie here and watch the lights come on in the darkening sky. As usual in cases of extreme fatigue, sleep does not come to me easily. Is this legitimate tiredness or a symptom of something else? I do not wish to take medication merely as a precaution, though, so I try thinking of nothing for a time. This does not work. I am overcome with the desire for a cup of hot tea. In its absence I swallow a jigger of brandy, which warms my insides for a time.

Still, sleep eludes me and I decide to tell myself a story as I did when I was very young and wanted to make the world turn into dream.

So . . . Upon a time during the troubles following the death of the Retired Emperor Sutoku a number of itinerant monks of various persuasions came this way, having met upon the road, traveling to seek respite from the wars, earthquakes, and whirlwinds which so disturbed the land. They hoped to found a religious community and pursue the meditative life in quiet and tranquillity. They came upon what appeared to be a deserted Shinto shrine near the seaside, and there they camped for the night, wondering what plague or misfortune might have carried off its attendants. The place was in good repair and no evidence of violence was to be seen. They discussed then the possibility of making this their retreat, of themselves becoming the shrine's attendants. They grew enthusiastic with the idea and spent much of the night talking over these plans. In the morning, however, an ancient priest appeared from within the shrine, as if to commence a day's duties. The monks asked him the story of the place, and he informed them that once there had been others to assist him in his duties but that they had long ago been taken by the sea during a storm, while about their peculiar devotions one night upon the shore. And no, it was not really a Shinto shrine, though in outward appearance it seemed such. It was actually the temple of a far older religion of which he could well be the last devotee.

They were welcome, however, to join him here and learn of it if they so wished. The monks discussed it quickly among themselves and decided that since it was a pleasant-seeming place, it might be well to stay and hear whatever teaching the old man possessed. So they became residents at the strange shrine. The place troubled several of them considerably at first, for at night they seemed to hear the calling of musical voices in the waves and upon the sea wind. And on occasion it seemed as if they could hear the old priest's voice responding to these calls. One night one of them followed the sounds and saw the old man standing upon the beach, his arms upraised. The monk hid himself and later fell asleep in a crevice in the rocks. When he awoke, a full moon stood high in the heavens and the old man was gone. The monk went down to the place where he had stood and there saw many marks in the sand, all of them the prints of webbed feet. Shaken, the monk returned and recited his experience to his fellows. They spent weeks thereafter trying to catch a glimpse of the old man's feet, which were always wrapped and bound. They did not succeed, but after a time it seemed to matter less and less. His teachings influenced them slowly but steadily. They began to assist him in his rituals to the Old Ones, and they learned the name of this promontory and its shrine. It was the last above-sea remnant of a large sunken island, which he assured them rose on certain wondrous occasions to reveal a lost city inhabited by the servants of his masters. The name of the place was R'lyeh and they would be happy to go there one day. By then it seemed a good idea, for they had noticed a certain thickening and extension of the skin between their fingers and toes, the digits themselves becoming sturdier and more elongated. By then, too, they were participating in all of the rites, which grew progressively abominable. At length, after a particularly gory ritual, the old priest's promise was fulfilled in reverse. Instead of the island rising, the promontory sank to join it, bearing the shrine and all of the monks along with it. So their abominations are primarily aquatic now. But once every century or so the whole island does indeed rise up for a night, and troops of them make their way ashore seeking victims. And of course, tonight is the night. . . .

A delicious feeling of drowsiness has finally come over me with this telling, based upon some of my favorite bedtime stories. My eyes are closed. I float on a cotton-filled raft . . . I—

A sound! Above me! Toward the sea. Something moving my way. Slowly, then quickly.

Adrenaline sends a circuit of fire through my limbs. I extend my hand carefully, quietly, and take hold of my staff.

Waiting. Why now, when I am weakened? Must danger always approach at the worst moment?

There is a thump as it strikes the ground beside me, and I let out the breath I have been holding.

It is the cat, little more than a kitten, which I had observed earlier. Purring, it approaches. I reach out and stroke it. It rubs against me. After a time I take it into the bag. It curls up at my side, still purring, warm. It is good to have something that trusts you and wants to be near you. I call the cat R'lyeh. Just for one night.

10. Mt. Fuji from Ejiri

I took the bus back this way. I was too tired to hike. I have taken my medicine as I probably should have been doing all along. Still, it could be several days before it brings me some relief, and this frightens me. I cannot really afford such a condition. I am not certain what I will do, save that I must go on.

The print is deceptive, for a part of its force lies in the effects of a heavy wind. Its skies are gray, Fuji is dim in the background, the people on the road and the two trees beside it all suffer from the wind's buffeting. The trees bend, the people clutch at their garments, there is a hat high in the air and some poor scribe or author has had his manuscript snatched skyward to flee from him across the land (reminding me of an old cartoon—Editor to Author: "A funny thing happened to your manuscript during the St. Patrick's Day Parade"). The scene which confronts me is less active at a meteorological level. The sky is indeed overcast but there is no wind, Fuji is darker, more clearly delineated than in the print, there are no struggling pedestrians in sight. There are many more trees near at hand. I stand near a small grove, in fact. There are some structures in the distance which are not present in the picture.

I lean heavily upon my staff. Live a little, die a little. I have reached my tenth station and I still do not know whether Fuji is giving me strength or taking it from me. Both, perhaps.

I head off into the wood, my face touched by a few raindrops as I go. There are no signs posted and no one seems to be about. I work my way back from the road, coming at last to a small clear area containing a few rocks and boulders. It will do as a campsite. I want nothing more than to spend the day resting.

I soon have a small fire going, my tiny teapot poised on rocks above it. A distant roll of thunder adds variety to my discomfort, but so far the rain has held off. The ground is damp, however. I spread my poncho and sit upon it while I wait. I hone a knife and put it away. I eat some biscuits and study a map. I suppose I should feel some satisfaction, in that things are proceeding somewhat as I intended. I wish that I could, but I do not.

An unspecified insect which has been making buzzing noises somewhere behind me ceases its buzzing. I hear a twig snap a moment later. My hand snakes out to fall upon my staff.

"Don't," says a voice at my back.

I turn my head. He is standing eight or ten feet from me, the man in black, earring in place, his right hand in his jacket pocket. And it looks as if there is more than his hand in there, pointed at me.

I remove my hand from my staff and he advances. With the side of his foot he sends the staff partway across the clearing, out of my reach. Then he removes his hand from his pocket, leaving behind whatever it held. He circles slowly to the other side of the fire, staring at me the while.

He seats himself upon a boulder, lets his hands rest upon his knees.

"Mari?" he asks then.

I do not respond to my name, but stare back. The light of Kokuzo's dream-sword flashes in my mind, pointing at him, and I hear the god speaking his name only not quite.

"Kotuzov!" I say then.

The man in black smiles, showing that the teeth I had broken once long ago are now neatly capped.

"I was not so certain of you at first either," he says.

Plastic surgery has removed at least a decade from his face, along with a lot of weathering and several scars. He is different about the eyes and cheeks, also. And his nose is smaller. It is a considerable improvement over the last time we met.

"Your water is boiling," he says then. "Are you going to offer me a cup of tea?"

"Of course," I reply, reaching for my pack, where I keep an extra cup.

"Slowly."

"Certainly."

I locate the cup, I rinse them both lightly with hot water, I prepare the tea.

"No, don't pass it to me," he says, and he reaches forward and takes the cup from where I had filled it.

I suppress a desire to smile.

"Would you have a lump of sugar?" he asks.

"Sorry."

He sighs and reaches into his other pocket, from which he withdraws a small flask.

"Vodka? In tea?"

"Don't be silly. My tastes have changed. It's Wild Turkey liqueur, a wonderful sweetener. Would you care for some?"

"Let me smell it."

There is a certain sweetness to the aroma.

"All right," I say, and he laces our tea with it.

We taste the tea. Not bad.

"How long has it been?" he asks.

"Fourteen years—almost fifteen," I tell him. "Back in the eighties."

"Yes."

He rubs his jaw. "I'd heard you'd retired."

"You heard right. It was about a year after our last—encounter."

"Turkey—yes. You married a man from your Code Section."

I nod.

"You were widowed three or four years later. Daughter born after your husband's death. Returned to the States. Settled in the country. That's all I know."

"That's all there is."

He takes another drink of tea.

"Why did you come back here?"

"Personal reasons. Partly sentimental."

"Under a false identity?"

"Yes. It involves my husband's family. I don't want them to know I'm here."

"Interesting. You mean that they would watch arrivals as closely as we have?"

"I didn't know you watched arrivals here."

"Right now we do."

"You've lost me. I don't know what's going on."

There is another roll of thunder. A few more drops spatter about us.

"I would like to believe that you are really retired," he says. "I'm getting near that point myself, you know."

"I have no reason to be back in business. I inherited a decent amount, enough to take care of me and my daughter."

He nods.

"If I had such an inducement I would not be in the field," he says. "I would rather sit home and read, play chess, eat and drink regularly. But you must admit it is quite a coincidence your being here when the future success of several nations is being decided."

I shake my head.

"I've been out of touch with a lot of things."

"The Osaka Oil Conference. It begins two weeks from Wednesday. You were planning perhaps to visit Osaka at about that time?"

"I will not be going to Osaka."

"A courier then. Someone from there will meet you, a simple tourist, at some point in your travels, to convey—"

"My God! Do you think everything's a conspiracy, Boris? I am just taking care of some personal problems and visiting some places that mean something to me. The conference doesn't."

"All right." He finishes his tea and puts the cup aside. "You know that we know you are here. A word to the Japanese authorities that you are traveling under false papers and they will kick you out. That would be simplest. No real harm done and one agent nullified. Only it would be a shame to spoil your trip if you are indeed only a tourist. . . ."

A rotten thought passes through my mind as I see where this is leading, and I know that my thought is far rottener than his. It is something I learned from a strange old woman I once worked with who did not look like an old woman.

I finish my tea and raise my eyes. He is smiling.

"I will make us some more tea," I say.

I see that the top button of my shirt comes undone while I am bent partly away from him. Then I lean forward with his cup and take a deep breath.

"You would consider not reporting me to the authorities?"

"I might," he says. "I think your story is probably true. And even if it is not, you would not take the risk of transporting anything now that I know about you."

"I really want to finish this trip," I say, blinking a few

extra times. "I would do anything not to be sent back now."

He takes hold of my hand.

"I am glad you said that, Maryushka," he replies. "I am lonely, and you are still a fine-looking woman."

"You think so?"

"I always thought so, even that day you bashed in my teeth."

"Sorry about that. It was strictly business, you know."

His hand moves to my shoulder.

"Of course. They looked better when they were fixed than they had before, anyway."

He moves over and sits beside me.

"I have dreamed of doing this many times," he tells me, as he unfastens the rest of the buttons on my shirt and unbuckles my belt.

He rubs my belly softly. It is not an unpleasant feeling. It has been a long time.

Soon we are fully undressed. He takes his time, and when he is ready I welcome him between my legs. All right, Boris. I give the ride, you take the fall. I could almost feel a little guilty about it. You are gentler than I'd thought you would be. I commence the proper breathing pattern, deep and slow. I focus my attention on my *hara* and his, only inches away. I feel our energies, dreamlike and warm, moving. Soon, I direct their flow. He feels it only as pleasure, perhaps more draining than usual. When he has done, though . . .

"You said you had some problem?" he inquires in that masculine coital magnanimity generally forgotten a few minutes afterward. "If it is something I could help you with, I have a few days off, here and there. I like you, Maryushka."

"It's something I have to do myself. Thanks anyway."

I continue the process.

Later, as I dress myself, he lies there looking up at me.

"I must be getting old, Maryushka," he reflects. "You have tired me. I feel I could sleep for a week."

"That sounds about right," I say. "A week and you should be feeling fine again."

"I do not understand . . ."

"You've been working too hard, I'm sure. That conference . . ."

He nods.

"You are probably right. You are not really involved . . . ?"

"I am really not involved."

"Good."

I clean the pot and my cups. I restore them to my pack.

"Would you be so kind as to move, Boris dear? I'll be needing the poncho very soon, I think."

"Of course."

He rises slowly and passes it to me. He begins dressing. His breathing is heavy.

"Where are you going from here?"

"Mishima-goe," I say, "for another view of my mountain."

He shakes his head. He finishes dressing and seats himself on the ground, his back against a treetrunk. He finds his flask and takes a swallow. He extends it then.

"Would you care for some?"

"Thank you, no. I must be on my way."

I retrieve my staff. When I look at him again, he smiles faintly, ruefully.

"You take a lot out of a man, Maryushka."

"I had to," I say.

I move off. I will hike twenty miles today, I am certain. The rain begins to descend before I am out of the grove; leaves rustle like the wings of bats.

11. Mt. Fuji from Mishima-goe

Sunlight. Clean air. The print shows a big cryptomeria tree, Fuji looming behind it, crowned with smoke. There is no smoke today, but I have located a big cryptomeria and positioned myself so that it cuts Fuji's shoulder to the left of the cone. There are a few clouds, not so popcorny as Hokusai's smoke (he shrugs at this), and they will have to do.

My stolen *ki* still sustains me, though the medication is working now beneath it. Like a transplanted organ, my body will soon reject the borrowed energy. By then, though, the drugs should be covering for me.

In the meantime, the scene and the print are close to each other. It is a lovely spring day. Birds are singing, butterflies stitch the air in zigzag patterns; I can almost hear the growth of plants beneath the soil. The world smells fresh and new. I am no longer being followed. Hello to life again.

I regard the huge old tree and listen for its echoes down the ages: Yggdrasil, the Golden Bough, the Yule tree, the Tree of the Knowledge of Good and Evil, the Bo beneath which Lord Gautama found his soul and lost it. . . .

I move forward to run my hand along its rough bark.

From that position I am suddenly given a new view of the valley below. The fields look like raked sand, the hills like rocks, Fuji a boulder. It is a garden, perfectly laid out. . . .

Later I notice that the sun has moved. I have been standing here for hours. My small illumination beneath a great tree. Older than my humanity, I do not know what I can do for it in return.

Stooping suddenly, I pick up one of its cones. A tiny thing, for such a giant. It is barely the size of my little fingernail. Delicately incised, as if sculpted by fairies.

I put it in my pocket. I will plant it somewhere along my way.

I retreat then, for I hear the sound of approaching bells and I am not yet ready for humanity to break my mood. But there was a small inn down the road which does not look to be part of a chain. I will bathe and eat there and sleep in a bed tonight.

I will still be strong tomorrow.

12. Mt. Fuji from Lake Kawaguchi

Reflections.

This is one of my favorite prints in the series: Fuji as seen from across the lake and reflected within it. There are green hills at either hand, a small village upon the far shore, a single small boat in sight upon the water. The most fascinating feature of the print is that the reflection of Fuji is not the same as the original; its position is wrong, its slope is wrong, it is snow-capped and the surface view of Fuji itself is not.

I sit in the small boat I have rented, looking back. The sky is slightly hazy, which is good. No glare to spoil the reflection. The town is no longer as quaint as in the print, and it has grown. But I am not concerned with details of this sort. Fuji is reflected more perfectly in my viewing, but the doubling is still a fascinating phenomenon for me.

Interesting, too ... In the print the village is not reflected, nor is there an image of the boat in the water. The only reflection is Fuji's. There is no sign of humanity.

I see the reflected buildings near the water's edge. And my mind is stirred by other images than those Hokusai would have known. Of course drowned R'lyeh occurs to me, but the place and the day are too idyllic. It fades from mind almost immediately, to be replaced by sunken Ys, whose bells still toll the hours beneath the sea. And Selma Lagerlöf's *Nils Holgersson*, the tale of the ship-wrecked sailor who finds himself in a sunken city at the bottom of the sea—a place drowned to punish its greedy, arrogant inhabitants, who still go about their business of cheating each other, though they are all of them dead. They wear rich, old-fashioned clothes and conduct their business as they once did above in this strange land beneath the waves. The sailor is drawn to them, but he knows that he must not be discovered or he will be turned into one of them, never to return to the earth, to see the sun. I suppose I think of this old children's story

because I understand now how the sailor must have felt.
My discovery, too, could result in a transformation I do
not desire.

And of course, as I lean forward and view my own
features mirrored in the water, there is the world of
Lewis Carroll beneath its looking-glass surface. To be an
Ama diving girl and descend ... To spin downward, and
for a few minutes to know the inhabitants of a land of
paradox and great charm ...

Mirror, mirror, why does the real world so seldom
cooperate with our aesthetic enthusiasms?

Halfway finished. I reach the midpoint of my pilgrimage to confront myself in a lake. It is a good time and
place to look upon my own countenance, to reflect upon
all of the things which have brought me here, to consider
what the rest of the journey may hold. Though images
may sometimes lie. The woman who looks back at me
seems composed, strong, and better-looking than I had
thought she would. I like you, Kawaguchi, lake with a
human personality. I flatter you with literary compliments
and you return the favor.

Meeting Boris lifted a burden of fear from my mind.
No human agents of my nemesis have risen to trouble
my passage. So the odds have not yet tipped so enor-
mously against me as they might.

Fuji and image. Mountain and soul. Would an evil
thing cast no reflection down here—some dark mountain
where terrible deeds were performed throughout history?
I am reminded that Kit no longer casts a shadow, has no
reflection.

Is he truly evil, though? By my lights he is. Especially
if he is doing the things I think he is doing.

He said that he loved me, and I did love him, once.
What will he say to me when we meet again, as meet
we must?

It will not matter. Say what he will, I am going to try
to kill him. He believes that he is invincible, indestructi-
ble. I do not, though I do believe that I am the only
person on earth capable of destroying him. It took a long

time for me to figure the means, an even longer time before the decision to try it was made for me. I must do it for Kendra as well as for myself. The rest of the world's population comes third.

I let my fingers trail in the water. Softly, I begin to sing an old song, a love song. I am loath to leave this place. Will the second half of my journey be a mirror-image of the first? Or will I move beyond the looking-glass, to pass into that strange realm where he makes his home?

I planted the cryptomeria's seed in a lonesome valley yesterday afternoon. Such a tree will look elegant there one day, outliving nations and armies, madmen and sages.

I wonder where R'lyeh is? She ran off in the morning after breakfast, perhaps to pursue a butterfly. Not that I could have brought her with me.

I hope that Kendra is well. I have written her a long letter explaining many things. I left it in the care of an attorney friend, who will be sending it to her one day in the not too distant future.

The prints of Hokusai . . . They could outlast the cryptomeria. I will not be remembered for any works.

Drifting between the worlds I formulate our encounter for the thousandth time. He will have to be able to duplicate an old trick to get what he wants. I will have to perform an even older one to see that he doesn't get it. We are both out of practice.

It has been long since I read *The Anatomy of Melancholy*. It is not the sort of thing I've sought to divert me in recent years. But I recall a line or two as I see fish dart by: "Polycrates Samius, that flung his ring into the sea, because he would participate in the discontent of others, and had it miraculously restored to him again shortly after, by a fish taken as he angled, was not free from melancholy dispositions. No man can cure himself . . ." Kit threw away his life and gained it. I kept mine and lost it. Are rings ever really returned to the proper people? And what about a woman curing herself? The cure I seek is a very special one.

Hokusai, you have shown me many things. Can you show me an answer?

Slowly, the old man raises his arm and points to his mountain. Then he lowers it and points to the mountain's image.

I shake my head. It is an answer that is no answer. He shakes his head back at me and points again.

The clouds are massing high above Fuji, but that is no answer. I study them for a long while but can trace no interesting images within.

Then I drop my eyes. Below me, inverted, they take a different form. It is as if they depict the clash of two armed hosts. I watch in fascination as they flow together, the forces from my right gradually rolling over and submerging those to my left. Yet in so doing, those from my right are diminished.

Conflict? That is the message? And both sides lose things they do not wish to lose? Tell me something I do not already know, old man.

He continues to stare. I follow his gaze again, upward. Now I see a dragon, diving into Fuji's cone.

I look below once again. No armies remain, only carnage; and here the dragon's tail becomes a dying warrior's arm holding a sword.

I close my eyes and reach for it. A sword of smoke for a man of fire.

13. Mt. Fuji from Koishikawa in Edo

Snow, on the roofs of houses, on evergreens, on Fuji—just beginning to melt in places, it seems. A windowful of women—geishas, I would say—looking out at it, one of them pointing at three dark birds high in the pale sky. My closest view of Fuji to that in the print is unfortunately snowless, geishaless, and sunny.

Details . . .

Both are interesting, and superimposition is one of the major forces of aesthetics. I cannot help but think of

the hot-spring geisha Komako in *Snow Country*—Yasu-
nari Kawabata's novel of loneliness and wasted, fading
beauty—which I have always felt to be the great anti-
love story of Japan. This print brings the entire tale to
mind for me. The denial of love. Kit was no Shimamura,
for he did want me, but only on his own highly special-
ized terms, terms that must remain unacceptable to me.
Selfishness or selflessness? It is not important . . .

And the birds at which the geisha points . . . ? "Thir-
teen Ways of Looking at a Blackbird?" To the point. We
could never agree on values.

The Twa Corbies? And throw in Ted Hughes's pugna-
cious Crow? Perhaps so, but I won't draw straws.—An
illusion for every allusion, and where's yesterday's snow?

I lean upon my staff and study my mountain. I wish
to make it to as many of my stations as possible before
ordering the confrontation. Is that not fair? Twenty-four
ways of looking at Mt. Fuji. It struck me that it would
be good to take one thing in life and regard it from many
viewpoints, as a focus for my being, and perhaps as a
penance for alternatives missed.

Kit, I am coming, as you once asked of me, but by my
own route and for my own reasons. I wish that I did not
have to, but you have deprived me of a real choice in
this matter. Therefore, my action is not truly my own,
but yours. I am become then your own hand turned
against you, representative of a kind of cosmic aikido.

I make my way through town after dark, choosing only
dark streets where the businesses are shut down. That
way I am safe. When I must enter town I always find a
protected spot for the day and do my traveling on these
streets at night.

I find a small restaurant on the corner of such a one
and I take my dinner there. It is a noisy place but the
food is good. I also take my medicine, and a little saké.

Afterward, I indulge in the luxury of walking rather
than take a taxi. I've a long way to go, but the night is
clear and star-filled and the air is pleasant.

I walk for the better part of ten minutes, listening to

the sounds of traffic, music from some distant radio or tape deck, a cry from another street, the wind passing high above me and rubbing its rough fur upon the sides of buildings.

Then I feel a sudden ionization in the air.

Nothing ahead. I turn, spinning my staff into a guard position.

An epigon with a six-legged canine body and a head like a giant fiery flower emerges from a doorway and sidles along the building's front in my direction.

I follow its progress with my staff, feinting as soon as it is near enough. I strike, unfortunately with the wrong tip, as it comes on. My hair begins to rise as I spin out of its way, cutting, retreating, turning, then striking again. This time the metal tip passes into that floral head.

I had turned on the batteries before I commenced my attack. The charge creates an imbalance. The epigon retreats, head ballooning. I follow and strike again, this time mid-body. It swells even larger, then collapses in a shower of sparks. But I am already turning away and striking again, for I had become aware of the approach of another even as I was dealing with the first.

This one advances in kangaroolike bounds. I brush it by with my staff, but its long bulbous tail strikes me as it passes. I recoil involuntarily from the shock I receive, my reflexes spinning the staff before me as I retreat. It turns quickly and rears then. This one is a quadruped, and its raised forelimbs are fountains of fire. Its faceful of eyes blazes and hurts to look upon.

It drops back onto its haunches then springs again.

I roll beneath it and attack as it descends. But I miss, and it turns to attack again even as I continue thrusting. It springs and I turn aside, striking upward. It seems that I connect, but I cannot be certain.

It lands quite near me, raising its forelimbs. But this time it does not spring. It simply falls forward, hind feet making a rapid shuffling movement the while, the legs seeming to adjust their lengths to accommodate a more perfect flow.

As it comes on, I catch it square in the midsection with the proper end of my staff. It keeps coming, or falling, even as it flares and begins to disintegrate. Its touch stiffens me for a moment, and I feel the flow of its charge down my shoulder and across my breast. I watch it come apart in a final photoflash instant and be gone.

I turn quickly again but there is no third emerging from the doorway. None overhead either. There is a car coming up the street, slowing, however. No matter. The terminal's potential must be exhausted for the moment, though I am puzzled by the consideration of how long it must have been building to produce the two I just dispatched. It is best that I be away quickly now.

As I resume my progress, though, a voice calls to me from the car, which has now drawn up beside me:

"Madam, a moment please."

It is a police car, and the young man who has addressed me wears a uniform and a very strange expression.

"Yes, officer?" I reply.

"I saw you just a few moments ago," he says. "What were you doing?"

I laugh.

"It is such a fine evening," I say then, "and the street was deserted. I thought I would do a *kata* with my *bo*."

"I thought at first that something was attacking you, that I saw something . . ."

"I am alone," I say, "as you can see."

He opens the door and climbs out. He flicks on a flashlight and shines its beam across the sidewalk, into the doorway.

"Were you setting off fireworks?"

"No."

"There were some sparkles and flashes."

"You must be mistaken."

He sniffs the air. He inspects the sidewalk very closely, then the gutter.

"Strange," he says. "Have you far to go?"

"Not too far."

"Have a good evening."

He gets back into the car. Moments later it is headed up the street.

I continue quickly on my way. I wish to be out of the vicinity before another charge can be built. I also wish to be out of the vicinity simply because being here makes me uneasy.

I am puzzled at the ease with which I was located. What did I do wrong?

"My prints," Hokusai seems to say, after I have reached my destination and drunk too much brandy. "Think, daughter, or they will trap you."

I try, but Fuji is crushing my head, squeezing off thoughts. Epigons dance on his slopes. I pass into a fitful slumber.

In tomorrow's light perhaps I shall see . . .

14. Mt. Fuji from Meguro in Edo

Again, the print is not the reality for me. It shows peasants amid a rustic village, terraced hillsides, a lone tree jutting from the slope of the hill to the right, a snowcapped Fuji partly eclipsed by the base of the rise.

I could not locate anything approximating it, though I do have a partly blocked view of Fuji—blocked in a similar manner, by a slope—from this bench I occupy in a small park. It will do.

Partly blocked, like my thinking. There is something I should be seeing but it is hidden from me. I felt it the moment the epigons appeared, like the devils sent to claim Faust's soul. But I never made a pact with the Devil . . . just Kit, and it was called marriage. I had no way of knowing how similar it would be.

Now . . . What puzzles me most is how my location was determined despite my precautions. My head-on encounter must be on my terms, not anyone else's. The reason for this transcends the personal, though I will not deny the involvement of the latter.

In *Hagakure*, Yamamoto Tsunetomo advised that the Way of the Samurai is the Way of Death, that one must live as though one's body were already dead in order to gain full freedom. For me, this attitude is not so difficult to maintain. The freedom part is more complicated, however; when one no longer understands the full nature of the enemy, one's actions are at least partly conditioned by uncertainty.

My occulted Fuji is still there in his entirety, I know, despite my lack of full visual data. By the same token I ought to be able to extend the lines I have seen thus far with respect to the power which now devils me. Let us return to death. There seems to be something there, though it also seems that there is only so much you can say about it and I already have.

Death . . . Come gentle . . . We used to play a parlor game, filling in bizarre causes on imaginary death certificates: "Eaten by the Loch Ness monster." "Stepped on by Godzilla." "Poisoned by a ninja." "Translated."

Kit had stared at me, brow knitting, when I'd offered that last one.

"What do you mean 'translated'?" he asked.

"Okay, you can get me on a technicality," I said, "but I still think the effect would be the same. 'Enoch was translated that he should not see death'—Paul's Epistle to the Hebrews, 11:5."

"I don't understand."

"It means to convey directly to heaven without messing around with the customary termination here on earth. Some Moslems believe that the Mahdi was translated."

"An interesting concept," he said. "I'll have to think about it."

Obviously, he did.

I've always thought that Kurosawa could have done a hell of a job with *Don Quixote*. Say there is this old gentleman living in modern times, a scholar, a man who is fascinated by the early days of the samurai and the

Code of Bushido. Say that he identifies so strongly with these ideals that one day he loses his senses and comes to believe that he *is* an old-time samurai. He dons some ill-fitting armor he had collected, takes up his *katana*, goes forth to change the world. Ultimately, he is destroyed by it, but he holds to the Code. That quality of dedication sets him apart and ennobles him, for all of his ludicrousness. I have never felt that *Don Quixote* was merely a parody of chivalry, especially not after I'd learned that Cervantes had served under Don John of Austria at the battle of Lepanto. For it might be argued that Don John was the last European to be guided by the medieval code of chivalry. Brought up on medieval romances, he had conducted his life along these lines. What did it matter if the medieval knights themselves had not? He believed and he acted on his belief. In anyone else it might simply have been amusing, save that time and circumstance granted him the opportunity to act on several large occasions, and he won. Cervantes could not but have been impressed by his old commander, and who knows how this might have influenced his later literary endeavor? Ortega y Gasset referred to Quixote as a Gothic Christ. Dostoevsky felt the same way about him, and in his attempt to portray a Christ-figure in Prince Myshkin he, too, felt that madness was a necessary precondition for this state in modern times.

All of which is preamble to stating my belief that Kit was at least partly mad. But he was no Gothic Christ. An Electronic Buddha would be much closer.

"Does the data-net have the Buddha-nature?" he asked me one day.

"Sure," I said. "Doesn't everything?" Then I saw the look in his eyes and added, "How the hell should I know?"

He grunted then and reclined his resonance couch, lowered the induction helmet, and continued his computer-augmented analysis of a Lucifer cipher with a 128-bit key. Theoretically, it would take thousands of years to crack it by brute force, but the answer was needed within two weeks. His nervous system coupled with the data-net, he was able to deliver.

I did not notice his breathing patterns for some time. It was not until later that I came to realize that after he had finished his work, he would meditate for increasingly long periods of time while still joined with the system.

When I realized this, I chided him for being too lazy to turn the thing off.

He smiled.

"The flow," he said. "You do not fixate at one point. You go with the flow."

"You could throw the switch before you go with the flow and cut down on our electric bill."

He shook his head, still smiling.

"But it is that particular flow that I am going with. I am getting farther and farther into it. You should try it sometime. There have been moments when I felt I could translate myself into it."

"Linguistically or theologically?"

"Both," he replied.

And one night he did indeed go with the flow. I found him in the morning—sleeping, I thought—in his resonance couch, the helmet still in place. This time, at least, he had shut down our terminal. I let him rest. I had no idea how late he might have been working. By evening, though, I was beginning to grow concerned and I tried to rouse him. I could not. He was in a coma.

Later, in the hospital, he showed a flat EEG. His breathing had grown extremely shallow, his blood pressure was very low, his pulse feeble. He continued to decline during the next two days. The doctors gave him every test they could think of but could determine no cause for his condition. In that he had once signed a document requesting that no heroic measures be taken to prolong his existence should something irreversible take him, he was not hooked up to respirators and pumps and IVs after his heart had stopped beating for the fourth time. The autopsy was unsatisfactory. The death certificate merely showed: "Heart stoppage. Possible cerebrovascular accident." The latter was pure speculation. They had found no sign of it. His organs were not distributed to the needy as he had once requested, for fear of some strange new virus which might be transmitted.

Kit, like Marley, was dead to begin with.

15. Mt. Fuji from Tsukudajima in Edo

Blue sky, a few low clouds, Fuji across the bay's bright water, a few boats and an islet between us. Again, dismissing time's changes, I find considerable congruence with reality. Again, I sit within a small boat. Here, however, I've no desire to dive beneath the waves in search of sunken splendor or to sample the bacteria-count with my person.

My passage to this place was direct and without incident. Preoccupied I came. Preoccupied I remain. My vitality remains high. My health is no worse. My concerns also remain the same, which means that my major question is still unanswered.

At least I feel safe out here on the water. "Safe," though, is a relative term. "Safer" then, than I felt ashore and passing among possible places of ambush. I have not really felt safe since that day after my return from the hospital. . . .

I was tired when I got back home, following several sleepless nights. I went directly to bed. I did not even bother to note the hour, so I have no idea how long I slept.

I was awakened in the dark by what seemed to be the ringing of the telephone. Sleepily, I reached for the instrument, then realized that it was not actually ringing. Had I been dreaming? I sat up in bed. I rubbed my eyes. I stretched. Slowly, the recent past filled my mind and I knew that I would not sleep again for a time. A cup of tea, I decided, might serve me well now. I rose, to go to the kitchen and heat some water.

As I passed through the work area, I saw that one of

the CRTs for our terminal was lit. I could not recall its
having been on but I moved to turn it off.

I saw then that its switch was not turned on. Puzzled,
I looked again at the screen and for the first time realized
that there was a display present:

MARI.
ALL IS WELL.
I AM TRANSLATED.
USE THE COUCH AND THE HELMET.
KIT

I felt my fingers digging into my cheeks and my chest
was tight from breath retained. Who had done this?
How? Was it perhaps some final delirious message left
by Kit himself before he went under?

I reached out and flipped the ON-OFF switch back
and forth several times, leaving it finally in the OFF
position.

The display faded but the light remained on. Shortly,
a new display was flashed upon the screen:

YOU READ ME. GOOD.
IT IS ALL RIGHT. I LIVE.
I HAVE ENTERED THE DATA-NET.
SIT ON THE COUCH AND USE THE HELMET.
I WILL EXPLAIN EVERYTHING.

I ran from the room. In the bathroom I threw up,
several times. Then I sat upon the toilet, shaking. Who
would play such a horrible joke upon me? I drank several
glasses of water and waited for my trembling to subside.

When it had, I went directly to the kitchen, made the
tea, and drank some. My thoughts settled slowly into the
channels of analysis. I considered possibilities. The one
that seemed more likely than most was that Kit had left
a message for me and that my use of the induction inter-
face gear would trigger its delivery. I wanted that message, whatever it might be, but I did not know whether
I possessed sufficient emotional fortitude to receive it at
the moment.

I must have sat there for the better part of an hour.
I looked out the window once and saw that the sky was

growing light. I put down my cup. I returned to the work area.

The screen was still lit. The message, though, had changed:

DO NOT BE AFRAID.
SIT ON THE COUCH AND USE THE HELMET.
THEN YOU WILL UNDERSTAND.

I crossed to the couch. I sat on it and reclined it. I lowered the helmet. At first there was nothing but field noise.

Then I felt his presence, a thing difficult to describe in a world customarily filled only with data flows. I waited. I tried to be receptive to whatever he had somehow left imprinted for me.

"I am not a recording, Mari," he seemed to say to me then. "I am really here."

I resisted the impulse to flee. I had worked hard for this composure and I meant to maintain it.

"I made it over," he seemed to say. "I have entered the net. I am spread out through many places. It is pure kundalini. I am nothing but flow. It is wonderful. I will be forever here. It is nirvana."

"It really is you," I said.

"Yes. I have translated myself. I want to show you what it means."

"Very well."

"I am gathered here now. Open the legs of your mind and let me in fully."

I relaxed and he flowed into me. Then I was borne away and I understood.

16. Mt. Fuji from Umezawa

Fuji across lava fields and wisps of fog, drifting clouds; birds on the wing and birds on the ground. This one at least is close. I lean on my staff and stare at his peaceful reaches across the chaos. The lesson is like that of a piece of music: I am strengthened in some fashion I cannot describe.

And I had seen blossoming cherry trees on the way over here, and fields purple with clover, cultivated fields yellow with rape-blossoms, grown for its oil, a few winter camellias still holding forth their reds and pinks, the green shoots of rice beds, here and there a tulip tree dashed with white, blue mountains in the distance, foggy river valleys. I had passed villages where colored sheet metal now covers the roofs' thatching—blue and yellow, green, black, red—and yards filled with the slate-blue rocks so fine for landscape gardening; an occasional cow, munching, lowing softly; scarlike rows of plastic-covered mulberry bushes where the silkworms are bred. My heart jogged at the sights—the tiles, the little bridges, the color. . . . It was like entering a tale by Lafcadio Hearn, to have come back.

My mind was drawn back along the path I had followed, to the points of its intersection with my electronic bane. Hokusai's warning that night I drank too much— that his prints may trap me—could well be correct. Kit had anticipated my passage a number of times. How could he have?

Then it struck me. My little book of Hokusai's prints— a small cloth-bound volume by the Charles E. Tuttle Company—had been a present from Kit.

It is possible that he was expecting me in Japan at about this time, because of Osaka. Once his epigons had spotted me a couple of times, probably in a massive scanning of terminals, could he have correlated my movements with the sequence of the prints in *Hokusai's Views of Mt. Fuji,* for which he knew my great fondness, and simply extrapolated and waited? I've a strong feeling that the answer is in the affirmative.

Entering the data-net with Kit was an overwhelming experience. That my consciousness spread and flowed I do not deny. That I was many places simultaneously, that I rode currents I did not at first understand, that knowledge and transcendence and a kind of glory were all about me and within me was also a fact of peculiar perception. The speed with which I was borne seemed instantaneous, and this was a taste of eternity. The access to multitudes of terminals and enormous memory banks seemed a measure of omniscience. The possibility of the manipulation of whatever I would change within this realm and its consequences at that place where I still felt my distant body seemed a version of omnipotence. And the feeling . . . I tasted the sweetness, Kit with me and within me. It was self surrendered and recovered in a new incarnation, it was freedom from mundane desire, liberation . . .

"Stay with me here forever," Kit seemed to say.

"No," I seemed to answer, dreamlike, finding myself changing even further. "I cannot surrender myself so willingly."

"Not for this? For unity and the flow of connecting energy?"

"And this wonderful lack of responsibility?"

"Responsibility? For what? This is pure existence. There is no past."

"Then conscience vanishes."

"What do you need it for? There is no future either."

"Then all actions lose their meaning."

"True. Action is an illusion. Consequence is an illusion."

"And paradox triumphs over reason."

"There is no paradox. All is reconciled."

"Then meaning dies."

"Being is the only meaning."

"Are you certain?"

"Feel it!"

"I do. But it is not enough. Send me back before I am changed into something I do not wish to be."

"What more could you desire than this?"

"My imagination will die, also. I can feel it."

"And what is imagination?"

"A thing born of feeling and reason."

"Does this not feel right?"

"Yes, it feels right. But I do not want that feeling unaccompanied. When I touch feeling with reason, I see that it is sometimes but an excuse for failing to close with complexity."

"You can deal with any complexity here. Behold the data! Does reason not show you that this condition is far superior to that you knew but moments ago?"

"Nor can I trust reason unaccompanied. Reason without feeling has led humanity to enact monstrosities. Do not attempt to disassemble my imagination this way."

"You retain your reason and your feelings!"

"But they are coming unplugged—with this storm of bliss, this shower of data. I need them conjoined, else my imagination is lost."

"Let it be lost, then. It has served its purpose. Be done with it now. What can you imagine that you do not already have here?"

"I cannot yet know, and that is its power. If there be a will with a spark of divinity to it, I know it only through my imagination. I can give you anything else but that I will not surrender."

"And that is all? A wisp of possibility?"

"No. But it alone is too much to deny."

"And my love for you?"

"You no longer love in the human way. Let me go back."

"Of course. You will think about it. You will return."

"Back! Now!"

I pushed the helmet from my head and rose quickly. I returned to the bathroom, then to my bed. I slept as if drugged, for a long while.

Would I have felt differently about possibilities, the future, imagination, had I not been pregnant—a thing I had suspected but not yet mentioned to him, and which he had missed learning with his attention focused upon our argument? I like to think that my answers would have been the same, but I will never know. My condition was confirmed by a local doctor the following day. I made the visit I had been putting off because my life required a certainty of something then—a certainty of anything. The screen in the work area remained blank for three days.

I read and I meditated. Then of an evening the light came on again:

ARE YOU READY?

I activated the keyboard. I typed one word:

NO.

I disconnected the induction couch and its helmet then. I unplugged the unit itself, also.

The telephone rang.

"Hello?" I said.

"Why not?" he asked me.

I screamed and hung up. He had penetrated the phone circuits, appropriated a voice.

It rang again. I answered again.

"You will never know rest until you come to me," he said.

"I will if you will leave me alone," I told him.

"I cannot. You are special to me. I want you with me. I love you."

I hung up. It rang again. I tore the phone from the wall.

I had known that I would have to leave soon. I was overwhelmed and depressed by all the reminders of our life together. I packed quickly and I departed. I took a room at a hotel. As soon as I was settled into it, the telephone rang and it was Kit again. My registration had gone into a computer and . . .

I had them disconnect my phone at the switchboard. I put out a Do Not Disturb sign. In the morning I saw a telegram protruding from beneath the door. From Kit. He wanted to talk to me.

I determined to go far away. To leave the country, to return to the States.

It was easy for him to follow me. We leave electronic tracks almost everywhere. By cable, satellite, optic fiber he could be wherever he chose. Like an unwanted suitor now he pestered me with calls, interrupted television shows to flash messages upon the screen, broke in on my own calls, to friends, lawyers, realtors, stores. Several times, horribly, he even sent me flowers. My electric bodhisattva, my hound of heaven, would give me no rest. It is a terrible thing to be married to a persistent data-net.

So I settled in the country. I would have nothing in my home whereby he could reach me. I studied ways of avoiding the system, of slipping past his many senses.

On those few occasions when I was careless he reached for me again immediately. Only he had learned a new trick, and I became convinced that he had developed it for the purpose of taking me into his world by force. He could build up a charge at a terminal, mold it into something like ball lightning and animallike, and send that short-lived artifact a little distance to do his will. I learned its weakness, though, in a friend's home when one came for me, shocked me, and attempted to propel me into the vicinity of the terminal, presumably for purposes of translation. I struck at the epigon—as Kit later referred to it in a telegram of explanation and apology— with the nearest object to hand—a lighted table lamp, which entered its field and blew a circuit immediately. The epigon was destroyed, which is how I discovered that a slight electrical disruption created an instability within the things.

I stayed in the country and raised my daughter. I read and I practiced my martial arts and I walked in the woods and climbed mountains and sailed and camped: rural occupations all, and very satisfying to me after a life of intrigue, conflict, plot and counterplot, violence, and then that small, temporary island of security with Kit. I was happy with my choice.

Fuji across the lava beds . . . Springtime . . . Now I am returned. This was not my choice.

17. Mt. Fuji from Lake Suwa

And so I come to Lake Suwa, Fuji resting small in the evening distance. It is no Kamaguchi of powerful reflections for me. But it is serene, which joins my mood in a kind of peace. I have taken the life of the spring into me now and it has spread through my being. Who would disrupt this world, laying unwanted forms upon it? Seal your lips.

Was it not in a quiet province where Bōtchan found his maturity? I've a theory concerning books like that one of Natsume Soseki's. Someone once told me that this is the one book you can be sure that every educated Japanese has read. So I read it. In the States I was told that *Huckleberry Finn* was the one book you could be sure that every educated Yankee had read. So I read it. In Canada it was Stephen Leacock's *Sunshine Sketches of a Little Town*. In France it was *Le Grand Meaulnes*. Other countries have their books of this sort. They are all of them pastorals, having in common a closeness to the countryside and the forces of nature in days just before heavy urbanization and mechanization. These things are on the horizon and advancing, but they only serve to add the spice of poignancy to the taste of simpler values. They are youthful books, of national heart and character, and they deal with the passing of innocence. I have given many of them to Kendra.

I lied to Boris. Of course I know all about the Osaka Conference. I was even approached by one of my former employers to do something along the lines Boris had guessed at. I declined. My plans are my own. There would have been a conflict.

Hokusai, ghost and mentor, you understand chance and purpose better than Kit. You know that human order must color our transactions with the universe, and that this is not only necessary but good, and that the light still comes through.

Upon this rise above the water's side I withdraw my

hidden blade and hone it once again. The sun falls away from my piece of the world, but the darkness, too, is here my friend.

18. Mt. Fuji from the Offing in Kanagawa

And so the image of death. The Big Wave, curling above, toppling upon, about to engulf the fragile vessels. The one print of Hokusai's that everyone knows.

I am no surfer. I do not seek the perfect wave. I will simply remain here upon the shore and watch the water. It is enough of a reminder. My pilgrimage winds down, though the end is not yet in sight.

Well . . . I see Fuji. Call Fuji the end. As with the barrel's hoop of the first print, the circle closes about him.

On my way to this place I halted in a small glade I came upon and bathed myself in a stream which ran through it. There I used the local wood to construct a low altar. Cleansing my hands each step of the way I set before it incense made from camphorwood and from white sandalwood; I also placed there a bunch of fresh violets, a cup of vegetables, and a cup of fresh water from the stream. Then I lit a lamp I had purchased and filled with rapeseed oil. Upon the altar I set my image of the god Kokuzo which I had brought with me from home, facing to the west where I stood. I washed again, then extended my right hand, middle finger bent to touch my thumb as I spoke the mantra for invoking Kokuzo. I drank some of the water. I lustrated myself with sprinklings of it and continued repetition of the mantra. Thereafter, I made the gesture of Kokuzo three times, hand to the crown of my head, to my right shoulder, left shoulder, heart and throat. I removed the white cloth in which Kokuzo's picture had been wrapped. When I had sealed the area with the proper repetitions, I meditated in the same position as Kokuzo in the picture and invoked him. After a time the mantra ran by itself, over and over.

Finally, there was a vision, and I spoke, telling all that had happened, all that I intended to do, and asking for strength and guidance. Suddenly, I saw his sword descending, descending like slow lightning, to sever a limb from a tree, which began to bleed. And then it was raining, both within the vision and upon me, and I knew that that was all to be had on the matter.

I wound things up, cleaned up, donned my poncho, and headed on my way.

The rain was heavy, my boots grew muddy, and the temperature dropped. I trudged on for a long while and the cold crept into my bones. My toes and fingers became numb.

I kept constant lookout for a shelter, but did not spot anyplace where I could take refuge from the storm. Later, it changed from a downpour to a drizzle to a weak, mistlike fall when I saw what could be a temple or shrine in the distance. I headed for it, hoping for some hot tea, a fire, and a chance to change my socks and clean my boots.

A priest stopped me at the gate. I told him my situation and he looked uncomfortable.

"It is our custom to give shelter to anyone," he said. "But there is a problem."

"I will be happy to make a cash donation," I said, "if too many others have passed this way and reduced your stores. I really just wanted to get warm."

"Oh no, it is not a matter of supplies," he told me, "and for that matter very few have been by here recently. The problem is of a different sort and it embarrasses me to state it. It makes us sound old-fashioned and superstitious, when actually this is a very modern temple. But recently we have been—ah—haunted."

"Oh?"

"Yes. Bestial apparitions have been coming and going from the library and record room beside the head priest's quarters. They stalk the shrine, pass through our rooms, pace the grounds, then return to the library or else fade away."

He studied my face, as if seeking derision, belief, disbelief—anything. I merely nodded.

"It is most awkward," he added. "A few simple exorcisms have been attempted but to no avail."

"For how long has this been going on?" I asked.

"For about three days," he replied.

"Has anyone been harmed by them?"

"No. They are very intimidating, but no one has been injured. They are distracting, too, when one is trying to sleep—that is, to meditate—for they produce a tingling feeling and sometimes cause the hair to rise up."

"Interesting," I said. "Are there many of them?"

"It varies. Usually just one. Sometimes two. Occasionally three."

"Does your library by any chance contain a computer terminal?"

"Yes, it does," he answered. "As I said, we are very modern. We keep our records with it, and we can obtain printouts of sacred texts we do not have on hand—and other things."

"If you will shut the terminal down for a day, they will probably go away," I told him, "and I do not believe they will return."

"I would have to check with my superior before doing a thing like that. You know something of these matters?"

"Yes, and in the meantime I would still like to warm myself, if I may."

"Very well. Come this way."

I followed him, cleaning my boots and removing them before entering. He led me around to the rear and into an attractive room which looked upon the temple's garden.

"I will go and see that a meal is prepared for you, and a brazier of charcoal that you may warm yourself," he said as he excused himself.

Left by myself I admired the golden carp drifting in a pond only a few feet away, its surface occasionally punctuated by raindrops, and a little stone bridge which crossed the pond, a stone pagoda, paths wandering among stones and shrubs. I wanted to cross that bridge—how unlike that metal span, thrusting, cold and dark!—and lose myself there for an age or two. Instead, I sat down and gratefully gulped the tea which arrived moments later, and I warmed my feet and dried my socks in the heat of the brazier which came a little while after that.

Later, I was halfway through a meal and enjoying a conversation with the young priest, who had been asked to keep me company until the head priest could come by and personally welcome me, when I saw my first epigon of the day.

It resembled a very small, triple-trunked elephant walking upright along one of the twisting garden paths, sweeping the air to either side of the trail with those snakelike appendages. It had not yet spotted me.

I called it to the attention of the priest, who was not faced in that direction.

"Oh my!" he said, fingering his prayer beads.

While he was looking that way, I shifted my staff into a readily available position beside me.

As it drifted nearer, I hurried to finish my rice and vegetables. I was afraid my bowl might be upset in the skirmish soon to come.

The priest glanced back when he heard the movement of the staff along the flagstones.

"You will not need that," he said. "As I explained, these demons are not aggressive."

I shook my head as I swallowed another mouthful.

"This one will attack," I said, "when it becomes aware of my presence. You see, I am the one it is seeking."

"Oh my!" he repeated.

I stood then as its trunks swayed in my direction and it approached the bridge.

"This one is more solid than usual," I commented. "Three days, eh?"

"Yes."

I moved about the tray and took a step forward. Suddenly, it was over the bridge and rushing toward me. I met it with a straight thrust, which it avoided. I spun the staff twice and struck again as it was turning. My blow landed and I was hit by two of the trunks simultaneously—once on the breast, once on the cheek. The epigon went out like a burned hydrogen balloon and I stood there rubbing my face, looking about me the while.

Another slithered into our room from within the temple. I lunged suddenly and caught it on the first stroke.

"I think perhaps I should be leaving now," I stated. "Thank you for your hospitality. Convey my regrets to the head priest that I did not get to meet him. I am warm and fed and I have learned what I wanted to know about your demons. Do not even bother about the terminal. They will probably cease to visit you shortly, and they should not return."

"You are certain?"

"I know them."

"I did not know the terminals were haunted. The salesman did not tell us."

"Yours should be all right now."

He saw me to the gate.

"Thank you for the exorcism," he said.

"Thanks for the meal. Good-bye."

I traveled for several hours before I found a place to camp in a shallow cave, using my poncho as a rain-screen.

And today I came here to watch for the wave of death. Not yet, though. No truly big ones in this sea. Mine is still out there, somewhere.

19. Mt. Fuji from Shichirigahama

Fuji past pine trees, through shadow, clouds rising beside him . . . It is getting on into the evening of things. The weather was good today, my health stable.

I met two monks upon the road yesterday and I traveled with them for a time. I was certain that I had seen them somewhere else along the way, so I greeted them and asked if this were possible. They said that they were on a pilgrimage of their own, to a distant shrine, and they admitted that I looked familiar, also. We took our lunch together at the side of the road. Our conversation was restricted to generalities, though they did ask me whether I had heard of the haunted shrine in Kanagawa. How quickly such news travels. I said that I had and we reflected upon its strangeness.

After a time I became annoyed. Every turning of the way that I took seemed a part of their route, also. While I'd welcomed a little company, I'd no desire for long-term companions, and it seemed their choices of ways approximated mine too closely. Finally, when we came to a split in the road I asked them which fork they were taking. They hesitated, then said that they were going right. I took the left-hand path. A little later they caught up with me. They had changed their minds, they said.

When we reached the next town, I offered a man in a car good sum of money to drive me to the next village. He accepted, and we drove away and left them standing there.

I got out before we reached the next town, paid him, and watched him drive off. Then I struck out upon a footpath I had seen, going in the general direction I desired. At one point I left the trail and cut through the woods until I struck another path.

I camped far off the trail when I finally bedded down, and the following morning I took pains to erase all sign of my presence there. The monks did not reappear. They may have been quite harmless, or their designs quite different, but I must be true to my carefully cultivated paranoia.

Which leads me to note that man in the distance—a Westerner, I'd judge, by his garments . . . He has been hanging around taking pictures for some time. I will lose him shortly, of course, if he is following me—or even if he isn't.

It is terrible to have to be this way for too long a period of time. Next I will be suspecting schoolchildren.

I watch Fuji as the shadows lengthen. I will continue to watch until the first star appears. Then I will slip away.

And so I see the sky darken. The photographer finally stows his gear and departs.

I remain alert, but when I see the first star, I join the shadows and fade like the day.

20. Mt. Fuji from Inume Pass

Through fog and above it. It rained a bit earlier. And there is Fuji, storm clouds above his brow. In many ways I am surprised to have made it this far. This view, though, makes everything worthwhile.

I sit upon a mossy rock and record in my mind the changing complexion of Fuji as a quick rain veils his countenance, ceases, begins again.

The winds are strong here. The fogbank raises ghostly limbs and lowers them. There is a kind of numb silence beneath the wind's monotone mantra.

I make myself comfortable, eating, drinking, viewing, as I go over my final plans once again. Things wind down. Soon the circle will be closed.

I had thought of throwing away my medicine here as an act of bravado, as a sign of full commitment. I see this now as a foolishly romantic gesture. I am going to need all of my strength, all of the help I can get, if I am to have a chance at succeeding. Instead of discarding the medicine here I take some.

The winds feel good upon me. They come on like waves, but they are bracing.

A few travelers pass below. I draw back, out of their line of sight. Harmless, they go by like ghosts, their words carried off by the wind, not even reaching this far. I feel a small desire to sing but I restrain myself.

I sit for a long while, lost in a reverie of the elements.

It has been good, this journey into the past, living at the edge once again . . .

Below me. Another vaguely familiar figure comes into view, lugging equipment. I cannot distinguish features from here, nor need I. As he halts and begins to set up his gear, I know that it is the photographer of Shichiriga-hama, out to capture another view of Fuji more permanent than any I desire.

I watch him for a time and he does not even glance my way. Soon I will be gone again, without his knowledge. I will allow this one as a coincidence. Provisionally, of course. If I see him again, I may have to kill him. I will be too near my goal to permit even the possibility of interference to exist.

I had better depart now, for I would rather travel before than behind him.

Fuji-from-on-high, this was a good resting place. We will see you again soon.

Come, Hokusai, let us be gone.

21. Mt. Fuji from the Tōtōmi Mountains

Gone the old sawyers, splitting boards from a beam, shaping them. Only Fuji, of snow and clouds, remains. The men in the print work in the old way, like the Owari barrel-maker. Yet, apart from those of the fishermen who merely draw their needs from nature, these are the only two prints in my book depicting people actively shaping something in their world. Their labors are too traditional for me to see the image of the Virgin and the Dynamo within them. They could have been performing the same work a thousand years before Hokusai.

Yet it is a scene of humanity shaping the world, and so it leads me down trails of years to this time, this day of sophisticated tools and large-scale changes. I see within it the image of what was later wrought, of the metal skin and pulsing flows the world would come to wear. And Kit is there, too, godlike, riding electronic waves.

Troubling. Yet bespeaking an ancient resilience, as if this, too, is but an eyeblink glimpse of humanity's movement in time, and whether I win or lose, the raw stuff remains and will triumph ultimately over any obstacle. I would really like to believe this, but I must leave certainty to politicians and preachers. My way is laid out and invested with my vision of what must be done.

I have not seen the photographer again, though I caught sight of the monks yesterday, camped on the side of a distant hill. I inspected them with my telescope and they were the same ones with whom I had traveled briefly. They had not noticed me and I passed them by way of a covering detour. Our trails have not crossed since.

Fuji, I have taken twenty-one of your aspects within me now. Live a little, die a little. Tell the gods, if you think of it, that a world is about to die.

I hike on, camping early in a field close to a monastery. I do not wish to enter there after my last experience in a modern holy place. I bed down in a concealed spot nearby, amid rocks and pine tree shoots. Sleep comes easily, lasts till some odd hour.

I am awake suddenly and trembling, in darkness and stillness. I cannot recall a sound from without or a troubling dream from within. Yet I am afraid, even to move. I breathe carefully and wait.

Drifting, like a lotus on a pond, it has come up beside me, towers above me, wears stars like a crown, glows with its own milky, supernal light. It is a delicate-featured image of a bodhisattva, not unlike Kwannon, in garments woven of moonbeams.

"Mari."

Its voice is soft and caressing.

"Yes?" I answer.

"You have returned to travel in Japan. You are coming to me, are you not?"

The illusion is broken. It is Kit. He has carefully sculpted this epigon-form and wears it himself to visit me. There must be a terminal in the monastery. Will he try to force me?

"I was on my way to see you, yes," I manage.

"You may join me now, if you would."

He extends a wonderfully formed hand, as in benediction.

"I've a few small matters I must clear up before we are reunited."

"What could be more important? I have seen the medical reports. I know the condition of your body. It would be tragic if you were to die upon the road, this close to your exaltation. Come now."

"You have waited this long, and time means little to you."

"It is you that I am concerned with."

"I assure you I shall take every precaution. In the meantime, there is something which has been troubling me."

"Tell me."

"Last year there was a revolution in Saudi Arabia. It seemed to promise well for the Saudis but it also threatened Japan's oil supply. Suddenly the new government began to look very bad on paper, and a new counterrevolutionary group looked stronger and better-tempered than it actually was. Major powers intervened successfully on the side of the counterrevolutionaries. Now they are in power and they seem even worse than the first government which had been overthrown. It seems possible, though incomprehensible to most, that computer readouts all over the world were somehow made to be misleading. And now the Osaka Conference is to be held to work out new oil agreements with the latest regime. It looks as if Japan will get a very good deal out of it. You once told me that you are above such mundane matters, but I wonder? You are Japanese, you loved your country. Could you have intervened in this?"

"What if I did? It is such a small matter in the light of eternal values. If there is a touch of sentiment for such things remaining within me, it is not dishonorable that I favor my country and my people."

"And if you did it in this, might you not be moved to intervene again one day, in some other matter where habit or sentiment tell you you should?"

"What of it?" he replies. "I but extend my finger and stir the dust of illusion a bit. If anything, it frees me even further."

"I see," I answer.

"I doubt that you do, but you will when you have joined me. Why not do it now?"

"Soon," I say. "Let me settle my affairs."

"I will give you a few more days," he says, "and then you must be with me forever."

I bow my head.

"I will see you again soon," I tell him.

"Good night, my love."

"Good night."

He drifts away then, his feet not touching the ground, and he passes through the wall of the monastery.

I reach for my medicine and my brandy. A double dose of each . . .

22. Mt. Fuji from the Sumida River in Edo

And so I come to the place of crossing. The print shows a ferryman bearing a number of people across the river into the city and evening. Fuji lies dark and brooding in the farthest distance. Here I do think of Charon, but the thought is not so unwelcome as it once might have been. I take the bridge myself, though.

As Kit has promised me a little grace, I walk freely the bright streets, to smell the smells and hear the noises and watch the people going their ways. I wonder what Hokusai would have done in contemporary times? He is silent on the matter.

I drink a little, I smile occasionally, I even eat a good meal. I am tired of reliving my life. I seek no consolations of philosophy or literature. Let me merely walk in the city tonight, running my shadow over faces and storefronts, bars and theaters, temples and offices. Anything which approaches is welcome tonight. I eat *sushi*, I gamble, I dance. There is no yesterday, there is no tomorrow for me now. When a man places his hand upon my shoulder and smiles, I move it to my breast and laugh. He is good for an hour's exercise and laughter in a small room he finds us. I make him cry out several times before I leave him, though he pleads with me to stay. Too much to do and see, love. A greeting and a farewell.

Walking. . . . Through parks, alleys, gardens, plazas. Crossing. . . . Small bridges and larger ones, streets and walkways. Bark, dog. Shout, child. Weep, woman. I come and go among you. I feel you with a dispassionate passion. I take all of you inside me that I may hold the world here, for a night.

I walk in a light rain and in its cool aftermath. My garments are damp, then dry again. I visit a temple. I pay a taximan to drive me about the town. I eat a late meal. I visit another bar. I come upon a deserted playground, where I swing and watch the stars.

And I stand before a fountain splaying its waters into the lightening sky, until the stars are gone and only their lost sparkling falls about me.

Then breakfast and a long sleep, another breakfast and a longer one . . .

And you, my father, there on the sad height? I must leave you soon, Hokusai.

23. Mt. Fuji from Edo

Walking again, within a cloudy evening. How long has it been since I spoke with Kit? Too long, I am sure. An epigon could come bounding my way at any moment.

I have narrowed my search to three temples—none of them the one in the print, to be sure, only that uppermost portion of it viewed from that impossible angle, Fuji back past its peak, smoke, clouds, fog between—but I've a feeling one of these three will do in the blue of evening.

I have passed all of them many times, like a circling bird. I am loath to do more than this, for I feel the right choice will soon be made for me. I became aware sometime back that I was being followed, really followed this time, on my rounds. It seems that my worst fear was not ungrounded; Kit is employing human agents as well as epigons. How he sought them and how he bound them to his service I do not care to guess. Who else would be following me at this point, to see that I keep my promise, to force me to it if necessary?

I slow my pace. But whoever is behind me does the same. Not yet. Very well.

Fog rolls in. The echoes of my footfalls are muffled. Also those at my back. Unfortunate.

I head for the other temple. I slow again when I come into its vicinity, all of my senses extended, alert.

Nothing. No one. It is all right. Time is no problem. I move on.

After a long while I approach the precincts of the third temple. This must be it, but I require some move from my pursuer to give me the sign. Then, of course, I must deal with that person before I make my own move. I hope that it will not be too difficult, for everything will turn upon that small conflict.

I slow yet again and nothing appears but the moisture of the fog upon my face and the knuckles of my hand wrapped about my staff. I halt. I seek in my pocket after a box of cigarettes I had purchased several days ago in my festive mood. I had doubted they would shorten my life.

As I raise one to my lips, I hear the words, "You desire a light, madam?"

I nod my head as I turn.

It is one of the two monks who extends a lighter to me and flicks forth its flame. I notice for the first time the heavy ridge of callus along the edge of his hand. He had kept it carefully out of sight before, as we sojourned together. The other monk appears to his rear, to his left.

"Thank you."

I inhale and send smoke to join the fog.

"You have come a long way," the man states.

"Yes."

"And your pilgrimage has come to an end."

"Oh? Here?"

He smiles and nods. He turns his head toward the temple.

"This is our temple," he says, "where we worship the new bodhisattva. He awaits you within."

"He can continue to wait, till I finish my cigarette," I say.

"Of course."

With a casual glance, I study the man. He is probably a very good *karateka*. I am very good with the *bo*. If it were only him, I would bet on myself. But two of them, and the other probably just as good as this one? Kokuzo, where is your sword? I am suddenly afraid.

I turn away, I drop the cigarette, I spin into my attack. He is ready, of course. No matter. I land the first blow.

By then, however, the other man is circling and I must wheel and move defensively, turning, turning. If this goes on for too long, they will be able to wear me down.

I hear a grunt as I connect with a shoulder. Something, anyway . . .

Slowly, I am forced to give way, to retreat toward the temple wall. If I am driven too near it, it will interfere with my strokes. I try again to hold my ground, to land a decisive blow. . . .

Suddenly, the man to my right collapses, a dark figure on his back. No time to speculate. I turn my attention to the first monk, and moments later I land another blow, then another.

My rescuer is not doing so well, however. The second monk has shaken him off and begins striking at him with bone-crushing blows. My ally knows something of unarmed combat, though, for he gets into a defensive stance and blocks many of these, even landing a few of his own. Still, he is clearly overmatched.

Finally I sweep a leg and deliver another shoulder blow. I try three strikes at my man while he is down, but he rolls away from all of them and comes up again. I hear a sharp cry from my right, but I cannot look away from my adversary.

He comes in again and this time I catch him with a sudden reversal and crush his temple with a follow-up. I spin then, barely in time, for my ally lies on the ground and the second monk is upon me.

Either I am lucky or he has been injured. I catch the

man quickly and follow up with a rapid series of strikes which take him down, out, and out for good.

I rush to the side of the third man and kneel beside him, panting. I had seen his gold earring as I moved about the second monk.

"Boris." I take his hand. "Why are you here?"

"I told you—I could take a few days—to help you," he says, blood trickling from the corner of his mouth. "Found you. Was taking pictures . . . And see . . . You needed me."

"I'm sorry," I say. "Grateful, but sorry. You're a better man than I thought."

He squeezes my hand. "I told you I liked you—Mary-ushka. Too bad . . . we didn't have—more time . . ."

I lean and kiss him, getting blood on my mouth. His hand relaxes within my own. I've never been a good judge of people, except after the fact.

And so I rise. I leave him there on the wet pavement. There is nothing I can do for him. I go into the temple.

It is dark near the entrance, but there are many votive lights to the rear. I do not see anyone about. I did not think that I would. It was just to have been the two monks, ushering me to the terminal. I head toward the lights. It must be somewhere back there.

I hear rain on the rooftop as I search. There are little rooms, off to either side, behind the lights.

It is there, in the second one. And even as I cross the threshold, I feel that familiar ionization which tells me that Kit is doing something here.

I rest my staff against the wall and go nearer. I place my hand upon the humming terminal.

"Kit," I say, "I have come."

No epigon grows before me, but I feel his presence and he seems to speak to me as he did on that night so long ago when I lay back upon the couch and donned the helmet:

"I knew that you would be here tonight."

"So did I," I reply.

"All of your business is finished?"

"Most of it."

"And you are ready now to be joined with me?"

"Yes."

Again I feel that movement, almost sexual in nature, as he flows into me. In a moment he would bear me away into his kingdom.

Tatemae is what you show to others. *Honne* is your real intention. As Musashi cautioned in the Book of Waters, I try not to reveal my *honne* even at this moment. I simply reach out with my free hand and topple my staff so that its metal tip, batteries engaged, falls against the terminal.

"Mari! What have you done?" he asks, within me now, as the humming ceases.

"I have cut off your line of retreat, Kit."

"Why?"

The blade is already in my hand.

"It is the only way for us. I give you this *jigai*, my husband."

"No!"

I feel him reaching for control of my arm as I exhale. But it is too late. It is already moving. I feel the blade enter my throat, well-placed.

"Fool!" he cries. "You do not know what you have done! I cannot return!"

"I know."

As I slump against the terminal I seem to hear a roaring sound, growing, at my back. It is the Big Wave, finally come for me. My only regret is that I did not make it to the final station, unless, of course, that is what Hokusai is trying to show me, there beside the tiny window, beyond the fog and the rain and the night.

24. Mt. Fuji in a Summer Storm

Paladin of the Lost Hour

by Harlan Ellison

This was an old man. Not an incredibly old man: obsolete, spavined; not as worn as the sway-backed stone steps ascending the Pyramid of the Sun to an ancient temple; not yet a relic. But even so, a *very* old man, this old man perched on an antique shooting stick, its handles opened to form a seat, its spike thrust at an angle into the soft ground and trimmed grass of the cemetery. Gray, thin rain misted down at almost the same angle as that at which the spike pierced the ground. The winter-barren trees lay flat and black against an aluminum sky, unmoving in the chill wind. An old man sitting at the foot of a grave mound whose headstone had tilted slightly when the earth had settled; sitting in the rain and speaking to someone below.

"They tore it down, Minna.

"I tell you, they must have bought off a councilman.

"Came in with bulldozers at six o'clock in the morning, and you *know* that's not legal. There's a Municipal Code. Supposed to hold off till at least seven on weekdays, eight on the weekend; but there they were at six, even *before* six, barely light for godsakes. Thought they'd sneak in and do it before the neighborhood got wind of it and called the landmarks committee. Sneaks: they come on *holidays*, can you imagine!

"But I was out there waiting for them, and I told them, 'You can't do it, that's Code number 91.3002, sub-section E,' and they lied and said they had special permission, so I said to the big muckymuck in charge, 'Let's see your waiver permit,' and he said the Code didn't apply in this case because it was supposed to be only for grading, and since they were demolishing and not grading, they could start whenever they felt like it. So I told him I'd call the police, then, because it came under the heading of Disturbing the Peace, and he said . . . well, I know you hate that kind of language, old girl, so I won't tell you what he said, but you can imagine.

"So I called the police, and gave them my name, and of course they didn't get there till almost quarter after seven (which is what makes me think they bought off a councilman), and by then those 'dozers had leveled most of it. Doesn't take long, you know that.

"And I don't suppose it's as great a loss as, maybe, say, the Great Library of Alexandria, but it was the last of the authentic Deco design drive-ins, and the carhops still served you on roller skates, and it was a landmark, and just about the only place left in the city where you could still get a decent grilled cheese sandwich pressed very flat on the grill by one of those weights they used to use, made with real cheese and not that rancid plastic they cut into squares and call it 'cheese food.'

"Gone, old dear, gone and mourned. And I understand they plan to put up another one of those mini-malls on the site, just ten blocks away from one that's already there, and you know what's going to happen: this new one will drain off the traffic from the older one, and then that one will fail the way they all do when the next one gets built, you'd think they'd see some history in it; but no, they never learn. And you should have seen the crowd by seven-thirty. All ages, even some of those kids painted like aborigines, with torn leather clothing. Even they came to protest. Terrible language, but at least they were concerned. And nothing could stop it. They just whammed it, and down it went.

"I do so miss you today, Minna. No more good grilled cheese." Said the *very* old man to the ground. And now he was crying softly, and now the wind rose, and the mist rain stippled his overcoat.

Nearby, yet at a distance, Billy Kinetta stared down at another grave. He could see the old man over there off to his left, but he took no further notice. The wind whipped the vent of his trenchcoat. His collar was up but rain trickled down his neck. This was a younger man, not yet thirty-five. Unlike the old man, Billy Kinetta neither cried nor spoke to memories of someone who had once listened. He might have been a geomancer, so silently did he stand, eyes toward the ground.

One of these men was black; the other was white.

Beyond the high, spiked-iron fence surrounding the cemetery two boys crouched, staring through the bars, through the rain; at the men absorbed by grave matters, by matters of graves. These were not really boys. They were legally young men. One was nineteen, the other two months beyond twenty. Both were legally old enough to vote, to drink alcoholic beverages, to drive a car. Neither would reach the age of Billy Kinetta.

One of them said, "Let's take the old man."

The other responded, "You think the guy in the trenchcoat'll get in the way?"

The first one smiled; and a mean little laugh. "I sure as shit hope so." He wore, on his right hand, a leather carnaby glove with the fingers cut off, small round metal studs in a pattern along the line of his knuckles. He made a fist, flexed, did it again.

They went under the spiked fence at a point where erosion had created a shallow gully. "Sonofabitch!" one of them said, as he slid through on his stomach. It was muddy. The front of his sateen roadie jacket was filthy. "Sonofabitch!" He was speaking in general of the fence, the sliding under, the muddy ground, the universe in total. And the old man, who would now *really* get the crap kicked out of him for making this fine sateen roadie jacket filthy.

They sneaked up on him from the left, as far from the young guy in the trenchcoat as they could. The first one kicked out the shooting stick with a short, sharp, downward movement he had learned in his Tae Kwon Do class. It was called the *yup-chagi*. The old man went over backward.

Then they were on him, the one with the filthy sonofabitch sateen roadie jacket punching at the old man's neck and the side of his face as he dragged him around by the collar of the overcoat. The other one began ransacking the coat pockets, ripping the fabric to get his hand inside.

The old man commenced to scream. "Protect me! You've got to protect me ... it's necessary to protect me!"

The one pillaging pockets froze momentarily. What the hell kind of thing is that for this old fucker to be saying? Who the hell does he think'll protect him? Is he asking *us* to protect him? I'll protect you, scumbag! I'll kick in your fuckin' lung! "Shut 'im up!" he whispered urgently to his friend. "Stick a fist in his mouth!" Then his hand, wedged in an inside jacket pocket, closed over something. He tried to get his hand loose, but the jacket and coat and the old man's body had wound around his wrist. "C'mon loose, motherfuckah!" he said to the very old man, who was still screaming for protection. The other young man was making huffing sounds, as dark as mud, as he slapped at the rain-soaked hair of his victim. "I can't ... he's all twisted 'round ... getcher hand outta there so's I can ..." Screaming, the old man had doubled under, locking their hands on his person.

And then the pillager's fist came loose, and he was clutching—for an instant—a gorgeous pocket watch.

What used to be called a turnip watch.

The dial face was *cloisonné*, exquisite beyond the telling.

The case was of silver, so bright it seemed blue.

The hands, cast as arrows of time, were gold. They formed a shallow V at precisely eleven o'clock. This was happening at 3:45 in the afternoon, with rain and wind.

The timepiece made no sound, no sound at all.

Then: there was space all around the watch, and in

that space in the palm of the hand, there was heat.
Intense heat for just a moment, just long enough for the
hand to open.

The watch glided out of the boy's palm and levitated.
"Help me! You *must* protect me!"

Billy Kinetta heard the shrieking, but did not see the
pocket watch floating in the air above the astonished
young man. It was silver, and it was end-on toward him,
and the rain was silver and slanting; and he did not see
the watch hanging free in the air, even when the furious
young man disentangled himself and leaped for it. Billy
did not see the watch rise just so much, out of reach of
the mugger.

Billy Kinetta saw two boys, two young men of ratpack
age, beating someone much older; and he went for them.
Pow, like that!

Thrashing his legs, the old man twisted around—over,
under—as the boy holding him by the collar tried to land
a punch to put him away. Who would have thought the
old man to have had so much battle in him?

A flapping shape, screaming something unintelligible,
hit the center of the group at full speed. The carnaby-
gloved hand reaching for the watch grasped at empty air
one moment, and the next was buried under its owner
as the boy was struck a crackback block that threw him
face-first into the soggy ground. He tried to rise, but
something stomped him at the base of his spine; something kicked him twice in the kidneys; something rolled
over him like a flash flood.

Twisting, twisting, the very old man put his thumb in
the right eye of the boy clutching his collar.

The great trenchcoated maelstrom that was Billy
Kinetta whirled into the boy as he let loose of the old
man on the ground and, howling, slapped a palm against
his stinging eye. Billy locked his fingers and delivered a
roundhouse wallop that sent the boy reeling backward to
fall over Minna's tilted headstone.

Billy's back was to the old man. He did not see the
miraculous pocket watch smoothly descend through rain

that did not touch it, to hover in front of the old man. He did not see the old man reach up, did not see the timepiece snuggle into an arthritic hand, did not see the old man return the turnip to an inside jacket pocket.

Wind, rain and Billy Kinetta pummeled two young men of a legal age that made them accountable for their actions. There was no thought of the knife stuck down in one boot, no chance to reach it, no moment when the wild thing let them rise. So they crawled. They scrabbled across the muddy ground, the slippery grass, over graves and out of his reach. They ran; falling, rising, falling again; away, without looking back.

Billy Kinetta, breathing heavily, knees trembling, turned to help the old man to his feet; and found him standing, brushing dirt from his overcoat, snorting in anger and mumbling to himself.

"Are you all right?"

For a moment the old man's recitation of annoyance continued, then he snapped his chin down sharply as if marking end to the situation, and looked at his cavalry to the rescue. "That was very good, young fella. Considerable style you've got there."

Billy Kinetta stared at him wide-eyed. "Are you sure you're okay?" He reached over and flicked several blades of wet grass from the shoulder of the old man's overcoat.

"I'm fine. I'm fine but I'm wet and I'm cranky. Let's go somewhere and have a nice cup of Earl Grey."

There had been a look on Billy Kinetta's face as he stood with lowered eyes, staring at the grave he had come to visit. The emergency had removed that look. Now it returned.

"No, thanks. If you're okay, I've got to do some things."

The old man felt himself all over, meticulously, as he replied, "I'm only superficially bruised. Now if I were an old woman, instead of a spunky old man, same age though, I'd have lost considerable of the calcium in my bones, and those two would have done me some mischief. Did you know that women lose a considerable part of their calcium when they reach my age? I read a report." Then he paused, and said shyly, "Come on, why don't you and I sit and chew the fat over a nice cup of tea?"

Billy shook his head with bemusement, smiling despite himself. "You're something else, Dad. I don't even know you."

"I like that."

"What: that I don't know you?"

"No, that you called me 'Dad' and not 'Pop.' I *hate* 'Pop.' Always makes me think the wise-apple wants to snap off my cap with a bottle opener. Now *Dad* has a ring of respect to it. I like that right down to the ground. Yes, I believe we should find someplace warm and quiet to sit and get to know each other. After all, you saved my life. And you know what that means in the Orient."

Billy was smiling continuously now. "In the first place, I doubt very much I saved your life. Your wallet, maybe. And in the second place, I don't even know your name; what would we have to talk about?"

"Gaspar," he said, extending his hand. "That's a first name. Gaspar. Know what it means?"

Billy shook his head.

"See, already we have something to talk about."

So Billy, still smiling, began walking Gaspar out of the cemetery. "Where do you live? I'll take you home."

They were on the street, approaching Billy Kinetta's 1979 Cutlass. "Where I live is too far for now. I'm beginning to feel a bit peaky. I'd like to lie down for a minute. We can just go on over to your place, if that doesn't bother you. For a few minutes. A cup of tea. Is that all right?"

He was standing beside the Cutlass, looking at Billy with an old man's expectant smile, waiting for him to unlock the door and hold it for him till he'd placed his still-calcium-rich but nonetheless old bones in the passenger seat. Billy stared at him, trying to figure out what was at risk if he unlocked that door. Then he snorted a tiny laugh, unlocked the door, held it for Gaspar as he

seated himself, slammed it and went around to unlock
the other side and get in. Gaspar reached across and
thumbed up the door lock knob. And they drove off
together in the rain.

Through all of this the timepiece made no sound, no
sound at all.

Like Gaspar, Billy Kinetta was alone in the world.

His three-room apartment was the vacuum in which
he existed. It was furnished, but if one stepped out into
the hallway and, for all the money in all the numbered
accounts in all the banks in Switzerland, one were asked
to describe those furnishings, one would come away no
richer than before. The apartment was charisma poor. It
was a place to come when all other possibilities had been
expended. Nothing green, nothing alive, existed in those
boxes. No eyes looked back from the walls. Neither
warmth nor chill marked those spaces. It was a place to
wait.

Gaspar leaned his closed shooting stick, now a walking
stick with handles, against the bookcase. He studied the
titles of the paperbacks stacked haphazardly on the
shelves.

From the kitchenette came the sound of water running
into a metal pan. Then tin on cast iron. Then the hiss of
gas and the flaring of a match as it was struck; and the
pop of the gas being lit.

"Many years ago," Gaspar said, taking out a copy of
Moravia's *The Adolescents* and thumbing it as he spoke,
"I had a library of books, oh, thousands of books—never
could bear to toss one out, not even the bad ones—and
when folks would come to the house to visit they'd look
around at all the nooks and crannies stuffed with books;
and if they were the sort of folks who don't snuggle with
books, they'd always ask the same dumb question." He
waited a moment for a response and when none was
forthcoming (the sound of china cups on sink tile), he
said, "Guess what the question was."

From the kitchen, without much interest: "No idea."

"They'd always ask it with the kind of voice people use in the presence of large sculptures in museums. They'd ask me, 'Have you read all these books?'" He waited again, but Billy Kinetta was not playing the game. "Well, young fella, after a while the same dumb question gets asked a million times, you get sorta snappish about it. And it came to annoy me more than a little bit. Till I finally figured out the right answer.

"And you know what that answer was? Go ahead, take a guess."

Billy appeared in the kitchenette doorway. "I suppose you told them you'd read a lot of them but not all of them."

Gaspar waved the guess away with a flapping hand. "Now what good would that have done? They wouldn't know they'd asked a dumb question, but I didn't want to insult them, either. So when they'd ask if I'd read all those books, I'd say, 'Hell, no. Who wants a library full of books you've already read?'"

Billy laughed despite himself. He scratched at his hair with idle pleasure, and shook his head at the old man's verve. "Gaspar, you are a wild old man. You retired?"

The old man walked carefully to the most comfortable chair in the room, an overstuffed Thirties-style lounge that had been reupholstered many times before Billy Kinetta had purchased it at the American Cancer Society Thrift Shop. He sank into it with a sigh. "No sir, I am not by any means retired. Still very active."

"Doing what, if I'm not prying?"

"Doing ombudsman."

"You mean, like a consumer advocate? Like Ralph Nader?"

"Exactly. I watch out for things. I listen, I pay some attention; and if I do it right, sometimes I can even make a little difference. Yes, like Mr. Nader. A very fine man."

"And you were at the cemetery to see a relative?"

Gaspar's face settled into an expression of loss. "My dear old girl. My wife, Minna. She's been gone, well, it was twenty years in January." He sat silently staring inward for a while, then: "She was everything to me. The nice part was that I knew how important we were to each other; we discussed, well, just *everything*. I miss that the most, telling her what's going on.

"I go to see her every other day.

"I used to go every day. But. It. Hurt. Too much."

They had tea. Gaspar sipped and said it was very nice, but had Billy ever tried Earl Grey? Billy said he didn't know what that was, and Gaspar said he would bring him a tin, that it was splendid. And they chatted. Finally, Gaspar asked, "And who were you visiting?"

Billy pressed his lips together. "Just a friend." And would say no more. Then he sighed and said, "Well, listen, I have to go to work."

"Oh? What do you do?"

The answer came slowly. As if Billy Kinetta wanted to be able to say that he was in computers, or owned his own business, or held a position of import. "I'm night manager at a 7-Eleven."

"I'll bet you meet some fascinating people coming in late for milk or one of those slushies," Gaspar said gently. He seemed to understand.

Billy smiled. He took the kindness as it was intended. "Yeah, the cream of high society. That is, when they're not threatening to shoot me through the head if I don't open the safe."

"Let me ask you a favor," Gaspar said. "I'd like a little sanctuary, if you think it's all right. Just a little rest. I could lie down on the sofa for a bit. Would that be all right? You trust me to stay here while you're gone, young fella?"

Billy hesitated only a moment. The very old man seemed okay, not a crazy, certainly not a thief. And what was there to steal? Some tea that wasn't even Earl Grey?

"Sure. That'll be okay. But I won't be coming back till two A.M. So just close the door behind you when you go; it'll lock automatically."

They shook hands, Billy shrugged into his still-wet trenchcoat, and he went to the door. He paused to look

back at Gaspar sitting in the lengthening shadows as evening came on. "It was nice getting to know you, Gaspar."

"You can make that a mutual pleasure, Billy. You're a
nice young fella."

And Billy went to work, alone as always.

When he came home at two, prepared to open a can
of Hormel chili, he found the table set for dinner; with
the scent of an elegant beef stew enriching the apartment. There were new potatoes and stir-fried carrots and
zucchini that had been lightly battered to delicate crisp-
ness. And cupcakes. White cake with chocolate frosting.
From a bakery.

And in that way, as gently as that, Gaspar insinuated
himself into Billy Kinetta's apartment and his life.

As they sat with tea and cupcakes, Billy said, "You
don't have anyplace to go, do you?"

The old man smiled and made one of those deprecat-
ing movements of the head. "Well, I'm not the sort of
fella who can bear to be homeless, but at the moment
I'm what vaudevillians used to call 'at liberty.'"

"If you want to stay on a time, that would be okay,"
Billy said. "It's not very roomy here, but we seem to get
on all right."

"That's strongly kind of you, Billy. Yes, I'd like to be
your roommate for a while. Won't be too long, though.
My doctor tells me I'm not long for this world." He
paused, looked into the teacup and said softly, "I have
to confess ... I'm a little frightened. To go. Having
someone to talk to would be a great comfort."

And Billy said, without preparation, "I was visiting the
grave of a man who was in my rifle company in Viet
Nam. I go there sometimes." But there was such pain in
his words that Gaspar did not press him for details.

So the hours passed, as they will with or without permission, and when Gaspar asked Billy if they could watch
the television, to catch an early newscast, and Billy tuned
in the old set just in time to pick up dire reports of
another aborted disarmament talk, and Billy shook his

head and observed that it wasn't only Gaspar who was frightened of something like death, Gaspar chuckled, patted Billy on the knee and said, with unassailable assurance, "Take my word for it, Billy ... it isn't going to happen. No nuclear holocaust. Trust me, when I tell you this: it'll never happen. Never, never, not ever."

Billy smiled wanly. "And why not? What makes *you* so sure ... got some special inside information?"

And Gaspar pulled out the magnificent timepiece, which Billy was seeing for the first time, and he said, "It's not going to happen because it's only eleven o'clock."

Billy stared at the watch, which read 11:00 precisely. He consulted his wristwatch. "Hate to tell you this, but your watch has stopped. It's almost five-thirty."

Gaspar smiled his own certain smile. "No, it's eleven."

And they made up the sofa for the very old man, who placed his pocket change and his fountain pen and the sumptuous turnip watch on the now-silent television set, and they went to sleep.

One day Billy went off while Gaspar was washing the lunch dishes, and when he came back, he had a large paper bag from Toys R Us.

Gaspar came out of the kitchenette rubbing a plate with a souvenir dish towel from Niagara Falls, New York. He stared at Billy and the bag. "What's in the bag?" Billy inclined his head, and indicated the very old man should join him in the middle of the room. Then he sat down crosslegged on the floor, and dumped the contents of the bag. Gaspar stared with startlement, and sat down beside him.

So for two hours they played with tiny cars that turned into robots when the sections were unfolded.

Gaspar was excellent at figuring out all the permutations of the Transformers, Starriors and GoBots. He played well.

Then they went for a walk. "I'll treat you to a matinee," Gaspar said. "But no films with Karen Black, Sandy

Dennis or Meryl Streep. They're always crying. Their noses are always red. I can't stand that."

They started to cross the avenue. Stopped at the light was this year's Cadillac Brougham, vanity license plates, ten coats of acrylic lacquer and two coats of clear (with a little retarder in the final "color coat" for a slow dry) of a magenta hue so rich that it approximated the shade of light shining through a decanter filled with Château Lafite-Rothschild 1945.

The man driving the Cadillac had no neck. His head sat thumped down hard on the shoulders. He stared straight ahead, took one last deep pull on the cigar, and threw it out the window. The still-smoking butt landed directly in front of Gaspar as he passed the car. The old man stopped, stared down at this coprolitic metaphor, and then stared at the driver. The eyes behind the wheel, the eyes of a macaque, did not waver from the stoplight's red circle. Just outside the window, someone was looking in, but the eyes of the rhesus were on the red circle.

A line of cars stopped behind the Brougham.

Gaspar continued to stare at the man in the Cadillac for a moment, and then, with creaking difficulty, he bent and picked up the smoldering butt of stogie.

The old man walked the two steps to the car—as Billy watched in confusion—thrust his face forward till it was mere inches from the driver's profile, and said with extreme sweetness, "I think you dropped this in our living room."

And as the glazed simian eyes turned to stare directly into the pedestrian's face, nearly nose-to-nose, Gaspar casually flipped the butt with its red glowing tip, into the back seat of the Cadillac, where it began to burn a hole in the fine Corinthian leather.

Three things happened simultaneously:

The driver let out a howl, tried to see the butt in his rearview mirror, could not get the angle, tried to look over his shoulder into the back seat but without a neck could not perform that feat of agility, put the car into neutral, opened his door and stormed into the street trying to grab Gaspar. "You fuckin' bastid, whaddaya think you're doin' tuh my car you asshole bastid, I'll kill ya . . ."

Billy's hair stood on end as he saw what Gaspar was doing; he rushed back the short distance in the crosswalk to grab the old man; Gaspar would not be dragged away, stood smiling with unconcealed pleasure at the mad bull rampaging and screaming of the hysterical driver. Billy yanked as hard as he could and Gaspar began to move away, around the front of the Cadillac, toward the far curb. Still grinning with octogeneric charm.

The light changed.

These three things happened in the space of five seconds, abetted by the impatient honking of the cars behind the Brougham; as the light turned green.

Screaming, dragging, honking, as the driver found he could not do three things at once: he could not go after Gaspar while the traffic was clanging at him; could not let go of the car door to crawl into the back seat from which now came the stench of charring leather that could not be rectified by an inexpensive Tijuana tuck-'n-roll; could not save his back seat and at the same time stave off the hostility of a dozen drivers cursing and honking. He trembled there, torn three ways, doing nothing.

Billy dragged Gaspar.

Out of the crosswalk. Out of the street. Onto the curb. Up the side street. Into the alley. Through a backyard. To the next street over away from the avenue.

Puffing with the exertion, Billy stopped at last, five houses up the street. Gaspar was still grinning, chuckling softly with unconcealed pleasure at his puckish ways. Billy turned on him with wild gesticulations and babble.

"You're *nuts!*"

"How about that?" the old man said, giving Billy an affectionate poke in the bicep.

"Nuts! Looney! That guy would've torn off your head! What the hell's wrong with you, old man? Are you out of your boots?"

"I'm not crazy. I'm responsible."

"Responsible!?! Responsible, fer chrissakes? For what? For all the butts every yotz throws into the street?"

The old man nodded. "For butts, and trash, and pollution, and toxic waste dumping in the dead of night; for bushes, and cactus, and the baobab tree; for pippin apples and even lima beans, which I despise. You show me someone who'll eat lima beans without being at gunpoint, I'll show you a pervert!"

Billy was screaming. "What the hell are you talking about?"

"I'm also responsible for dogs and cats and guppies and cockroaches and the President of the United States and Jonas Salk and your mother and the entire chorus line at the Sands Hotel in Las Vegas. Also their choreographer."

"Who do you think you are? God?"

"Don't be sacrilegious. I'm too old to wash your mouth out with laundry soap. Of course I'm not God. I'm just an old man. *But I'm responsible.*"

Gaspar started to walk away, toward the corner and the avenue, and a resumption of their route. Billy stood where the old man's words had pinned him.

"Come on, young fella," Gaspar said, walking backward to speak to him, "we'll miss the beginning of the movie. I hate that."

Billy had finished eating, and they were sitting in the dimness of the apartment, only the lamp in the corner lit. The old man had gone to the County Art Museum and had bought inexpensive prints—Max Ernst, Gérôme, Richard Dadd, a subtle Feininger—which he had mounted in Insta-Frames. They sat in silence for a time, relaxing; then murmuring trivialities in a pleasant undertone.

Finally, Gaspar said, "I've been thinking a lot about my dying. I like what Woody Allen said."

Billy slid to a more comfortable position in the lounger. "What was that?"

"He said: I don't mind dying, I just don't want to be there when it happens."

Billy snickered.

"I feel something like that, Billy. I'm not afraid to go, but I don't want to leave Minna entirely. The times I spend with her, talking to her, well, it gives me the feeling we're still in touch. When I go, that's the end of Minna. She'll be well and truly dead. We never had any children, almost everyone who knew us is gone, no relatives. And we never did anything important that anyone would put in a record book, so that's the end of us. For me, I don't mind; but I wish there was someone who knew about Minna . . . she was a remarkable person."

So Billy said, "Tell me. I'll remember for you."

Memories in no particular order. Some as strong as ropes that could pull the ocean ashore. Some that shimmered and swayed in the faintest breeze like spiderwebs. The entire person, all the little movements, that dimple that appeared when she was amused at something foolish he had said. Their youth together, their love, the procession of their days toward middle age. The small cheers and the pain of dreams never realized. So much about *him*, as he spoke of *her*. His voice soft and warm and filled with a longing so deep and true that he had to stop frequently because the words broke and would not come out till he had thought away some of the passion. He thought of her and was glad. He had gathered her together, all her dowry of love and taking care of him, her clothes and the way she wore them, her favorite knickknacks, a few clever remarks: and he packed it all up and delivered it to a new repository.

The very old man gave Minna to Billy Kinetta for safekeeping.

Dawn had come. The light filtering in through the blinds was saffron. "Thank you, Dad," Billy said. He could not name the feeling that had taken him hours earlier. But he said this: "I've never had to be responsible for anything, or anyone, in my whole life. I never belonged to anybody ... I don't know why. It didn't bother me, because I didn't know any other way to be."

Then his position changed, there in the lounger. He sat up in a way that Gaspar thought was important. As if Billy were about to open the secret box buried at his center. And Billy spoke so softly the old man had to strain to hear him.

"I didn't even know him.

"We were defending the airfield at Danang. Did I tell you we were 1st Battalion, 9th Marines? Charlie was massing for a big push out of Quang Ngai province, south of us. Looked as if they were going to try to take the provincial capital. My rifle company was assigned to protect the perimeter. They kept sending in patrols to bite us. Every day we'd lose some poor bastard who scratched his head when he shouldn't of. It was June, late in June, cold and a lot of rain. The foxholes were hip-deep in water.

"Flares first. Our howitzers started firing. Then the sky was full of tracers, and I started to turn toward the bushes when I heard something coming, and these two main-force regulars in dark blue uniforms came toward me. I could see them so clearly. Long black hair. All crouched over. And they started firing. And that goddam carbine seized up, wouldn't fire; and I pulled out the banana clip, tried to slap in another, but they saw me and just turned a couple of AK-47s on me ... God, I remember everything slowed down ... I looked at those things, seven-point-six-two-millimeter assault rifles they were ... I got crazy for a second, tried to figure out in my own mind if they were Russian-made, or Chinese, or Czech, or North Korean. And it was so bright from the flares I could see them starting to squeeze off the rounds, and then from out of nowhere this lance corporal jumped out at them and yelled somedamnthing like, 'Hey, you VC fucks, looka here!' except it wasn't that ... I never could recall what he said actually ... and they turned to brace him ... and they opened him up like a Baggie full of blood . . . and he was all over me, and the bushes, and oh god there was pieces of him floating on the water I was standing in . . ."

Billy was heaving breath with impossible weight. His hands moved in the air before his face without pattern or goal. He kept looking into far corners of the dawn-lit room as if special facts might present themselves to fill out the reasons behind what he was saying.

"Aw, geezus, he was *floating* on the water . . . aw, christ, *he got in my boots!*" Then a wail of pain so loud it blotted out the sound of traffic beyond the apartment; and he began to moan, but not cry; and the moaning kept on; and Gaspar came from the sofa and held him and said such words as *it's all right*, but they might not have been those words, or *any* words.

And pressed against the old man's shoulder, Billy Kinetta ran on only half sane: "He wasn't my friend, I never knew him, I'd never talked to him, but I'd seen him, he was just this guy, and there wasn't any reason to do that, he didn't know whether I was a good guy or a shit or anything, so why did he do that? He didn't need to do that. They wouldn't of seen him. He was dead before I killed them. He was gone already. I never got to say thank you or thank you or . . . *anything!*

"Now he's in that grave, so I came here to live, so I can go there, but I try and try to say thank you, and he's dead, and he can't hear me, he can't hear nothin', he's just down there, down in the ground, and I can't say thank you . . . oh, geezus, geezus, why don't he hear me, I just want to say thanks . . ."

Billy Kinetta wanted to assume the responsibility for saying thanks, but that was possible only on a night that would never come again; and this was the day.

Gaspar took him to the bedroom and put him down to sleep in exactly the same way he would soothe an old, sick dog.

Then he went to his sofa, and because it was the only thing he could imagine saying, he murmured, "He'll be all right, Minna. Really he will."

°   °   °

When Billy left for the 7-Eleven the next evening, Gaspar was gone. It was an alternate day, and that meant he was out at the cemetery. Billy fretted that he shouldn't be there alone, but the old man had a way of taking care of himself. Billy was not smiling as he thought of his friend, and the word *friend* echoed as he realized that, yes, this was his friend, truly and really his friend. He wondered how old Gaspar was, and how soon Billy Kinetta would be once again what he had always been: alone.

When he returned to the apartment at two-thirty, Gaspar was asleep, cocooned in his blanket on the sofa. Billy went in and tried to sleep, but hours later, when sleep would not come, when thoughts of murky water and calcium night light on dark foliage kept him staring at the bedroom ceiling, he came out of the room for a drink of water. He wandered around the living room, not wanting to be by himself even if the only companionship in this sleepless night was breathing heavily, himself in sleep.

He stared out the window. Clouds lay in chiffon strips across the sky. The squealing of tires from the street.

Sighing, idle in his movement around the room, he saw the old man's pocket watch lying on the coffee table beside the sofa. He walked to the table. If the watch was still stopped at eleven o'clock, perhaps he would borrow it and have it repaired. It would be a nice thing to do for Gaspar. The old man loved that beautiful timepiece.

Billy bent to pick it up.

The watch, stopped at the V of eleven precisely, levitated at an angle, floating away from him.

Billy Kinetta felt a shiver travel down his back to burrow in at the base of his spine. He reached for the watch hanging in air before him. It floated away just enough that his fingers massaged empty space. He tried to catch it. The watch eluded him, lazily turning away like an opponent who knows he is in no danger of being struck from behind.

Then Billy realized Gaspar was awake. Turned away

from the sofa, nonetheless he knew the old man was observing him. And the blissful floating watch.

He looked at Gaspar.

They did not speak for a long time.

Then: "I'm going back to sleep," Billy said. Quietly.

"I think you have some questions," Gaspar replied.

"Questions? No, of course not, Dad. Why in the world would I have questions? I'm still asleep." But that was not the truth, because he had not been asleep that night.

"Do you know what 'Gaspar' means? Do you remember the three wise men of the Bible, the Magi?"

"I don't want any frankincense and myrrh. I'm going back to bed. I'm going now. You see, I'm going right now."

" 'Gaspar' means master of the treasure, keeper of the secrets, paladin of the palace." Billy was staring at him, not walking into the bedroom; just staring at him. As the elegant timepiece floated to the old man, who extended his hand palm-up to receive it. The watch nestled in his hand, unmoving, and it made no sound, no sound at all.

"You go back to bed. But will you go out to the cemetery with me tomorrow? It's important."

"Why?"

"Because I believe I'll be dying tomorrow."

It was a nice day, cool and clear. Not at all a day for dying, but neither had been many such days in Southeast Asia, and death had not been deterred.

They stood at Minna's gravesite, and Gaspar opened his shooting stick to form a seat; and he thrust the spike into the ground; and he settled onto it, and sighed, and said to Billy Kinetta, "I'm growing cold as that stone."

"Do you want my jacket?"

"No, I'm cold inside." He looked around at the sky, at the grass, at the rows of markers. "I've been responsible, for all of this, and more."

"You've said that before."

"Young fella, are you by any chance familiar, in your reading, with an old novel by James Hilton called *Lost*

Horizon? Perhaps you saw the movie. It was a wonderful movie, actually much better than the book. Mr. Capra's greatest achievement. A human testament. Ronald Colman was superb. Do you know the story?"

"Yes."

"Do you remember the High Lama, played by Sam Jaffe? His name was Father Perrault?"

"Yes."

"Do you remember how he passed on the caretakership of that magical hidden world, Shangri-La, to Ronald Colman?"

"Yes, I remember that." Billy paused. "Then he died. He was very old, and he died."

Gaspar smiled up at him. "Very good, Billy. I knew you were a good boy. So now, if you remember all that, may I tell you a story? It's not a very long story."

Billy nodded, smiling at his friend.

"In 1582 Pope Gregory XIII decreed that the civilized world would no longer observe the Julian calendar. October 4th, 1582 was followed, the next day, by October 15th. Eleven days vanished from the world. One hundred and seventy years later, the British Parliament followed suit, and September 2nd, 1752 was followed, the next day, by September 14th. Why did he do that, the Pope?"

Billy was bewildered by the conversation. "Because he was bringing it into synch with the real world. The solstices and equinoxes. When to plant, when to harvest."

Gaspar waggled a finger at him with pleasure. "Excellent, young fella. And you're correct when you say Gregory abolished the Julian calendar because its error of one day in every one hundred and twenty-eight years had moved the vernal equinox to March 11th. That's what the history books say. It's what *every* history book says. But what if?"

"What if *what*? I don't know what you're talking about."

"What if: Pope Gregory had the knowledge revealed to him that he *must* readjust time in the minds of men? What if: the excess time in 1582 was eleven days and one hour? What if: he accounted for those eleven days, vanished those eleven days, but that one hour slipped free, was left loose to bounce through eternity? A very special hour . . . an hour that must *never* be used . . . an hour that must never toll. What if?"

Billy spread his hands. "What if, what if, what if! It's all just philosophy. It doesn't mean anything. Hours aren't real, time isn't something that you can bottle up. So what if there *is* an hour out there somewhere that . . ."

And he stopped.

He grew tense, and leaned down to the old man. "The watch. Your watch. It doesn't work. It's stopped."

Gaspar nodded. "At eleven o'clock. My watch works; it keeps very special time, for one very special hour."

Billy touched Gaspar's shoulder. Carefully he asked, "Who are you, Dad?"

The old man did not smile as he said, "Gaspar. Keeper. Paladin. Guardian."

"Father Perrault was hundreds of years old."

Gaspar shook his head with a wistful expression on his old face. "I'm eighty-six years old, Billy. You asked me if I thought I was God. Not God, not Father Perrault, not an immortal, just an old man who will die too soon. Are you Ronald Colman?"

Billy nervously touched his lower lip with a finger. He looked at Gaspar as long as he could, then turned away. He walked off a few paces, stared at the barren trees. It seemed suddenly much chillier here in this place of entombed remembrances. From a distance he said, "But it's only . . . what? A chronological convenience. Like daylight saving time; Spring forward, Fall back. We don't actually *lose* an hour; we get it back."

Gaspar stared at Minna's grave. "At the end of April I lost an hour. If I die now, I'll die an hour short in my life. I'll have been cheated out of one hour I want, Billy." He swayed toward all he had left of Minna. "One last hour I could have with my old girl. That's what I'm afraid of, Billy. I have that hour in my possession. I'm afraid I'll use it, god help me, I want so much to use it."

Billy came to him. Tense, and chilled, he said, "Why must that hour never toll?"

Gaspar drew a deep breath and tore his eyes away from the grave. His gaze locked with Billy's. And he told him.

The years, all the days and hours, exist. As solid and as real as mountains and oceans and men and women and the baobab tree. Look, he said, at the lines in my face and deny that time is real. Consider these dead weeds that were once alive and try to believe it's all just vapor or the mutual agreement of Popes and Caesars and young men like you.

"The lost hour must never come, Billy, for in that hour it all ends. The light, the wind, the stars, this magnificent open place we call the universe. It all ends, and in its place—waiting, always waiting—is eternal darkness. No new beginnings, no world without end, just the infinite emptiness."

And he opened his hand, which had been lying in his lap, and there, in his palm, rested the watch, making no sound at all, and stopped dead at eleven o'clock. "Should it strike twelve, Billy, eternal night falls; from which there is no recall."

There he sat, this very old man, just a perfectly normal old man. The most recent in the endless chain of keepers of the lost hour, descended in possession from Caesar and Pope Gregory XIII, down through the centuries of men and women who had served as caretakers of the excellent timepiece. And now he was dying, and now he wanted to cling to life as every man and woman clings to life no matter how awful or painful or empty, even if it is for one more hour. The suicide, falling from the bridge, at the final instant, tries to fly, tries to climb back up the sky. This weary old man, who only wanted to stay one brief hour more with Minna. Who was afraid that his love would cost the universe.

He looked at Billy, and he extended his hand with the watch waiting for its next paladin. So softly Billy could barely hear him, knowing that he was denying himself what he most wanted at this last place in his life, he whispered, "If I die without passing it on . . . it will begin to tick."

"Not me," Billy said. "Why did you pick me? I'm no one special. I'm not someone like you. I run an all-night service mart. There's nothing special about me the way there is about you! I'm *not* Ronald Colman! I don't want to be responsible, I've *never* been responsible!"

Gaspar smiled gently. "You've been responsible for me."

Billy's rage vanished. He looked wounded.

"Look at us, Billy. Look at what color you are; and look at what color I am. You took me in as a friend. I think of you as worthy, Billy. Worthy."

They remained there that way, in silence, as the wind rose. And finally, in a timeless time, Billy nodded.

Then the young man said, "You won't be losing Minna, Dad. Now you'll go to the place where she's been waiting for you, just as she was when you first met her. There's a place where we find everything we've ever lost through the years."

"That's good, Billy, that you tell me that. I'd like to believe it, too. But I'm a pragmatist. I believe in what exists . . . like rain and Minna's grave and the hours that pass that we can't see, but they *are*. I'm afraid, Billy. I'm afraid this will be the last time I can speak to her. So I ask a favor. As payment, in return for my life spent protecting the watch.

"I ask for one minute of the hour, Billy. One minute to call her back, so we can stand face-to-face and I can touch her and say goodbye. You'll be the new protector of this watch, Billy, so I ask you please, just let me steal one minute."

Billy could not speak. The look on Gaspar's face was without horizon, empty as tundra, bottomless. The child left alone in darkness; the pain of eternal waiting. He knew he could never deny this old man, no matter what he asked, and in the silence he heard a voice say: "*No!*" And it was his own.

He had spoken without conscious volition. Strong and determined, and without the slightest room for reversal. If a part of his heart had been swayed by compassion, that part had been instantly overridden. No. A final, unshakeable no.

For an instant Gaspar looked crestfallen. His eyes

clouded with tears; and Billy felt something twist and break within himself at the sight. He knew he had hurt the old man. Quickly, but softly, he said urgently, "You know that would be wrong, Dad. We mustn't . . ."

Gaspar said nothing. Then he reached out with his free hand and took Billy's. It was an affectionate touch. "That was the last test, young fella. Oh, you know I've been testing you, don't you? This important item couldn't go to just anyone.

"And you passed the test, my friend: my last, best friend. When I said I could bring her back from where she's gone, here in this place we've both come to so often, to talk to someone lost to us, I knew you would understand that *anyone* could be brought back in that stolen minute. I knew you wouldn't use it for yourself, no matter how much you wanted it; but I wasn't sure that as much as you like me, it might not sway you. But you wouldn't even give it to *me*, Billy."

He smiled up at him, his eyes now clear and steady.

"I'm content, Billy. You needn't have worried. Minna and I don't need that minute. But if you're to carry on for me, I think you *do* need it. You're in pain, and that's no good for someone who carries this watch. You've got to heal, Billy.

"So I give you something you would never take for yourself. I give you a going-away present . . ."

And he started the watch, whose ticking was as loud and as clear as a baby's first sound; and the sweep-second hand began to move away from eleven o'clock.

Then the wind rose, and the sky seemed to cloud over, and it grew colder, with a remarkable silver-blue mist that rolled across the cemetery; and though he did not see it emerge from that grave at a distance far to the right, Billy Kinetta saw a shape move toward him. A soldier in the uniform of a day past, and his rank was Lance Corporal. He came toward Billy Kinetta, and Billy went to meet him as Gaspar watched.

They stood together and Billy spoke to him. And the man whose name Billy had never known when he was alive, answered. And then he faded, as the seconds ticked away. Faded, and faded, and was gone. And the silver-blue mist rolled through them, and past them, and was gone; and the soldier was gone.

Billy stood alone.

When he turned back to look across the grounds to his friend, he saw that Gaspar had fallen from the shooting-stick. He lay on the ground. Billy rushed to him, and fell to his knees and lifted him onto his lap. Gaspar was still.

"Oh, god, Dad, you should have heard what he said. Oh, geez, he let me go. He let me go so I didn't even have to say I was sorry. He told me he didn't even *see* me in that foxhole. He never knew he'd saved my life. I said thank you and he said no, thank *you*, that he hadn't died for nothing. Oh, please, Dad, please don't be dead yet. I want to tell you . . ."

And, as it sometimes happens, rarely but wonderfully, sometimes they come back for a moment, for an instant before they go, the old man, this very old man, opened his eyes, just before going on his way, and he looked through the dimming light at his friend, and he said, "May I remember you to my old girl, Billy?"

And his eyes closed again, after only a moment; and his caretakership was at an end; as his hand opened and the most excellent timepiece, now stopped again at one minute past eleven, floated from his palm and waited till Billy Kinetta extended his hand; and then it floated down and lay there silently, making no sound, no sound at all. Safe. Protected.

There in the place where all lost things returned, the young man sat on the cold ground, rocking the body of his friend. And he was in no hurry to leave. There was time.

A blessing of the 18th Egyptian Dynasty:

> *God be between you and harm in*
> *all the empty places you walk.*

The author gratefully acknowledges the importance of a discussion with Ms. Ellie Grossman in the creation of this work of fiction.

Fermi and Frost

by Frederik Pohl

On Timothy Clary's ninth birthday he got no cake. He spent all of it in a bay of the TWA terminal at John F. Kennedy airport in New York, sleeping fitfully, crying now and then from exhaustion or fear. All he had to eat was stale Danish pastries from the buffet wagon and not many of them, and he was fearfully embarrassed because he had wet his pants. Three times. Getting to the toilets over the packed refugee bodies was just about impossible. There were twenty-eight hundred people in a space designed for a fraction that many, and all of them with the same idea. Get away! Climb the highest mountain! Drop yourself splat, sprang, right in the middle of the widest desert! Run! Hide!—

And pray. Pray as hard as you can, because even the occasional planeload of refugees that managed to fight their way aboard and even take off had no sure hope of refuge when they got wherever the plane was going. Families parted. Mothers pushed their screaming children aboard a jet and melted back into the crowd before screaming, more quietly, themselves.

Because there had been no launch order yet, or none that the public had heard about anyway, there might still be time for escape. A little time. Time enough for the TWA terminal, and every other airport terminal everywhere, to jam up with terrified lemmings. There was no doubt that the missiles were poised to fly. The attempted Cuban coup had escalated wildly, and one nuclear sub had attacked another with a nuclear charge. That, everyone agreed, was the signal. The next event would be the final one.

Timothy knew little of this, but there would have been

103

nothing he could have done about it—except perhaps cry, or have nightmares, or wet himself, and young Timothy was doing all of those anyway. He did not know where his father was. He didn't know where his mother was, either, except that she had gone somewhere to try to call his father, but then there had been a surge that could not be resisted when three 747s at once had announced boarding, and Timothy had been carried far from where he had been left. Worse than that. Wet as he was, with a cold already, he was beginning to be very sick. The young woman who had brought him the Danish pastries put a worried hand to his forehead and drew it away helplessly. The boy needed a doctor. But so did a hundred others, elderly heart patients and hungry babies and at least two women close to childbirth.

If the terror had passed and the frantic negotiations had succeeded, Timothy might have found his parents again in time to grow up and marry and give them grandchildren. If one side or the other had been able to preempt, and destroy the other, and save itself. Timothy forty years later might have been a graying, cynical colonel in the American military government of Leningrad. (Or body servant to a Russian one in Detroit.) Or if his mother had pushed just a little harder earlier on, he might have wound up in the plane of refugees that reached Pittsburgh just in time to become plasma. Or if the girl who was watching him had became just a little more scared, and a little more brave, and somehow managed to get him through the throng to the improvised clinics in the main terminal, he might have been given medicine, and found somebody to protect him, and take him to a refuge, and lived. . . .

But that is in fact what did happen!

Because Harry Malibert was on his way to a British Interplanetary Society seminar in Portsmouth, he was already sipping Beefeater Martinis in the terminal's Ambassador Club when the unnoticed TV at the bar suddenly made everybody notice it.

Those silly nuclear-attack communications systems that the radio station tested out every now and then, and nobody paid any attention to any more—why, this time it was real! They were serious! Because it was winter and snowing heavily Malibert's flight had been delayed anyway. Before its rescheduled departure time came, all flights had been embargoed. Nothing would leave Kennedy until some official somewhere decided to let them go.

Almost at once the terminal began to fill with would-be refugees. The Ambassador Club did not fill at once. For three hours the ground-crew stew at the desk resolutely turned away everyone who rang the bell who could not produce the little red card of admission; but when the food and drink in the main terminals began to run out the Chief of Operations summarily opened the club to everyone. It didn't help relieve the congestion outside, it only added to what was within. Almost at once a volunteer doctors' committee seized most of the club to treat the ill and injured from the thickening crowds, and people like Harry Malibert found themselves pushed into the bar area. It was one of the Operations staff, commandeering a gin and tonic at the bar for the sake of the calories more than the booze, who recognized him. "You're Harry Malibert. I heard you lecture once, at Northwestern."

Malibert nodded. Usually when someone said that to him he answered politely, "I hope you enjoyed it," but this time it did not seem appropriate to be normally polite. Or normal at all.

"You showed slides of Arecibo," the man said dreamily. "You said that radio telescope could send a message as far as the Great Nebula in Andromeda, two million light-years away—if only there was another radio telescope as good as that one there to receive it."

"You remember very well," said Malibert, surprised.

"You made a big impression, Dr. Malibert." The man glanced at his watch, debated, took another sip of his drink. "It really sounded wonderful, using the big telescopes to listen for messages from alien civilizations somewhere in space—maybe hearing some, maybe making contact, maybe not being alone in the universe any more. You made me wonder why we hadn't seen some of these people already, or anyway heard from them—but maybe," he finished, glancing bitterly at the ranked and guarded aircraft outside, "maybe now we know why."

Malibert watched him go, and his heart was leaden. The thing he had given his professional career to—SETI, the Search for Extra-Terrestrial Intelligence—no longer seemed to matter. If the bombs went off, as everyone said they must, then that was ended for a good long time, at least—

Gabble of voices at the end of the bar; Malibert turned, leaned over the mahogany, peered. The *Please Stand By* slide had vanished, and a young black woman with pomaded hair, voice trembling, was delivering a news bulletin:

"—the president has confirmed that a nuclear attack has begun against the United States. Missiles have been detected over the Arctic, and they are incoming. Everyone is ordered to seek shelter and remain there pending instructions—"

Yes, It was ended, thought Malibert, at least for a good long time.

The surprising thing was that the news that it had begun changed nothing. There were no screams, no hysteria. The order to seek shelter meant nothing to John F. Kennedy Airport, where there was no shelter any better than the building they were in. And that, no doubt, was not too good. Malibert remembered clearly the strange aerodynamic shape of the terminal's roof. Any blast anywhere nearby would tear that off and send it sailing over the bay to the Rockaways, and probably a lot of the people inside with it.

But there was nowhere else to go.

There were still camera crews at work, heaven knew why. The television set was showing crowds in Times

Square and Newark, a clot of automobiles stagnating on the George Washington Bridge, their drivers abandoning them and running for the Jersey shore. A hundred people were peering around each other's heads to catch glimpses of the screen, but all that anyone said was to call out when he recognized a building or a street.

Orders rang out: "You people will have to move back! We need the room! Look, some of you, give us a hand with these patients." Well, that seemed useful, at least. Malibert volunteered at once and was given the care of a young boy, teeth chattering, hot with fever. "He's had tetracycline," said the doctor who turned the boy over to him. "Clean him up if you can, will you? He ought to be all right if—"

If any of them were, thought Malibert, not requiring her to finish the sentence. How did you clean a young boy up? The question answered itself when Malibert found the boy's trousers soggy and the smell told him what the moisture was. Carefully he laid the child on a leather love seat and removed the pants and sopping undershorts. Naturally the boy had not come with a change of clothes. Malibert solved that with a pair of his own jockey shorts out of his briefcase—far too big for the child, of course, but since they were meant to fit tightly and elastically they stayed in place when Malibert pulled them up to the waist. Then he found paper towels and pressed the blue jeans as dry as he could. It was not very dry. He grimaced, laid them over a bar stool and sat on them for a while, drying them with body heat. They were only faintly wet ten minutes later when he put them back on the child—

San Francisco, the television said, had ceased to transmit.

Malibert saw the Operations man working his way toward him and shook his head. "It's begun," Malibert said, and the man looked around. He put his face close to Malibert's.

"I can get you out of here," he whispered. "There's an Icelandic DC-8 loading right now. No announcement.

They'd be rushed if they did. There's room for you, Dr. Malibert."

It was like an electric shock. Malibert trembled. Without knowing why he did it, he said, "Can I put the boy on instead?"

The Operations man looked annoyed. "Take him with you, of course," he said. "I didn't know you had a son."

"I don't," said Malibert. But not out loud. And when they were in the jet he held the boy in his lap as tenderly as though he were his own.

If there was no panic in the Ambassador Club at Kennedy there was plenty of it everywhere else in the world. What everyone in the superpower cities knew was that their lives were at stake. Whatever they did might be in vain, and yet they had to do something. Anything! Run, hide, dig, brace, stow . . . pray. The city people tried to desert the metropolises for the open safety of the country, and the farmers and the exurbanites sought the stronger, safer buildings of the cities.

And the missiles fell.

The bombs that had seared Hiroshima and Nagasaki were struck matches compared to the hydrogen-fusion flares that ended eighty million lives in those first hours. Firestorms fountained above a hundred cities. Winds of three hundred kilometers an hour pulled in cars and debris and people, and they all became ash that rose to the sky. Splatters of melted rock and dust sprayed into the air.

The sky darkened.

Then it grew darker still.

When the Icelandic jet landed at Keflavik Airport Malibert carried the boy down the passage to the little stand marked *Immigration*. The line was long, for most of the passengers had no passports at all, and the immigration woman was very tired of making out temporary entrance permits by the time Malibert reached her. "He's my son," Malibert lied. "My wife has his passport, but I don't know where my wife is."

She nodded wearily. She pursed her lips, looked toward the door beyond which her superior sat sweating and initialing reports, then shrugged and let them through. Malibert took the boy to a door marked *Snirtling*, which seemed to be the Icelandic word for toilets, and was relieved to see that at least Timothy was able to stand by himself while he urinated, although his eyes stayed half closed. His head was very hot. Malibert prayed for a doctor in Reykjavik.

In the bus the English-speaking tour guide in charge of them—she had nothing else to do, for her tour would never arrive—sat on the arm of a first-row seat with a microphone in her hand and chatted vivaciously to the refugees. "Chicago? Ya, is gone, Chicago. And Detroit and Pitts-burrug—is bad. New York? Certainly New York too!" she said severely, and the big tears rolling down her cheek made Timothy cry too.

Malibert hugged him. "Don't worry, Timmy," he said. "No one would bother bombing Reykjavik." And no one would have. But when the bus was ten miles farther along there was a sudden glow in the clouds ahead of them that made them squint. Someone in the USSR had decided that it was time for neatening up loose threads. That someone, whoever remained in whatever remained of their central missile control, had realized that no one had taken out that supremely, insultingly dangerous bastion of imperialist American interests in the North Atlantic, the United States airbase at Keflavik.

Unfortunately, by then EMP and attrition had compromised the accuracy of their aim. Malibert had been right. No one would have bothered bombing Reykjavik—on purpose—but a forty-mile miss did the job anyway, and Reykjavik ceased to exist.

They had to make a wide detour inland to avoid the fires and the radiation. And as the sun rose on their first day in Iceland, Malibert, drowsing over the boy's bed after the Icelandic nurse had shot him full of antibiotics, saw the daybreak in awful, sky-drenching red.

It was worth seeing, for in the days to come there was no daybreak at all.

The worst was the darkness, but at first that did not seem urgent. What was urgent was rain. A trillion trillion dust particles nucleated water vapor. Drops formed. Rain fell—torrents of rain, sheets and cascades of rain. The rivers swelled. The Mississippi overflowed, and the Ganges, and the Yellow. The High Dam at Aswan spilled water over its lip, then crumbled. The rains came where rains came never. The Sahara knew flash floods. The Flaming Mountains at the edge of the Gobi flamed no more; a ten-year supply of rain came down in a week and rinsed the dusty slopes bare.

And the darkness stayed.

The human race lives always eighty days from starvation. That is the sum of stored food, globe wide. It met the nuclear winter with no more and no less.

The missiles went off on the 11th of June. If the world's larders had been equally distributed, on the 30th of August the last mouthful would have been eaten. The starvation deaths would have begun and ended in the next six weeks; exit the human race.

The larders were not equally distributed. The Northern Hemisphere was caught on one foot, fields sown, crops not yet grown. Nothing did grow there. The seedlings poked up through the dark earth for sunlight, found none, died. Sunlight was shaded out by the dense clouds of dust exploded out of the ground by the H-bombs. It was the Cretaceous repeated; extinction was in the air.

There were mountains of stored food in the rich countries of North American and Europe, of course, but they melted swiftly. The rich countries had much stored wealth in the form of their livestock. Every steer was a million calories of protein and fat. When it was slaughtered, it saved thousands of other calories of grain and roughage for every day lopped off its life in feed. The

cattle and pigs and sheep—even the goats and horses;
even the pet bunnies and the chicks; even the very kittens and hamsters—they all died quickly and were eaten,
to eke out the stores of canned foods and root vegetables
and grain. There was no rationing of the slaughtered
meat. It had to be eaten before it spoiled.

Of course, even in the rich countries the supplies were
not equally distributed. The herds and the grain elevators
were not located on Times Square or in the Loop. It
took troops to convoy corn from Iowa to Boston and
Dallas and Philadelphia. Before long, it took killing. Then
it could not be done at all.

So the cities starved first. As the convoys of soldiers
made the changeover from seizing food for the cities to
seizing food for themselves, the riots began, and the next
wave of mass death. These casualties didn't usually die
of hunger. They died of someone else's.

It didn't take long. By the end of "summer" the frozen
remnants of the cities were all the same. A few thousand
skinny, freezing desperadoes survived in each, sitting
guard over their troves of canned and dried and frozen
foodstuffs.

Every river in the world was running sludgy with mud
to its mouth, as the last of the trees and grasses died and
relaxed their grip on the soil. Every rain washed dirt
away. As the winter dark deepened the rains turned to
snow. The Flaming Mountains were sheeted in ice now,
ghostly, glassy fingers uplifted to the gloom. Men could
walk across the Thames at London now, the few men
who were left. And across the Hudson, across the Whang-
poo, across the Missouri between the two Kansas Cities.
Avalanches rumbled down on what was left of Denver. In
the stands of dead timber grubs flourished. The starved
predators scratched them out and devoured them. Some
of the predators were human. The last of the Hawaiians
were finally grateful for their termites.

A Western human being—comfortably pudgy on a diet
of 2800 calories a day, resolutely jogging to keep the flab
away or mournfully conscience-stricken at the thickening

thighs and the waistbands that won't quite close—can survive for forty-five days without food. By then the fat is gone. Protein reabsorption of the muscles is well along. The plump housewife or businessman is a starving scarecrow. Still, even then care and nursing can still restore health.

Then it gets worse.

Dissolution attacks the nervous system. Blindness begins. The flesh of the gums recedes, and the teeth fall out. Apathy becomes pain, then agony, then coma.

Then death. Death for almost every person on Earth. . . .

For forty days and forty nights the rain fell, and so did the temperature. Iceland froze over.

To Harry Malibert's astonishment and dawning relief, Iceland was well equipped to do that. It was one of the few places on Earth that could be submerged in snow and ice and still survive.

There is a ridge of volcanoes that goes almost around the Earth. The part that lies between America and Europe is called the Mid-Atlantic Ridge, and most of it is under water. Here and there, like boils erupting along a forearm, volcanic islands poke up above the surface. Iceland is one of them. It was because Iceland was volcanic that it could survive when most places died of freezing, but it was also because it had been cold in the first place.

The survival authorities put Malibert to work as soon as they found out who he was. There was no job opening for a radio astronomer interested in contacting far-off (and very likely non-existent) alien races. There was, however, plenty of work for persons with scientific training, especially if they had the engineering skills of a man who had run Arecibo for two years. When Malibert was not nursing Timothy Clary through the slow and silent convalescence from his pneumonia, he was calculating heat losses and pumping rates for the piped geothermal water.

Iceland filled itself with enclosed space. It heated the spaces with water from the boiling underground springs.

Of heat it had plenty. Getting the heat from the geyser fields to the enclosed spaces was harder. The hot water was as hot as ever, since it did not depend at all on sunlight for its calories, but it took a lot more of it to keep out a -30°C chill than a +5°C one. It wasn't just to keep the surviving people warm that they needed energy. It was to grow food.

Iceland had always had a lot of geothermal greenhouses. The flowering ornamentals were ripped out and food plants put in their place. There was no sunlight to make the vegetables and grains grow, so the geothermal power-generating plants were put on max output. Solar-spectrum incandescents flooded the trays with photons. Not just in the old greenhouses. Gymnasia, churches, schools—they all began to grow food under the glaring lights. There was other food, too, metric tons of protein baaing and starving in the hills. The herds of sheep were captured and slaughtered and dressed—and put outside again, to freeze until needed. The animals that froze to death on the slopes were bulldozed into heaps of a hundred, and left where they were. Geodetic maps were carefully marked to show the location of each heap.

It was, after all, a blessing that Reykjavik had been nuked. That meant half a million fewer people for the island's resources to feed.

When Malibert was not calculating load factors, he was out in the desperate cold, urging on the workers. Sweating navvies tried to muscle shrunken fittings together in icy foxholes that their body heat kept filling with icewater. They listened patiently as Malibert tried to give orders—his few words of Icelandic were almost useless, but even the navvies sometimes spoke tourist-English. They checked their radiation monitors, looked up at the storms overhead, returned to their work and prayed. Even Malibert almost prayed when one day, trying to locate the course of the buried coastal road, he looked out on the sea ice and saw a gray-white ice hummock that was not an ice hummock. It was just at the limits of visibility, dim on the fringe of the road crew's work lights,

and it moved. "A polar bear!" he whispered to the head
of the work crew, and everyone stopped while the beast
shambled out of sight.

From then on they carried rifles.

When Malibert was not (incompetent) technical advi-
sor to the task of keeping Iceland warm or (almost
incompetent, but learning) substitute father to Timothy
Clary, he was trying desperately to calculate survival
chances. Not just for them; for the entire human race.
With all the desperate flurry of survival work, the Ice-
landers spared time to think of the future. A study team
was created, physicists from the University of Reykjavik,
the surviving Supply officer from the Keflavik airbase, a
meteorologist on work-study from the University of
Leyden to learn about North Atlantic air masses. They
met in the gasthuis where Malibert lived with the boy,
and usually Timmy sat silent next to Malibert while they
talked. What they wanted was to know how long the dust
cloud would persist. Some day the particles would finish
dropping from the sky, and then the world could be
reborn—if enough survived to parent a new race, anyway.
But when? They could not tell. They did not know how
long, how cold, how killing the nuclear winter would be.
"We don't know the megatonnage," said Malibert, "we
don't know what atmospheric changes have taken place,
we don't know the rate of insolation. We only know it
will be bad."

"It is already bad," grumbled Thorsid Magnesson,
Director of Public Safety. (Once that office had had
something to do with catching criminals, when the major
threat to safety was crime.)

"It will get worse," said Malibert, and it did. The cold
deepened. The reports from the rest of the world dwin-
dled. They plotted maps to show what they knew to
show. One set of missile maps, to show where the strikes
had been—within a week that no longer mattered,
because the deaths from cold already began to outweigh
those from blast. They plotted isotherm maps, based on

the scattered weather reports that came in—maps that had to be changed every day, as the freezing line marched toward the Equator. Finally the maps were irrelevant. The whole world was cold then. They plotted fatality maps—the percentages of deaths in each area, as they could infer them from the reports they received, but those maps soon became too frightening to plot.

The British Isles died first, not because they were nuked but because they were not. There were too many people alive there. Britain never owned more than a four-day supply of food. When the ships stopped coming they starved. So did Japan. A little later, so did Bermuda and Hawaii and Canada's off-shore provinces; and then it was the continents' turn.

And Timmy Clary listened to every word.

The boy didn't talk much. He never asked after his parents, not after the first few days. He did not hope for good news, and did not want bad. The boy's infection was cured, but the boy himself was not. He ate half of what a hungry child should devour. He ate that only when Malibert coaxed him.

The only thing that made Timmy look alive was the rare times when Malibert could talk to him about space. There were many in Iceland who knew about Harry Malibert and SETI, and a few who cared about it almost as much as Malibert himself. When time permitted they would get together, Malibert and his groupies. There was Lars the postman (now pick-and-shovel ice excavator, since there was no mail), Ingar the waitress from the Loftleider Hotel (now stitching heavy drapes to help insulate dwelling walls), Elda the English teacher (now practical nurse, frostbite cases a specialty). There were others, but those three were always there when they could get away. They were Harry Malibert fans who had read his books and dreamed with him of radio messages from weird aliens from Aldebaran, or worldships that could carry million-person populations across the galaxy, on voyages of a hundred thousand years. Timmy listened, and drew sketches of the worldships. Malibert supplied him with dimensions. "I talked to Gerry Webb," he said, "and he'd worked it out in detail. It is a matter of rotation rates and strength of materials. To provide the proper simulated gravity for the people in the ships, the shape has to be a cylinder and it has to spin—sixteen kilometers is what the diameter must be. Then the cylinder must be long enough to provide space, but not so long that the dynamics of spin cause it to wobble or bend—perhaps sixty kilometers long. One part to live in. One part to store fuel. And at the end, a reaction chamber where hydrogen fusion thrusts the ship across the Galaxy."

"Hydrogen bombs," said the boy. "Harry? Why don't the bombs wreck the worldship?"

"It's engineering," said Malibert honestly, "and I don't know the details. Gerry was going to give his paper at the Portsmouth meeting; it was one reason I was going." But, of course, there would never be a British Interplanetary Society meeting in Portsmouth now, ever again.

Elda said uneasily, "It is time for lunch soon. Timmy? Will you eat some soup if I make it?" And did make it, whether the boy promised or not. Elda's husband had worked at Keflavik in the PX, an accountant; unfortunately he had been putting in overtime there when the follow-up missile did what the miss had failed to do, and so Elda had no husband left, not enough even to bury.

Even with the earth's hot water pumped full velocity through the straining pipes it was not warm in the gasthuis. She wrapped the boy in blankets and sat near him while he dutifully spooned up the soup. Lars and Ingar sat holding hands and watching the boy eat. "To hear a voice from another star," Lars said suddenly, "that would have been fine."

"There are no voices," said Ingar bitterly. "Not even ours now. We have the answer to the Fermi paradox."

And when the boy paused in his eating to ask what that was, Harry Malibert explained it as carefully as he could:

"It is named after Enrico Fermi, a scientist. He said, 'We know that there are many billions of stars like our sun. Our sun has planets, therefore it is reasonable to assume that some of the other stars do also. One of our planets has living things on it. Us, for instance, as well as trees and germs and horses. Since there are so many stars, it seems almost certain that some of them, at least, have also living things. People. People as smart as we are—or smarter. People who can build spaceships, or send radio messages to other stars, as we can.' Do you understand so far, Timmy?" The boy nodded, frowning, but—Malibert was delighted to see—kept on eating his soup. "Then, the question Fermi asked was, 'Why haven't some of them come to see us?' "

"Like in the movies," the boy nodded. "The flying saucers."

"All those movies are made-up stories, Timmy. Like Jack and the Beanstalk, or Oz. Perhaps some creatures from space have come to see us sometime, but there is no good evidence that this is so. I feel sure there would be evidence if it had happened. There would have to be. If there were many such visits, ever, then at least one would have dropped the Martian equivalent of a McDonald's Big Mac box, or a used Sirian flash cube, and it would have been found and shown to be from somewhere other than the Earth. None ever has. So there are only three possible answers to Dr. Fermi's question. One, there is no other life. Two, there is, but they want to leave us alone. They don't want to contact us, perhaps because we frighten them with our violence, or for some reason we can't even guess at. And the third reason—" Elda made a quick gesture, but Malibert shook his head—"is that perhaps as soon as any people get smart enough to do all those things that get them into space— when they have all the technology we do—they also have such terrible bombs and weapons that they can't control them any more. So a war breaks out. And they kill themselves off before they are fully grown up."

"Like now," Timothy said, nodding seriously to show he understood. He had finished his soup, but instead of taking the plate away Elda hugged him in her arms and tried not to weep.

The world was totally dark now. There was no day or night, and would not be again for no one could say how long. The rains and snows had stopped. Without sunlight to suck water up out of the oceans there was no moisture left in the atmosphere to fall. Floods had been replaced by freezing droughts. Two meters down the soil of Iceland was steel hard, and the navvies could no longer dig. There was no hope of laying additional pipes. When more heat was needed all that could be done was to close off buildings and turn off their heating pipes. Elda's patients now were less likely to be frostbite and more to be the listlessness of radiation sickness as volunteers raced in and out of the Reykjavik ruins to find medicine and food. No one was spared that job. When Elda came back on a snowmobile from a foraging trip to the Loftleider Hotel she brought back a present for the boy. Candy bars and postcards from the gift shop; the candy bars had to be shared, but the postcards were all for him. "Do you know what these are?" she asked. The cards showed huge, squat, ugly men and women in costumes of a thousand years ago. "They're trolls. We have myths in Iceland that the trolls lived here. They're still here, Timmy, or so they say; the mountains are trolls that just got too old and tired to move any more."

"They're made-up stories, right?" the boy asked seriously, and did not grin until she assured him they were. Then he made a joke. "I guess the trolls won," he said.

"Ach, Timmy!" Elda was shocked. But at least the boy was capable of joking, she told herself, and even graveyard humor was better than none. Life had become a little easier for her with the new patients—easier because for the radiation-sick there was very little that could be done—and she bestirred herself to think of ways to entertain the boy.

And found a wonderful one.

Since fuel was precious there were no excursions to see the sights of Iceland-under-the-ice. There was no way to see them anyway in the eternal dark. But when a hospital chopper was called up to travel empty to Stokksnes on the eastern shore to bring back a child with a broken back, she begged space for Malibert and Timmy. Elda's own ride was automatic, as duty nurse for the wounded child. "An avalanche crushed his house," she explained. "It is right under the mountains, Stokksnes, and landing there will be a little tricky, I think. But we can come in from the sea and make it safe. At least in the landing lights of the helicopter something can be seen."

They were luckier than that. There was more light. Nothing came through the clouds, where the billions of particles that had once been Elda's husband added to the trillions of trillions that had been Detroit and Marseilles and Shanghai to shut out the sky. But in the clouds and under them were snakes and sheets of dim color, sprays of dull red, fans of pale green. The aurora borealis did not give much light. But there was no other light at all except for the faint glow from the pilot's instrument panel. As their eyes widened they could see the dark shapes of the Vatnajökull slipping by below them. "*Big trolls*," cried the boy happily, and Elda smiled too as she hugged him.

The pilot did as Elda had predicted, down the slopes of the eastern range, out over the sea, and cautiously back in to the little fishing village. As they landed, red-tipped flashlights guiding them, the copter's landing lights picked out a white lump, vaguely saucer-shaped. "Radar dish," said Malibert to the boy, pointing.

Timmy pressed his nose to the freezing window. "Is it one of them, Daddy Harry? The things that could talk to the stars?"

The pilot answered: "Ach, no, Timmy—military, it is." And Malibert said:

"They wouldn't put one of those here, Timothy. It's too far north. You wanted a place for a big radio telescope that could search the whole sky, not just the little piece of it you can see from Iceland."

And while they helped slide the stretcher with the broken child into the helicopter, gently, kindly as they could be, Malibert was thinking about those places, Arecibo and Woomara and Socorro and all the others. Every one of them was now dead and certainly broken with a weight of ice and shredded by the mean winds. Crushed, rusted, washed away, all those eyes on space were blinded now; and the thought saddened Harry Malibert, but not for long. More gladdening than anything sad was the fact that, for the first time, Timothy had called him "Daddy."

In one ending to the story, when at last the sun came back it was too late. Iceland had been the last place where human beings survived, and Iceland had finally starved. There was nothing alive anywhere on Earth that spoke, or invented machines, or read books. Fermi's terrible third answer was the right one after all.

But there exists another ending. In this one the sun came back in time. Perhaps it was just barely in time, but the food had not yet run out when daylight brought the first touches of green in some parts of the world, and plants began to grow again from frozen or hoarded seed. In this ending Timothy lived to grow up. When he was old enough, and after Malibert and Elda had got around to marrying, he married one of their daughters. And of their descendants—two generations or a dozen generations later—one was alive on that day when Fermi's paradox became a quaintly amusing old worry, as irrelevant and comical as a fifteenth-century mariner's fear of falling off the edge of the flat Earth. On that day the skies spoke, and those who lived in them came to call.

Perhaps that is the true ending of the story, and in it the human race chose not to squabble and struggle within itself, and so extinguish itself finally into the dark.

In this ending human beings survived, and saved all the science and beauty of life, and greeted their star-born visitors with joy. . . .

But that is in fact what did happen!

At least, one would like to think so.

1987
45th World SF
Convention
Brighton

Gilgamesh in the Outback
   by Robert Silverberg
Permafrost by Roger Zelazny
Tangents by Greg Bear

Gilgamesh in the Outback

by Robert Silverberg

> *Faust.* First I will question thee about hell.
>   Tell me, where is the place that men call hell?
> *Meph.* Under the heavens.
> *Faust.* Ay, but whereabout?
> *Meph.* Within the bowels of these elements,
>   Where we are tortur'd and remain for ever:
>   Hell hath no limits, nor is circumscrib'd
>   In one self place; for where we are is hell,
>   And where hell is, there must we ever be:
>   And, to conclude, when all the world dissolves,
>   And every creature shall be purified,
>   All places shall be hell that are not heaven.
> *Faust.* Come, I think hell's a fable.
> *Meph.* Ay, think so still, till experience change thy
>   mind.
>
> Marlowe: *Dr. Faustus*

Jagged green lightning danced on the horizon and the wind came ripping like a blade out of the east, skinning the flat land bare and sending up clouds of gray-brown dust. Gilgamesh grinned broadly. By Enlil, now that was a wind! A lion-killing wind it was, a wind that turned the air dry and crackling. The beasts of the field gave you the greatest joy in their hunting when the wind was like that, hard and sharp and cruel.

He narrowed his eyes and stared into the distance, searching for this day's prey. His bow of several fine woods, the bow that no man but he was strong enough to draw—no man but he and Enkidu his beloved thrice-lost friend—hung loosely from his hand. His body was poised and ready. Come now, you beasts! Come and be slain! It is Gilgamesh, king of Uruk, who would make his sport with you this day!

Other men in this land, when they went about their hunting, made use of guns, those foul machines that the New Dead had brought, which hurled death from a great distance along with much noise and fire and smoke; or they employed the even deadlier laser devices from whose ugly snouts came spurts of blue-white flame. Cowardly things, all those killing machines! Gilgamesh loathed them, as he did most instruments of the New Dead, those slick and bustling Johnny-come-latelies of Hell. He would not touch them if he could help it. In all the thousands of years he had dwelled in this nether world he had never used any weapons but those he had known during his first lifetime: the javelin, the spear, the double-headed axe, the hunting bow, the good bronze sword. It took some skill, hunting with such weapons as those. And there was physical effort; there was more than a little risk. Hunting was a contest, was it not? Then it must make demands. Why, if the idea was merely to slaughter one's prey in the fastest and easiest and safest way, then the sensible thing to do would be to ride high above the hunting grounds in a weapons platform and drop a little nuke, eh, and lay waste five kingdoms' worth of beasts at a single stroke!

He knew that there were those who thought him a fool for such ideas. Caesar, for one. Cocksure cold-blooded Julius with the gleaming pistols thrust into his belt and the submachine gun slung across his shoulders. "Why don't you admit it?" Caesar had asked him once, riding up in his jeep as Gilgamesh was making ready to set forth toward Hell's open wilderness. "It's a pure affectation, Gilgamesh, all this insistence on arrows and javelins and spears. This isn't old Sumer you're living in now."

Gilgamesh spat. "Hunt with 9-millimeter automatics?

Hunt with grenades and cluster bombs and lasers? You call that sport, Caesar?"

"I call it acceptance of reality. Is it technology you hate? What's the difference between using a bow and arrow and using a gun? They're both technology, Gilgamesh. It isn't as though you kill the animals with your bare hands."

"I have done that, too," said Gilgamesh.

"Bah! I'm on to your game. Big hulking Gilgamesh, the simple innocent oversized Bronze Age hero! That's just an affectation, too, my friend! You pretend to be a stupid, stubborn thick-skulled barbarian because it suits you to be left alone to your hunting and your wandering, and that's all you claim that you really want. But secretly you regard yourself as superior to anybody who lived in an era softer than your own. You mean to restore the bad old filthy ways of the ancient ancients, isn't that so? If I read you the right way you're just biding your time, skulking around with your bow and arrow in the dreary Outback until you think it's the right moment to launch the *putsch* that carries you to supreme power here. Isn't that it, Gilgamesh? You've got some crazy fantasy of overthrowing Satan himself and lording it over all of us. And then we'll live in mud cities again and make little chicken scratches on clay tablets, the way we were meant to do. What do you say?"

"I say this is great nonsense, Caesar."

"Is it? This place is full of kings and emperors and sultans and pharaohs and shahs and presidents and dictators, and every single one of them wants to be Number One again. My guess is that you're no exception."

"In this you are very wrong."

"I doubt that. I suspect you believe you're the best of us all; you, the sturdy warrior, the great hunter, the maker of bricks, the builder of vast temples and lofty walls, the shining beacon of ancient heroism. You think we're all decadent rascally degenerates and that you're the one true virtuous man. But you're as proud and ambitious as any of us. Isn't that how it is? You're a fraud, Gilgamesh, a huge musclebound fraud!"

"At least I am no slippery tricky serpent like you, Caesar, who dons a wig and spies on women at their mysteries if it pleases him."

Caesar looked untroubled by the thrust. "And so you pass three-quarters of your time killing stupid monstrous creatures in the Outback and you make sure everyone knows that you're too pious to have anything to do with modern weapons while you do it. You don't fool me. It isn't virtue that keeps you from doing your killing with a decent double-barreled .470 Springfield. It's intellectual pride, or maybe simple laziness. The bow just happens to be the weapon you grew up with, who knows how many thousands of years ago. You like it because it's familiar. But what language are you speaking now, eh? Is it your thick-tongued Euphrates gibberish? No, it seems to be English, doesn't it? Did you grow up speaking English too, Gilgamesh? Did you grow up riding around in jeeps and choppers? Apparently *some* of the new ways are acceptable to you."

Gilgamesh shrugged. "I speak English with you because that is what is spoken now in this place. In my heart I speak the old tongue, Ceasar. In my heart I am still Gilgamesh of Uruk, and I will hunt as I hunt."

"Uruk's long gone to dust. This is the life after life, my friend. We've been here a long time. We'll be here for all time to come, unless I miss my guess. New people constantly bring new ideas to this place, and it's impossible to ignore them. Even you can't do it. Isn't that a wristwatch I see on your arm, Gilgamesh? A *digital* watch, no less?"

"I will hunt as I hunt," said Gilgamesh. "There is no sport in it, when you do it with guns. There is no grace in it."

Caesar shook his head. "I never could understand hunting for sport, anyway. Killing a few stags, yes, or a boar or two, when you've bivouacked in some dismal Gaulish forest and your men want meat. But hunting?

Slaughtering hideous animals that aren't even edible? By Apollo, it's all nonsense to me!"

"My point exactly."

"But if you must hunt, to scorn the use of a decent hunting rifle—"

"You will never convince me."

"No," Caesar said with a sigh. "I suppose I won't. I should know better than to argue with a reactionary."

"Reactionary! In my time I was thought to be a radical," said Gilgamesh. "When I was king in Uruk—"

"Just so," Caesar said, laughing. "King in Uruk. Was there ever a king who wasn't reactionary? You put a crown on your head and it addles your brains instantly. Three times Antonius offered me a crown, Gilgamesh. Three times, and—"

"—you did thrice refuse it, yes. I know all that. 'Was this ambition?' You thought you'd have the power without the emblem. Who were you fooling, Caesar? Not Brutus, so I hear. Brutus said you were ambitious. And Brutus—"

That stung him. "Damn you, don't say it!"

"—was an honorable man," Gilgamesh concluded, enjoying Caesar's discomfiture.

Caesar groaned. "If I hear that line once more—"

"Some say this is a place of torment," said Gilgamesh serenely. "If in truth it is, yours is to be swallowed up in another man's poetry. Leave me to my bows and arrows, Caesar, and return to your jeep and your trivial intrigues. I am a fool and a reactionary, yes. But you know nothing of hunting. Nor do you understand anything of me."

All that had been a year ago, or two, or maybe five— with or without a wristwatch, there was no keeping proper track of time in Hell, where the unmoving ruddy eye of the sun never budged from the sky—and now Gilgamesh was far from Caesar and all his minions, far from the troublesome center of Hell and the tiresome squabbling of those like Caesar and Alexander and Napoleon and that sordid little Guevara man who maneuvered for power in this place.

Let them maneuver all they liked, those shoddy new men of the latter days. Some day they might learn wisdom, and was not that the purpose of this place, if it had any purpose at all?

Gilgamesh preferred to withdraw. Unlike the rest of those fallen emperors and kings and pharaohs and shahs, he felt no yearning to reshape Hell in his own image. Caesar was as wrong about Gilgamesh's ambitions as he was about the reasons for his preferences in hunting gear. Out here in the Outback, in the bleak dry chilly hinterlands of Hell, Gilgamesh hoped to find peace. That was all he wanted now: peace. He had wanted much more, once, but that had been long ago.

There was a stirring in the scraggly underbrush.

A lion, maybe?

No, Gilgamesh thought. There were no lions to be found in Hell, only the strange nether-world beasts. Ugly hairy things with flat noses and many legs and dull baleful eyes, and slick shiny things with the faces of women and the bodies of malformed dogs, and worse, much worse. Some had drooping leathery wings, and some were armed with spiked tails that rose like a scorpion's, and some had mouths that opened wide enough to swallow an elephant at a gulp. They all were demons of one sort or another, Gilgamesh knew. No matter. Hunting was hunting; the prey was the prey; all beasts were one in the contest of the field. That fop Caesar could never begin to comprehend that.

Drawing an arrow from his quiver, Gilgamesh laid it lightly across his bow and waited.

"If you ever had come to Texas, H.P., this here's a lot like what you'd have seen," said the big barrel-chested man with the powerful arms and the deeply tanned skin. Gesturing sweepingly with one hand, he held the wheel of the Land Rover lightly with three fingers of the other, casually guiding the vehicle in jouncing zigs and zags over the flat trackless landscape. Gnarled gray-green shrubs matted the gritty ground. The sky was black with swirling dust. Far off in the distance barren mountains rose like dark jagged teeth. "Beautiful. Beautiful. As close to Texas in look as makes no never mind, this countryside is."

"Beautiful?" said the other man uncertainly. "Hell?"

"This stretch sure is. But if you think Hell's beautiful, you should have seen Texas!"

The burly man laughed and gunned the engine, and the Land Rover went leaping and bouncing onward at a stupefying speed.

His traveling companion, a gaunt, lantern-jawed man as pale as the other was bronzed, sat very still in the passenger seat, knees together and elbows digging in against his ribs, as if he expected a fiery crash at any moment. The two of them had been journeying across the interminable parched wastes of the Outback for many days now—how many, not even the Elder Gods could tell. They were ambassadors, these two: Their Excellencies Robert E. Howard and H.P. Lovecraft of the Kingdom of New Holy Diabolic England, envoys of His Britannic Majesty Henry VIII to the court of Prester John.

In another life they had been writers, fantasists, inventors of fables; but now they found themselves caught up in something far more fantastic than anything to be found in any of their tales, for this was no fable, this was no fantasy. This was the reality of Hell.

"Robert—" said the pale man nervously.

"A lot like Texas, yes," Howard went on, "only Hell's just a faint carbon copy of the genuine item. Just a rough first draft, is all. You see that sandstorm rising out thataway? We had sandstorms, they covered entire counties! You see that lightning? In Texas that would be just a flicker!"

"If you could drive just a little more slowly, Bob—"

"More slowly? Cthulhu's whiskers, man, I am driving slowly!"

"Yes, I'm quite sure you believe that you are."

"And the way I always heard it, H.P., you loved for people to drive you around at top speed. Seventy, eighty miles an hour, that was what you liked best, so the story goes."

"In the other life one dies only once, and then all pain ceases," Lovecraft replied. "But here, where one can go to the Undertaker again and again, and when one returns one remembers every final agony in the brightest of hues—here, dear friend Bob, death's much more to be feared, for the pain of it stays with one forever, and one may die a thousand deaths." Lovecraft managed a pale baleful smile. "Speak of that to some professional warrior, Bob, some Trojan or Hun or Assyrian—or one of the gladiators, maybe, someone who has died and died and died again. Ask him about it: the dying and the rebirth, and the pain, the hideous torment, reliving every detail. It is a dreadful thing to die in Hell. I fear dying here far more than I ever did in life. I will take no needless risks here."

Howard snorted. "Gawd, try and figure you out! When you thought you lived only once, you made people go roaring along with you on the highway a mile a minute. Here where no one stays dead for very long you want me to drive like an old woman. Well, I'll attempt it, H.P., but everything in me cries out to go like the wind. When you live in big country, you learn to cover the territory the way it has to be covered. And Texas is the biggest country there is. It isn't just a place, it's a state of mind."

"As is Hell," said Lovecraft. "Though I grant you that Hell isn't Texas."

"Texas!" Howard boomed. "God damn, I wish you could have seen it! By god, H.P., what a time we'd have had, you and me, if you'd come to Texas. Two gentlemen of letters like us riding together all to hell and gone from Corpus Christi to El Paso and back again, seeing it all and telling each other wondrous stories all the way! I swear, it would have enlarged your soul, H.P. Beauty such as perhaps even you couldn't have imagined. That big sky. That blazing sun. And the open space! Whole empires could fit into Texas and never be seen again! That Rhode Island of yours, H.P.—we could drop it down just back of Cross Plains and lose it behind a medium-size prickly pear! What you see here, it just gives you the merest idea of that glorious beauty. Though I admit this is plenty beautiful itself, this here."

"I wish I could share your joy in this landscape, Robert," Lovecraft said quietly, when it seemed that Howard had said all he meant to say.

"You don't care for it?" Howard asked, sounding surprised and a little wounded.

"I can say one good thing for it: at least it's far from the sea."

"You'll give it that much, will you?"

"You know how I hate the sea and all that the sea contains! Its odious creatures—that hideous reek of salt air hovering above it—" Lovecraft shuddered fastidiously. "But this land—this bitter desert—you don't find it somber? You don't find it forbidding?"

"It's the most beautiful place I've seen since I came to Hell."

"Perhaps the beauty is too subtle for my eye. Perhaps it escapes me altogether. I was always a man for cities, myself."

"What you're trying to say, I reckon, is that all this looks real hateful to you. Is that it? As grim and ghastly as the Plateau of Leng, eh, H.P.?" Howard laughed. " 'Sterile hills of gray granite . . . dim wastes of rock and ice and snow . . . ' " Hearing himself quoted, Lovecraft laughed too, though not exuberantly. Howard went on. "I look around at the Outback of Hell and I see something a whole lot like Texas, and I love it. For you it's as sinister as dark frosty Leng, where people have horns and hooves and munch on corpses and sing hymns to Nyarlathotep. Oh, H.P., H.P., there's no accounting for tastes, is there? Why, there's even some people who—whoa, now! Look there!"

He braked the Land Rover suddenly and brought it to

a jolting halt. A small malevolent-looking something with blazing eyes and a scaly body had broken from cover and gone scuttering across the path just in front of them. Now it faced them, glaring up out of the road, snarling and hissing flame.

"Hell-cat!" Howard cried. "Hell-coyote! *Look* at that critter, H.P. You ever see so much ugliness packed into such a small package? Scare the toenails off a shoggoth, that one would!"

"Can you drive past it?" Lovecraft asked, looking dismayed.

"I want a closer look, first." Howard rummaged down by his boots and pulled a pistol from the clutter on the floor of the car. "Don't it give you the shivers, driving around in a land full of critters that could have come right out of one of your stories, or mine? I want to look this little ghoul-cat right in the eye."

"Robert—"

"You wait here. I'll only be but a minute."

Howard swung himself down from the Land Rover and marched stolidly toward the hissing little beast, which stood its ground. Lovecraft watched fretfully. At any moment the creature might leap upon Bob Howard and rip out his throat with a swipe of its horrid yellow talons, perhaps—or burrow snout-deep into his chest, seeking the Texan's warm, throbbing heart—

They stood staring at each other, Howard and the small monster, no more than a dozen feet apart. For a long moment neither one moved. Howard, gun in hand, leaned forward to inspect the beast as one might look at a feral cat guarding the mouth of an alleyway. Did he mean to shoot it? No, Lovecraft thought: beneath his bluster the robust Howard seemed surprisingly squeamish about bloodshed and violence of any sort.

Then things began happening very quickly. Out of a thicket to the left a much larger animal abruptly emerged: a ravening Hell-creature with a crocodile head and powerful thick-thighed legs that ended in monstrous curving claws. An arrow ran through the quivering dewlaps of its heavy throat from side to side, and a hideous dark ichor streamed from the wound down the beast's repellent blue-gray fur. The small animal, seeing the larger one wounded this way, instantly sprang upon its back and sank its fangs joyously into its shoulder. But a moment later there burst from the same thicket a man of astonishing size, a great dark-haired black-bearded man clad only in a bit of cloth about his waist. Plainly he was the huntsman who had wounded the larger monster, for there was a bow of awesome dimensions in his hand and a quiver of arrows on his back. In utter fearlessness the giant plucked the foul little creature from the wounded beast's back and hurled it far out of sight; then, swinging around, he drew a gleaming bronze dagger, and with a single fierce thrust, drove it into the breast of his prey as the coup de grace that brought the animal crashing heavily down.

All this took only an instant. Lovecraft, peering through the window of the Land Rover, was dazzled by the strength and speed of the dispatch and awed by the size and agility of the half-naked huntsman. He glanced toward Howard, who stood to one side, his own considerable frame utterly dwarfed by the black-bearded man.

For a moment Howard seemed dumbstruck, paralyzed with wonder and amazement. But then he was the first to speak.

"By Crom," he muttered, staring at the giant. "Surely this is Conan of Aquilonia and none other!" He was trembling. He took a lurching step toward the huge man, holding out both his hands in a strange gesture—submission, was it? "Lord Conan?" Howard murmured. "Great king, is it you? Conan? Conan?" And before Lovecraft's astounded eyes Howard fell to his knees next to the dying beast, and looked up with awe and something like rapture in his eyes at the towering huntsman.

It had been a decent day's hunting so far. Three beasts brought down after long and satisfying chase; every shaft fairly placed; each animal skillfully dressed, the meat set out as bait for other hell-beasts, the hide and head carefully put aside for proper cleaning at nightfall. There was true pleasure in work done so well.

Yet there was a hollowness at the heart of it all, Gilgamesh thought, that left him leaden and cheerless no matter how cleanly his arrows sped to their mark. He never felt that true fulfillment, that clean sense of completion, that joy of accomplishment, which was ultimately the only thing he sought.

Why was that? Was it—as the Christian dead so drearily insisted—because this was Hell, where by definition there could be no delight?

To Gilgamesh that was foolishness. Those who came here expecting eternal punishment did indeed get eternal punishment, and it was even more horrendous than anything they had anticipated. It served them right, those true believers, those gullible New Dead, that army of credulous Christians.

He had been amazed when their kind first came flocking into Hell, Enki only knew how many thousands of years ago. The things they talked of! Rivers of boiling oil! Lakes of pitch! Demons with pitchforks! That was what they expected, and the Administration was happy to oblige them. There were Torture Towns aplenty for those who wanted them. Gilgamesh had trouble understanding why anyone would. Nobody among the Old Dead really could figure them out, those absurd New Dead with their obsession with punishment. What was it Sargon called them? Masochists, that was the word. Pathetic masochists. But then that sly little Machiavelli had begged to disagree, saying, "No, my lord, it would be a violation of the nature of Hell to send a true masochist off to the torments. The only ones who go are the strong ones—the bullies, the braggarts, the ones who are cowards at the core of their souls." Augustus had had something to say on the matter too, and Caesar, and that Egyptian bitch Hatshepsut had butted in, she of the false beard and the startling eyes, and then all of them had jabbered at once, trying yet again to make sense of the Christian New Dead. Until finally Gilgamesh had said, before stalking out of the room, "The trouble with all of you is that you keep trying to make sense out of this place. But when you've been here as long as I have—"

Well, perhaps Hell *was* a place of punishment. Certainly there were some disagreeable aspects to it. The business about sex, for example. Never being able to come, even if you pumped away all day and all night. And the whole digestive complication, allowing you to eat real food but giving you an unholy hard time when it came to passing the stuff through your gut. But Gilgamesh tended to believe that those were merely the incidental consequences of being dead: this place was not, after all, the land of the living, and there was no reason why things should work the same way here as they did back there.

He had to admit that the reality of Hell had turned out to be nothing at all like what the priests had promised it would be. The House of Dust and Darkness, was what they had called it in Uruk long ago. A place where the dead lived in eternal night and sadness, clad like birds, with wings for garments. Where the dwellers had dust for their bread, and clay for their meat. Where the kings of the earth, the masters, the high rulers, lived humbly without their crowns, and were forced to wait on the demons like servants. Small wonder that he had dreaded death as he had, believing that that was what awaited him for all time to come!

Well, in fact all that had been mere myth and folly. Gilgamesh could still remember Hell as it had been when he first had come to it: a place much like Uruk, so it seemed, with low flat-roofed buildings of whitewashed brick, and temples rising on high platforms of many steps. And there he found all the heroes of olden days, living as they had always lived: Lugalbanda, his father; and Enmerkar, his father's father; and Ziusudra who built the vessel by which mankind survived the Flood; and others on and on, back to the dawn of time. At least that was what it was like where Gilgamesh first found himself; there were other districts, he discovered later, that were quite different—places where people lived in caves, or in pits in the ground, or in flimsy houses of reeds, and still other places where the Hairy Men dwelled and had no houses at all. Most of that was gone now, greatly transformed by all those who had come to Hell in the latter days, and indeed a lot of nonsensical ugliness and ideological foolishness had entered in recent centuries in the baggage of the New Dead. But still, the idea that this whole vast realm—infinitely bigger than his own beloved Land of the Two Rivers—existed merely for the sake of chastising the dead for their sins, struck Gilgamesh as too silly for serious contemplation.

Why, then, was the joy of his hunting so pale and hollow? Why none of the old ecstasy when spying the prey, when drawing the great bow, when sending the arrow true to its mark?

Gilgamesh thought he knew why, and it had nothing to do with punishment. There had been joy aplenty in the hunting for many a thousand years of his life in Hell. If the joy had gone from it now, it was only that in these latter days he hunted alone; that Enkidu—his friend, his true brother, his other self—was not with him. That and nothing but that: for he had never felt complete without Enkidu since they first had met and wrestled and come to love one another after the manner of brothers, long ago in the city of Uruk. That great burly man, broad and tall and strong as Gilgamesh himself, that shaggy wild creature out of the high ridges: Gilgamesh had never loved anyone as he loved Enkidu.

But it was the fate of Gilgamesh, so it seemed, to lose him again and again. Enkidu had been ripped from him the first time long ago when they still dwelled in Uruk, on that dark day when the gods had had revenge upon them for their great pride and had sent the fever to take Enkidu's life. In time Gilgamesh too had yielded to death and was taken into Hell, which he found nothing at all like the Hell that the scribes and priests of the Land had taught; and there he had searched for Enkidu, and one glorious day he had found him. Hell had been a much smaller place, then, and everyone seemed to know everyone else; but even so it had taken an age to track him down. Oh, the rejoicing that day in Hell! Oh, the singing and the dancing, the vast festival that went on and on! There was great kindliness among the denizens of Hell in those days, and everyone was glad for Gilgamesh and Enkidu. Minos of Crete gave the first great party in honor of their reunion, and then it was Amenhotep's turn, and then Agamemnon's. And on the fourth day the host was dark slender Varuna, the Meluhhan king, and then on the fifth the heroes gathered in the ancient hall of the Ice-Hunter folk where one-eyed Vy-otin was chieftain and the floor was strewn with mammoth tusks, and after that—

Well, and it went on for some long time, the great celebration of the reunion. This was long before the hordes of New Dead had come, all those grubby little unheroic people out of unheroic times, carrying with them their nasty little demons and their dark twisted apparatus of damnation and punishment. Before they had come, Hell had simply been a place to live in the time after life. It was all very different then, a far happier place.

For uncountable years Gilgamesh and Enkidu dwelled together in Gilgamesh's palace in Hell as they had in the old days in the Land of the Two Rivers. And all was well with them, with much hunting and feasting, and they were happy in Hell even after the New Dead began to come in, bringing all their terrible changes.

They were shoddy folk, these New Dead, confused of soul and flimsy of intellect, and their petty trifling rivalries and vain strutting poses were a great nuisance. But Gilgamesh and Enkidu kept their distance from them while they replayed all the follies of their lives, their nonsensical Crusades and their idiotic trade wars and their preposterous theological squabbles. The trouble was that they had brought not only their lunatic ideas to Hell but also their accursed diabolical modern gadgets, and the worst of those were the vile weapons called guns, that slaughtered noisily from afar in the most shameful cowardly way. Heroes know how to parry the blow of a battle-ax or the thrust of a sword; but what can even a hero do about a bullet from afar? It was Enkidu's bad luck to fall between two quarreling bands of these gun-wielders, a flock of babbling Spaniards and a rabble of arrogant Englanders, for whom he tried to make peace. Of course they would have no peace, and soon shots were flying, and Gilgamesh arrived at the scene just as a bolt from an arquebus tore through his dear Enkidu's noble heart.

No one dies in Hell forever; but some are dead a long time, and that was how it was with Enkidu. It pleased the Undertaker this time to keep him in limbo some hundreds of years, or however many it was—tallying such matters in Hell is always difficult. It was, at any rate, a dreadful long while, and Gilgamesh once more felt that terrible inrush of loneliness that only the presence of Enkidu might cure. Hell continued to change, and now the changes were coming at a stupefying, overwhelming rate. There seemed to be far more people in the world than there ever had been in the old days, and great armies of them marched into Hell every day, a swarming rabble of uncouth strangers who after only a little interval of disorganization and bewilderment would swiftly set out to reshape the whole place into something as discordant and repellent as the world they had left behind. The steam engine came, with its clamor and clangor, and something called the dynamo, and then harsh glittering electrical lights blazed in every street where the lamps had been, and factories arose and began pouring out all manner of strange things. And more and more and more, relentlessly, unceasingly. Railroads. Telephones. Automobiles. Noise, smoke, soot everywhere, and no way to hide from it. The Industrial Revolution, they called it. Satan and his swarm of Administration bureaucrats seemed to love all the new things, and so did almost everyone else, except for Gilgamesh and a few other cranky conservatives. "What are they trying to do?" Rabelais asked one day. "Turn the place into Hell?" Now the New Dead were bringing in such devices as radios and helicopters and computers, and everyone was speaking English, so that once again Gilgamesh, who had grudgingly learned the new-fangled Greek long ago when Agamemnon and his crew had insisted on it, was forced to master yet another tongue-twisting, intricate language. It was a dreary time for him. And then at last did Enkidu reappear, far away in one of the cold northern domains. He made his way south, and for a time, they were reunited again, and once more all was well for Gilgamesh of Uruk in Hell.

But now they were separated again, this time by something colder and more cruel than death itself. It was beyond all belief, but they had quarreled. There had been words between them, ugly words on both sides—such a dispute as never in thousands of years had passed between them in the land of the living or in the land of Hell—and at last Enkidu had said that which Gilgamesh had never dreamed he would ever hear, which was, "I want no more of you, king of Uruk. If you cross my path again I will have your life." Could that have been Enkidu speaking, or was it, Gilgamesh wondered, some demon of Hell in Enkidu's form?

In any case he was gone. He vanished into the turmoil and intricacy of Hell and placed himself beyond Gilgamesh's finding. And when Gilgamesh sent forth inquiries, back came only the report, "He will not speak with you. He has no love for you, Gilgamesh."

It could not be. It must be a spell of witchcraft, thought Gilgamesh. Surely this was some dark working of the Hell of the New Dead, that could turn brother against brother and lead Enkidu to persist in his wrath. In time, Gilgamesh was sure, Enkidu would be triumphant over this sorcery that gripped his soul, and he would open himself once more to the love of Gilgamesh. But time went on, after the strange circuitous fashion of Hell, and Enkidu did not return to his brother's arms.

What was there to do but hunt, and wait, and hope?

• • •

So this day Gilgamesh hunted in Hell's parched outback. He had killed and killed and killed again, and now late in the day he had put his arrow through the throat of a monster more foul even than the usual run of creatures of Hell; but there was a terrible vitality to the thing, and it went thundering off, dripping dark blood from its pierced maw.

Gilgamesh gave pursuit. It is sinful to strike and wound and not to kill. For a long weary hour he ran, crisscrossing this harsh land. Thorny plants slashed at him with the malevolence of imps, and the hard wind flailed him with clouds of dust sharp as whips. Still the evil-looking beast outpaced him, though its blood drained in torrents from it to the dry ground.

Gilgamesh would not let himself tire, for there was god-power in him by virtue of his descent from the divine Lugalbanda, his great father who was both king and god. But he was hard pressed to keep going. Three times he lost sight of his quarry, and tracked it only by the spoor of its blood-droppings. The bleak red motionless eye that was the sun of Hell seemed to mock him, hovering forever before him as though willing him to run without cease.

Then he saw the creature, still strong but plainly staggering, lurching about at the edge of a thicket of little twisted, greasy-leaved trees. Unhesitatingly Gilgamesh plunged forward. The trees stroked him lasciviously, coating him with their slime, trying like raucous courtesans to insinuate their leaves between his legs; but he slapped them away, and emerged finally into a clearing where he could confront his animal.

Some repellent little hell-beast was clinging to the back of his prey, ripping out bloody gobbets of flesh and ruining the hide. A Land Rover was parked nearby, and a pale, strange-looking man with a long jaw was peering from its window. A second man, red-faced and beefy-looking, stood close by Gilgamesh's roaring, snorting quarry.

First things first. Gilgamesh reached out, scooped the foul hissing little carrion-seeker from the bigger animal's back, flung it aside. Then with all his force he rammed his dagger toward what he hoped was the heart of the wounded animal. In the moment of his thrust Gilgamesh felt a great convulsion within the monster's breast and its hell-life left it in an instant.

The work was done. Again, no exultation, no sense of fulfillment; only a kind of dull ashen release from an unfinished chore. Gilgamesh caught his breath and looked around.

What was this? The red-faced man seemed to be having a crazy fit. Quivering, shaking, sweating, dropping to his knees, his eyes gleaming insanely—

"Lord Conan?" the man cried. "Great king?"

"Conan is not one of my titles," said Gilgamesh, mystified. "And I was a king once in Uruk, but I reign over nothing at all in this place. Come, man, get off your knees!"

"But you are Conan to the life!" moaned the red-faced man hoarsely. "To the absolute life!"

Gilgamesh felt a surge of intense dislike for this fellow. He would be slobbering in another moment. Conan? Conan? That name meant nothing at all. No, wait; he had known a Conan once, some little Celtic fellow he had encountered in a tavern, a chap with a blunt nose and heavy cheekbones and dark hair tumbling down his face, a drunken twitchy little man forever invoking forgotten godlets of no consequence—yes, he had called himself Conan, so Gilgamesh thought. Drank too much, caused trouble for the barmaid, even took a swing at her, that was the one. Gilgamesh had dropped him down an open cesspool to teach him manners. But how could this blustery-faced fellow here mistake me for that one? He was still mumbling on, too, babbling about lands whose names meant nothing to Gilgamesh—Cimmeria, Aquilonia, Hyrkania, Zamora. Total nonsense. There were no such places.

And that glow in the fellow's eyes—what sort of look

was that? A look of adoration, almost the sort of look a woman might give a man when she has decided to yield herself utterly to his will.

Gilgamesh had seen such looks aplenty in his day, from women and men both; and he had welcomed them from women, but never from a man. He scowled. What does he think I am? Does he think, as so many have wrongly thought, that because I loved Enkidu with so great a love that I am a man who will embrace a man in the fashion of men and women? Because it is not so. Not even here in Hell is it so, said Gilgamesh to himself. Nor will it ever be.

"Tell me everything!" the red-faced man was imploring. "All those exploits that I dreamed in your name, Conan: Tell me how they really were! That time in the snow fields, when you met the frost giant's daughter—and when you sailed the *Tigress* with the Black Coast's queen—and that time you stormed the Aquilonian capital, and slew King Numedides on his own throne—"

Gilgamesh stared in distaste at the man groveling at his feet.

"Come, fellow, stop this blather now," he said sourly. "Up with you! You mistake me greatly, I think."

The second man was out of the Land Rover now, and on his way over to join them. An odd-looking creature he was, too, skeleton-thin and corpse-white, with a neck like a water-bird's that seemed barely able to support his long, big-chinned head. He was dressed oddly too, all in black, and swathed in layer upon layer as if he dreaded the faintest chill. Yet he had a gentle and thoughtful way about him, quite unlike the wild-eyed and feverish manner of his friend. He might be a scribe, Gilgamesh thought, or a priest; but what the other one could be, the gods alone would know.

The thin man touched the other's shoulder and said, "Take command of yourself, man. This is surely not your Conan here."

"To the life! To the very life! His size—his grandeur—the way he killed that beast—"

"Bob—Bob, Conan's a figment! Conan's a fantasy! You spun him out of whole cloth. Come, now. Up. Up." To Gilgamesh he said, "A thousand pardons, good sir. My friend is—sometimes excitable—"

Gilgamesh turned away, shrugging, and looked to his quarry. He had no need for dealings with these two. Skinning the huge beast properly might take him the rest of the day; and then to haul the great hide back to his camp, and determine what he wanted of it as a trophy—

Behind him he heard the booming voice of the red-faced man. "A figment, H.P.? How can you be sure of that? I thought I invented Conan, too; but what if he really lived, what if I had merely tapped into some powerful primordial archetype, what if the authentic Conan stands here before us this very moment—"

"Dear Bob, your Conan had blue eyes, did he not? And this man's eyes are dark as night."

"Well—" Grudgingly.

"You were so excited you failed to notice. But I did. This is some barbarian warrior, yes, some great huntsman beyond any doubt—a Nimrod, an Ajax. But not Conan, Bob! Grant him his own identity. He's no invention of yours." Coming up beside Gilgamesh, the long-jawed man said, speaking in a formal and courtly way, "Good sir, I am Howard Phillips Lovecraft, formerly of Providence, Rhode Island, and my companion is Robert E. Howard of Texas, whose other life was lived, as was mine, in the twentieth century after Christ. At that time we were tale-tellers by trade, and I think he confuses you with a hero of his own devising. Put his mind at ease, I pray you, and let us know your name."

Gilgamesh looked up. He rubbed his wrist across his forehead to clear it of a smear of the monster's gore and met the other man's gaze evenly. This one, at least, was no madman, strange though he looked.

Quietly Gilgamesh said, "I think his mind may be beyond putting at any ease. But know you that I am called Gilgamesh, the son of Lugalbanda."

"Gilgamesh the Sumerian?" Lovecraft whispered. "Gilgamesh who sought to live forever?"

"Gilgamesh am I, yes, who was king in Uruk when that was the greatest city of the Land of the Two Rivers, and who in his folly thought there was a way of cheating death."

"Do you hear that, Bob?"

"Incredible. Beyond all belief!" muttered the other.

Rising until he towered above them both, Gilgamesh drew in his breath deeply and said with awesome resonance, "I am Gilgamesh to whom all things were made known, the secret things, the truths of life and death, most especially those of death. I have coupled with Inanna the goddess in the bed of the Sacred Marriage; I have slain demons and spoken with gods; I am two parts god myself, and only one part mortal." He paused and stared at them, letting it sink in, those words that he had recited so many times in situations much like this. Then in a quieter tone he went on, "When death took me I came to this nether world they call Hell, and here I pass my time as a huntsman, and I ask you now to excuse me, for as you see I have my tasks."

Once more he turned away.

"Gilgamesh!" said Lovecraft again in wonder. And the other said, "If I live here till the end of time, H.P., I'll never grow used to it. This is more fantastic than running into Conan would have been! Imagine it: *Gilgamesh!*"

A tiresome business, Gilgamesh thought: all this awe, all this adulation.

The problem was that damned epic, of course. He could see why Caesar grew so irritable when people tried to suck up to him with quotations out of Shakespeare's verses. "Why, man, he doth bestride the narrow world like a Colossus," and all that: Caesar grew livid by the third syllable. Once they put you into poetry, Gilgamesh had discovered, as had Odysseus and Achilles and Caesar after him and many another, your own real self can begin to disappear and the self of the poem overwhelms you entirely and turns you into a walking cliche. Shakespeare had been particularly villainous that way, Gilgamesh thought: ask Richard III, ask Macbeth, ask Owen Glendower. You found them skulking around Hell with perpetual chips on their shoulders, because every time they opened their mouths people expected them to say something like "My kingdom for a horse!" or "Is this a dagger which I see before me?" or "I can call spirits from the vasty deep." Gilgamesh had had to live with that kind of thing almost from the time he had first come to Hell, for they had written the poems about him soon after. All that pompous brooding stuff, a whole raft of Gilgamesh tales of varying degrees of basis in reality. And then the Babylonians and the Assyrians, and even those smelly garlic-gobbling Hittites, had gone on translating and embroidering them for another thousand years so that everybody from one end of the known world to the other knew them by heart. And even after all those peoples were gone and their languages had been forgotten, there was no surcease, because these twentieth-century folk had found the whole thing and deciphered the text somehow and made it famous all over again. Over the centuries they had turned him into everybody's favorite all-purpose hero, which was a hell of a burden to bear: there was a piece of him in the Prometheus legend, and in the Heracles stuff, and in that story of Odysseus' wanderings, and even in the Celtic myths, which was probably why this creepy Howard fellow kept calling him Conan. At least that other Conan, that ratty little sniveling drunken one, had been a Celt. Enlil's ears, but it was wearying to have everyone expecting you to live up to the mythic exploits of twenty or thirty very different culture-heroes! And embarrassing, too, considering that the original non-mythical Heracles and Odysseus and some of the others dwelled here too and tended to be pretty possessive about the myths that had attached to *them*, even when they were simply variants on his own much older ones.

There was substance to the Gilgamesh stories, of course, especially the parts about him and Enkidu. But the poet had salted the story with a lot of pretentious arty nonsense too, as poets always will, and in any case you got very tired of having everybody boil your long and complex life down into the same twelve chapters and the same little turns of phrase. It got so that Gilgamesh found himself quoting the main Gilgamesh poem too, the one about his quest for eternal life—well, that one wasn't too far from the essence of the truth, though they had mucked up a lot of the details with precious little "imaginative" touches—by way of making introduction for himself: "I am the man to whom all things were made known, the secret things, the truths of life and death." Straight out of the poet's mouth, those lines. Tiresome. Tiresome. Angrily he jabbed his dagger beneath the dead monster's hide, and set about his task of flaying, while the two little men behind him went on muttering and mumbling to one another in astonishment at having run into Gilgamesh of Uruk in this bleak and lonely corner of Hell.

There were strange emotions stirring in Robert Howard's soul, and he did not care for them at all. He could forgive himself for believing for that one giddy moment that this Gilgamesh was his Conan. That was nothing more than the artistic temperament at work, sweeping him up in a bit of rash feverish enthusiasm. To come suddenly upon a great muscular giant of a man in a loincloth who was hacking away at some fiendish monster with a little bronze dagger, and to think that he must surely be the mighty Cimmerian—well, that was a pardonable enough thing. Here in Hell you learned very quickly that you might run into anybody at all. You could find yourself playing at dice with Lord Byron or sharing a mug of mulled wine with Menelaos or arguing with Plato about the ideas of Nietzsche, who was standing right there making faces, and after a time you came to take most such things for granted, more or less.

So why not think that this fellow was Conan? No matter that Conan's eyes had been of a different color. That was a trifle. He looked like Conan in all the important ways. He was of Conan's size and strength. And he was kingly in more than physique. He seemed to have Conan's cool intelligence and complexity of soul, his regal courage and indomitable spirit.

The trouble was that Conan, the wondrous Cimmerian warrior from 19,000 B.C., had never existed except in Howard's own imagination. And there were no fictional characters in Hell. You might meet Richard Wagner, but you weren't likely to encounter Siegfried. Theseus was here somewhere, but not the Minotaur. William the Conqueror, yes; William Tell, no.

That was all right, Howard told himself. His little fantasy of meeting Conan here in Hell was nothing but a bit of mawkish narcissism: he was better off without it. Coming across the authentic Gilgamesh—ah, how much more interesting that was! A genuine Sumerian king—an actual titan out of history's dawn, not some trumped-up figure fashioned from cardboard and hard-breathing wish-fulfilling dreams. A flesh-and-blood mortal who lived a lusty life and had fought great battles and had walked eye to eye with the ancient gods. A man who had struggled against the inevitability of death, and who in dying had taken on the immortality of mythic archetype—ah, now there was someone worth getting to know! Whereas Howard had to admit that he would learn no more from a conversation with Conan than he could discover by interrogating his own image in the mirror. Or else a meeting with the "real" Conan, if it was in any way possible, would surely cast him into terrible confusions and contradictions of soul from which there would be no recovering. No, Howard thought. Better that this man be Gilgamesh than Conan, by all means. He was reconciled to that.

But this other business—this sudden bewildering urge to throw himself at the giant's feet, to be swept up in his arms, to be crushed in a fierce embrace—

What was that? Where had *that* come from? By the blazing Heart of Ahriman, what could it mean?

Howard remembered a time in his former life when he had gone down to the Cisco Dam and watched the construction men strip and dive in: well-built men, confident, graceful, at ease in their bodies. For a short while he had looked at them and had reveled in their physical perfection. They could have been naked Greek statues come alive, a band of lusty Apollos and Zeuses. And then as he listened to them shouting and laughing and crying out in their foul-mouthed way he began to grow angry, suddenly seeing them as mere thoughtless animals who were the natural enemies of dreamers like himself. He hated them as the weak always must hate the strong, those splendid swine who could trample the dreamers and their dreams as they wished. But then he had reminded himself that he was no weakling himself, that he who once had been spindly and frail had by hard effort made himself big and strong and burly. Not beautiful of body as these men were—too fleshy for that, too husky—but nevertheless, he had told himself, there was no man there whose ribs he could not crush if it came to a struggle. And he had gone away from that place full of rage and thoughts of bloody violence.

What had that been all about? That barely suppressed fury—was it some sort of dark hidden lust, some craving for the most bestial sort of sinfulness? Was the anger that had arisen in him masking an anger he should have directed at himself, for looking upon those naked men and taking pleasure in it?

No. No. No. No. He wasn't any kind of degenerate. He was certain of that.

The desire of men for men was a mark of decadence, of the decline of civilization. He was a man of the frontier, not some feeble limp-wristed sodomite who reveled in filth and wanton evil. If he had never in his short life known a woman's love, it was for lack of opportunity, not out of a preference for that other shameful kind. Living out his days in that small and remote prairie town, devoting himself to his mother and to his writing, he had chosen not to avail himself of prostitutes or shallow women, but he was sure that if he had lived a few years longer and the woman who was his true mate had ever made herself known to him, he would certainly have reached toward her in passion and high abandon.

And yet—and yet—that moment when he first spied the giant Gilgamesh, and thought he was Conan—

That surge of electricity through his entire body, and most intensely through his loins—what else could it have been but desire, instant and intense and overwhelming? For a *man?* Unthinkable! Even this glorious hero—even this magnificent kingly creature—

No. No. No. No.

I am in Hell, and this is my torment, Howard told himself.

He paced furiously up and down alongside the Land Rover. Desperately he fought off the black anguish that threatened to settle over him now, as it had done so many times in his former life and in this life after life. These sudden corrupt and depraved feelings, Howard thought: they are nothing but diabolical perversions of my natural spirit, intended to cast me into despair and self-loathing! By Crom, I will resist! By the breasts of Ishtar, I will not yield this foulness!

All the same he found his eyes straying to the edge of the nearby thicket, where Gilgamesh still knelt over the animal he had killed.

What extraordinary muscles rippling in that broad back, in those iron-hard thighs! What careless abandon in the way he was peeling back the creature's shaggy hide, though he had to wallow in dark gore to do it! That cascade of lustrous black hair lightly bound by a jewelled circlet, that dense black beard curling in tight ringlets—

Howard's throat went dry. Something at the base of his belly was tightening into a terrible knot.

Lovecraft said, "You want a chance to talk with him, don't you?"

Howard swung around. He felt his cheeks go scarlet. He was utterly certain that his guilt must be emblazoned incontrovertibly on his face.

"What the hell do you mean?" he growled. His hands knotted of their own accord into fists. There seemed to be a band of fire across his forehead. "What would I want to talk with him about, anyway?"

Lovecraft looked startled by the ferocity of Howard's tone and posture. He took a step backward and threw up his hand almost as though to protect himself. "What a strange thing to say! You, of all people, with your love of antique times, your deep and abiding passion for the lost mysteries of those steamy Oriental empires that perished so long ago! Why, man, is there nothing you want to know about the kingdoms of Sumer? Uruk, Nippur, Ur of the Chaldees? The secret rites of the goddess Inanna in the dark passageways beneath the ziggurat? The incantations that opened the gates of the Underworld, the libations that loosed and bound the demons of the worlds beyond the stars? Who knows what he could tell us? There stands a man six thousand years old, a hero from the dawn of time, Bob!"

Howard snorted. "I don't reckon that oversized son of a bitch would want to tell us a damned thing. All that interests him is getting the hide off that bloody critter of his."

"He's nearly done with that. Why not wait, Bob? And invite him to sit with us a little while. And draw him out, lure him into telling us tales of life beside the Euphrates!" Now Lovecraft's dark eyes were gleaming as though he too felt some strange lust, and his forehead was surprisingly bright with uncharacteristic perspiration; but Howard knew that in Lovecraft's case what had taken possession of him was only the lust for knowledge, the hunger for the arcane lore of high antiquity that Lovecraft imagined would spill from the lips of this Mesopotamian hero. That same lust ached in him as well. To speak with this man who had lived before Babylon was, who had walked the streets of Ur when Abraham was yet unborn—

But there were other lusts besides that hunger for

knowledge, sinister lusts that must be denied at any cost—

"No," said Howard brusquely. "Let's get the hell out of here right now, H.P. This damned foul bleak country-side is getting on my nerves."

Lovecraft gave him a strange look. "But weren't you just telling me how beautiful—

"Damnation take whatever I was telling you! King Henry's expecting us to negotiate an alliance for him. We aren't going to get the job done out here in the boondocks."

"The what?"

"Boondocks. Wild uncivilized country. Term that came into use after our time, H.P. The backwoods, you know? You never did pay much heed to the vernacular, did you?" He tugged at Lovecraft's sleeve. "Come on. That big bloody ape over there isn't going to tell us a thing about his life and times, I guarantee. Probably doesn't remember anything worth telling, anyway. And he bores me. Pardon me, H.P., but I find him an enormous pain in the butt, all right? I don't have any further hankering for his company. Do you mind, H.P.? Can we move along, do you think?"

"I must confess that you mystify me sometimes, Bob. But of course if you—" Suddenly Lovecraft's eyes wid-ened in amazement. "Get down, Bob! Behind the car! Fast!"

"What—"

An arrow came singing through the air and passed just alongside Howard's left ear. Then another, and another. One arrow ricocheted off the flank of the Land Rover with a sickening thunking sound. Another struck straight on and stuck quivering an inch deep in the metal.

Howard whirled. He saw horsemen—a dozen, perhaps a dozen and a half—bearing down on them out of the darkness to the east, loosing shafts as they came.

They were lean compact men of some Oriental stock in crimson leather jerkins, riding like fiends. Their mounts were little flat-headed, fiery-eyed gray Hell-horses that moved as if their short, fiercely pistoning legs could carry them to the far boundaries of the nether world without the need of a moment's rest.

Chanting, howling, the yellow-skinned warriors seemed to be in a frenzy of rage. Mongols? Turks? Whoever they were, they were pounding toward the Land Rover like the emissaries of Death himself. Some brandished long wickedly curved blades, but most wielded curious-looking small bows from which they showered one arrow after another with phenomenal rapidity.

Crouching behind the Land Rover with Lovecraft beside him, Howard gaped at the attackers in a paralysis of astonishment. How often had he written of scenes like this? Waving plumes, bristling lances, a whistling cloud of cloth-yard shafts! Thundering hooves, wild war cries, the thunk of barbarian arrowheads against Aquilonian shields! Horses rearing and throwing their riders. . . . Knights in bloodied armor tumbling to the ground. . . . Steel-clad forms littering the slopes of the battlefield. . . .

But this was no swashbuckling tale of Hyborean derring-do that was unfolding now. Those were real horsemen—as real as anything was, in this place—rampaging across this chilly wind-swept plain in the outer reaches of Hell. Those were real arrows; and they would rip their way into his flesh with real impact and inflict real agony of the most frightful kind.

He looked across the way at Gilgamesh. The giant Sumerian was hunkered down behind the overturned bulk of the animal he had slain. His mighty bow was in his hand. As Howard watched in awe, Gilgamesh aimed and let fly. The shaft struck the nearest horseman, traveling through jerkin and rib cage and all, and emerging from the man's back. But still the onrushing warrior managed to release one last arrow before he fell. It traveled on an erratic trajectory, humming quickly toward Gilgamesh on a wild wobbly arc and skewering him through the flesh of his left forearm.

Coolly the Sumerian glanced down at the arrow jutting from his arm. He scowled and shook his head, the way

he might if he had been stung by a hornet. Then—as
Conan might have done, how very much like Conan!—
Gilgamesh inclined his head toward his shoulder and *bit*
the arrow in half just below the fletching. Bright blood
spouted from the wound as he pulled the two pieces of
the arrow from his arm.

As though nothing very significant had happened, Gilgamesh lifted his bow and reached for a second shaft.
Blood was streaming in rivulets down his arm, but he
seemed not even to be aware of it.

Howard watched as if in a stupor. He could not move;
he barely had the will to draw breath. A haze of nausea
threatened to overwhelm him. It had been nothing at all
for him to heap up great bloody mounds of severed heads
and arms and legs with cheerful abandon in his stories;
but in fact, real bloodshed and violence of any sort had
horrified him whenever he had even a glimpse of it.

"The gun, Bob!" said Lovecraft urgently beside him.
"Use the *gun!*"

"What?"

"There. There."

Howard looked down. Thrust through his belt was the
pistol he had taken from the Land Rover when he had
come out to investigate that little beast in the road. He
drew it now and stared at it, glassy-eyed, as though it
were a basilisk's egg that rested on the palm of his hand.

"What are you doing?" Lovecraft asked. "Ah. Ah. Give
it to me." He snatched the gun impatiently from Howard's frozen fingers and studied it a moment as though
he had never held a weapon before. Perhaps he never
had. But then, grasping the pistol with both his hands,
he rose warily above the hood of the Land Rover and
squeezed off a shot.

The tremendous sound of an explosion cut through the
shrill cries of the horsemen. Lovecraft laughed. "Got one!
Who would ever have imagined—"

He fired again. In the same moment Gilgamesh
brought down one more of the attackers with his bow.

"They're backing off!" Lovecraft cried. "By Alhazred,

they didn't expect *this,* I wager!" He laughed again and poked the gun up into a firing position. "*Ia!*" he cried, in a voice Howard had never heard out of the shy and scholarly Lovecraft before. "*Shub-Niggurath!*" Lovecraft fired a third time. "*Ph'nglui mglw'nafh Cthulhu R'lyeh wgah'nagl fhtagn!*"

Howard felt sweat rolling down his body. This inaction of his—this paralysis, this shame—what would Conan make of it? What would Gilgamesh? And Lovecraft, that timid and sheltered man, he who dreaded the fishes of the sea and the cold winds of his New England winters and so many other things, was laughing and bellowing his wondrous gibberish and blazing away like any gangster, having the time of his life—

Shame! Shame!

Heedless of the risk, Howard scrambled up into the cab of the Land Rover and groped around for the second gun that was lying down there on the floor somewhere. He found it and knelt beside the window. Seven or eight of the Asiatic horsemen lay strewn about, dead or dying, within a hundred-yard radius of the car. The others had withdrawn to a considerable distance and were cantering in uneasy circles. They appeared taken aback by the unexpectedly fierce resistance they had encountered on what they had probably expected to have been an easy bit of jolly slaughter in these untracked frontierlands.

What were they doing now? Drawing together, a tight little ground, horses nose to nose. Conferring. And now two of them were pulling what seemed to be some sort of war-banner from a saddlebag and hoisting it between them on bamboo poles: a long yellow streamer with fluttering blood-red tips, on which bold Oriental characters were painted in shining black. Serious business, obviously. Now they were lining themselves up in a row, facing the Land Rover. Getting ready for a desperate suicide charge—that was the way things appeared.

Gilgamesh, standing erect in full view, calmly nocked yet another arrow. He took aim and waited for them to come. Lovecraft, looking flushed with excitement, wholly transformed by the alien joys of armed combat, was leaning forward, staring intently, his pistol cocked and ready.

Howard shivered. Shame rode him with burning spurs. How *could* he cower here while those two bore the brunt of the struggle? Though his hand was shaking, he thrust the pistol out the window and drew a bead on the closest horseman. His finger tightened on the trigger. Would it be possible to score a hit at such a distance? Yes. Yes. Go ahead. You know how to use a gun, all right. High time you put some of that skill to use. Knock that little yellow bastard off his horse with one bark of the Colt .380, yes. Send him straight to Hell—no, he's in Hell already, send him off to the Undertaker for recycling. Yes, that's it. Ready—aim—

"Wait," Lovecraft said. "Don't shoot."

What was this? As Howard, with an effort, lowered his gun and let his rigid quivering hand go slack, Lovecraft, shading his eyes against the eerie glare of the motionless sun, peered closely at the enemy warriors a long silent moment. Then he turned, reached up into the rear of the Land Rover, groped around for a moment, finally pulled out the manila envelope that held their royal commission from King Henry.

And then—what was he doing?

Stepping out into plain view, arms raised high, waving the envelope around, walking toward the enemy?

"They'll kill you, H.P.! Get down! Get down!"

Lovecraft, without looking back, gestured brusquely for Howard to be silent. He continued to walk steadily toward the far-off horsemen. They seemed just as mystified as Howard was. They sat without moving, their bows held stiffly out before them, a dozen arrows trained on the middle of Lovecraft's body.

He's gone completely off the deep end, Howard thought in dismay. He never was really well balanced, was he? Half believing all his stuff about Elder Gods and dimensional gateways and blasphemous rites on dark New England hillsides. And now all this shooting—the excitement—

"Hold your weapons, all of you!" Lovecraft cried in a voice of amazing strength and presence. "In the name of Prester John, I bid you hold your weapons! We are not your enemies! We are embassadors to your emperor!"

Howard gasped. He began to understand. No, Lovecraft hadn't gone crazy after all!

He took another look at that long yellow war-banner. Yes, yes, it bore the emblems of Prester John! These berserk horsemen must be part of the border patrol of the very nation whose ruler they had traveled so long to find. Howard felt abashed, realizing that in the fury of the battle Lovecraft had had the sense actually to pause long enough to give the banner's legend close examination—and the courage to walk out there waving his diplomatic credentials. The parchment scroll of their royal commission was in his hand, and he was pointing to the little red-ribboned seal of King Henry.

The horsemen stared, muttered among themselves, lowered their bows. Gilgamesh, lowering his great bow also, looked on in puzzlement. "Do you see?" Lovecraft called. "We are heralds of King Henry! We claim the protection of your master the August Sovereign Yeh-lu Ta-shih!" Glancing back over his shoulder, he called to Howard to join him; and after only an instant's hesitation, Howard leaped down from the Land Rover and trotted forward. It was a giddy feeling, exposing himself to those somber yellow archers this way. It felt almost like standing on the edge of some colossal precipice.

Lovecraft smiled. "It's all going to be all right, Bob! That banner they unfurled, it bears the markings of Prester John—"

"Yes, yes. I see."

"And look—they're making a safe-conduct sign. They understand what I'm saying, Bob! They believe me!"

Howard nodded. He felt a great upsurge of relief and even a sort of joy. He clapped Lovecraft lustily on the back. "Fine going, H.P.! I didn't think you had it in you!" Coming up out of his funk, now, he felt a manic exuberance seize his spirit. He gestured to the horsemen,

wigwagging his arms with wild vigor. "Hoy! Royal com-
missioners!" he bellowed. "Envoys from His Britannic
Majesty King Henry VIII! Take us to your emperor!"
Then he looked toward Gilgamesh, who stood frowning,
his bow still at the ready. "Hoy there, king of Uruk! Put
away the weapons! Everything's all right now! We're
going to be escorted to the court of Prester John!"

Gilgamesh wasn't at all sure why he had let himself go
along. He had no interest in visiting Prester John's court,
or anybody else's. He wanted nothing more than to be
left alone to hunt and roam in the wilderness and thereby
to find some ease for his sorrows.

But the gaunt long-necked man and his blustery red-
faced friend had beckoned him to ride with them in their
Land Rover, and while he stood there frowning over that,
the ugly flat-featured little yellow warriors had indicated
with quick impatient gestures that he should get in. And
he had. They looked as though they would try to compel
him to get in if he balked; and though he had no fear
of them, none whatever, some impulse that he could not
begin to understand had led him to step back from the
likelihood of yet another battle and simply climb aboard
the vehicle. Perhaps he had had enough of solitary hunting for a while. Or perhaps it was just that the wound
in his arm was beginning to throb and ache, now that
the excitement of the fray was receding, and it seemed
like a good idea to have it looked after by a surgeon.
The flesh all around it was badly swollen and bruised.
That arrow had pierced him through and through. He
would have the wound cleaned and dressed, and then he
would move along.

Well, then, so he was going to the court of Prester
John. Here he was, sitting back silent and somber in the
rear of this musty, mildew-flecked car, riding with these
two very odd New Dead types, these scribes or tale-
tellers or whatever it was they claimed to be, as the
horsemen of Prester John led them to the encampment
of their monarch.

The one who called himself Howard, the one who could not help stealing sly little glances at him like an infatuated schoolgirl, was at the wheel. Glancing back at his passenger now, he said, "Tell me, Gilgamesh: have you had dealings with Prester John before?"

"I have heard the name, that much I know," replied the Sumerian. "But it means little to me."

"The legendary Christian emperor," said the other, the thin one, Lovecraft. "He who was said to rule a secret kingdom somewhere in the misty hinterlands of Central Asia—although it was in Africa, according to some—"

Asia, Africa—names, only names, Gilgamesh thought bleakly. They were places somewhere in the other world, but he had no idea where they might be.

Such a multitude of places, so many names! It was impossible to keep it all straight. There was no sense of any of it. The world—his world, the Land—had been bordered by the Two Rivers, the Idigna and the Buranunu, which the Greeks had preferred to call the Tigris and the Euphrates. Who were the Greeks, and by what right had they renamed the rivers? Everyone used those names now, even Gilgamesh himself, except in the inwardness of his soul.

And beyond the Two Rivers? Why, there was the vassal state of Aratta far to the east, and in that direction also lay the Land of Cedars, where the fire-breathing demon Huwawa roared and bellowed, and in the eastern mountains lay the kingdom of the barbaric Elamites. To the north was the land called Uri, and in the deserts of the west the wild Martu people dwelled, and in the south was the blessed isle Dilmun, which was like a paradise. Was there anything more to the world than that? Why, there was Meluhha far away beyond Elam, where the people had black skins and fine features, and there was Punt in the south, where they were black also, with flat noses and thick lips. And there was another land even beyond Meluhha, with folk of yellow skins who mined a precious green stone. And that was the world. Where could all these other latter-day places be—this Africa and this Asia and Europe and the rest, Rome, Greece, England? Perhaps some of them were mere new names for old places. The Land itself had had a host of names since his own time—Babylonia, Mesopotamia, Iraq, and more. Why had it needed all those names? He had no idea. New men made up new names: that seemed to be the way of the world. This Africa, this Asia—America, China, Russia. A little man named Herodotos, a Greek, had tried to explain it all to him once—the shape of the world and the names of the places in it, sketching a map for him on an old bit of parchment—and much later a stolid fellow named Mercator had done the same, and once after that he had spoken of such matters with an Englishman called Cook; but the things they told him all conflicted with one another and he could make no sense out of any of it. It was too much to ask, making sense of these things. Those myriad nations that had arisen after his time, those empires that had arisen and fallen and been forgotten, all those lost dynasties, the captains and the kings—he had tried from time to time to master the sequence of them, but it was no use. Once in his former life he had sought to make himself the master of all knowledge, yes. His appetites had been boundless: for knowledge, for wealth, for power, for women, for life itself. Now all that seemed only the merest folly to him. That jumble of confused and confusing places, all those great realms and far-off kingdoms, were in another world: what could they matter to him now?

"Asia?" he said. "Africa?" Gilgamesh shrugged. "Prester John?" He prowled the turbulent cluttered recesses of his memory. "Ah. There's a Prester John, I think, lives in New Hell. A dark-skinned man, a friend of that gaudy old liar Sir John Mandeville." It was coming back now. "Yes, I've seen them together many times, in that dirty squalid tavern where Mandeville's always to be found. The two of them telling outlandish stories back and forth, each a bigger fraud than the other."

"A different Prester John," said Lovecraft.

"That one is Susenyos the Ethiop, I think," Howard

said. "A former African tyrant, and lover of the Jesuits, now far gone in whiskey. He's one of many. There are seven, nine, a dozen Prester Johns in Hell, to my certain knowledge. And maybe more."

Gilgamesh contemplated that notion blankly. Fire was running up and down his injured arm now.

Lovecraft was saying, "—not a true name, but merely a title, and a corrupt one at that. There never was a *real* Prester John, only various rulers in various distant places, whom it pleased the tale-spinners of Europe to speak of as Prester John, the Christian emperor, the great mysterious unknown monarch of a fabulous realm. And here in Hell there are many who choose to wear the name. There's power in it, do you see?"

"Power and majesty!" Howard cried. "And poetry, by God!"

"So this Prester John whom we are to visit," said Gilgamesh, "he is not in fact Prester John?"

"Yeh-lu Ta-shih's his name," said Howard. "Chinese. Manchurian, actually, twelfth century A.D. First emperor of the realm of Kara-Khitai, with his capital at Samarkand. Ruled over a bunch of Mongols and Turks, mainly, and they called him Gur Khan, which means 'supreme ruler,' and somehow that turned into 'John' by the time it got to Europe. And they said he was a Christian priest, too, *Presbyter Joannes,* 'Prester John.'" Howard laughed. "Damned silly bastards. He was no more a Christian than you were. A Buddhist, he was, a bloody shamanistic Buddhist."

"Then why—"

"Myth and confusion!" Howard said. "The great human nonsense factory at work! And wouldn't you know it, but when he got to Hell this Yeh-lu Ta-shih founded himself another empire right away in the same sort of territory he'd lived in back there, and when Richard Burton came out this way and told him about Prester John and how Europeans long ago had spoken of him by that name and ascribed all sorts of fabulous accomplishments to him he said, 'Yes, yes, I am Prester John indeed.' And so he styles himself that way now, he and nine or ten others, most of them Ethiopians like that friend of your friend Mandeville."

"They are no friends of mine," said Gilgamesh stiffly. He leaned back and massaged his aching arm. Outside the Land Rover the landscape was changing now: more hilly, with ill-favored fat-trunked little trees jutting at peculiar angles from the purple soil. Here and there in the distance his keen eyes made out scattered groups of black tents on the hillsides, and herds of the little Hell-horses grazing near them. Gilgamesh wished now that he hadn't let himself be inveigled into this expedition. What need had he of Prester John? One of these upstart New Dead potentates, one of the innumerable little princelings who had set up minor dominions for themselves out here in the vast measureless wastelands of the Outback— and reigning under a false name, at that—one more shoddy scoundrel, one more puffed-up little nobody swollen with unearned pride—

Well, and what difference did it make? He would sojourn a while in the land of this Prester John, and then he would move on, alone, apart from others, mourning as always his lost Enkidu. There seemed no escaping that doom that lay upon him, that bitter solitude, whether he reigned in splendor in Uruk or wandered in the wastes of Hell.

"Their Excellencies P.E. Lovecraft and Howard E. Robert," cried the major-domo grandly though inaccurately, striking three times on the black marble floor of Prester John's throne-chamber with his gold-tipped staff of pale green jade. "Envoys Plenipotentiary of His Britannic Majesty King Henry VIII of the Kingdom of New Holy Diabolic England."

Lovecraft and Howard took a couple of steps forward. Yeh-lu Ta-shih nodded curtly and waved one elegant hand, resplendent with inch-long fingernails, in casual acknowledgment. The envoys plenipotentiary did not seem to hold much interest for him, nor, apparently, did whatever it was that had caused His Britannic Majesty King Henry to send them here.

The emperor's cool imperious glance turned toward Gilgamesh, who was struggling to hold himself erect. He was beginning to feel feverish and dizzy and he wondered when anyone would notice that there was an oozing hole in his arm. Even he had limits to his endurance, after all, though he usually tried to conceal that fact. He didn't know how much longer he could hold out. There were times when behaving like a hero was a heroic pain in the ass, and this was one of them.

"—and his Late Highness Gilgamesh of Uruk, son of Lugalbanda, great king, king of Uruk, king of kings, lord of the Land of the Two Rivers by merit of Enlil and An," boomed the major-domo in the same splendid way, looking down only once at the card he held in his hand.

"Great king?" said Yeh-lu Ta-shih, fixing Gilgamesh with one of the most intensely penetrating stares the Sumerian could remember ever having received. "King of kings? Those are very lofty titles, Gilgamesh of Uruk."

"A mere formula," Gilgamesh replied, "which I thought appropriate when being presented at your court. In fact I am king of nothing at all now."

"Ah," said Yeh-lu Ta-shih. "King of Nothing-at-all."

And so are you, my lord Prester John. Gilgamesh did not let himself say it, though the words bubbled toward the roof of his mouth and begged to be uttered. *And so are all the self-appointed lords and masters of the many realms of Hell.*

The slender amber-hued man on the throne leaned forward. "And where then, I pray, is Nothing-at-all?"

Some of the courtiers began to snicker. But Prester John looked to be altogether in earnest, though it was impossible to be completely certain of that. He was plainly a formidable man, Gilgamesh had quickly come to see: sly, shrewd, self-contained, with a tough and sinewy intelligence. Not at all the vain little cock-of-the-walk Gilgamesh had expected to find in this bleak and remote corner of Hell. However small and obscure his principality might be, Prester John ruled it, obviously, with a firm grasp. The grandeur of the glittering palace that his scruffy subjects had built for him here on the edge of nowhere, and the solidity of the small but substantial city surrounding it, testified to that. Gilgamesh knew something about the building of cities and palaces. Prester John's capital bore the mark of the steady toil of centuries.

The long stare was unrelenting. Gilgamesh, fighting back the blazing pain in his arm, met the emperor's gaze with an equally earnest one of his own and said:

"Nothing-at-all? It is a land that never was, and will always be, my lord. Its boundaries are nowhere and its capital city is everywhere, nor do any of us ever leave it."

"Ah. Ah. Indeed. Nicely put. You are Old Dead, are you?"

"Very old, my lord."

"Older than Ch'in Shih Huang Ti? Older than the Lords of Shang and Hsia?"

Gilgamesh turned in puzzlement toward Lovecraft, who told him in a half-whisper, "Ancient kings of China. Your time was even earlier."

Shrugging, Gilgamesh replied, "They are not known to me, my lord, but you hear what the Britannic ambassador says. He is a man of learning: it must be so. I will tell you that I am older than Caesar by far, older than Agamemnon and the Supreme Commander Rameses, older even than Sargon. By a great deal."

Yeh-lu Ta-shih considered that a moment. Then he made another of his little gestures of dismissal, as though brushing aside the whole concept of relative ages in Hell. With a dry laugh he said, "So you are very old, King Gilgamesh. I congratulate you. And yet the Ice-Hunter folk would tell us that you and I and Rameses and Sargon all arrived here only yesterday; and to the Hairy Men, the Ice-Hunters themselves are mere newcomers. And so on and so on. There's no beginning to it, is there? Any more than there's an end."

Without waiting for an answer he asked Gilgamesh, "How did you come by that gory wound, great king of Nothing-at-all?"

At least he's noticed it, Gilgamesh thought.

"A misunderstanding, my lord. It may be that your border patrol is a little overzealous at times."

One of the courtiers learned toward the emperor and murmured something. Prester John's serene brow grew furrowed. He lifted a flawlessly contoured eyebrow ever so slightly.

"Killed nine of them, did you?"

"They attacked us before we had the opportunity of showing our diplomatic credentials," Lovecraft put in quickly. "It was entirely a matter of self-defense, my lord Prester John."

"I wouldn't doubt it." The emperor seemed to contemplate for a moment, but only for a moment, the skirmish that had cost the lives of nine of his horsemen; and then quite visibly he dismissed that matter too from the center of his attention. "Well, now, my lords ambassador—"

Abruptly Gilgamesh swayed, tottered, started to fall. He checked himself just barely in time, seizing a massive porphyry column and clinging to it until he felt more steady. Beads of sweat trickled down his forehead into his eyes. He began to shiver. The huge stone column seemed to be expanding and contracting. Waves of vertigo were rippling through him and he was seeing double, suddenly. Everything was blurring and multiplying. He drew his breath in deeply, again, again, forcing himself to hold on. He wondered if Prester John was playing some kind of game with him, trying to see how long his strength could last. Well, if he had to, Gilgamesh swore, he would stand here forever in front of Prester John without showing a hint of weakness.

But now Yeh-lu Ta-shih was at last willing to extend compassion. With a glance toward one of his pages the emperor said, "Summon my physician, and tell him to bring his tools and his potions. That wound should have been dressed an hour ago."

"Thank you, my lord," Gilgamesh muttered, trying to keep the irony from his tone.

The doctor appeared almost at once, as though he had been waiting in an antechamber. Another of Prester John's little games, perhaps? He was a burly, broad-shouldered, bushy-haired man of more than middle years, with a manner about him that was brisk and bustling but nevertheless warm, concerned, reassuring. Drawing Gilgamesh down beside him on a low divan covered with the gray-green hide of some scaly Hell-dragon, he peered into the wound, muttered something unintelligible to himself in a guttural language unknown to the Sumerian, and pressed his thick fingers around the edges of the torn flesh until fresh blood flowed. Gilgamesh hissed sharply but did not flinch.

"*Ach, mein lieber Freund,* I must hurt you again, but it is for your own good. *Verstehen sie?*"

The doctor's fingers dug in more deeply. He was spreading the wound, swabbing it, cleansing it with some clear fluid that stung like a hot iron. The pain was so intense that there was almost a kind of pleasure in it: it was a purifying kind of pain, a purging of the soul.

Prester John said, "How bad is it, Dr. Schweitzer?"

"*Gott sei dank,* it is deep but clean. He will heal without damage."

He continued to probe and cleanse; murmuring softly to Gilgamesh as he worked: "*Bitte. Bitte. Einen Augenblick, mein Freund.*" To Prester John he said, "This man is made of steel. No nerves at all, immense resistance to pain. We have one of the great heroes here, *nicht wahr?* You are Roland, are you? Achilles, perhaps?"

"Gilgamesh is his name," said Yeh-lu Ta-shih.

The doctor's eyes grew bright. "Gilgamesh! Gilgamesh of Sumer? *Wunderbar! Wunderbar!* The very man. The seeker after life. *Ach,* we must talk, my friend, you and I, when you are feeling better." From his medical kit he now produced a frightful-looking hypodermic syringe.

Gilgamesh watched as though from a vast distance, as though that throbbing swollen arm belonged to someone else. "*Ja, ja,* certainly we must talk, of life, of death, or philosophy, *mein Freund,* of *philosophy!* There is so very much for us to discuss!" He slipped the needle beneath Gilgamesh's skin. "There. *Genug.* Sit. Rest. The healing now begins."

Robert Howard had never seen anything like it. It could have been something straight from the pages of one of his Conan stories. The big ox had taken an arrow right through the fat part of his arm, and he had simply yanked it out and gone right on fighting. Then, afterward, he had behaved as if the wound were nothing more than a scratch, all that time while they were driving hour after hour toward Prester John's city and then undergoing lengthy interrogation by the court officials and then standing through this whole endless ceremony at court— God almighty, what a display of endurance! True, Gilgamesh had finally gone a little wobbly and had actually seemed on the verge of passing out. But any ordinary mortal would have conked out long ago. Heroes really *were* different. They were another breed altogether. Look at him now, sitting there casually while that old German medic swabs him out and stitches him up in that slapdash cavalier way, and not a whimper out of him. Not a whimper!

Suddenly Howard found himself wanting to go over there to Gilgamesh, to comfort him, to let him lean his head back against him while the doctor worked him over, to wipe the sweat from his brow—

Yes, to comfort him in an open, rugged, manly way— No. No. No. No.

There it was again, the horror, the unspeakable thing, the hideous crawling Hell-borne impulse rising out of the cesspools of his soul—

Howard fought it back. Blotted it out, hid it from view. Denied that it had ever entered his mind.

To Lovecraft he said, "That's some doctor! Took his medical degree at the Chicago slaughterhouses, I reckon!"

"Don't you know who he is, Bob?"

"Some old Dutchman who wandered in here during a sandstorm and never bothered to leave."

"Does the name Dr. Schweitzer mean nothing to you?"

Howard gave Lovecraft a blank look. "Guess I never heard it much in Texas."

"Oh, Bob, Bob, why must you always pretend to be such a cowboy? Can you tell me you've never heard of Schweitzer? *Albert* Schweitzer? The great philosopher, theologian, musician—there never was a greater interpreter of Bach, and don't tell me you don't know Bach either—"

"She-it, H.P., you talking about that old country doctor there?"

"Who founded the leprosy clinic in Africa, at Lambarene, yes. Who devoted his life to helping the sick, under the most primitive conditions, in the most remote forests of—"

"Hold on, H.P. That can't be so."

"That one man could achieve so much? I assure you, Bob, he was quite well known in our time—perhaps not in Texas, I suppose, but nevertheless—"

"No. Not that he could do all that. But that he's here. In Hell. If that old geezer's everything you say, then he's a goddamned *saint*. Unless he beat his wife when no one was looking, or something like that. What's a saint doing in Hell, H.P.?"

"What are *we* doing in Hell?" Lovecraft asked.

Howard reddened and looked away. "Well, I suppose, there were things in our lives—things that might be considered sins, in the strictest sense—"

"No one understands the rules of Hell, Bob," said Lovecraft gently. "Sin may have nothing to do with it. Gandhi is here, do you realize that? Confucius. Were *they* sinners? Was Moses? Abraham? We've tried to impose our own pitiful shallow beliefs, our pathetic grade-school notions of punishment for bad behavior, on this incredibly bizarre place where we find ourselves. By what right? We don't begin to comprehend what Hell really is. All we know is that it's full of heroic villains and villainous heroes—and people like you and me— and it seems that Albert Schweitzer is here, too. A great mystery. But perhaps someday—"

"Shh," Howard said. "Prester John's talking to us."

"My lords ambassador—"

Hastily they turned toward him. "Your majesty?" Howard said.

"This mission that has brought you here: your king wants an alliance, I suppose? What for? Against whom? Quarreling with some pope again, is he?"

"With his daughter, I'm afraid," said Howard.

Prester John looked bored. He toyed with his emerald scepter. "Mary, you mean?"

"Elizabeth, your majesty," Lovecraft said.

"Your king's a most quarrelsome man. I'd have thought there were enough popes in Hell to keep him busy, though, and no need to contend with his daughters."

"They are the most contentious women in Hell," Lovecraft said. "Blood of his blood, after all, and each of them a queen with a noisy, brawling kingdom of her own. Elizabeth, my lord, is sending a pack of her explorers to the Outback, and King Henry doesn't like the idea."

"Indeed," said Yeh-lu Ta-shih, suddenly interested again. "And neither do I. She has no business in the Outback. It's not her territory. The rest of Hell should be big enough for Elizabeth. What is she looking for here?"

"The sorcerer John Dee has told her that the way out of Hell is to be found in these parts."

"There is no way out of Hell."

Lovecraft smiled. "I'm not any judge of that, your majesty. Queen Elizabeth, in any event, has given credence to the notion. Her Walter Raleigh directs the expedition, and the geographer Hakluyt is with him, and a force of five hundred soldiers. They move diagonally across the Outback just to the south of your domain, following some chart that Dr. Dee had obtained for them. He had it from Cagliostro, they say, who bought it from Hadrian when Hadrian was still supreme commander of Hell's legions. It is allegedly an official Satanic document."

Prester John did not appear to be impressed. "Let us say, for argument's sake, that there *is* an exit from Hell. Why would Queen Elizabeth desire to leave? Hell's not so bad. It has its minor discomforts, yes, but one learns to cope with them. Does she think she'd be able to reign in Heaven as she does here—assuming there's a Heaven at all, which is distinctly not proven?"

"Elizabeth has no real interest in leaving Hell herself, majesty," Howard said. "What King Henry fears is that if she does find the way out, she'll claim it for her own and set up a colony around it, and charge a fee for passing through the gate. No matter where it takes you, the king reckons there'll be millions of people willing to risk it, and Elizabeth will wind up cornering all the money in Hell. He can't abide that notion, d'ye see? He thinks she's already too smart and aggressive by half, and he hates the idea that she might get even more powerful. There's something mixed into it having to do with Queen Elizabeth's mother, too—that was Anne Boleyn, Henry's second wife. She was a wild and wanton one, and he cut her head off for adultery, and now he thinks that Anne's behind Elizabeth's maneuvers, trying to get even with him by—"

"Spare me these details," said Ye-luh Ta-shih with some irritation. "What does Henry expect me to do?"

"Send troops to turn the Raleigh expedition back before it can find anything useful to Elizabeth."

"And in what way do I gain from this?"

"If the exit from Hell's on your frontier, your majesty, do you really want a bunch of Elizabethan Englishmen setting up a colony next door to you?"

"There is no exit from Hell," Prester John said complacently once again.

"But if they set up a colony anyway?"

Prester John was silent a moment. "I see," he said finally.

"In return for your aid," Howard said, "we're empowered to offer you a trade treaty on highly favorable terms."

"Ah."

"And a guarantee of military protection in the event of the invasion of your realm by a hostile power."

"If King Henry's armies are so mighty, why does he not deal with the Raleigh expedition himself?"

"There was no time to outfit and dispatch an army across such a great distance," said Lovecraft. "Elizabeth's people had already set out before anything was known of the scheme."

"Ah," said Yeh-lu Ta-shih.

"Of course," Lovecraft went on, "there were other princes of the Outback that King Henry might have approached. Moammar Khadafy's name came up, and one of the Assyrians—Assurnasirpal, I think—and someone mentioned Mao Tse-tung. No, King Henry said, let us ask the aid of Prester John, for he is a monarch of great puissance and grandeur, whose writ is supreme throughout the far reaches of Hell. Prester John, indeed, that is the one whose aid we must seek!"

A strange new sparkle had came into Ye-luh Ta-shih's eyes. "You were considering an alliance with Mao Tsetung?"

"It was merely a suggestion, your majesty."

"Ah. I see." The emperor rose from his throne. "Well, we must consider these matters more carefully, eh? We must not come hastily to a decision." He looked across the great vaulted throne room to the divan where Dr. Schweitzer still labored over Gilgamesh's wound. "Your patient, doctor—what's the report?"

"A man of steel, majesty, a man of steel! *Gott sei dank*, he heals before my eyes!"

"Indeed. Come, then. You will all want to rest, I think; and then you shall know the full hospitality of Prester John."

•   •   •

The full hospitality of Prester John, Gilgamesh soon discovered, was no trifling affair.

He was led off to a private chamber with walls lined with black felt—a kind of indoor tent—where three serving-girls who stood barely hip-high to him surrounded him, giggling, and took his clothing from him. Gently they pushed him into a huge marble cistern full of warm milk, where they bathed him lovingly and massaged his aching body in the most intimate manner. Afterward they robed him in intricate vestments of yellow silk.

Then they conveyed him to the emperor's great hall, where the whole court was gathered, a glittering and resplendent multitude. Some sort of concert was under way, seven solemn musicians playing harsh screeching twanging music. Gongs crashed, a trumpet blared, pipes uttered eerie piercing sounds. Servants showed Gilgamesh to a place of honor atop a pile of furry blankets heaped high with velvet cushions.

Lovecraft and Howard were already there, garbed like Gilgamesh in magnificent silks. Both of them looked somewhat unsettled—unhinged, even. Howard, flushed and boisterous, could barely sit still: he laughed and waved his arms and kicked his heels against the furs, like a small boy who has done something very naughty and is trying to conceal it by being over-exuberant. Lovecraft, on the other hand, seemed dazed and dislocated, with the glassy-eyed look of someone who has recently been clubbed.

These are two very odd men indeed, Gilgamesh thought.

One works hard at being loud and lusty, and now and then gives you a glimpse of a soul boiling with wild fantasies of swinging swords and rivers of blood. But in reality he seems terrified of everything. The other, though he is weirdly remote and austere, is apparently not quite as crazy, but he too gives the impression of being at war with himself, in terror of allowing any sort of real human

feeling to break through the elaborate facade of his man-
nerisms. The poor fools must have been scared silly when
the serving-girls started stripping them and pouring warm
milk over them and stroking their bodies. No doubt they
haven't recovered yet from all that nasty pleasure, Gilgamesh thought. He could imagine their cries of horror
as the little Mongol girls started going to work on them.
What are you doing? *Leave my trousers alone! Don't
touch me there! Please—no—ooh—ah—*ooh! *Oooh!*

Yeh-lu Ta-shih, seated upon a high throne of ivory and
onyx, waved grandly to him, one great king to another.
Gilgamesh gave him an almost imperceptible nod by way
of acknowledgment. All this pomp and formality bored
him hideously. He had endured so much of it in his
former life, after all. And then *he* had been the one on
the high throne, but even then it had been nothing but
a bore. And now—

But this was no more boring than anything else. Gilgamesh had long ago decided that that was the true curse
of Hell: all striving was meaningless here, mere thunder
without the lightning. And there was no end to it. You
might die again now and then if you were careless or
unlucky, but back you came for another turn, sooner or
later, at the Undertaker's whim. There was no release
from the everlastingness of it all. Once he had yearned
desperately for eternal life, and he had learned that he
could not have such a thing, at least not in the world of
mortal men. But now indeed he had come to a place
where he would live forever, so it seemed, and yet there
was no joy in it. His fondest dream now was simply to
serve his time in Hell and be allowed to sleep in peace
forever. He saw no way of attaining that. Life here just
went on and on—very much like this concert, this endless
skein of twangs and plinks and screeches.

Someone with the soft face of a eunuch came by and
offered him a morsel of grilled meat. Gilgamesh knew
he would pay for it later—you always did, when you ate
something in Hell—but he was hungry now, and he gob-

bled it. And another, and another, and a flagon of fermented mare's milk besides.

A corps of dancers appeared, men and women in flaring filmy robes. They were doing things with swords and flaming torches. A second eunuch brought Gilgamesh a tray of mysterious sugary delicacies, and he helped himself with both hands, heedless of the consequences. He was ravenous. His body, as it healed, was calling furiously for fuel. Beside him, the man Howard was swilling down the mare's milk as if it were water and getting tipsier and tipsier, and the other, the one called Lovecraft, sat morosely staring at the dancers without touching a thing. He seemed to be shivering as though in the midst of a snowstorm.

Gilgamesh beckoned for a second flagon. Just then the doctor arrived and settled down cheerfully on the heap of blankets next to him. Schweitzer grinned his approval as Gilgamesh took a hearty drink. "*Fuhlen Sie sich besser, mein Held, eh?* The arm, it no longer gives you pain? Already the wound is closing. So quickly you repair yourself! Such strength, such power and healing! You are God's own miracle, dear Gilgamesh. The blessing of the Almighty is upon you." He seized a flagon of his own from a passing servant, quaffed it, made a face. "*Ach,* this milk-wine of theirs! And *ach, ach,* this *verfluchte* music! What I would give for the taste of decent Moselle on my tongue now, eh, and the sound of the D minor toccata and fugue in my ears! Bach—do you know him?"

"Who?"

"Bach! Bach, Johann Sebastian Bach. The greatest of musicians, God's own poet in sound. I saw him once, just once, years ago." Schweitzer's eyes were glowing. "I was new here. Not two weeks had I been here. It was at the villa of King Friedrich—Frederick the Great, you know him? No? The king of Prussia? *Der alte Fritz?* No matter. No matter. *Er macht nichts.* A man entered, ordinary, you would never notice him in a crowd, yes? And began to play the harpsichord, and he had not played three measures when I said, 'This is Bach, this

must be the actual Bach,' and I would have dropped
down on my knees before him but that I was ashamed.
And it was he. I said to myself, 'Why is it that Bach is
in Hell?' But then I said, as perhaps you have said, as I
think everyone here must say at one time or another,
'Why is it that *Schweitzer* is in Hell?' And I knew that
it is that God is mysterious. Perhaps I was sent here to
minister to the damned. Perhaps it is that Bach was also.
Or perhaps we are damned also; or perhaps no one here
is damned. *Es macht nichts aus*, all this speculation. It
is a mistake, or even *vielleicht* a sin, to imagine that we
can comprehend the workings of the mind of God. We
are here. We have our tasks. That is enough for me to
know."

"I felt that way once," said Gilgamesh. "When I was
king in Uruk, and finally came to understand that I must
die, that there was no hiding from that. What is the
purpose, then, I asked myself? And I told myself: The
gods have put us here to perform our tasks, and that is
the purpose. And so I lived thereafter and so I died."
Gilgamesh's face darkened. "But here—here—"

"Here, too, we have our tasks," Schweitzer said.

"You do, perhaps. For me there is only the task of
passing the time. I had a friend to bear the burden with
me once—"

"Enkidu."

Gilgamesh seized the doctor's sturdy wrist with sudden
fierce intensity. "You know of Enkidu?"

"From the poem, yes. The poem is very famous."

"Ah. Ah. The poem. But the actual man—"

"I know nothing of him, *nein*."

"He is of my stature, very large. His beard is thick,
his hair is shaggy, his shoulders are wider even than
mine. We journeyed everywhere together. But then we
quarreled, and he went from me in anger, saying, 'Never
cross my path again.' Saying, 'I have no love for you,
Gilgamesh.' Saying, 'If we meet again I will have your
life.' And I have heard nothing of him since."

Schweitzer turned and stared closely at Gilgamesh.

"How is this possible? All the world knows the love of Enkidu for Gilgamesh!"

Gilgamesh called for yet another flagon. This conversation was awakening an ache within his breast, an ache that made the pain that his wound had caused seem like nothing more than an itch. Nor would the drink soothe it; but he would drink all the same.

He took a deep draught and said somberly, "We quarreled. There were hot words between us. He said he had no love for me any longer."

"This cannot be true."

Gilgamesh shrugged and made no reply.

"You wish to find him again?" Schweitzer asked.

"I desire nothing else."

"Do you know where he is?"

"Hell is larger even than the world. He could be anywhere."

"You will find him."

"If you knew how I have searched for him—"

"You will find him. That I know."

Gilgamesh shook his head. "If Hell is a place of torment, then this is mine, that I will never find him again. Or if I do, that he will spurn me. Or raise his hand against me."

"This is not so," said Schweitzer "I think he longs for you even as you do for him."

"Then why does he keep himself from me?"

"This is Hell," said Schweitzer gently. "You are being tested, my friend, but no test lasts forever. Not even in Hell. Not even in Hell. Even though you are in Hell, have faith in the Lord: You will have your Enkidu soon enough, *um Himmels Willen*." Smiling, Schweitzer said, "The emperor is calling you. Go to him. I think he has something to tell you that you will want to hear."

Prester John said, "You are a warrior, are you not?"

"I was," replied Gilgamesh indifferently.

"A general? A leader of men?"

"All that is far behind me," Gilgamesh said. "This is

the life after life. Now I go my own way and I take on no tasks for others. Hell has plenty of generals."

"I am told that you were a leader among leaders. I am told that you fought like the god of war. When you took the field, whole nations laid down their arms and knelt before you."

Gilgamesh waited, saying nothing.

"You miss the glory of the battlefield, don't you, Gilgamesh?"

"Do I?"

"What if I were to offer you the command of my army?"

"Why would you do that? What am I to you? What is your nation to me?"

"In Hell we take whatever citizenship we wish. What would you say, if I offered you the command?"

"I would tell you that you are making a great mistake."

"It isn't a trivial army. Ten thousand men. Adequate air support. Tactical nukes. The strongest firepower in the Outback."

"You misunderstand," said Gilgamesh. "Warfare doesn't interest me. I know nothing of modern weapons and don't care to learn. You have the wrong man, Prester John. If you need a general, send for Wellington. Send for Marlborough. Rommel. Tiglath-Pileser."

"Or for Enkidu?"

The unexpected name hit Gilgamesh like a battering ram. At the sound of it his face grew hot and his entire body trembled convulsively.

"What do you know about Enkidu?"

Prester John held up one superbly manicured hand. "Allow me the privilege of asking the questions, great king."

"You spoke the name of Enkidu. What do you know about Enkidu?"

"First let us discuss the matters which are of—"

"Enkidu," said Gilgamesh implacably. "Why did you mention his name?"

"I know that he was your friend—"

"*Is.*"

"Very well, *is* your friend. And a man of great valor and strength. Who happens to be a guest at this very moment at the court of the great enemy of my realm. And who, so I understand it, is preparing just now to make war against me."

"*What?*" Gilgamesh stared. "Enkidu is in the service of Queen Elizabeth?"

"I don't recall having said that."

"Is it not Queen Elizabeth who even now has sent an army to encroach on your domain?"

Yeh-lu Ta-shih laughed. "Raleigh and his five hundred fools? That expedition's an absurdity. I'll take care of them in an afternoon. I mean another enemy altogether. Tell me this: do you know of Mao Tse-tung?"

"These princes of the New Dead—there are so many names—"

"A Chinese, a man of Han. Emperor of the Marxist Dynasty, long after my time. Crafty, stubborn, tough. More than a little crazy. He runs something called the Celestial People's Republic, just north of here. What he tells his subjects is that we can turn Hell into Heaven by collectivizing it."

"Collectivizing?" said Gilgamesh uncomprehendingly.

"To make all the peasants into kings, and the kings into peasants. As I say: more than a little crazy. But he has his hordes of loyal followers, and they do whatever he says. He means to conquer all the Outback, beginning right here. And after that, all of Hell will be subjected to his lunatic ideas. I fear that Elizabeth's in league with him—that this nonsense of looking for a way out of Hell is only a ruse, that in fact her Raleigh is spying out my weaknesses for her so that she can sell the information to Mao."

"But if this Mao is the enemy of all kings, why would Elizabeth ally herself with—"

"Obviously they mean to use each other. Elizabeth aiding Mao to overthrow me, Mao aiding Elizabeth to push her father from his throne. And then afterward, who knows? But I mean to strike before either of them can harm me."

"What about Enkidu?" Gilgamesh said. "Tell me about Enkidu."

Prester John opened a scroll of computer printout. Skimming through it, he read, "The Old Dead warrior Enkidu of Sumer—Sumer, that's your nation, isn't it?— arrived at court of Mao Tse-tung on such-and-such a date—ostensible purpose of visit, Outback hunting expedition—accompanied by American spy posing as journalist and hunter, one E. Hemingway—secret meeting with Kublai Khan, Minister of War for the Celestial People's Republic—now training Communist troops in preparation for invasion of New Kara-Khitai—" The emperor looked up. "Is this of interest to you, Gilgamesh?"

"What is it you want from me?"

"This man is your famous friend. You know his mind as you do your own. Defend us from him and I'll give you anything you desire."

"What I desire," said Gilgamesh, "is nothing more than the friendship of Enkidu."

"Then I'll give you Enkidu on a silver platter. Take the field for me against Mao's troops. Help me anticipate whatever strategies your Enkidu has been teaching them. We'll wipe the Marxist bastards out and capture their generals, and then Enkidu will be yours. I can't guarantee that he'll want to be your friend again, but he'll be yours. What do you say, Gilgamesh? What do you say?"

Across the gray plains of Hell from horizon to horizon sprawled the legions of Prester John. Scarlet-and-yellow banners fluttered against the somber sky. At the center of the formation stood a wedge of horseborne archers in leather armor; on each flank was a detachment of heavy infantry; the emperor's fleet of tanks was in the vanguard, rolling unhurriedly forward over the rough, broken terrain. A phalanx of transatmospheric weapons platforms provided air cover far overhead.

A cloud of dust in the distance gave evidence of the oncoming army of the Celestial People's Republic.

"By all the demons of Stygia, did you ever see such a cockeyed sight?" Robert Howard cried. He and Lovecraft had a choice view of the action from their place in the imperial command post, a splendid pagoda protected by a glowing force-shield. Gilgamesh was there, too, just across the way with Prester John and the officers of the Kara-Khitai high command. The emperor was peering into a bank of television monitors and one of his aides was feverishly tapping out orders on a computer terminal. "Makes no goddamned sense," said Howard. "Horsemen, tanks, weapons platforms, all mixing it up at the same time—is that how these wild sons of bitches fight a war?"

Lovecraft touched his forefinger to his lips. "Don't shout so, Bob. Do you want Prester John to hear you? We're his guests, remember. And King Henry's ambassadors."

"Well, if he hears me, he hears me. Look at that crazy mess! Doesn't Prester John realize that he's got a twentieth-century Bolshevik Chinaman coming to attack him with twentieth-century weapons? What good are mounted horsemen, for God's sake? A cavalry charge into the face of heavy artillery. Bows and arrows against howitzers?" Howard guffawed. "Nuclear-tipped arrows, is that the trick?"

Softly Lovecraft said, "For all we know, that's what they are."

"You know that can't be, H.P. I'm surprised at you, a man with your scientific background. I know all this nuke stuff is after our time, but surely you've kept up with the theory. Critical mass at the tip of an arrow? No, H.P., you know as well as I do that it just can't work. And even if it could—"

In exasperation Lovecraft waved to him to be silent. He pointed across the room to the main monitor in front of Prester John. The florid face of a heavyset man with a thick white beard had appeared on the screen.

"Isn't that Hemingway?" Lovecraft asked.

"Who?"

"Ernest Hemingway. The writer. *A Farewell to Arms. The Sun Also Rises.*"

"Never could stand his stuff," said Howard. "Sick crap about a bunch of drunken weaklings. You sure that's him?"

"Weaklings, Bob?" said Lovecraft in astonishment.

"I read only the one book, about those Americans in Europe who go to the bullfights and get drunk and fool around with each other's women, and that was all of Mr. Hemingway that I cared to experience. I tell you, H.P., it disgusted me. And the way it was written! All those short little sentences—no magic, no poetry, H.P.—"

"Let's talk about it some other time, Bob."

"No vision of heroism—no awareness of the higher passions that ennoble and—"

"Bob—please—"

"A fixation on the sordid, the slimy, the depraved—"

"You're being absurd, Bob. You're completely misinterpreting his philosophy of life. If you had simply taken the trouble to read *A Farewell to Arms*—" Lovecraft shook his head angrily. "This is no time for a literary discussion. Look—look there." He nodded toward the far side of the room. "One of the emperor's aides is calling over. Something's going on."

Indeed there had been a development of some sort. Yeh-lu Ta-shih seemed to be conferring with four or five aides at once. Gilgamesh, red-faced, agitated, was striding swiftly back and forth in front of the computer bank. Hemingway's face was still on the screen and he too looked agitated.

Hastily Howard and Lovecraft crossed the room. The emperor turned to them. "There's been a request for a parley in the field," Prester John said, "Kublai Khan is on his way over. Dr. Schweitzer will serve as my negotiator. The man Hemingway's going to be an impartial observer—*their* impartial observer. I need an impartial observer, too. Will you two go down there too, as diplomats from a neutral power, to keep an eye on things?"

"An honor to serve," said Howard grandly.

"And for what purpose, my lord, has the parley been called?" Lovecraft asked.

Yeh-lu Ta-shih gestured toward the screen. "Hemingway has had the notion that we can settle this thing by single combat—Gilgamesh versus Enkidu. Save on ammunition, spare the Undertaker a devil of a lot of toil. But there's a disagreement over the details." Delicately he smothered a yawn. "Perhaps it can all be worked out by lunchtime."

It was an oddly assorted group. Mao Tse-tung's chief negotiator was the plump, magnificently dressed Kublai Khan, whose dark sly eyes gave evidence of much cunning and force. He had been an emperor in his own right in his former life, but evidently had preferred less taxing responsibilities here. Next to him was Hemingway, big and heavy, with a deep voice and an easy, almost arrogant manner. Mao had also sent four small men in identical blue uniforms with red stars on their breasts—"Party types," someone murmured—and, strangely, a Hairy Man, big-browed and chinless, one of those creatures out of deepest antiquity. He too wore the Communist emblem on his uniform.

And there was one more to the group—the massive, deep-chested man of dark brow and fierce and smouldering eyes, who stood off by himself at the far side—

Gilgamesh could barely bring himself to look at him. He too stood apart from the group a little way, savoring the keen edge of the wind that blew across the field of battle. He longed to rush toward Enkidu, to throw his arms around him, to sweep away in one jubilant embrace all the bitterness that had separated them—

If only it could be as simple as that!

The voices of Mao's negotiators and the five that Prester John had sent—Schweitzer, Lovecraft, Howard, and a pair of Kara-Khitai officers—drifted to Gilgamesh above the howling of the wind.

Hemingway seemed to be doing most of the talking.

"Writers, are you? Mr. Howard, Mr. Lovecraft? I regret I haven't had the pleasure of encountering your work."

"Fantasy, it was," said Lovecraft. "Fables. Visions."

"That so? You publish in *Argosy*? The *Post*?"

"Five to *Argosy*, but they were westerns," Howard said. "Mainly we wrote for *Weird Tales*. And H.P., a few in *Astounding Stories*."

"*Weird Tales*," Hemingway said. "*Astounding Stories*." A shadow of distaste flickered across his face. "Mmm. Don't think I knew those magazines. But you wrote well, did you, gentlemen? You set down what you truly felt, the real thing, and you stated it purely? Of course you did. I know you did. You were honest writers or you'd never have gone to Hell. That goes almost without saying." He laughed, rubbed his hands in glee, effusively threw his arms around the shoulders of Howard and Lovecraft. Howard seemed alarmed by that and Lovecraft looked as though he wanted to sink into the ground. "Well, gentlemen," Hemingway boomed, "what shall we do here? We have a little problem. The one hero wishes to fight with bare hands, the other with—what did he call it?—a disruptor pistol? You would know more about that than I do: something out of *Astounding Stories*, is how it sounds to me. But we can't have this, can we? Bare hands against fantastic future science? There is a good way to fight and that is equal to equal, and all other ways are the bad ways."

"Let him come to me with his fists," Gilgamesh called from the distance. "As we fought the first time, in the Market-of-the-Land, when my path crossed his in Uruk."

"He is afraid to use the new weapons," Enkidu replied.

"*Afraid?*"

"I brought a shotgun to him, a fine 12-gauge weapon, a gift to my brother Gilgamesh. He shrank from it as though I had given him a venomous serpent."

"Lies!" roared Gilgamesh. "I had no fear of it! I despised it because it was cowardly!"

"He fears anything which is new," said Enkidu. "I never thought Gilgamesh of Uruk would know fear, but he fears the unfamiliar. He called me a coward, because I would hunt with a shotgun. But I think he was the coward. And now he fears to fight me with the unfamiliar. He knows that I'll slay him. He fears death even here, do you know that? Death has always been his great terror. Why is that? Because it is an insult to his pride? I think that is it. Too proud to die—too proud to accept the decree of the gods—"

"I will break you with my hands alone!" Gilgamesh bellowed.

"Give us disruptors," said Enkidu. "Let us see if he dares to touch such a weapon."

"A coward's weapon!"

"Again you call me a coward? You, Gilgamesh, you are the one who quivers in fear—"

"Gentlemen! Gentlemen!"

"You fear my strength, Enkidu!"

"You fear my skill. You with your pathetic old sword, your pitiful bow—"

"Is this the Enkidu I loved, mocking me so?"

"You were the first to mock, when you threw back the shotgun into my hands, spurning my gift, calling me a coward—"

"The weapon, I said, was cowardly. Not you, Enkidu."

"It was the same thing."

"*Bitte, bitte,*" said Schweitzer. "This is not the way!"

And again from Hemingway: "Gentlemen, please!"

They took no notice.

"I meant—"

"You said—"

"Shame—"

"Fear—"

"Three times over a coward!"

"Five times five a traitor!"

"False friend!"

"Vain braggart!"

"Gentlemen, I have to ask you—"

But Hemingway's voice, loud and firm though it was, was altogether drowned out by the roar of rage that came from the throat of Gilgamesh. Dizzying throbs of anger pounded in his breast, his throat, his temples. He could take no more. This was how it had begun the first time, when Enkidu had come to him with that shotgun and he had given it back and they had fallen into dispute. At first merely a disagreement, and then a hot debate, and then a quarrel, and then the hurling of bitter accusations. And then such words of anger as had never passed between them before, they who had been closer than brothers.

That time they hadn't come to blows. Enkidu had simply stalked away, declaring that their friendship was at an end. But now—hearing all the same words again, stymied by this quarrel even over the very method by which they were to fight—Gilgamesh could no longer restrain himself. Overmastered by fury and frustration, he rushed forward.

Enkidu, eyes gleaming, was ready for him.

Hemingway attempted to come between them. Big as he was, he was like a child next to Gilgamesh and Enkidu, and they swatted him to one side without effort. With a jolt that made the ground itself reverberate, Gilgamesh went crashing into Enkidu and laid hold of him with both hands.

Enkidu laughed. "So you have your way after all, King Gilgamesh! Bare hands it is!"

"It is the only way," said Gilgamesh.

At last. At last. There was no wrestler in this world or the other who could contend with Gilgamesh of Uruk. I will break him, Gilgamesh thought, as he broke our friendship. I will snap his spine. I will crush his chest.

As once they had done long ago, they fought like maddened bulls. They stared eye to eye as they contended. They grunted; they bellowed, they roared. Gilgamesh shouted out defiance in the language of Uruk and in any other language he could think of; and Enkidu muttered and stormed at Gilgamesh in the language of the beasts that once he had spoken when he was a wild man, the harsh growling of the lion of the plains.

Gilgamesh yearned to have Enkidu's life. He loved this man more dearly than life itself, and yet he prayed that it would be given him to break Enkidu's back, to hear the sharp snapping sound of his spine, to toss him aside like a worn-out cloak. So strong was his love that it had turned to the brightest of hatreds. I will send him to the Undertaker once again, Gilgamesh thought. I will hurl him from Hell.

But though he struggled as he had never struggled in combat before, Gilgamesh was unable to budge Enkidu. Veins bulged in his forehead; the sutures that held his wound burst and blood flowed down his arm; and still he strained to throw Enkidu to the ground, and still Enkidu held his place. And matched him, strength for strength, and kept him at bay. They stood locked that way a long moment, staring into each other's eyes, locked in unbreakable stalemate.

Then after a long while Enkidu said, as once he had said long ago, "Ah, Gilgamesh! There is not another one like you in all the world! Glory to the mother who bore you!"

It was like the breaking of a dam, and a rush of life-giving waters tumbling out over the summer-parched fields of the Land.

And from Gilgamesh in that moment of release and relief came twice-spoken words also:

"There is one other who is like me. But only one."

"No, for Enlil has given you the kingship."

"But you are my brother," said Gilgamesh, and they laughed and let go of each other and stepped back, as if seeing each other for the first time, and laughed again.

"This is great foolishness, this fighting between us," Enkidu cried.

"Very great foolishness indeed, brother."

"What need have you of shotguns and disruptors?"

"And what do I care if you choose to play with such toys?"

"Indeed, brother."

"Indeed!"

Gilgamesh looked away. They were all staring—the four party men, Lovecraft, Howard, the Hairy Man, Kublai Khan, Hemingway—all astonished, mouths drooping open. Only Schweitzer was beaming. The doctor came up to them and said quietly, "You have not injured each other? No. *Gut. Gut.* Then leave here, the two of you, together. Now. What do you care for Prester John and his wars, or for Mao and his? This is no business of yours. Go. Now."

Enkidu grinned. "What do you say, brother? Shall we go off hunting together?"

"To the end of the Outback, and back again. You and I, and no one else."

"And we will hunt only with our bows and spears?"

Gilgamesh shrugged. "With disruptors, if that is how you would have it. With cannons. With nuke grenades. Ah, Enkidu, Enkidu—!"

"Gilgamesh!"

"Go," Schweitzer whispered. "Now. Leave this place and never look back. *Auf Wiedersehen! Gluckliche Reise! Gottes Name,* go now!"

Watching them take their leave, seeing them trudge off together into the swirling winds of the Outback, Robert Howard felt a sudden sharp pang of regret and loss. How beautiful they had been, those two heroes, those two giants, as they strained and struggled! And then that sudden magic moment when the folly of their quarrel came home to them, when they were enemies no longer and brothers once more—

And now they were gone, and here he stood amidst these others, these strangers—

He had wanted to be Gilgamesh's brother, or perhaps—he barely comprehended it—something more than a brother. But that could never have been. And, knowing that it could never have been, knowing that that man who seemed so much like his Conan was lost to him forever, Howard felt tears beginning to surge within him.

"Bob?" Lovecraft said. "Bob, are you all right?"

She-it, Howard thought. *A man don't cry. Especially in front of other men.*

He turned away, into the wind, so Lovecraft could not see his face.

"Bob? Bob?"

She-it, Howard thought again. And he let the tears come.

Permafrost

by Roger Zelazny

High upon the western slope of Mount Kilimanjaro is the dried and frozen carcass of a leopard. An author is always necessary to explain what it was doing there because stiff leopards don't talk much.

THE MAN. The music seems to come and go with a will of its own. At least turning the knob on the bedside unit has no effect on its presence or absence. A half-familiar, alien tune, troubling in a way. The phone rings, and he answers it. There is no one there. Again.

Four times during the past half hour, while grooming himself, dressing and rehearsing his arguments, he has received noncalls. When he checked with the desk he was told there were no calls. But that damned clerk-thing had to be malfunctioning—like everything else in this place.

The wind, already heavy, rises, hurling particles of ice against the building with a sound like multitudes of tiny claws scratching. The whining of steel shutters sliding into place startles him. But worst of all, in his reflex glance at the nearest window, it seems he has seen a face.

Impossible of course. This is the third floor. A trick of light upon hard-driven flakes: Nerves.

Yes. He has been nervous since their arrival this morning. Before then, even . . .

He pushes past Dorothy's stuff upon the countertop, locates a small package among his own articles. He unwraps a flat red rectangle about the size of his thumbnail. He rolls up his sleeve and slaps the patch against the inside of his left elbow.

The tranquilizer discharges immediately into his bloodstream. He takes several deep breaths, then peels off the patch and drops it into the disposal unit. He rolls his sleeve down, reaches for his jacket.

The music rises in volume, as if competing with the blast of the wind, the rattle of the icy flakes. Across the room the videoscreen comes on of its own accord.

The face. The same face. Just for an instant. He is certain. And then channelless static, wavy lines. Snow. He chuckles.

All right, play it that way, nerves, he thinks. *You've every reason. But the trank's coming to get you now. Better have your fun quick. You're about to be shut down.*

The videoscreen cuts into a porn show.

Smiling, the woman mounts the man . . .

The picture switches to a voiceless commentator on something or other.

He will survive. He is a survivor. He, Paul Plaige, has done risky things before and has always made it through. It is just that having Dorothy along creates a kind of déjà vu that he finds unsettling. No matter.

She is waiting for him in the bar. Let her wait. A few drinks will make her easier to persuade—unless they make her bitchy. That sometimes happens, too. Either way, he has to talk her out of the thing.

Silence. The wind stops. The scratching ceases. The music is gone.

The whirring. The window screens dilate upon the empty city.

Silence, under totally overcast skies. Mountains of ice ringing the place. Nothing moving. Even the video has gone dead.

He recoils at the sudden flash from a peripheral unit far to his left across the city. The laser beam hits a key point on the glacier, and its face falls away.

Moments later he hears the hollow, booming sound of the crashing ice. A powdery storm has risen like surf at the ice mount's foot. He smiles at the power, the timing, the display. Andrew Aldon . . . always on the job, dueling with the elements, stalemating nature herself, immortal guardian of Playpoint. At least Aldon never malfunctions.

The silence comes again. As he watches the risen snows settle he feels the tranquilizer beginning to work. It will be good not to have to worry about money again. The past two years have taken a lot out of him. Seeing all of his investments fail in the Big Washout— that was when his nerves had first begun to act up. He has grown softer than he was a century ago—a young, rawboned soldier of fortune then, out to make his bundle and enjoy it. And he had. Now he has to do it again, though this time will be easier—except for Dorothy.

He thinks of her. A century younger than himself, still in her twenties, sometimes reckless, used to all of the good things in life. There is something vulnerable about Dorothy, times when she lapses into such a strong dependence that he feels oddly moved. Other times, it just irritates the hell out of him. Perhaps this is the closest he can come to love now, an occasional ambivalent response to being needed. But of course she is loaded. That breeds a certain measure of necessary courtesy. Until he can make his own bundle again, anyway. But none of these things are the reason he has to keep her from accompanying him on his journey. It goes beyond love or money. It is survival.

The laser flashes again, this time to the right. He waits for the crash.

THE STATUE. It is not a pretty pose. She lies frosted in an ice cave, looking like one of Rodin's less comfortable figures, partly propped on her left side, right elbow raised above her head, hand hanging near her face, shoulders against the wall, left leg completely buried.

She has on a gray parka, the hood slipped back to reveal twisted strands of dark blond hair; and she wears blue trousers; there is a black boot on the one foot that is visible.

She is coated with ice, and within the much-refracted light of the cave what can be seen of her features is not unpleasant but not strikingly attractive either. She looks to be in her twenties.

There are a number of fracture lines within the cave's walls and floor. Overhead, countless icicles hang like stalactites, sparkling jewellike in the much-bounced light. The grotto has a stepped slope to it with the statue at its higher end, giving to the place a vaguely shrinelike appearance.

On those occasions when the cloud cover is broken at sundown, a reddish light is cast about her figure.

She has actually moved in the course of a century—a few inches, from a general shifting of the ice. Tricks of the light make her seem to move more frequently, however.

The entire tableau might give the impression that this is merely a pathetic woman who had been trapped and frozen to death here, rather than the statue of the living goddess in the place where it all began.

THE WOMAN. She sits in the bar beside a window. The patio outside is gray and angular and drifted with snow; the flowerbeds are filled with dead plants—stiff, flattened, and frozen. She does not mind the view. Far from it. Winter is a season of death and cold, and she likes being reminded of it. She enjoys the prospect of pitting herself against its frigid and very visible fangs. A faint flash of light passes over the patio, followed by a distant roaring sound. She sips her drink and licks her lips and listens to the soft music that fills the air.

She is alone. The bartender and all of the other help here are of the mechanical variety. If anyone other than Paul were to walk in, she would probably scream. They are the only people in the hotel during this long off-season. Except for the sleepers, they are the only people in all of Playpoint.

And Paul . . . He will be along soon to take her to the dining room. There they can summon holo-ghosts to people the other tables if they wish. She does not wish.

She likes being alone with Paul at a time like this, on the eve of a great adventure.

He will tell her his plans over coffee, and perhaps even this afternoon they might obtain the necessary equipment to begin the exploration for that which would put him on his feet again financially, return to him his self-respect. It will of course be dangerous and very rewarding. She finishes her drink, rises, and crosses to the bar for another.

And Paul ... She had really caught a falling star, a swashbuckler on the way down, a man with a glamorous past just balanced on the brink of ruin. The teetering had already begun when they had met two years before, which had made it even more exciting. Of course, he needed a woman like her to lean upon at such a time. It wasn't just her money. She could never believe the things her late parents had said about him. No, he does care for her. He is strangely vulnerable and dependent.

She wants to turn him back into the man he once must have been, and then of course that man will need her, too. The thing he had been—that is what she needs most of all—a man who can reach up and bat the moon away. He must have been like that long ago.

She tastes her second drink.

The son of a bitch had better hurry, though. She is getting hungry.

THE CITY. Playpoint is located on the world known as Balfrost, atop a high peninsula that slopes down to a now-frozen sea. Playpoint contains all of the facilities for an adult playground, and it is one of the more popular resorts in this sector of the galaxy from late spring through early autumn—approximately fifty Earth years. Then winter comes on like a period of glaciation, and everybody goes away for half a century—or half a year, depending on how one regards such matters. During this time Playpoint is given into the care of its automated defense and maintenance routine. This is a self-repairing system, directed toward cleaning, plowing, thawing, melting, warming everything in need of such care, as well as directly combating the encroaching ice and snow. And all of these functions are done under the supervision of a well-protected central computer that also studies the weather and climate patterns, anticipating as well as reacting.

This system has worked successfully for many centuries, delivering Playpoint over to spring and pleasure in reasonably good condition at the end of each long winter.

There are mountains behind Playpoint, water (or ice, depending on the season) on three sides, weather and navigation satellites high above. In a bunker beneath the administration building is a pair of sleepers—generally a man and a woman—who awaken once every year or so to physically inspect the maintenance system's operations and to deal with any special situations that might have arisen. An alarm may arouse them for emergencies at any time. They are well paid, and over the years they have proven worth the investment. The central computer has at its disposal explosives and lasers as well as a great variety of robots. Usually it keeps a little ahead of the game, and it seldom falls behind for long.

At the moment, things are about even because the weather has been particularly nasty recently.

Zzzzt! Another block of ice has become a puddle.

Zzzzt! The puddle has been evaporated. The molecules climb toward a place where they can get together and return as snow.

The glaciers shuffle their feet, edge forward. *Zzzzt!* Their gain has become a loss.

Andrew Aldon knows exactly what he is doing.

CONVERSATIONS. The waiter, needing lubrication, rolls off after having served them, passing through a pair of swinging doors.

She giggles. "Wobbly," she says.

"Old World charm," he agrees, trying and failing to catch her eye as he smiles.

"You have everything worked out?" she asks after they have begun eating.

"Sort of," he says, smiling again.

"Is that a yes or a no?"

"Both. I need more information. I want to go and check things over first. Then I can figure the best course of action."

"I note your use of the singular pronoun," she says steadily, meeting his gaze at last.

His smile freezes and fades.

"I was referring to only a little preliminary scouting," he says softly.

"No," she says. "We. Even for a little preliminary scouting."

He sighs and sets down his fork.

"This will have very little to do with anything to come later," he begins. "Things have changed a lot. I'll have to locate a new route. This will just be dull work and no fun."

"I didn't come along for fun," she replies. "We were going to share everything, remember? That includes boredom, danger, and anything else. That was the understanding when I agreed to pay our way."

"I'd a feeling it would come to that," he says, after a moment.

"Come to it? It's always been there. That was our agreement."

He raises his goblet and sips the wine.

"Of course. I'm not trying to rewrite history. It's just that things would go faster if I could do some of the initial looking around myself. I can move more quickly alone."

"What's the hurry?" she says. "A few days this way or that. I'm in pretty good shape. I won't slow you down all that much."

"I'd the impression you didn't particularly like it here. I just wanted to hurry things up so we could get the hell out."

"That's very considerate," she says, beginning to eat

again. "But that's my problem, isn't it?" She looks up at him. "Unless there's some other reason you don't want me along?"

He drops his gaze quickly, picks up his fork. "Don't be silly."

She smiles. "Then that's settled. I'll go with you this afternoon to look for the trail."

The music stops, to be succeeded by a sound as of the clearing of a throat. Then, "Excuse me for what may seem like eavesdropping," comes a deep, masculine voice. "It is actually only a part of a simple monitoring function I keep in effect—"

"Aldon!" Paul exclaims.

"At your service, Mr. Plaige, more or less. I choose to make my presence known only because I did indeed overhear you, and the matter of your safety overrides the good manners that would otherwise dictate reticence. I've been receiving reports that indicate we could be hit by some extremely bad weather this afternoon. So if you were planning an extended sojourn outside, I would recommend you postpone it."

"Oh," Dorothy says.

"Thanks," Paul says.

"I shall now absent myself. Enjoy your meal and your stay."

The music returns.

"Aldon?" Paul asks.

There is no reply.

"Looks as if we do it tomorrow or later."

"Yes," Paul agrees, and he is smiling his first relaxed smile of the day. And thinking fast.

THE WORLD. Life on Balfrost proceeds in peculiar cycles. There are great migrations of animal life and quasi-animal life to the equatorial regions during the long winter. Life in the depths of the seas goes on. And the permafrost vibrates with its own style of life.

The permafrost. Throughout the winter and on through the spring the permafrost lives at its peak. It is laced with mycelia—twining, probing, touching, knotting themselves into ganglia, reaching out to infiltrate other systems. It girds the globe, vibrating like a collective unconscious throughout the winter. In the spring it sends up stalks which develop gray, flowerlike appendages for a few days. These blooms then collapse to reveal dark pods which subsequently burst with small, popping sounds, releasing clouds of sparkling spores that the winds bear just about everywhere. These are extremely hardy, like the mycelia they will one day become.

The heat of summer finally works its way down into the permafrost, and the strands doze their way into a long period of quiescence. When the cold returns, they are roused, spores send forth new filaments that repair old damages, create new synapses. A current begins to flow. The life of summer is like a fading dream. For eons this had been the way of things upon Balfrost, within Balfrost. Then the goddess decreed otherwise. Winter's queen spread her hands, and there came a change.

THE SLEEPERS. Paul makes his way through swirling flakes to the administration building. It has been a simpler matter than he had anticipated, persuading Dorothy to use the sleep-induction unit to be well rested for the morrow. He had pretended to use the other unit himself, resisting its blandishments until he was certain she was asleep and he could slip off undetected.

He lets himself into the vaultlike building, takes all of the old familiar turns, makes his way down a low ramp. The room is unlocked and a bit chilly, but he begins to perspire when he enters. The two cold lockers are in operation. He checks their monitoring systems and sees that everything is in order.

All right, go! Borrow the equipment now. They won't be using it.

He hesitates.

He draws nearer and looks down through the view plates at the faces of the sleepers. No resemblance, thank God. He realizes then that he is trembling. He backs away, turns, and flees toward the storage area.

Later, in a yellow snowslider, carrying special equipment, he heads inland.

As he drives, the snow ceases falling and the winds die down. He smiles. The snows sparkle before him, and landmarks do not seem all that unfamiliar. Good omens, at last.

Then something crosses his path, turns, halts, and faces him.

ANDREW ALDON. Andrew Aldon, once a man of considerable integrity and resource, had on his deathbed opted for continued existence as a computer program, the enchanted loom of his mind shuttling and weaving thereafter as central processing's judgmental program in the great guardian computerplex at Playpoint. And there he functions as a program of considerable integrity and resource. He maintains the city, and he fights the elements. He does not merely respond to pressure, but he anticipates structural and functional needs; he generally outguesses the weather. Like the professional soldier he once had been, he keeps himself in a state of constant alert—not really difficult considering the resources available to him. He is seldom wrong, always competent, and sometimes brilliant. Occasionally he resents his fleshless state. Occasionally he feels lonely.

This afternoon he is puzzled by the sudden veering off of the storm he had anticipated and by the spell of clement weather that has followed this meteorological quirk. His mathematics were elegant, but the weather was not. It seems peculiar that this should come at a time of so many other little irregularities, such as unusual ice adjustments, equipment glitches, and the peculiar behavior of machinery in the one occupied room of the hotel— a room troublesomely tenanted by a *non grata* ghost from the past.

So he watches for a time. He is ready to intervene when Paul enters the administration building and goes to the bunkers. But Paul does nothing that might bring harm to the sleepers. His curiosity is dominant when

Paul draws equipment. He continues to watch. This is because in his judgment, Paul bears watching.

Aldon decides to act only when he detects a development that runs counter to anything in his experience. He sends one of his mobile units to intercept Paul as the man heads out of town. It catches up with him at a bending of the way and slides into his path with one appendage upraised.

"Stop!" Aldon calls through the speaker.

Paul brakes his vehicle and sits for a moment regarding the machine.

Then he smiles faintly. "I assume you have good reason for interfering with a guest's freedom of movement."

"Your safety takes precedence."

"I am perfectly safe."

"At the moment."

"What do you mean?"

"This weather pattern has suddenly become more than a little unusual. You seem to occupy a drifting island of calm while a storm rages about you."

"So I'll take advantage of it now and face the consequences later, if need be."

"It is your choice. I wanted it to be an informed one, however."

"All right. You've informed me. Now get out of my way."

"In a moment. You departed under rather unusual circumstances the last time you were here—in breach of your contract."

"Check your legal bank if you've got one. The statute's run for prosecuting me on that."

"There are some things on which there is no statute of limitations."

"What do you mean by that? I turned in a report on what happened that day."

"One which—conveniently—could not be verified. You were arguing that day . . ."

"We always argued. That's just the way we were. If you have something to say about it, say it."

"No, I have nothing more to say about it. My only intention is to caution you—"

"Okay, I'm cautioned."

"To caution you in more ways than the obvious."

"I don't understand."

"I am not certain that things are the same here now as when you left last winter."

"Everything changes."

"Yes, but that is not what I mean. There is something peculiar about this place now. The past is no longer a good guide for the present. More and more anomalies keep cropping up. Sometimes it feels as if the world is testing me or playing games with me."

"You're getting paranoid, Aldon. You've been in that box too long. Maybe it's time to terminate."

"You son of a bitch, I'm trying to tell you something. I've run a lot of figures on this, and all this shit started shortly after you left. The human part of me still has hunches, and I've a feeling there's a connection. If you know all about this and can cope with it, fine. If you don't, I think you should watch out. Better yet, turn around and go home."

"I can't."

"Even if there is something out there, something that is making it easy for you—for the moment?"

"What are you trying to say?"

"I am reminded of the old Gaia hypothesis—Lovelock, twentieth century . . ."

"Planetary intelligence. I've heard of it. Never met one, though."

"Are you certain? I sometimes feel I'm confronting one."

"What if something is out there and it wants you—is leading you on like a will-o'-the-wisp?"

"It would be my problem, not yours."

"I can protect you against it. Go back to Playpoint."

"No thanks. I will survive."

"What of Dorothy?"

"What of her?"

"You would leave her alone when she might need you?"

"Let me worry about that."

"Your last woman didn't fare too well."

"Damn it! Get out of my way, or I'll run you down!"

The robot withdraws from the trail. Through its sensors Aldon watches Paul drive away.

Very well, he decides. *We know where we stand, Paul. And you haven't changed. That makes it easier.*

Aldon further focuses his divided attention. To Dorothy now. Clad in heated garments. Walking. Approaching the building from which she had seen Paul emerge on his vehicle. She had hailed and cursed him, but the winds had carried her words away. She, too, had only feigned sleep. After a suitable time, then, she sought to follow. Aldon watches her stumble once and wants to reach out to assist her, but there is no mobile unit handy. He routes one toward the area against future accidents.

"Damn him!" she mutters as she passes along the street, ribbons of snow rising and twisting away before her.

"Where are you going, Dorothy?" Aldon asks over a nearby PA speaker.

She halts and turns. "Who—?"

"Andrew Aldon," he replies. "I have been observing your progress."

"Why?" she asks.

"Your safety concerns me."

"That storm you mentioned earlier?"

"Partly."

"I'm a big girl. I can take care of myself. What do you mean *partly?*"

"You move in dangerous company."

"Paul? How so?"

"He once took a woman into that same wild area he is heading for now. She did not come back."

"He told me all about that. There was an accident."

"And no witnesses."

"What are you trying to say?"

"It is suspicious. That is all."

She begins moving again, toward the administrative building. Aldon switches to another speaker, within its entrance.

"I accuse him of nothing. If you choose to trust him, fine. But don't trust the weather. It would be best for you to return to the hotel."

"Thanks but no thanks," she says, entering the building.

He follows her as she explores, is aware of her quickening pulse when she halts beside the cold bunkers.

"These are the sleepers?"

"Yes. Paul held such a position once, as did the unfortunate woman."

"I know. Look, I'm going to follow him whether you approve or not. So why not just tell me where those sleds are kept?"

"Very well. I will do even more than that. I will guide you."

"What do you mean?"

"I request a favor—one that will actually benefit you."

"Name it."

"In the equipment locker behind you, you will find a remote-sensor bracelet. It is also a two-way communication link. Wear it. I can be with you then. To assist you. Perhaps even to protect you."

"You can help me to follow him?"

"Yes."

"All right. I can buy that."

She moves to the locker, opens it.

"Here's something that looks like a bracelet, with doodads."

"Yes. Depress the red stud."

She does. His voice now emerges clearly from the unit.

"Put it on, and I'll show you the way."

"Right."

SNOWSCAPE. Sheets and hills of white, tufts of evergreen shrubbery, protruding joints of rock, snowdevils twirled like tops beneath wind's lash . . . light and shade.

Cracking sky. Tracks in sheltered areas, smoothness beyond.

She follows, masked and bundled.

"I've lost him," she mutters, hunched behind the curved windscreen of her yellow, bullet-shaped vehicle.

"Straight ahead, past those two rocks. Stay in the lee of the ridge. I'll tell you when to turn. I've a satellite overhead. If the clouds stay parted—strangely parted . . ."

"What do you mean?"

"He seems to be enjoying light from the only break in the cloud cover over the entire area."

"Coincidence."

"I wonder."

"What else could it be?"

"It is almost as if something had opened a door for him."

"Mysticism from a computer?"

"I am not a computer."

"I'm sorry, Mr. Aldon. I know that you were once a man . . ."

"I am still a man."

"Sorry."

"There are many things I would like to know. Your arrival here comes at an unusual time of year. Paul took some prospecting equipment with him . . ."

"Yes. It's not against the law. In fact, it is one of the vacation features here, isn't it?"

"Yes. There are many interesting minerals about, some of them precious."

"Well, Paul wants some more, and he didn't want a crowd around while he was looking."

"More?"

"Yes, he made a strike here years ago. Yndella crystals."

"I see. Interesting."

"What's in this for you, anyway?"

"Protecting visitors is a part of my job. In your case, I feel particularly protective."

"How so?"

"In my earlier life I was attracted to women of your—specifications. Physical, as well as what I can tell of the rest."

Two-beat pause, then, "You are blushing."

"Compliments do that to me," she says, "and that's a hell of a monitoring system you have. What's it like?"

"Oh, I can tell your body temperature, your pulse rate—"

"No, I mean, what's it like being—what you are?"

Three-beat pause. "Godlike in some ways. Very human in others—almost exaggeratedly so. I feel something of an amplification of everything I was earlier. Perhaps it's a compensation or a clinging to things past. You make me feel nostalgic—among other things. Don't fret. I'm enjoying it."

"I'd like to have met you then."

"Mutual."

"What were you like?"

"Imagine me as you would. I'll come off looking better that way."

She laughs. She adjusts her filters. She thinks about Paul.

"What was *he* like in his earlier days—Paul?" she asks.

"Probably pretty much the way he is now, only less polished."

"In other words, you don't care to say."

The trail turns upward more steeply, curves to the right. She hears winds but does not feel them. Cloud-shadow grayness lies all about, but her trail/*his* trail is lighted.

"I don't really know," Aldon says, after a time, "and I will not guess, in the case of someone you care about."

"Gallant," she observes.

"No, just fair," he replies. "I might be wrong."

They continue to the top of the rise, where Dorothy draws a sharp breath and further darkens her goggles against the sudden blaze where a range of ice fractures rainbows and strews their shards like confetti in all directions.

"God!" she says.

"Or goddess," Aldon replies.

"A goddess, sleeping in a circle of flame?"

"Not sleeping."

"That would be a lady for you, Aldon—if she existed. God and goddess."

"I do not want a goddess."

"I can see his tracks, heading into that."

"Not swerving a bit, as if he knows where he's going."

She follows, tracing slopes like the curves of a pale torso. The world is stillness and light and whiteness. Aldon on her wrist hums softly now, an old tune, whether of love or martial matters she isn't certain. Distances are distorted, perspectives skewed. She finds herself humming softly along with him, heading for the place where Paul's tracks find their vanishing point and enter infinity.

THE LIMP WATCH HUNG UPON THE TREE LIMB. *My lucky day. The weather . . . trail clean. Things changed but not so out of shape I can't tell where it is. The lights! God, yes! Iceshine, mounds of prisms . . . If only the opening is still there. . . . Should have brought explosives. There has been shifting, maybe a collapse. Must get in. Return later with Dorothy. But first—clean up, get rid of . . . it. If she's still there. . . . Swallowed up maybe. That would be good, best. Things seldom are, though. I—When it happened. Wasn't as if. Wasn't what. Was. . . . Was shaking the ground. Cracking, splitting. Icicles ringing, rattling, banging about. Thought we'd go under. Both of us. She was going in. So was the bag of the stuff. Grabbed the stuff. Only because it was nearer. Would have helped her if—Couldn't. Could I? Ceiling was slipping. Get out. No sense both of us getting it. Got out. She'd've done the same. Wouldn't she? Her eyes. . . . Glenda! Maybe . . . No! Couldn't have. Just couldn't. Could I? Silly. After all these years. There was a moment. Just a moment, though. A lull. If I'd known it was com-*

ing, I might have. No. Ran. Your face at the window, on the screen, in a sometime dream. Glenda. It wasn't that I didn't. Blaze of hills. Fire and eyes. Ice. Ice. Fire and snow. Blazing hearthful. Ice. Ice. Straight through the ice the long road lies. The fire hangs high above. The screaming. The crash. And the silence. Get out. Yet. Different? No. It could never have. That was the way. Not my fault. . . . Damn it. Everything I could. Glenda. Up ahead. Yes. Long curve. Then down. Winding back in there. The crystals will. . . . I'll never come back to this place.

THE LIMP TREE LIMB HUNG UPON THE WATCH. *Gotcha! Think I can't see through the fog? Can't sneak up on me on little cat feet. Same for your partner across the way. I'll melt off a little more near your bases, too. A lot of housecleaning backed up here . . . Might as well take advantage of the break. Get those streets perfect. . . . How long? Long. . . . Long legs parting. . . . Long time since. Is it not strange that desire should so many years outlive performance? Unnatural. This weather. A sort of spiritual spring. . . . Extend those beams. Burn. Melt in my hot, red-fingered hands. Back off. I say. I rule here. Clear that courtyard. Unplug that drain. Come opportunity, let me clasp thee. Melt. Burn. I rule here, goddess. Draw back. I've a bomb for every tower of ice, a light for any darkness. Tread carefully here. I feel I begin to know thee. I see thy signature in cloud and fog bank, trace thy icy tresses upon the blowing wind. Thy form lies contoured all about me, white as shining death. We're due an encounter. Let the clouds spiral, ice ring, Earth heave. I rush to meet thee, death or maiden, in halls of crystal upon the heights. Not here. Long, slow fall, ice facade, crashing. Melt. Another. . . . Gotcha!*

FROZEN WATCH EMBEDDED IN PERMAFROST. *Bristle and thrum. Coming now. Perchance. Perchance. Perchance. I say. Throstle. Crack. Sunder. Split. Open. Coming. Beyond the ice in worlds I have known. Returning. He. Throstle. The mind the mover. To open the way. Come now. Let not to the meeting impediments. Admit. Open. Cloud stand thou still, and wind be leashed. None dare oppose thy passage returning, my killer love. It was but yesterday. A handful of stones. . . . Come singing fresh-armed from the warm places. I have looked upon thy unchanged countenance. I open the way. Come to me. Let not to the mating. I—Girding the globe, I have awakened in all of my places to receive thee. But here, here this special spot, I focus, mind the mover, in place where it all began, my bloody handed, Paul my love, calling, back, for the last good-bye, ice kiss, fire touch, heart stop, blood still, soul freeze, embrace of world and my hate with thy fugitive body, elusive the long year now. Come into the place it has waited. I move there again, up sciatic to spine, behind the frozen eyeballs, waiting and warming. To me. To me now. Throstle and click, bristle and thrum. And runners scratching the snow, my heart slashing parallel. Cut.*

PILGRIMAGE. He swerves, turns, slows amid the ragged prominences—ice fallen, ice heaved—in the fields where mountain and glacier wrestle in slow motion, to the accompaniment of occasional cracking and pinging sounds, crashes, growls, and the rattle of blown ice crystals. Here the ground is fissured as well as greatly uneven, and Paul abandons his snowslider. He secures some tools to his belt and his pack, anchors the sled, and commences the trek.

At first, he moves slowly and carefully, but old reflexes return, and soon he is hurrying. Moving from dazzle to shade, he passes among ice forms like grotesque statues of glass. The slope is changed from the old one he remembers, but it feels right. And deep, below, to the right. . . .

Yes. That darker place. The canyon or blocked pass, whichever it was. That seems right, too. He alters his course slightly. He is sweating now within his protective clothing, and his breath comes faster as he increases his pace. His vision blurs, and for a moment, somewhere between glare and shadow, he seems to see. . . .

He halts, sways a moment, then shakes his head, snorts, and continues.

Another hundred meters and he is certain. Those rocky ribs to the northeast, snow rivulets diamond hard between them. . . . He has been here before.

The stillness is almost oppressive. In the distance he sees spumes of windblown snow jetting off and eddying down from a high, white peak. If he stops and listens carefully, he can even hear the far winds.

There is a hole in the middle of the clouds, directly overhead. It is as if he were looking downward upon a lake in a crater.

More than unusual. He is tempted to turn back. His trank has worn off, and his stomach feels unsettled. He half-wishes to discover that this is not the place. But he knows that feelings are not very important. He continues until he stands before the opening.

There has been some shifting, some narrowing of the way. He approaches slowly. He regards the passage for a full minute before he moves to enter.

He pushes back his goggles as he comes into the lessened light. He extends a gloved hand, places it upon the facing wall, pushes. Firm. He tests the one behind him. The same.

Three paces forward and the way narrows severely. He turns and sidles. The light grows dimmer, the surface beneath his feet, more slick. He slows. He slides a hand along either wall as he advances. He passes through a tiny spot of light beneath an open ice chimney. Overhead, the wind is howling a high note now, almost whistling it.

The passage begins to widen. As his right hand falls away from the more sharply angling wall, his balance is tipped in that direction. He draws back to compensate, but his left foot slides backward and falls. He attempts to rise, slips, and falls again.

Cursing, he begins to crawl forward. This area had not been slick before. . . . He chuckles. Before? A century ago. Things do change in a span like that. They—

The wind begins to howl beyond the cave mouth as he sees the rise of the floor, looks upward along the slope. She is there.

He makes a small noise at the back of his throat and stops, his right hand partly raised. She wears the shadows like veils, but they do not mask her identity. He stares. It's even worse than he had thought. Trapped, she must have lived for some time after. . . .

He shakes his head.

No use. She must be cut loose and buried now—disposed of.

He crawls forward. The icy slope does not grow level until he is quite near her. His gaze never leaves her form as he advances. The shadows slide over her. He can almost hear her again.

He thinks of the shadows. She couldn't have moved just then. . . . He stops and studies her face. It is not frozen. It is puckered and sagging as if waterlogged. A caricature of the face he had so often touched. He grimaces and looks away. The leg must be freed. He reaches for his ax.

Before he can take hold of the tool, he sees movement of the hand, slow and shaking. It is accompanied by a throaty sigh.

"No. . . ." he whispers, drawing back.

"Yes," comes the reply.

"Glenda."

"I am here." Her head turns slowly. Reddened, watery eyes focus upon his own. "I have been waiting."

"This is insane."

The movement of the face is horrible. It takes him some time to realize that it is a smile.

"I knew that one day you would return."

"How?" he says. "How have you lasted?"

"The body is nothing," she replies. "I had all but forgotten it. I live within the permafrost of this world. My buried foot was in contact with its filaments. It was alive, but it possessed no consciousness until we met. I live everywhere now."

"I am—happy—that you—survived."

She laughs slowly, dryly.

"Really, Paul? How could that be when you left me to die?"

"I had no choice, Glenda. I couldn't save you."

"There was an opportunity. You preferred the stones to my life."

"That's not true!"

"You didn't even try." The arms are moving again, less jerkily now. "You didn't even come back to recover my body."

"What would have been the use? You were dead—or I thought you were."

"Exactly. You didn't know, but you ran out anyway. I loved you, Paul. I would have done anything for you."

"I cared about you, too, Glenda. I would have helped you if I could have. If—"

"*If?* Don't give me *ifs.* I know what you are."

"I loved you," Paul says. "I'm sorry."

"You loved me? You never said it."

"It's not the sort of thing I talk about easily. Or think about, even."

"Show me," she says. "Come here."

He looks away. "I can't."

She laughs. "You said you loved me."

"You—you don't know how you look. I'm sorry."

"You fool!" Her voice grows hard, imperious. "Had you done it, I would have spared your life. It would have shown me that some tiny drop of affection might truly have existed. But you lied. You only used me. You didn't care."

"You're being unfair!"

"Am I? Am I really?" she says. There comes a sound like running water from somewhere nearby. "*You* would speak to me of fairness? I have hated you, Paul, for nearly a century. Whenever I took a moment from regulating the life of this planet to think about it, I would curse you. In the spring as I shifted my consciousness toward the poles and allowed a part of myself to dream, my nightmares were of you. They actually upset the ecology somewhat, here and there. I have waited, and now you are here. I see nothing to redeem you. I shall use you as you used me—to your destruction. Come to me!"

He feels a force enter into his body. His muscles twitch. He is drawn up to his knees. Held in that position for long moments, then he beholds her as she also rises, drawing a soaking leg from out of the crevice where it had been held. He had heard the running water. She had somehow melted the ice. . . .

She smiles and raises her pasty hands. Multitudes of dark filaments extend from her freed leg down into the crevice.

"Come!" she repeats.

"Please . . . ," he says.

She shakes her head. "Once you were so ardent. I cannot understand you."

"If you're going to kill me, then kill me, damn it! But don't— "

Her features begin to flow. Her hands darken and grow firm. In moments she stands before him looking as she did a century ago.

"Glenda!" He rises to his feet.

"Yes. Come now."

He takes a step forward. Another.

Shortly, he holds her in his arms, leans to kiss her smiling face.

"You forgive me . . . ," he says.

Her face collapses as he kisses her. Corpselike, flaccid, and pale once more, it is pressed against his own.

"No!"

He attempts to draw back, but her embrace is inhumanly strong.

"Now is not the time to stop," she says.

"Bitch! Let me go! I hate you!"

"I know that, Paul. Hate is the only thing we have in common."

". . . Always hated you," he continues, still struggling. "You always were a bitch!"

Then he feels the cold lines of control enter his body again.

"The greater my pleasure, then," she replies, as his hands drift forward to open her parka.

ALL OF THE ABOVE. Dorothy struggles down the icy slope, her sled parked beside Paul's. The winds lash at her, driving crystals of ice like microbullets against her struggling form. Overhead, the clouds have closed again. A curtain of white is drifting slowly in her direction.

"It waited for him," comes Aldon's voice, above the screech of the wind.

"Yes. Is this going to be a bad one?"

"A lot depends on the winds. You should get to shelter soon, though."

"I see a cave. I wonder whether that's the one Paul was looking for?"

"If I had to guess, I'd say yes. But right now it doesn't matter. Get there."

When she finally reaches the entrance, she is trembling. Several paces within she leans her back against the icy wall, panting. Then the wind changes direction and reaches her. She retreats farther into the cave.

She hears a voice: "Please . . . don't."

"Paul?" she calls.

There is no reply. She hurries.

She puts out a hand and saves herself from falling as she comes into the chamber. There she beholds Paul in necrophiliac embrace with his captor.

"Paul! What is it?" she cries.

"Get out!" he says. "Hurry!"

Glenda's lips form the words. "What devotion. Rather, let her stay, if you would live."

Paul feels her clasp loosen slightly.

"What do you mean?" he asks.

"You may have your life if you will take me away—in her body. Be with me as before."

It is Aldon's voice that answers, "No!" in reply. "You can't have her. Gaia!"

"Call me Glenda. I know you. Andrew Aldon. Many times have I listened to your broadcasts. Occasionally have I struggled against you when our projects were at odds. What is this woman to you?"

"She is under my protection."

"That means nothing. I am stronger here. Do you love her?"

"Perhaps I do. Or could."

"Fascinating. My nemesis of all these years, with the analog of a human heart within your circuits. But the decision is Paul's. Give her to me if you would live."

The cold rushes into his limbs. His life seems to contract to the center of his being. His consciousness begins to fade.

"Take her," he whispers.

"I forbid it!" rings Aldon's voice.

"You have shown me again what kind of man you are," Glenda hisses, "my enemy. Scorn and undying hatred are all I will ever have for you. Yet you shall live."

"I will destroy you," Aldon calls out, "if you do this thing!"

"What a battle that would be!" Glenda replies. "But I've no quarrel with you here. Nor will I grant you one with me. Receive my judgment."

Paul begins to scream. Abruptly this ceases. Glenda releases him, and he turns to stare at Dorothy. He steps in her direction.

"Don't—don't do it, Paul. Please."

"I am—not Paul," he replies, his voice deeper, "and I would never hurt you. . . ."

"Go now," says Glenda. "The weather will turn again, in your favor."

"I don't understand," Dorothy says, staring at the man before her.

"It is not necessary that you do," says Glenda. "Leave this planet quickly."

Paul's screaming commences once again, this time emerging from Dorothy's bracelet.

"I will trouble you for that bauble you wear, however. Something about it appeals to me."

FROZEN LEOPARD. He has tried on numerous occasions to relocate the cave, with his eyes in the sky and his robots and flyers, but the topography of the place was radically altered by a severe icequake, and he has met with no success. Periodically he bombards the general area. He also sends thermite cubes melting their ways down through the ice and the permafrost, but this has had no discernible effect.

This is the worst winter in the history of Balfrost. The winds howl constantly and waves of snow come on like surf. The glaciers have set speed records in their advance upon Playpoint. But he has held his own against them, with electricity, lasers, and chemicals. His supplies are virtually inexhaustible now, drawn from the planet itself, produced in his underground factories. He has also designed and is manufacturing more sophisticated weapons. Occasionally he hears her laughter over the missing communicator. "Bitch!" he broadcasts then. "Bastard!" comes the reply. He sends another missile into the mountains. A sheet of ice falls upon his city. It will be a long winter.

Andrew Aldon and Dorothy are gone. He has taken up painting, and she writes poetry now. They live in a warm place.

Sometimes Paul laughs over the broadcast band when he scores a victory. "Bastard!" comes the immediate response. "Bitch!" he answers, chuckling. He is never bored, however, or nervous. In fact . . . let it be.

When spring comes, the goddess will dream of this conflict while Paul turns his attention to his more immediate duties. But he will be planning and remembering, also. His life has a purpose to it now. And if anything, he is more efficient than Aldon. But the pods will bloom and burst despite his herbicides and fungicides. They will mutate just sufficiently to render the poisons innocuous.

"Bastard," she will mutter sleepily.

"Bitch," he will answer softly.

The night may have a thousand eyes and the day but one. The heart, often, is better blind to its own workings, and I would sing of arms and the man and the wrath of the goddess, not the torment of love unsatisfied, or satisfied, in the frozen garden of our frozen world. And that, leopard, is all.

Tangents

by Greg Bear

The nut-brown boy stood in the California field, his Asian face shadowed by a hardhat, his short stocky frame clothed in a T-shirt and a pair of brown shorts. He squinted across the hip-high grass at the spraddled old two-story ranch house, whistling a few bars from a Haydn piano sonata.

Out of the upper floor of the house came a man's high, frustrated "Bloody hell!" and the sound of a fist slamming on a solid surface. Silence for a minute. Then, more softly, a woman's question, "Not going well?"

"No. I'm swimming in it, but I don't see it."

"The encryption?" the woman asked timidly.

"The tesseract. If it doesn't gel, it isn't aspic."

The boy squatted in the grass and listened.

"And?" the woman encouraged.

"Ah, Lauren, it's still cold broth."

The boy lay back in the grass. He had crept over the split-rail and brick-pylon fence from the new housing project across the road. School was out for the summer and his mother—foster mother—did not like him around the house all day. Or at all.

Behind his closed eyes, a huge piano keyboard appeared, with him dancing on the keys. He loved music.

He opened his eyes and saw a thin, graying lady in a tweed suit leaning over him, staring. "You're on private land," she said, brows knit.

He scrambled up and brushed grass from his pants. "Sorry."

"I thought I saw someone out here. What's your name?"

"Pal," he replied.

219

"Is that a name?" she asked querulously.

"Pal Tremont. It's not my real name. I'm Korean."

"Then what's your real name?"

"My folks told me not to use it anymore. I'm adopted. Who are you?"

The gray woman looked him up and down. "My name is Lauren Davies," she said. "You live near here?"

He pointed across the fields at the close-packed tract homes.

"I sold the land for those homes ten years ago," she said. She seemed to be considering something. "I don't normally enjoy children trespassing."

"Sorry," Pal said.

"Have you had lunch?"

"No."

"Will a grilled cheese sandwich do?"

He squinted at her and nodded.

In the broad, red-brick and tile kitchen, sitting at an oak table with his shoulders barely rising above the top, he ate the slightly charred sandwich and watched Lauren Davies watching him.

"I'm trying to write about a child," she said. "It's difficult. I'm a spinster and I don't understand children."

"You're a writer?" he asked, taking a swallow of milk. She sniffed. "Not that anyone would know."

"Is that your brother, upstairs?"

"No," she said. "That's Peter. We've been living together for twenty years."

"But you said you're a spinster . . . isn't that someone who's never married, or never loved?" Pal asked.

"Never married. And never you mind. Peter's relationship to me is none of your concern." She placed a bowl of soup and a tuna salad sandwich on a lacquer tray. "His lunch," she said. Without being asked, Pal trailed up the stairs after her.

"This is where Peter works," Lauren explained. Pal stood in the doorway, eyes wide. The room was filled with electronics gear, computer terminals, and bookcases with geometric cardboard sculptures sharing each shelf with books and circuit boards. She rested the tray precariously on a pile of floppy disks atop a rolling cart.

"Time for a break," she told a thin man seated with his back toward them.

The man turned around on his swivel chair, glanced briefly at Pal and the tray and shook his head. The hair on top of his head was a rich, glossy black; on the close-cut sides, the color changed abruptly to a startling white. He had a small thin nose and large green eyes. On the desk before him was a high-resolution computer monitor. "We haven't been introduced," he said, pointing to Pal.

"This is Pal Tremont, a neighborhood visitor. Pal, this is Peter Tuthy. Pal's going to help me with that character we discussed this morning."

Pal looked at the monitor curiously. Red and green lines shadowed each other through some incomprehensible transformation on the screen, then repeated.

"What's a 'tesseract'?" Pal asked, remembering what he had heard as he stood in the field.

"It's a four-dimensional analog of a cube. I'm trying to teach myself to see it in my mind's eye," Tuthy said. "Have you ever tried that?"

"No," Pal admitted.

"Here," Tuthy said, handing him the spectacles. "As in the movies."

Pal donned the spectacles and stared at the screen. "So?" he said. "It folds and unfolds. It's pretty—it sticks out at you, and then it goes away." He looked around the workshop. "Oh, wow!" The boy ran to a yard-long black music keyboard propped in one corner. "A Tronclavier! With all the switches! My mother had me take piano lessons, but I'd rather play this. Can you play it?"

"I toy with it," Tuthy said, exasperated. "I toy with all sorts of electronic things. But what did you see on the screen?" He glanced up at Lauren, blinking. "I'll eat the food, I'll eat it. Now please don't bother us."

"He's supposed to be helping *me*," Lauren complained.

Peter smiled at her. "Yes, of course. I'll send him downstairs in a little while."

When Pal descended an hour later, he came into the kitchen to thank Lauren for lunch. "Peter's a real flake," he said confidentially. "He's trying to learn to see in weird directions."

"I know," Lauren said, sighing.

"I'm going home now," Pal said. "I'll be back, though . . . if it's all right with you. Peter invited me."

"I'm sure it will be fine," Lauren said dubiously.

"He's going to let me learn the Tronclavier." With that, Pal smiled radiantly and exited through the kitchen door, just as he had come in.

When she retrieved the tray, she found Peter leaning back in his chair, eyes closed. The figures on the screen were still folding and unfolding.

"What about Hockrum's work?" she asked.

"I'm on it," Peter replied, eyes still closed.

Lauren called Pal's foster mother on the second day to apprise them of their son's location, and the woman assured her it was quite all right. "Sometimes he's a little pest. Send him home if he causes trouble . . . but not right away! Give me a rest," she said, then laughed nervously.

Lauren drew her lips together tightly, thanked the woman, and hung up.

Peter and the boy had come downstairs to sit in the kitchen, filling up paper with line drawings. "Peter's teaching me how to use his program," Pal said.

"Did you know," Tuthy said, assuming his highest Cambridge professorial tone, "that a cube, intersecting a flat plane, can be cut through a number of geometrically different cross-sections?"

Pal squinted at the sketch Tuthy had made. "Sure," he said.

"If shoved through the plane the cube can appear, to a two-dimensional creature living on the plane—let's call him a 'Flatlander'—to be either a triangle, a rectangle, a trapezoid, a rhombus, or a square. If the two-dimensional being observes the cube being pushed through all the way, what he sees is one or more of these objects growing larger, changing shape suddenly, shrinking, and disappearing."

"Sure," Pal said, tapping his sneakered toe. "That's easy. Like in that book you showed me."

"And a sphere pushed through a plane would appear, to the hapless flatlander, first as an 'invisible' point (the two-dimensional surface touching the sphere, tangential), then as a circle. The circle would grow in size, then shrink back to a point and disappear again." He sketched two-dimensional stick figures looking in awe at such an intrusion.

"Got it," Pal said. "Can I play with the Tronclavier now?"

"In a moment. Be patient. So what would a tesseract look like, coming into our three-dimensional space? Remember the program, now . . . the pictures on the monitor."

Pal looked up at the ceiling. "I don't know," he said, seeming bored.

"Try to think," Tuthy urged him.

"It would . . ." Pal held his hands out to shape an angular object. "It would look like one of those Egyptian things, but with three sides . . . or like a box. It would look like a weird-shaped box, too, not square. And if *you* were to fall through a flatland . . ."

"Yes, that would look very funny," Peter acknowledged with a smile. "Cross-sections of arms and legs and body, all surrounded by skin . . ."

"And a head!" Pal enthused. "With eyes and a nose."

The doorbell rang. Pal jumped off the kitchen chair. "Is that my mom?" he asked, looking worried.

"I don't think so," Lauren said. "More likely it's Hockrum." She went to the front door to answer. She returned a moment later with a small, pale man behind her. Tuthy stood and shook the man's hand. "Pal Tremont, this is Irving Hockrum," he introduced, waving his hand between them. Hockrum glanced at Pal and blinked a long, cold blink.

"How's the work coming?" he asked Tuthy.

"It's finished," Tuthy said. "It's upstairs. Looks like your savants are barking up the wrong logic tree." He retrieved a folder of papers and printouts and handed them to Hockrum.

Hockrum leafed through the printouts. "I can't say this makes me happy. Still, I can't find fault. Looks like the work is up to your usual brilliant standards. Here's your check." He handed Tuthy an envelope. "I just wish you'd given it to us sooner. It would have saved me some grief—and the company quite a bit of money."

"Sorry," Tuthy said.

"Now I have an important bit of work for you . . ." And Hockrum outlined another problem. Tuthy thought it over for several minutes and shook his head.

"Most difficult, Irving. Pioneering work there. Take at least a month to see if it's even feasible."

"That's all I need to know for now—whether it's feasible. A lot's riding on this, Peter." Hockrum clasped his hands together in front of him, looking even more pale and worn than when he had entered the kitchen. "You'll let me know soon?"

"I'll get right on it," Tuthy said.

"Protégé?" he asked, pointing to Pal. There was a speculative expression on his face, not quite a leer.

"No, a young friend. He's interested in music," Tuthy said. "Damned good at Mozart, in fact."

"I help with his tesseracts," Pal asserted.

"I hope you don't interrupt Peter's work. Peter's work is important."

Pal shook his head solemnly. "Good," Hockrum said, and then left the house with the folder under his arm.

Tuthy returned to his office, Pal in train. Lauren tried to work in the kitchen, sitting with fountain pen and pad of paper, but the words wouldn't come. Hockrum always worried her. She climbed the stairs and stood in the open doorway of the office. She often did that; her presence did not disturb Tuthy, who could work under all sorts of adverse conditions.

"Who was that man?" Pal was asking Tuthy.

"I work for him," Tuthy said. "He's employed by a big electronics firm. He loans me most of the equipment I use. The computers, the high-resolution monitors. He brings me problems and then takes my solutions back to his bosses and claims he did the work."

"That sounds stupid," Pal said. "What kind of problems?"

"Codes, encryptions. Computer security. That was my expertise, once."

"You mean, like fencerail, that sort of thing?" Pal asked, face brightening. "We learned some of that in school."

"Much more complicated, I'm afraid," Tuthy said, grinning. "Did you ever hear of the German 'Enigma,' or the 'Ultra' project?"

Pal shook his head.

"I thought not. Let's try another figure now." He called up another routine on the four-space program and sat Pal before the screen. "So what would a hypersphere look like if it intruded into our space?"

Pal thought a moment. "Kind of weird," he said.

"Not really. You've been watching the visualizations."

"Oh, in *our* space. That's easy. It just looks like a balloon, blowing up from nothing and then shrinking again. It's harder to see what a hypersphere looks like when it's real. Reft of us, I mean."

"Reft?" Tuthy said.

"Sure. Reft and light. Dup and owwen. Whatever the directions are called."

Tuthy stared at the boy. Neither of them had noticed Lauren in the doorway. "The proper terms are *ana* and *kata*," Tuthy said. "What does it look like?"

Pal gestured, making two wide wings with his arms. "It's like a ball and it's like a horseshoe, depending on how you look at it. Like a balloon stung by bees, I guess, but it's smooth all over, not lumpy."

Tuthy continued to stare, then asked quietly, "You actually see it?"

"Sure," Pal said. "Isn't that what your program is supposed to do—make you see things like that?"

Tuthy nodded, flabbergasted.

"Can I play the Tronclavier now?"

Lauren backed out of the doorway. She felt she had eavesdropped on something momentous, but beyond her. Tuthy came downstairs an hour later, leaving Pal to pick out Telemann on the synthesizer. He sat at the kitchen table with her. "The program works," he said. "It doesn't work for me, but it works for him. I've just been showing him reverse-shadow figures. He caught on right away, and then he went off to play Haydn. He's gone through all my sheet music. The kid's a genius."

"Musical, you mean?"

He glanced directly at her and frowned. "Yes, I suppose he's remarkable at that, too. But spacial relations—coordinates and motion in higher dimensions . . . Did you know that if you take a three-dimensional object and rotate it in the fourth dimension, it will come back with left-right reversed? So if I were to take my hand"—he held up his right hand—"and lift it *dup*"—he enunciated the word clearly, *dup*—"or drop it *owwen*, it would come back like this?" He held his left hand over his right, balled the right up into a fist, and snuck it away behind his back.

"I didn't know that," Lauren said. "What are *dup* and *owwen*?"

"That's what Pal calls movement along the fourth dimension. *Ana* and *kata* to purists. Like up and down to a flatlander, who only comprehends left and right, back and forth."

She thought about the hands for a moment. "I still can't see it," she said.

"I've tried, but neither can I," Tuthy admitted. "Our circuits are just too hard-wired, I suppose."

Upstairs, Pal had switched the Tronclavier to a cathedral organ and steel guitar combination and was playing variations on Pergolesi.

"Are you going to keep working for Hockrum?" Lauren asked. Tuthy didn't seem to hear her.

"It's remarkable," he murmured. "The boy just walked in here. You brought him in by accident. Remarkable."

"Can you show me the direction, point it out to me?" Tuthy asked the boy three days later.

"None of my muscles move that way," the boy replied. "I can see it, in my head, but . . ."

"What is it like, seeing that direction?"

Pal squinted. "It's a lot bigger. We're sort of stacked up with other places. It makes me feel lonely."

"Why?"

"Because I'm stuck here. Nobody out there pays any attention to us."

Tuthy's mouth worked. "I thought you were just intuiting those directions in your head. Are you telling me . . . you're actually *seeing* out there?"

"Yeah. There's people out there, too. Well, not people, exactly. But it isn't my eyes that see them. Eyes are like muscles—they can't point those ways. But the head—the brain, I guess—can."

"Bloody hell," Tuthy said. He blinked and recovered. "Excuse me. That's rude. Can you show me the people . . . on the screen?"

"Shadows, like we were talking about," Pal said.

"Fine. Then draw the shadows for me."

Pal sat down before the terminal, fingers pausing over the keys. "I can show you, but you have to help me with something."

"Help you with what?"

"I'd like to play music for them . . . out there. So they'll notice us."

"The people?"

"Yeah. They look really weird. They stand on us, sort of. They have hooks in our world. But they're tall . . . high dup. They don't notice us because we're so small, compared to them."

"Lord, Pal, I haven't the slightest idea how we'd send

music out to them . . . I'm not even sure I believe they exist."

"I'm not lying," Pal said, eyes narrowing. He turned his chair to face a mouse on a black-ruled pad and began sketching shapes on the monitor. "Remember, these are just shadows of what they look like. Next I'll draw the dup and owwen lines to connect the shadows."

The boy shaded the shapes he drew to make them look solid, smiling at his trick but explaining it was necessary because the projection of a four-dimensional object in normal space was, of course, three-dimensional.

"They look like you take the plants in a garden, flowers and such, and giving them lots of arms and fingers . . . and it's kind of like seeing things in an aquarium," Pal explained.

After a time, Tuthy suspended his disbelief and stared in open-mouthed wonder at what the boy was re-creating on the monitor.

"I think you're wasting your time, that's what I think," Hockrum said. "I needed that feasibility judgment by today." He paced around the living room before falling as heavily as his light frame permitted into a chair.

"I *have* been distracted," Tuthy admitted.

"By that boy?"

"Yes, actually. Quite a talented fellow—"

"Listen, this is going to mean a lot of trouble for me. I guaranteed the study would be finished by today. It'll make me look bad." Hockrum screwed his face up in frustration. "What in hell are you doing with that boy?"

"Teaching him, actually. Or rather, he's teaching me. Right now, we're building a four-dimensional cone, part of a speaker system. The cone is three-dimensional, the material part, but the magnetic field forms a fourth-dimensional extension—"

"Do you ever think how it looks, Peter?" Hockrum asked.

"It looks very strange on the monitor, I grant you—"

"I'm talking about you and the boy."

Tuthy's bright, interested expression fell slowly into long, deep-lined dismay. "I don't know what you mean."

"I know a lot about you, Peter. Where you come from, why you had to leave . . . It just doesn't look good."

Tuthy's face flushed crimson.

"Keep him away from here," Hockrum advised.

Tuthy stood. "I want you out of this house," he said quietly. "Our relationship is at an end."

"I swear," Hockrum said, his voice low and calm, staring up at Tuthy from under his brows, "I'll tell the boy's parents. Do you think they'd want their kid hanging around an old—pardon the expression—queer? I'll tell them if you don't get the feasibility judgment made. I think you can do it by the end of this week—two days. Don't you?"

"No, I don't think so," Tuthy said. "Please leave."

"I know you're here illegally. There's no record of you entering the country. With the problems you had in England, you're certainly not a desirable alien. I'll pass word to the INS. You'll be deported."

"There isn't time to do the work," Tuthy said.

"Make time. Instead of 'educating' that kid."

"Get out of here."

"Two days, Peter."

Over dinner that evening, Tuthy explained to Lauren the exchange he had had with Hockrum. "He thinks I'm buggering Pal. Unspeakable bastard. I will never work for him again."

"We'd better talk to a lawyer, then," Lauren said. "You're sure you can't make him . . . happy, stop all this trouble?"

"I could solve his little problem for him in just a few hours. But I don't want to see him or speak to him again."

"He'll take your equipment away."

Tuthy blinked and waved one hand through the air helplessly. "Then we'll just have to work fast, won't we?

Ah, Lauren, you were a fool to bring me here. You should have left me to rot."

"They ignored everything you did for them," Lauren said bitterly. "You saved their hides during the war, and then ... They would have shut you up in prison." She stared through the kitchen window at the overcast sky and woods outside.

The cone lay on the table near the window, bathed in morning sun, connected to both the mini-computer and the Tronclavier. Pal arranged the score he had composed on a music stand before the synthesizer. "It's like Bach," he said, "but it'll play better for them. It has a kind of over-rhythm that I'll play on the dup part of the speaker."

"Why are we doing this, Pal?" Tuthy asked as the boy sat down to the keyboard.

"You don't belong here, really, do you, Peter?" Pal asked in turn. Tuthy stared at him.

"I mean, Miss Davies and you get along okay—but do you belong *here,* now?"

"What makes you think I don't belong?"

"I read some books in the school library. About the war and everything. I looked up 'Enigma' and 'Ultra.' I found a fellow named Peter Thornton. His picture looked like you. The books made him seem like a hero."

Tuthy smiled wanly.

"But there was this note in one book. You disappeared in 1965. You were being prosecuted for something. They didn't say what you were being prosecuted for."

"I'm a homosexual," Tuthy said quietly.

"Oh. So what?"

"Lauren and I met in England in 1964. We became good friends. They were going to put me in prison, Pal. She smuggled me into the U.S. through Canada."

"But you said you're a homosexual. They don't like women."

"Not at all true, Pal. Lauren and I like each other very much. We could talk. She told me about her dreams of being a writer, and I talked to her about mathematics, and about the war. I nearly died during the war."

"Why? Were you wounded?"

"No. I worked too hard. I burned myself out and had a nervous breakdown. My lover—a man—kept me alive throughout the forties. Things were bad in England after the war. But he died in 1963. His parents came in to settle the estate, and when I contested the settlement in court, I was arrested. So I suppose you're right, Pal. I don't really belong here."

"I don't, either. My folks don't care much. I don't have too many friends. I wasn't even born here, and I don't know anything about Korea."

"Play," Tuthy said, his face stony. "Let's see if they'll listen."

"Oh, they'll listen," Pal said. "It's like the way they talk to each other."

The boy ran his fingers over the keys on the Tronclavier. The cone, connected with the keyboard through the mini-computer, vibrated tinnily.

For an hour, Pal paged back and forth through his composition, repeating and trying variations. Tuthy sat in a corner, chin in hand, listening to the mousy squeaks and squeals produced by the cone. *How much more difficult to interpret a four-dimensional sound,* he thought. *Not even visual clues . . .*

Finally the boy stopped and wrung his hands, then stretched his arms. "They must have heard. We'll just have to wait and see." He switched the Tronclavier to automatic playback and pushed the chair away from the keyboard.

Pal stayed until dusk, then reluctantly went home. Tuthy sat in the office until midnight, listening to the tinny sounds issuing from the speaker cone.

All night long, the Tronclavier played through its pre-programmed selection of Pal's compositions. Tuthy lay in bed in his room, two doors down from Lauren's room, watching a shaft of moonlight slide across the wall. *How far would a four-dimensional being have to travel to get here?*

How far have I come to get here?

Without realizing he was asleep, he dreamed, and in his dream a wavering image of Pal appeared, gesturing with both arms as if swimming, eyes wide. *I'm okay*, the boy said without moving his lips. *Don't worry about me . . . I'm okay. I've been back to Korea to see what it's like. It's not bad, but I like it better here. . . .*

Tuthy awoke sweating. The moon had gone down and the room was pitch-black. In the office, the hyper-cone continued its distant, mouse-squeak broadcast.

Pal returned early in the morning, repetitively whistling a few bars from Mozart's Fourth Violin Concerto. Lauren let him in and he joined Tuthy upstairs. Tuthy sat before the monitor, replaying Pal's sketch of the four-dimensional beings.

"Do you see anything?" he asked the boy.

Pal nodded. "They're coming closer. They're interested. Maybe we should get things ready, you know . . . be prepared." He squinted. "Did you ever think what a four-dimensional footprint would look like?"

Tuthy considered for a moment. "That would be most interesting," he said. "It would be solid."

On the first floor, Lauren screamed.

Pal and Tuthy almost tumbled over each other getting downstairs. Lauren stood in the living room with her arms crossed above her bosom, one hand clamped over her mouth. The first intrusion had taken out a section of the living-room floor and the east wall.

"Really clumsy," Pal said. "One of them must have bumped it."

"The music," Tuthy said.

"What in HELL is going on?" Lauren demanded, her voice starting as a screech and ending as a roar.

"Better turn the music off," Tuthy elaborated.

"Why?" Pal asked, face wreathed in an excited smile. "Maybe they don't like it."

A bright filmy blue blob rapidly expanded to a yard in diameter just beside Tuthy. The blob turned red, wriggled, froze, and then just as rapidly vanished.

"That was like an elbow," Pal explained. "One of its arms. I think it's listening. Trying to find out where the music is coming from. I'll go upstairs."

"Turn it off!" Tuthy demanded.

"I'll play something else." The boy ran up the stairs. From the kitchen came a hideous hollow crashing, then the sound of a vacuum being filled—a reverse-pop, ending in a hiss—followed by a low-frequency vibration that set their teeth on edge . . .

The vibration caused by a four-dimensional creature *scraping* across its "floor," their own three-dimensional space. Tuthy's hands shook with excitement.

"Peter—" Lauren bellowed, all dignity gone. She unwrapped her arms and held clenched fists out as if she were about to start exercising, or boxing.

"Pal's attracted visitors," Tuthy explained.

He turned toward the stairs. The first four steps and a section of floor spun and vanished. The rush of air nearly drew him down the hole. Regaining his balance, he knelt to feel the precisely cut, concave edge. Below lay the dark basement.

"Pal!" Tuthy called out.

"I'm playing something original for them," Pal shouted back. "I think they like it."

The phone rang. Tuthy was closest to the extension at the bottom of the stairs and instinctively reached out to answer it. Hockrum was on the other end, screaming.

"I can't talk now—" Tuthy said. Hockrum screamed again, loud enough for Lauren to hear. Tuthy abruptly hung up. "He's been fired, I gather," he said. "He seemed angry." He stalked back three paces and turned, then ran forward and leaped the gap to the first intact step. "Can't talk." He stumbled and scrambled up the stairs, stopping on the landing. "Jesus," he said, as if something had suddenly occurred to him.

"He'll call the government," Lauren warned.

Tuthy waved that off. "I know what's happening. They're knocking chunks out of three-space, into the fourth. The fourth dimension. Like Pal says: clumsy brutes. They could kill us!"

Sitting before the Tronclavier, Pal happily played a new melody. Tuthy approached and was abruptly blocked by a thick green column, as solid as rock and with a similar texture. It vibrated and ascribed an arc in the air. A section of the ceiling four feet wide was kicked out of three-space. Tuthy's hair lifted in the rush of wind. The column shrank to a broomstick and hairs sprouted all over it, writhing like snakes.

Tuthy edged around the hairy broomstick and pulled the plug on the Tronclavier. A cage of zeppelin-shaped brown sausages encircled the computer, spun, elongated to reach the ceiling, the floor, and the top of the monitor's table, and then pipped down to tiny strings and was gone.

"They can't see too clearly here," Pal said, undisturbed that his concert was over. Lauren had climbed the outside stairs and stood behind Tuthy. "Gee, I'm sorry about the damage."

In one smooth curling motion, the Tronclavier and cone and all the wiring associated with them were peeled away as if they had been stick-on labels hastily removed from a flat surface.

"Gee," Pal said, his face suddenly registering alarm.

Then it was the boy's turn. He was removed more slowly, with greater care. The last thing to vanish was his head, which hung suspended in the air for several seconds.

"I think they liked the music," he said, grinning.

Head, grin and all, dropped away in a direction impossible for Tuthy or Lauren to follow. The air in the room sighed.

Lauren stood her ground for several minutes, while Tuthy wandered through what was left of the office, passing his hand through mussed hair.

"Perhaps he'll be back," Tuthy said. "I don't even

know ..." But he didn't finish. Could a three-dimensional boy survive in a four-dimensional void, or whatever lay dup ... or owwen?

Tuthy did not object when Lauren took it upon herself to call the boy's foster parents and the police. When the police arrived, he endured the questions and accusations stoically, face immobile, and told them as much as he knew. He was not believed; nobody knew quite what to believe. Photographs were taken. The police left.

It was only a matter of time, Lauren told him, until one or the other or both of them were arrested. "Then we'll make up a story," he said. "You'll tell them it was my fault."

"I will *not*," Lauren said. "But where *is* he?"

"I'm not positive," Tuthy said. "I think he's all right, however."

"How do you *know*?"

He told her about the dream.

"But that was before," she said.

"Perfectly allowable in the fourth dimension," he explained. He pointed vaguely up, then down, and shrugged.

On the last day, Tuthy spent the early morning hours bundled in an overcoat and bathrobe in the drafty office, playing his program again and again, trying to visualize *ana* and *kata*. He closed his eyes and squinted and twisted his head, intertwined his fingers and drew odd little graphs on the monitors, but it was no use. His brain was hard-wired.

Over breakfast, he reiterated to Lauren that she must put all the blame on him.

"Maybe it will all blow over," she said. "They haven't got a case. No evidence ... nothing."

"All blow *over*," he mused, passing his hand over his head and grinning ironically. "How *over*, they'll never know."

The doorbell rang. Tuthy went to answer it, and Lauren followed a few steps behind.

Tuthy opened the door. Three men in gray suits, one with a briefcase, stood on the porch. "Mr. Peter Thornton?" the tallest asked.

"Yes," Tuthy acknowledged.

A chunk of the door frame and wall above the door vanished with a roar and a hissing pop. The three men looked up at the gap. Ignoring what was impossible, the tallest man returned his attention to Tuthy and continued, "We have information that you are in this country illegally."

"Oh?" Tuthy said.

Beside him, an irregular filmy blue cylinder grew to a length of four feet and hung in the air, vibrating. The three men backed away on the porch. In the middle of the cylinder, Pal's head emerged, and below that, his extended arm and hand.

"It's fun here," Pal said. "They're friendly."

"I believe you," Tuthy said.

"Mr. Thornton," the tallest man continued valiantly.

"Won't you come with me?" Pal asked.

Tuthy glanced back at Lauren. She gave him a small fraction of a nod, barely understanding what she was assenting to, and he took Pal's hand. "Tell them it was all my fault," he said.

From his feet to his head, Peter Tuthy was peeled out of this world. Air rushed in. Half of the brass lamp to one side of the door disappeared.

The INS men returned to their car without any further questions, with damp pants and embarrassed, deeply worried expressions. They drove away, leaving Lauren to contemplate the quiet. They did not return.

She did not sleep for three nights, and when she did sleep, Tuthy and Pal visited her, and put the question to her.

Thank you, but I prefer it here, she replied.

It's a lot of fun, the boy insisted. *They like music.*

Lauren shook her head on the pillow and awoke. Not

very far away, there was a whistling, tinny kind of sound, followed by a deep vibration.

To her, it sounded like applause.

She took a deep breath and got out of bed to retrieve her notebook.

1988
46th World SF
Convention
New Orleans

Eye for Eye by Orson Scott Card
Buffalo Gals, Won't You Come Out Tonight
by Ursula K. Le Guin
Why I Left Harry's All-Night Hamburgers
by Lawrence Watt-Evans

Eye for Eye

by Orson Scott Card

Just talk, Mick. Tell us everything. We'll listen.

Well to start with I know I was doing terrible things.
If you're a halfway decent person, you don't go looking
to kill people. Even if you can do it without touching
them. Even if you can do it so as nobody even guesses
they was murdered, you still got to try not to do it.

Who taught you that?

Nobody. I mean it wasn't in the books in the Baptist
Sunday School—they spent all their time telling us not
to lie or break the sabbath or drink liquor. Never did
mention killing. Near as I can figure, the Lord thought
killing was pretty smart sometimes, like when Samson
done it with a donkey's jaw. A thousand guys dead, but
that was okay cause they was Philistines. And lighting
foxes' tails on fire. Samson was a sicko, but he still got
his pages in the Bible.

I figure Jesus was about the only guy got much space
in the Bible telling people not to kill. And even then,
there's that story about how the Lord struck down a guy
and his wife cause they held back on their offerings to
the Christian church. Oh, Lord, the TV preachers did go
on about that. No, it wasn't cause I got religion that I
figured out not to kill people.

You know what I think it was? I think it was Vondel
Cone's elbow. At the Baptist Children's Home in Eden,
North Carolina, we played basketball all the time. On a
bumpy dirt court, but we figured it was part of the game,
never knowing which way the ball would bounce. Those
boys in the NBA, they play a sissy game on that flat
smooth floor.

We played basketball because there wasn't a lot else

241

to do. Only thing they ever had on TV was the preachers. We got it all cabled in—Falwell from up in Lynchburg, Jim and Tammy from Charlotte, Jimmy Swaggart looking hot, Ernest Ainglee looking carpeted, Billy Graham looking like God's executive vice-president—that was all our TV ever showed, so no wonder we lived on the basketball court all year.

Anyway, Vondel Cone wasn't particularly tall and he wasn't particularly good at shooting and on the court nobody was even halfway good at dribbling. But he had elbows. Other guys, when they hit you it was an accident. But when Vondel's elbow met up with your face, he like to pushed your nose out your ear. You can bet we all learned real quick to give him room. He got to take all the shots and get all the rebounds he wanted.

But we got even. We just didn't count his points. We'd call out the score, and any basket he made it was like it never happened. He'd scream and he'd argue and we'd all stand there and nod and agree so he wouldn't punch us out, and then as soon as the next basket was made, we'd call out the score—still not counting Vondel's points. Drove that boy crazy. He screamed till his eyes bugged out, but nobody ever counted his cheating points.

Vondel died of leukemia at the age of fourteen. You see, I never did like that boy.

But I learned something from him. I learned how unfair it was for somebody to get his way just because he didn't care how much he hurt other people. And when I finally realized that I was just about the most hurtful person in the whole world, I knew then and there that it just wasn't right. I mean, even in the Old Testament, Moses said the punishment should fit the crime. Eye for eye, tooth for tooth. Even Steven, that's what Old Peleg said before I killed him of prostate cancer. It was when Peleg got took to the hospital that I left the Eden Baptist Children's Home. Cause I wasn't Vondel. I *did* care how much I hurt folks.

But that doesn't have nothing to do with anything. I don't know what all you want me to talk about.

Just talk, Mick. Tell us whatever you want.

Well I don't aim to tell you my whole life story. I mean I didn't really start to figure out anything till I got on that bus in Roanoke, and so I can pretty much start there I guess. I remember being careful not to get annoyed when the lady in front of me didn't have the right change for the bus. And I didn't get angry when the bus driver got all snotty and told the lady to get off. It just wasn't worth killing for. That's what I always tell myself when I get mad. It isn't worth killing for, and it helps me calm myself down. So anyway I reached past her and pushed a dollar bill through the slot.

"This is for both of us," I says.

"I don't make change," says he.

I could've just said "Fine" and left it at that, but he was being such a prick that I had to do something to make him see how ignorant he was. So I put another nickel in the slot and said, "That's thirty-five for me, thirty-five for her, and thirty-five for the next guy gets on without no change."

So maybe I provoked him. I'm sorry for that, but I'm human, too, I figure. Anyway he was mad. "Don't you smart off with me, boy. I don't have to let you ride, fare or no fare."

Well, fact was he did, that's the law, and anyway I was white and my hair was short so his boss would probably do something if I complained. I could have told him what for and shut his mouth up tight. Except that if I did, I would have gotten too mad, and no man deserves to die just for being a prick. So I looked down at the floor and said, "Sorry, sir." I didn't say "Sorry *sir*" or anything snotty like that. I said it all quiet and sincere.

If he just *dropped* it, everything would have been fine, you know? I was mad, yes, but I'd gotten okay at bottling it in, just kind of holding it tight and then waiting for it to ooze away where it wouldn't hurt nobody. But just as I turned to head back toward a seat, he lurched that bus forward so hard that it flung me down and I only caught myself from hitting the floor by catching the handhold on a seatback and half-smashing the poor lady sitting there.

Some other people said, "Hey!" kind of mad, and I realize now that they was saying it to the driver, cause they was on my side. But at the time I thought they was mad at *me*, and that plus the scare of nearly falling and how mad I already was, well, I lost control of myself. I could just feel it in me, like sparklers in my blood veins, spinning around my whole body and then throwing off this pulse that went and hit that bus driver. He was behind me, so I didn't see it with my eyes. But I could feel that sparkiness connect up with him, and twist him around inside, and then finally it came loose from me, I didn't feel it no more. I wasn't mad no more. But I knew I'd done him already.

I even knew where. It was in his liver. I was a real expert on cancer by now. Hadn't I seen everybody I ever knew die of it? Hadn't I read every book in the Eden Public Library on cancer? You can live without kidneys, you can cut out a lung, you can take out a colon and live with a bag in your pants, but you can't live without a liver and they can't transplant it either. That man was dead. Two years at the most, I gave him. Two years, all because he was in a bad mood and lurched his bus to trip up a smartmouth kid.

I felt like piss on a flat rock. On that day I had gone nearly eight months, since before Christmas, the whole *year* so far without hurting anybody. It was the best I'd ever done, and I thought I'd licked it. I stepped across the lady I smashed into and sat by the window, looking out, not seeing anything. All I could think was I'm sorry I'm sorry I'm sorry. Did he have a wife and kids? Well, they'd be a widow and orphans soon enough, because of me. I could feel him from clear over here. The sparkiness of his belly, making the cancer grow and keeping his body's own natural fire from burning it out. I wanted with all my heart to take it back, but I couldn't. And like so many times before, I thought to myself that if I had any guts I'd kill myself. I couldn't figure why I hadn't died of my own cancer already. I sure enough hated myself a lot worse than I ever hated anybody else.

The lady beside me starts to talk. "People like that are so annoying, aren't they?"

I didn't want to talk to anybody, so I just grunted and turned away.

"That was very kind of you to help me," she says.

That's when I realized she was the same lady who didn't have the right fare. "Nothing," I says.

"No, you didn't have to do that." She touched my jeans.

I turned to look at her. She was older, about twenty-five maybe, and her face looked kind of sweet. She was dressed nice enough that I could tell it wasn't cause she was poor that she didn't have bus fare. She also didn't take her hand off my knee, which made me nervous, because the bad thing I do is a lot stronger when I'm actually touching a person, and so I mostly don't touch folks and I don't feel safe when they touch me. The fastest I ever killed a man was when he felt me up in a bathroom at a rest stop on I-85. He was coughing blood when I left that place, I really tore him up that time, I still have nightmares about him gasping for breath there with his hand on me.

So anyway that's why I felt real nervous her touching me there on the bus, even though there was no harm in it. Or anyway that's half why I was nervous, and the other half was that her hand was real light on my leg and out of the corner of my eye I could see how her chest moved when she breathed, and after all I'm seventeen and normal most ways. So when I wished she'd move her hand, I only *half* wished she'd move it back to her own lap.

That was up till she smiles at me and says, "Mick, I want to help you."

It took me a second to realize she spoke my name. I didn't know many people in Roanoke, and she sure wasn't one of them. Maybe she was one of Mr. Kaiser's customers, I thought. But they hardly ever knew my name. I kind of thought, for a second, that maybe she had seen me working in the warehouse and asked Mr. Kaiser all about me or something. So I says, "Are you one of Mr. Kaiser's customers?"

"Mick Winger," she says. "You got your first name from a note pinned to your blanket when you were left at the door of the sewage plant in Eden. You chose your last name when you ran away from the Eden Baptist Children's Home, and you probably chose it because the first movie you ever saw was *An Officer and a Gentleman*. You were fifteen then, and now you're seventeen, and you've killed more people in your life than Al Capone."

I got nervous when she knew my whole name and how I got it, cause the only way she could know that stuff was if she'd been following me for years. But when she let on she knew I killed people, I forgot all about feeling mad or guilty or horny. I pulled the cord on the bus, practically crawled over her to get out, and in about three seconds I was off that bus and hit the ground running. I'd been afraid of it for years, somebody finding out about me. But it was all the more scary seeing how she must have known about me for so *long*. It made me feel like somebody'd been peeking in the bathroom window all my life and I only just now found out about it.

I ran for a long time, which isn't easy because of all the hills in Roanoke. I ran mostly downhill, though, into town, where I could dodge into buildings and out their back doors. I didn't know if she was following me, but she'd been following me for a long time, or someone had, and I never even guessed it, so how did I know if they was following me now or not?

And while I ran, I tried to figure where I could go now. I had to leave town, that was sure. I couldn't go back to the warehouse, not even to say good-bye, and that made me feel real bad, cause Mr. Kaiser would think I just run off for no reason, like some kid who didn't care nothing about people counting on him. He might even worry about me, never coming to pick up my spare clothes from the room he let me sleep in.

Thinking about what Mr. Kaiser might think about me

going was pretty strange. Leaving Roanoke wasn't going to be like leaving the orphanage, and then leaving Eden, and finally leaving North Carolina. I never had much to let go of in those places. But Mr. Kaiser had always been real straight with me, a nice steady old guy, never bossed me, never tried to take me down, even stuck up for me in a quiet kind of way by letting it be known that he didn't want nobody teasing me. Hired me a year and a half ago, even though I was lying about being sixteen and he must've known it. And in all that time, I never once got mad at work, or at least not so mad I couldn't stop myself from hurting people. I worked hard, built up muscles I never thought I'd have, and I also must've grown five inches, my pants kept getting so short. I sweated and I ached most days after work, but I earned my pay and kept up with the older guys, and Mr. Kaiser never once made me feel like he took me on for charity, the way the orphanage people always did, like I should thank them for not letting me starve. Kaiser's Furniture Warehouse was the first peaceful place I ever spent time, the first place where nobody died who was my fault.

I knew all that before, but right till I started running I never realized how bad I'd feel about leaving Roanoke. Like somebody dying. It got so bad that for a while I couldn't hardly see which way I was going, not that I out and out cried or nothing.

Pretty soon I found myself walking down Jefferson Street, where it cuts through a woody hill before it widens out for car dealers and Burger Kings. There was cars passing me both ways, but I was thinking about other things now. Trying to figure why I never got mad at Mr. Kaiser. Other people treated me nice before, it wasn't like I got beat up every night or nobody ever gave me seconds or I had to eat dogfood or nothing. I remembered all those people at the orphanage, they was just trying to make me grow up Christian and educated. They just never learned how to be nice without also being nasty. Like Old Peleg, the black caretaker, he was a nice old coot and told us stories, and I never let nobody call him nigger even behind his back. But he was a racist himself, and I knew it on account of the time he caught me and Jody Capel practicing who could stop pissing the most times in a single go. We both done the same thing didn't we? But he just sent me off and then started whaling on Jody, and Jody was yelling like he was dying, and I kept saying, "It ain't fair! I done it too! You're only beating on him cause he's black!" but he paid no mind, it was so crazy, I mean it wasn't like I wanted him to beat me too, but it made me so *mad* and before I knew it, I felt so sparky that I couldn't hold it in and I was hanging on him, trying to pull him away from Jody, so it hit him hard.

What could I say to him then? Going into the hospital, where he'd lie there with a tube in his arm and a tube in his nose sometimes. He told me stories when he could talk, and just squoze my hand when he couldn't. He used to have a belly on him, but I think I could have tossed him in the air like a baby before he died. And I did it to him, not that I meant to, I couldn't help myself, but that's the way it was. Even people I purely loved, they'd have mean days, and God help them if I happened to be there, because I was like God with a bad mood, that's what I was, God with no mercy, because I couldn't give them nothing, but I sure as hell could take away. Take it all away. They told me I shouldn't visit Old Peleg so much cause it was sick to keep going to watch him waste away. Mrs. Howard and Mr. Dennis both got tumors from trying to get me to stop going. So many people was dying of cancer in those days they came from the county and tested the water for chemicals. It wasn't no chemicals, I knew that, but I never did tell them, cause they'd just lock me up in the crazy house and you can bet that crazy house would have a *epidemic* before I been there a week if that ever happened.

Truth was I didn't know, I just didn't know it was me doing it for the longest time. It's just people kept dying on me, everybody I ever loved, and it seemed like they always took sick after I'd been real mad at them once,

and you know how little kids always feel guilty about
yelling at somebody who dies right after. The counselor
even told me that those feelings were perfectly natural,
and of course it wasn't my fault, but I couldn't shake it.
And finally I began to realize that other people didn't
feel that sparky feeling like I did, and they couldn't tell
how folks was feeling unless they looked or asked. I
mean, I knew when my lady teachers was going to be on
the rag before *they* did, and you can bet I stayed away
from them the best I could on those crabby days. I could
feel it, like they was giving off sparks. And there was
other folks who had a way of sucking you to them, without saying a thing, without doing a thing, you just went
into a room and couldn't take your eyes off them, you
wanted to be close—I saw that other kids felt the same
way, just automatically liked them, you know? But I
could feel it like they was on fire, and suddenly I was
cold and needed to warm myself. And I'd say something
about it and people would look at me like I was crazy
enough to lock right up, and I finally caught on that I
was the only one that had those feelings.

Once I knew that, then all those deaths began to fit
together. All those cancers, those days they lay in hospital
beds turning into mummies before they was rightly dead,
all the pain until they drugged them into zombies so they
wouldn't tear their own guts out just trying to get to the
place that hurt so bad. Torn up, cut up, drugged up,
radiated, bald, skinny, praying for death, and I knew I
did it. I began to tell the minute I did it. I began to
know what kind of cancer it would be, and where, and
how bad. And I was always right.

Twenty-five people I knew of, and probably more I
didn't.

And it got even worse when I ran away. I'd hitch rides
because how else was I going to get anywheres? But I
was always scared of the people who picked me up, and
if they got weird or anything I sparked them. And cops
who run me out of a place, they got it. Until I figured I
was just Death himself, with his bent-up spear and a

hood over his head, walking around and whoever came near him bought the farm. That was me. I was the most terrible thing in the world, I was families broke up and children orphaned and mamas crying for their dead babies, I was everything that people hate most in all the world. I jumped off a overpass once to kill myself but I just sprained my ankle. Old Peleg always said I was like a cat, I wouldn't die lessen somebody skinned me, roasted the meat and ate it, then tanned the hide, made it into slippers, wore them slippers clean out, and then burned them and raked the ashes, that's when I'd finally die. And I figure he's right, cause I'm still alive and that's a plain miracle after the stuff I been through lately.

Anyway that's the kind of thing I was thinking, walking along Jefferson, when I noticed that a car had driven by going the other way and saw me and turned around and came back up behind me, pulled ahead of me and stopped. I was so spooked I thought it must be that lady finding me again, or maybe somebody with guns to shoot me all up like on "Miami Vice," and I was all set to take off up the hill till I saw it was just Mr. Kaiser.

He says, "I was heading the other way, Mick. Want a ride to work?"

I couldn't tell him what I was doing. "Not today, Mr. Kaiser," I says.

Well, he knew by my look or something, cause he says, "You quitting on me, Mick?"

I was just thinking, don't argue with me or nothing, Mr. Kaiser, just let me go, I don't want to hurt you, I'm so fired up with guilt and hating myself that I'm just death waiting to bust out and blast somebody, can't you see sparks falling off me like spray off a wet dog? I just says, "Mr. Kaiser, I don't want to talk right now, I really don't."

Right then was the moment for him to push. For him to lecture me about how I had to learn responsibility, and if I didn't talk things through how could anybody ever make things right, and life ain't a free ride so sometimes you got to do things you don't want to do, and I been nicer to you than you deserve, you're just what they warned me you'd be, shiftless and ungrateful and a bum in your soul.

But he didn't say none of that. He just says, "You had some bad luck? I can advance you against wages, I know you'll pay back."

"I don't owe no money," I says.

And he says, "Whatever you're running away from, come home with me and you'll be safe."

What could I say? You're the one who needs protecting, Mr. Kaiser, and I'm the one who'll probably kill you. So I didn't say nothing, until finally he just nodded and put his hand on my shoulder and said, "That's okay, Mick. If you ever need a place or a job, you just come on back to me. You find a place to settle down for a while, you write to me and I'll send you your stuff."

"You just give it to the next guy," I says.

"A son-of-a-bitch stinking mean old Jew like me?" he says. "I don't give nothing to nobody."

Well I couldn't help but laugh, cause that's what the foreman always called Mr. Kaiser whenever he thought the old guy couldn't hear him. And when I laughed, I felt myself cool off, just like as if I had been on fire and somebody poured cold water over my head.

"Take care of yourself, Mick," he says. He give me his card and a twenty and tucked it into my pocket when I told him no. Then he got back into his car and made one of his insane U-turns right across traffic and headed back the other way.

Well if he did nothing else he got my brain back in gear. There I was walking along the highway where anybody at all could see me, just like Mr. Kaiser did. At least till I was out of town I ought to stay out of sight as much as I could. So there I was between those two hills, pretty steep, and all covered with green, and I figured I could climb either one. But the slope on the other side of the road looked somehow better to me, it looked more like I just ought to go there, and I figured that was as good a reason to decide as any I ever heard of, and so I dodged my way across Jefferson Street and went right into the kudzu caves and clawed my way right up. It was dark under the leaves, but it wasn't much cooler than right out in the sun, particularly cause I was working so hard. It was a long way up, and just when I got to the top the ground started shaking. I thought it was an earthquake I was so edgy, till I heard the train whistle and then I knew it was one of those coal-hauling trains, so heavy it could shake ivy off a wall when it passed. I just stood there and listened to it, the sound coming from every direction all at once, there under the kudzu. I listened till it went on by, and then I stepped out of the leaves into a clearing.

And there she was, waiting for me, sitting under a tree.

I was too wore out to run, and too scared, coming on her sudden like that, just when I thought I was out of sight. It was just as if I'd been aiming straight at her, all the way up the hill, just as if she somehow tied a string to me and pulled me across the street and up the hill. And if she could do that, how could I run away from her, tell me that? Where could I go? I'd just turn some corner and there she'd be, waiting. So I says to her, "All right, what do you want?"

She just waved me on over. And I went, too, but not very close, cause I didn't know what she had in mind. "Sit down, Mick," says she. "We need to talk."

Now I'll tell you that I didn't want to sit, and I didn't want to talk, I just wanted to get out of there. And so I did, or at least I thought I did. I started walking straight away from her, I thought, but in three steps I realized that I wasn't walking away, I was walking around her. Like that planet thing in science class, the more I moved, the more I got nowhere. It was like she had more say over what my legs did than me.

So I sat down.

"You shouldn't have run off from me," she says.

What I mostly thought of now was to wonder if she was wearing anything under that shirt. And then I thought, what a stupid time to be thinking about that. But I still kept thinking about it.

"Do you promise to stay right there till I'm through talking?" she says.

When she moved, it was like her clothes got almost transparent for a second, but not quite. Couldn't take my eyes off her. I promised.

And then all of a sudden she was just a woman. Not ugly, but not all that pretty, neither. Just looking at me with eyes like fire. I was scared again, and I wanted to leave, especially cause now I began to think she really was doing something to me. But I promised, so I stayed.

"That's how it began," she says.

"What's how what began?" says I.

"What you just felt. What I made you feel. That only works on people like you. Nobody else can feel it."

"Feel what?" says I. Now, I knew what she meant, but I didn't know for sure if she meant what I knew. I mean, it bothered me real bad that she could tell how I felt about her those few minutes there.

"Feel that," she says, and there it is again, all I can think about is her body. But it only lasted a few seconds, and then I knew for sure that she was doing it to me.

"Stop it," I says, and she says, "I already did."

I ask her, "How do you do that?"

"Everybody can do it, just a little. A woman looks at a man, she's interested, and so the bio-electrical system heats up, causes some odors to change, and he smells them and notices her and he pays attention."

"Does it work the other way?"

"Men are always giving off those odors, Mick. Makes no difference. It isn't a man's stink that gives a woman her ideas. But like I said, Mick, that's what everybody can do. With some men, though, it isn't a woman's smell that draws his eye. It's the bio-electrical system itself. The smell is nothing. You can feel the heat of the fire. It's the same thing as when you kill people, Mick. If you couldn't kill people the way you do, you also couldn't feel it so strong when I give off magnetic pulses."

Of course I didn't understand all that the first time, and maybe I'm remembering it now with words she didn't teach me until later. At the time, though, I was scared, yes, because she knew, and because she could do things to me, but I was also excited, because she sounded like she had some answers, like she knew why it was that I killed people without meaning to.

But when I asked her to explain everything, she couldn't. "We're only just beginning to understand it ourselves, Mick. There's a Swedish scientist who is making some strides that way. We've sent some people over to meet with him. We've read his book, and maybe even some of us understand it. I've got to tell you, Mick, just because we can do this thing doesn't mean that we're particularly smart or anything. It doesn't get us through college any faster or anything. It just means that teachers who flunk us tend to die off a little younger."

"You're like me! You can do it too!"

She shook her head. "Not likely," she says. "If I'm really furious at somebody, if I really hate him, if I really *try*, and if I keep it up for weeks, I can maybe give him an ulcer. You're in a whole different league from me. You and your people."

"I got no people," I says.

"I'm here, Mick, because you got people. People who knew just exactly what you could do from the minute you were born. People who knew that if you didn't get a tit to suck you wouldn't just cry, you'd kill. Spraying out death from your cradle. So they planned it all from the beginning. Put you in an orphanage. Let other people, all those do-gooders, let them get sick and die, and then when you're old enough to have control over it, then they look you up, they tell you who you are, they bring you home to live with them."

"So you're my kin?" I ask her.

"Not so you'd notice," she says. "I'm here to warn you about your kin. We've been watching you for years, and now it's time to warn you."

"*Now* it's time? I spent fifteen years in that children's

home killing everybody who ever cared about me, and if they'd just come along—or you, or anybody, if you just said, Mick, you got to control your temper or you'll hurt people, if somebody just said to me, Mick, we're your people and we'll keep you safe, then maybe I wouldn't be so scared all the time, maybe I wouldn't go killing people so much, did you ever think of that?" Or maybe I didn't say all that, but that's what I was feeling, and so I said a lot, I chewed her up and down.

And then I saw how scared she was, because I was all sparky, and I realized I was just about to shed a load of death onto her, and so I kind of jumped back and yelled at her to leave me alone, and then she does the craziest thing, she reaches out toward me, and I scream at her, "Don't you touch me!" cause if she touches me I can't hold it in, it'll just go all through her and tear up her guts inside, but she just keeps reaching, leaning toward me, and so I kind of crawled over toward a tree, and I hung onto that tree, I just held on and let the tree kind of soak up all my sparkiness, almost like I was burning up the tree. Maybe I killed it, for all I know. Or maybe it was so big, I couldn't hurt it, but it took all the fire out of me, and then she *did* touch me, like nobody ever touched me, her arm across my back, and hand holding my shoulder, her face right up against my ear, and she says to me, "Mick, you didn't hurt me."

"Just leave me alone," says I.

"You're not like them," she says. "Don't you see that? They love the killing. They *use* the killing. Only they're not as strong as you. They have to be touching, for one thing, or close to it. They have to keep it up longer. They're stronger than *I* am, but not as strong as you. So they'll want you, that's for sure, Mick, but they'll also be scared of you, and you know what'll scare them most? That you didn't kill me, that you can *control* it like that."

"I can't always. That bus driver today."

"So you're not perfect. But you're trying. Trying not to kill people. Don't you see, Mick? You're not like them.

They may be your blood family, but you don't belong with them, and they'll see that, and when they do—"

All I could think about was what she said, my blood family. "My Mama and Daddy, you telling me I'm going to meet them?"

"They're calling you now, and that's why I had to warn you."

"Calling me?"

"The way I called you up this hill. Only it wasn't just me, of course, it was a bunch of us."

"I just decided to come up here, to get off the road."

"You just decided to cross the highway and climb this hill, instead of the other one? Anyway, that's how it works. It's part of the human race for all time, only we never knew it. A bunch of people kind of harmonize their bio-electrical systems, to call for somebody to come home, and they come home, after a while. Or sometimes a whole nation unites to hate somebody. Like Iran and the Shah, or the Philippines and Marcos."

"They just kicked them out," I says.

"But they were already dying, weren't they? A whole nation, hating together, they make a constant interference with their enemy's bio-electrical system. A constant noise. All of them together, millions of people, they are finally able to match what you can do with one flash of anger."

I thought about that for a few minutes, and it came back to me all the times I thought how I wasn't even human. So maybe I *was* human, after all, but human like a guy with three arms is human, or one of those guys in the horror movies I saw, gigantic and lumpy and going around hacking up teenagers whenever they was about to get laid. And in all those movies they always try to kill the guy only they can't, he gets stabbed and shot and burned up and he still comes back, and that's like me, I must have tried to kill myself so many times only it never worked.

No. Wait a minute.

I got to get this straight, or you'll think I'm crazy or a

liar. I didn't jump off that highway overpass like I said. I stood on one for a long time, watching the cars go by. Whenever a big old semi came along I'd say, this one, and I'd count, and at the right second I'd say, now. Only I never did jump. And then afterward I dreamed about jumping, and in all those dreams I'd just bounce off the truck and get up and limp away. Like the time I was a kid and sat in the bathroom with the little gardening shears, the spring-loaded kind that popped open, I sat there thinking about jamming it into my stomach right under the breastbone, and then letting go of the handle, it'd pop right open and make a bad wound and cut open my heart or something. I was there so long I fell asleep on the toilet, and later I dreamed about doing it but no blood ever came out, because I couldn't die.

So I never tried to kill myself. But I thought about it all the time. I was like those monsters in those movies, just killing people but secretly hoping somebody would catch on to what was going on and kill me first.

And so I says to her, "Why didn't you just kill me?"

And there she was with her face close to mine and she says, just like it was love talk, she says, "I've had you in my rifle sights, Mick, and then I didn't do it. Because I saw something in you. I saw that maybe you were trying to control it. That maybe you didn't want to use your power to kill. And so I let you live, thinking that one day I'd be here like this, telling you what you are, and giving you a little hope."

I thought she meant I'd hope because of knowing my Mama and Daddy were alive and wanted me.

"I hoped for a long time, but I gave it up. I don't want to see my Mama and Daddy, if they could leave me there all those years. I don't want to see you, neither, if you didn't so much as warn me not to get mad at Old Peleg. I didn't want to kill Old Peleg, and I couldn't even help it! You didn't help me a bit!"

"We argued about it," she says. "We knew you were killing people while you tried to sort things out and get control. Puberty's the worst time, even worse than in-

fancy, and we knew that if we didn't kill you a lot of
people would die—and mostly they'd be the people you
loved best. That's the way it is for most kids your age,
they get angriest at the people they love most, only you
couldn't help killing them, and what does that do to your
mind? What kind of person do you become? There was
some who said we didn't have the right to leave you alive
even to study you, because it would be like having a cure
for cancer and then not using it on people just to see
how fast they'd die. Like that experiment where the government left syphilis cases untreated just to see what the
final stages of the disease were like, even though they
could have cured those people at any time. But some of
us told them, Mick isn't a disease, and a bullet isn't
penicillin. I told them, Mick is something special. And
they said, yes, he's special, he kills more than any of
those other kids, and we shot *them* or ran them over
with a truck or drowned them, and here we've got the
worst one of all and you want to keep him alive."

And I was crying cause I wished they *had* killed me,
but also because it was the first time I ever thought there
was people arguing that I ought to be alive, and even
though I didn't rightly understand then or even now why
you didn't kill me, I got to tell you that knowing somebody knew what I was and still chose not to blast my
head off, that done me in, I just bawled like a baby.

One thing led to another, there, my crying and her
holding me, and pretty soon I figured out that she pretty
much wanted to get laid right there. But that just made
me sick, when I knew that. "How can you want to do
that!" I says to her. "I can't get married! I can't have no
kids! They'd be like me!"

She didn't argue with me or say nothing about birth
control, and so I figured out later that I was right, she
wanted to have a baby, and that told me plain that she
was crazy as a loon. I got my pants pulled back up and
my shirt on, and I wouldn't look at her getting dressed
again, neither.

"I could make you do it," she says to me. "I could do

that to you. The ability you have that lets you kill also makes you sensitive. I can make you lose your mind with desire for me."

"Then why don't you?" I says.

"Why don't you kill if you can help it?" she says.

"Cause nobody has the right," says I.

"That's right," she says.

"Anyway you're ten years older than me," I tell her.

"Fifteen," she says. "Almost twice your age. But that don't mean nothing." Or I guess she actually said, "That *doesn't* mean nothing," or probably, "that doesn't mean *anything*." She talks better than I do but I can't always remember the fancy way. "That doesn't mean a thing," she says. "You'll go to your folks, and you can bet they'll have some pretty little girl waiting for you, and she'll know how to do it much better than me, she'll turn you on so your pants unzip themselves, cause that's what they want most from you. They want your babies. As many as they can get, because you're the strongest they've produced in all the years since Grandpa Jake realized that the cursing power went father to son, mother to daughter, and that he could breed for it like you breed dogs or horses. They'll breed you like a stud, but then when they find out that you don't like killing people and you don't want to play along and you aren't going to take orders from whoever's in charge there now, they'll kill you. That's why I came to warn you. We could feel them just starting to call you. We knew it was time. And I came to warn you."

Most of this didn't mean much to me yet. Just the idea of having kinfolk was still so new I couldn't exactly get worried about whether they'd kill me or put me out for stud or whatever. Mostly what I thought about was her, anyway. "I might have killed you, you know."

"Maybe I didn't care," she says. "And maybe I'm not so easy to kill."

"And maybe you ought to tell me your name," says I.

"Can't," she says.

"How come?" says I.

"Because if you decide to put in with them, and you know my name, then I *am* dead."

"I wouldn't let anybody hurt you," says I.

She didn't answer that. She just says to me, "Mick, you don't know my name, but you remember this. I have hopes for you, cause I know you're a good man and you never meant to kill nobody. I could've made you love me, and I didn't, because I want you to do what you do by your own choice. And most important of all, if you come with me, we have a chance to see if maybe your ability doesn't have a good side."

You think I hadn't thought of that before? When I saw Rambo shooting down all those little brown guys, I thought, I could do that, and without no gun, either. And if somebody took me hostage like the Achille Lauro thing, we wouldn't have to worry about the terrorists going unpunished. They'd all be rotting in a hospital in no time. "Are you with the government?" I ask her.

"No," she says.

So they didn't want me to be a soldier. I was kind of disappointed. I kind of thought I might be useful that way. But I couldn't volunteer or nothing, cause you don't walk into the recruiting office and say, I've killed a couple dozen people by giving sparks off my body, and I could do it to Castro and Qaddafi if you like. Cause if they believe you, then you're a murderer, and if they don't believe you, they lock you up in a nuthouse.

"Nobody's been calling me, anyway," I says. "If I didn't see you today, I wouldn't've gone nowhere. I would've stayed with Mr. Kaiser."

"Then why did you take all your money out of the bank?" she says. "And when you ran away from me, why did you run toward the highway where you can hitch a ride at least to Madison and then catch another on in to Eden?"

And I didn't have no answer for her then, cause I didn't know rightly why I took my money out of the bank lessen it was like she said, and I was planning to leave town. It was just an impulse, to close that account, I didn't think nothing of it, just stuffed three hundreds into my wallet and come to think of it I really was heading toward Eden, I just didn't *think* of it, I was just *doing* it. Just the way I climbed up that hill.

"They're stronger than we are," she says. "So we can't hold you here. You have to go anyway, you have to work this thing out. The most we could do was just get you on the bus next to me, and then call you up this hill."

"Then why don't you come with me?" I says.

"They'd kill me in two seconds, right in front of your eyes, and none of this cursing stuff, either, Mick. They'd just take my head off with a machete."

"Do they know you?"

"They know *us*," she says. "We're the only ones that know your people exist, so we're the only ones working to stop them. I won't lie to you, Mick. If you join them, you can find us, you'll learn how, it isn't hard, and you can do this stuff from farther away, you could really take us apart. But if you join *us*, the tables are turned."

"Well maybe I don't want to be on either side in this war," I says. "And maybe now I won't go to Eden, neither. Maybe I'll go up to Washington D.C. and join the CIA."

"Maybe," she says.

"And don't try to stop me."

"I wouldn't try," she says.

"Damn straight," I says. And then I just walked on out, and this time I didn't walk in no circles, I just headed north, past her car, down the railroad right of way. And I caught a ride heading up toward D.C., and that was that.

Except that along about six o'clock in the evening I woke up and the car was stopping and I didn't know where I was, I must have slept all day, and the guy says to me, "Here you are, Eden, North Carolina."

And I about messed my pants. "Eden!" I says.

"It wasn't far out of my way," he says. "I'm heading for Burlington, and these country roads are nicer than the freeway, anyway. Don't mind if I never drive I-85 again, to tell the truth."

But that was the very guy who told me he had business in D.C., he was heading there from Bristol, had to see somebody from a government agency, and here he was in Eden. It made no sense at all, except for what that woman told me. Somebody was calling me, and if I wouldn't come, they'd just put me to sleep and call whoever was driving. And there I was. Eden, North Carolina. Scared to death, or at least scared a little, but also thinking, if what she said was true, my folks was coming, I was going to meet my folks.

Nothing much changed in the two years since I ran off from the orphanage. Nothing much ever changes in Eden, which isn't a real town anyway, just cobbled together from three little villages that combined to save money on city services. People still mostly think of them as three villages. There wasn't nobody who'd get too excited about seeing me, and there wasn't nobody I wanted to see. Nobody living, anyway. I had no idea how my folks might find me, or how I might find them, but in the meantime I went to see about the only people I ever much cared about. Hoping that they wouldn't rise up out of the grave to get even with me for killing them.

It was still full day that time of year, but it was whippy weather, the wind gusting and then holding still, a big row of thunderclouds off to the southwest, the sun sinking down to get behind them. The kind of afternoon that promises to cool you off, which suited me fine. I was still pretty dusty from my climb up the hill that morning, and I could use a little rain. Got a coke at a fast food place and then walked on over to see Old Peleg.

He was buried in a little cemetery right by an old Baptist Church. Not Southern Baptist, *Black* Baptist, meaning that it didn't have no fancy building with classrooms and a rectory, just a stark-white block of a building with a little steeple and a lawn that looked like it'd been clipped by hand. Cemetery was just as neat-kept. Nobody around, and it was dim cause of the thunderclouds moving through, but I wasn't afraid of the graves there, I just went to Old Peleg's cross. Never knew his last name was Lindley. Didn't sound like a black man's name, but then when I thought about it I realized that *no* last name sounded like a black man's name, because Eden is still just old-fashioned enough that an old black man doesn't get called by his last name much. He grew up in a Jim Crow state, and never got around to insisting on being called Mr. Lindley. Old Peleg. Not that he ever hugged me or took me on long walks or gave me that tender loving care that makes people get all teary-eyed about how wonderful it is to have parents. He never tried to be my dad or nothing. And if I hung around him much, he always gave me work to do and made damn sure I did it right, and mostly we didn't talk about anything except the work we was doing, which made me wonder, standing there, why I wanted to cry and why I hated myself worse for killing Old Peleg than for any of the other dead people under the ground in that city.

I didn't see them and I didn't hear them coming and I didn't smell my mama's perfume. But I knew they was coming, because I felt the prickly air between us. I didn't turn around, but I knew just where they were, and just how far off, because they was *lively*. Shedding sparks like I never saw on any living soul except myself, just walking along giving off light. It was like seeing myself from the outside for the first time in my life. Even when she was making me get all hot for her, that lady in Roanoke wasn't as lively as them. They was just like me.

Funny thing was, that wrecked everything. I didn't want them to be like me. I *hated* my sparkiness, and there they were, showing it to me, making me see how a killer looks from the outside. It took a few seconds to realize that they was *scared* of me, too. I recognized how scaredness looks, from remembering how my own bio-electrical system got shaped and changed by fear. Course I didn't think of it as a bio-electrical system then, or maybe I did cause she'd already told me, but you know what I mean. They was afraid of me. And I knew that was because I was giving off all the sparks I shed when I feel so mad at myself that I could bust. I was standing there at Old Peleg's grave, hating myself, so naturally they saw me like I was ready to kill half a city. They didn't know that it was me I was hating. Naturally they figured I might be mad at *them* for leaving me at that orphanage seventeen years ago. Serve them right, too, if I gave them a good hard twist in the gut, but I don't do that, I honestly don't, not any more, not standing there by Old Peleg who I loved a lot more than these two strangers, I don't act out being a murderer when my shadow's falling across his grave.

So I calmed myself down as best I could and I turned around and there they was, my mama and my daddy. And I got to tell you I almost laughed. All those years I watched them TV preachers, and we used to laugh till our guts ached about how Tammy Bakker always wore makeup so thick she could be a nigger underneath (it was okay to say that cause Old Peleg himself said it first) and here was my mama, wearing just as much makeup and her hair sprayed so thick she could work construction without a hardhat. And smiling that same sticky phony smile, and crying the same gooey oozey black tears down her cheeks, and reaching out her hands just the right way so I halfway expected her to say, "Praise to Lord Jesus," and then she actually *says* it, "Praise to Lord Jesus, it's my boy," and comes up and lays a kiss on my cheek with so much spit in it that it dripped down my face.

I wiped the slobber with my sleeve and felt my daddy have this little flash of anger, and I knew that he thought I was judging my mama and he didn't like it. Well, I was, I got to admit. Her perfume was enough to knock me over, I swear she must've mugged an Avon lady. And there was my daddy in a fine blue suit like a business-man, his hair all blow-dried, so it was plain he knew just as well as I did the way real people are supposed to look. Probably he was plain embarrassed to be seen in public with Mama, so why didn't he ever just say, Mama, you wear too much makeup? That's what I thought, and it wasn't till later that I realized that when your woman is apt to give you cancer if you rile her up, you don't go telling her that her face looks like she slept in wet sawdust and she smells like a whore. White trash, that's what my mama was, sure as if she was still wearing the factory label.

"Sure am glad to see you, son," says my daddy.

I didn't know what to say, tell the truth. I *wasn't* glad to see them, now that I saw them, because they wasn't exactly what a orphan boy dreams his folks is like. So I kind of grinned and looked back down at Old Peleg's grave.

"You don't seem too surprised to see *us*," he says.

I could've told him right then about the lady in Roanoke, but I didn't. Just didn't feel right to tell him. So I says, "I felt like somebody was calling me back here. And you two are the only people I met who's as sparky as me. If you all say you're my folks, then I figure it must be so."

Mama giggled and she says to him, "Listen, Jesse, he calls it 'sparky.' "

"The word we use is 'dusty,' son," says Daddy. "We say a body's looking dusty when he's one of us."

"You were a very dusty baby," says Mama. "That's why we knew we couldn't keep you. Never seen such a dusty baby before. Papa Lem made us take you to the orphanage before you even sucked one time. You never sucked even once." And her mascara just flooded down her face.

"Now Deeny," says Daddy, "no need telling him everything right here."

Dusty. That was no sense at all. It didn't look like *dust*, it was flecks of light, so bright on me that sometimes I had to squint just to see my own hands through the dazzle. "It don't *look* like dust," I says.

And Daddy says, "Well what do *you* think it looks like?"

And I says, "Sparks. That's why I call it being sparky."

"Well that's what it looks like to us, too," says Daddy.

"But we've been calling it 'dusty' all our lives, and so I figure it's easier for one boy to change than for f—for lots of other folks."

Well, now, I learned a lot of things right then from what he said. First off, I knew he was lying when he said it looked like sparks to them. It didn't. It looked like what they called it. Dust. And that meant that I was seeing it a whole lot *brighter* than they could see it, and that was good for me to know, especially because it was plain that Daddy *didn't* want me to know it and so he pretended that he saw it the same way. He wanted me to think he was just as good at seeing as I was. Which meant that he sure wasn't. And I also learned that he didn't want me to know how many kinfolk I had, cause he started to say a number that started with F, and then caught himself and didn't say it. Fifty? Five hundred? The number wasn't half so important as the fact that he didn't want me to know it. They didn't trust me. Well, why should they? Like the lady said, I was better at this than they were, and they didn't know how mad I was about being abandoned, and the last thing they wanted to do was turn me loose killing folks. Especially themselves.

Well I stood there thinking about that stuff and pretty soon it makes them nervous and Mama says, "Now, Daddy, he can call it whatever he wants, don't go making him mad or something."

And Daddy laughs and says, "He isn't mad, are you, son?"

Can't they see for themselves? Course not. Looks like *dust* to them, so they can't see it clear at all.

"You don't seem too happy to see us," says Daddy.

"Now, Jesse," says Mama, "don't go pushing. Papa Lem said don't you push the boy, you just make his acquaintance, you let him know why we had to push him out of the nest so young, so now you explain it, Daddy, just like Papa Lem said to."

For the first time right then it occurred to me that my own folks didn't *want* to come fetch me. They came because this Papa Lem made them do it. And you can bet they hopped and said yes, knowing how Papa Lem used his—but I'll get to Papa Lem in good time, and you said I ought to take this all in order, which I'm mostly trying to do.

Anyway Daddy explained it just like the lady in Roanoke, except he didn't say a word about bio-electrical systems, he said that I was "plainly chosen" from the moment of my birth, that I was "one of the elect," which I remembered from Baptist Sunday School meant that I was one that God had saved, though I never heard of anybody who was saved the minute they was born and not even baptized or nothing. They saw how dusty I was and they knew I'd kill a lot of people before I got old enough to control it. I asked them if they did it a lot, putting a baby out to be raised by strangers.

"Oh, maybe a dozen times," says Daddy.

"And it always works out okay?" says I.

He got set to lie again, I could see it by ripples in the light, I didn't know lying could be so plain, which made me glad they saw dust instead of sparks. "Most times," he says.

"I'd like to meet one of them others," says I. "I figure we got a lot in common, growing up thinking our parents hated us, when the truth was they was scared of their own baby."

"Well they're mostly grown up and gone off," he says, but it's a lie, and most important of all was the fact that here I as much as said I thought they wasn't worth horse pucky as parents and the only thing Daddy can think of to say is why I can't see none of the other "orphans," which tells me that whatever he's lying to cover up must be real important.

But I didn't push him right then, I just looked back down at Old Peleg's grave and wondered if he ever told a lie in his life.

Daddy says, "I'm not surprised to find you here." I guess he was nervous, and had to change the subject. "He's one you dusted, isn't he?"

Dusted. That word made me so mad. What I done to

Old Peleg wasn't *dusting*. And being mad must have changed me enough they could see the change. But they didn't know what it meant, cause Mama says to me, "Now, son, I don't mean to criticize, but it isn't right to take pride in the gifts of God. That's why we came to find you, because we need to teach you why God chose you to be one of the elect, and you shouldn't glory in yourself because you could strike down your enemies. Rather you should give all glory to the Lord, praise his name, because we are his servants."

I like to puked, I was so mad at that. Glory! Old Peleg, who was worth ten times these two phony white people who tossed me out before I ever sucked tit, and they thought I should give the *glory* for his terrible agony and death to *God*? I didn't know God all that well, mostly because I thought of him as looking as pinched up and serious as Mrs. Bethel who taught Sunday School when I was little, until she died of leukemia, and I just never had a thing to say to God. But if God gave me that power to strike down Old Peleg, and God wanted the glory for it when I was done, then I *did* have a few words to say to God. Only I didn't believe it for a minute. Old Peleg believed in God, and the God he believed in didn't go striking an old black man dead because a dumb kid got pissed off at him.

But I'm getting off track in the story, because that was when my father touched me for the first time. His hand was shaking. And it had every right to shake, because I was so mad that a year ago he would've been bleeding from the colon before he took his hand away. But I'd got so I could keep from killing whoever touched me when I was mad, and the funny thing was that his hand *shaking* kind of changed how I felt anyway. I'd been thinking about how mad I was that they left me and how mad I was that they thought I'd be proud of killing people but now I realized how brave they was to come fetch me, cause how did they know I wouldn't kill them? But they came anyway. And that's something. Even if Papa Lem told them to do it, they came, and now I realized that it was real brave for Mama to come kiss me on the cheek right then, because if I was going to kill her, she touched me and gave me a chance to do it before she even tried to explain anything. Maybe it was her strategy to win me over or something, but it was still brave. And she also didn't approve of people being proud of murder, which was more points in her favor. And she had the guts to tell me so right to my face. So I chalked up some points for Mama. She might look like as sickening as Tammy Bakker, but she faced her killer son with more guts than Daddy had.

He touched my shoulder and they led me to their car. A Lincoln Town Car, which they probably thought would impress me, but all I thought about was what it would've been like at the Children's Home if we'd had the price of that car, even fifteen years ago. Maybe a paved basketball court. Maybe some decent toys that wasn't broken-up hand-me-downs. Maybe some pants with knees in them. I never felt so poor in my life as when I slid onto that fuzzy seat and heard the stereo start playing elevator music in my ear.

There was somebody else in the car. Which made sense. If I'd killed them or something, they'd need somebody else to drive the car home, right? He wasn't much, when it came to being dusty or sparky or whatever. Just a little, and in rhythms of fear, too. And I could see *why* he was scared, cause he was holding a blindfold in his hands, and he says, "Mr. Yow, I'm afraid I got to put this on you."

Well, I didn't answer for a second, which made him more scared cause he thought I was mad, but mostly it took me that long to realize he meant *me* when he said "Mr. Yow."

"That's our name, son," says my daddy. "I'm Jesse Yow, and your mother is Minnie Rae Yow, and that makes you Mick Yow."

"Don't it figure," says I. I was joking, but they took it wrong, like as if I was making fun of their name. But I been Mick Winger so long that it just feels silly calling myself Yow, and the fact is it *is* a funny name. They said it like I should be proud of it, though, which makes me laugh, but to them it was the name of God's Chosen People, like the way the Jews called themselves Israelites in the Bible. I didn't know that then, but that's the way they said it, real proud. And they was ticked off when I made a joke, so I helped them feel better by letting Billy put on—Billy's the name of the man in the car—put on the blindfold.

It was a lot of country roads, and a lot of country talk. About kinfolk I never met, and how I'd love this person and that person, which sounded increasingly unlikely to me, if you know what I mean. A long-lost child is coming home and you put a *blindfold* on him. I knew we were going mostly east, cause of the times I could feel the sun coming in my window and on the back of my neck, but that was about it, and that wasn't much. They lied to me, they wouldn't show me nothing, they was scared of me. I mean, any way you look at it, they wasn't exactly killing the fatted calf for the prodigal son. I was definitely on probation. Or maybe even on trial. Which, I might point out, is exactly the way you been treating me, too, and I don't like it much better now than I did then, if you don't mind me putting some personal complaints into this. I mean, somewhere along the line somebody's going to have to decide whether to shoot me or let me go, because I can't control my temper forever locked up like a rat in a box, and the difference is a rat can't reach out of the box and blast you the way I can, so somewhere along the way somebody's going to have to figure out that you better either trust me or kill me. My personal preference is for trusting me, since I've given you more reason to trust me than you've given me to trust *you* so far.

But anyway I rode along in the car for more than an hour. We could have gotten to Winston or Greensboro or Danville by then, it was so long, and by the time we got there nobody was talking and from the snoring, Billy was even asleep. I wasn't asleep, though. I was watching.

Cause I don't see sparks with my eyes, I see it with
something else, like as if my sparks see other folks'
sparks, if you catch my drift, and so that blindfold
might've kept me from seeing the road, but it sure didn't
keep me from seeing the other folks in the car with me.
I knew right where they were, and right what they were
feeling. Now, I've always had a knack for telling things
about people, even when I couldn't see nary a spark or
nothing, but this was the first time I ever saw anybody
who was sparky besides me. So I sat there watching how
Mama and Daddy acted with each other even when they
wasn't touching or saying a thing, just little drifts of anger
or fear or—well, I looked for love, but I didn't see it,
and I know what it looks like, cause I've felt it. They
were like two armies camped on opposite hills, waiting
for the truce to end at dawn. Careful. Sending out little
scouting parties.

Then the more I got used to understanding what my
folks was thinking and feeling, toward each other, the
easier it got for me to read what Billy had going on inside
him. It's like after you learn to read big letters, you can
read little letters, too, and I wondered if maybe I could
even learn to understand people who didn't have hardly
any sparks at all. I mean that occurred to me, anyway,
and since then I've found out that it's mostly true. Now
that I've had some practice I can read a sparky person
from a long ways off, and even regular folks I can do a
little reading, even through walls and windows. But I
found that out later. Like when you guys have been
watching me through mirrors. I can also see your microphone wires in the walls.

Anyway it was during that car ride that I first started
seeing what I could see with my eyes closed, the shape
of people's bio-electrical system, the color and spin of it,
the speed and the flow and the rhythm and whatever, I
mean those are the words I use, cause there isn't exactly
a lot of books I can read on the subject. Maybe that
Swedish doctor has fancy words for it. I can only tell you
how it feels to me. And in that hour I got to be good

enough at it that I could tell Billy was scared, all right,
but he *wasn't* all that scared of me, he was mostly scared
of Mama and Daddy. Me he was jealous of, angry kind
of. Scared a little, too, but mostly mad. I thought maybe
he was mad cause I was coming in out of nowhere
already sparkier than him, but then it occurred to me
that he probably couldn't even tell how sparky I was,
because to him it'd look like dust, and he wouldn't have
enough of a knack at it to see much distinction between
one person and another. It's like the more light you give
off, the clearer you can see other people's light. So I was
the one with the blindfold on, but I could see clearer
than anybody else in that car.

We drove on gravel for about ten minutes, and then
on a bumpy dirt road, and then suddenly on asphalt again,
smooth as you please, for about a hundred yards, and
then we stopped. I didn't wait for a by-your-leave, I had
that blindfold off in half a second.

It was like a whole town of houses, but right among
the trees, not a gap in the leaves overhead. Maybe fifty,
sixty houses, some of them pretty big, but the trees made
them half invisible, it being summer. Children running
all over, scruffy dirty kids from diapered-up snot-nose
brats to most-growed kids not all that much younger than
me. They sure kept us cleaner in the Children's Home.
And they was all sparky. Mostly like Billy, just a little,
but it explained why they wasn't much washed. There
isn't many a mama who'd stuff her kid in a tub if the
kid can make her sick just by getting mad.

It must've been near eight-thirty at night, and even
the little kids still wasn't in bed. They must let their kids
play till they get wore out and drop down and fall asleep
by themselves. It came to me that maybe I wasn't so bad
off growing up in an orphanage. At least I knew manners
and didn't whip it out and pee right in front of company,
the way one little boy did, just looking at me while I got
out of the car, whizzing away like he wasn't doing nothing
strange. Like a dog marking trees. He needed to so he

done it. If I ever did that at the Children's Home they'd've slapped me silly.

I know how to act with strangers when I'm hitching a ride, but not when I'm being company, cause orphans don't go calling much so I never had much experience. So I'd've been shy no matter what, even if there wasn't no such thing as sparkiness. Daddy was all set to take me to meet Papa Lem right off, but Mama saw how I wasn't cleaned up and maybe she guessed I hadn't been to the toilet in a while and so she hustled me into a house where they had a good shower and when I came out she had a cold ham sandwich waiting for me on the table. On a plate, and the plate was setting on a linen place mat, and there was a tall glass of milk there, so cold it was sweating on the outside of the glass. I mean, if an orphan kid ever dreamed of what it might be like to have a Mama, that was the dream. Never mind that she didn't look like a model in the Sears Catalog. I felt clean, the sandwich tasted good, and when I was done eating she even offered me a cookie.

It felt good, I'll admit that, but at the same time I felt cheated. It was just too damn late. I needed it to be like this when I was seven, not seventeen.

But she was trying, and it wasn't all her fault, so I ate the cookie and drank off the last of the milk and my watch said it was after nine. Outside it was dusk now, and most of the kids were finally gone off to bed, and Daddy comes in and says, "Papa Lem says he isn't getting any younger."

He was outside, in a big rocking chair sitting on the grass. You wouldn't call him fat, but he did have a belly on him. And you wouldn't call him old, but he was bald on top and his hair was wispy yellow and white. And you wouldn't call him ugly, but he had a soft mouth and I didn't like the way it twisted up when he talked.

Oh, hell, he was fat, old, and ugly, and I hated him from the first time I saw him. A squishy kind of guy. Not even as sparky as my daddy, neither, so you didn't get to be in charge around here just by having more of what-

ever it was made us different. I wondered how close kin
he was to me. If he's got children, and they look like
him, they ought to drown them out of mercy.

"Mick Yow," he says to me, "Mick my dear boy, Mick
my dear cousin."

"Good evening, sir," says I.

"Oh, and he's got manners," says he. "We were right
to donate so much to the Children's Home. They took
excellent care of you."

"You donated to the home?" says I. If they did, they
sure didn't give *much*.

"A little," he says. "Enough to pay for your food, your
room, your Christian education. But no luxuries. You
couldn't grow up soft, Mick. You had to grow up lean
and strong. And you had to know suffering, so you could
be compassionate. The Lord God has given you a marvel-
ous gift, a great helping of his grace, a heaping plateful
of the power of God, and we had to make sure you were
truly worthy to sit up to the table at the banquet of the
Lord."

I almost looked around to see if there was a camera,
he sounded so much like the preachers on TV.

And he says, "Mick, you have already passed the first
test. You have forgiven your parents for leaving you to
think you were an orphan. You have kept that holy com-
mandment, Honor thy father and mother, that thy days
may be long upon the land which the Lord thy God hath
given thee. You know that if you had raised a hand
against them, the Lord would have struck you down. For
verily I say unto you that there was two rifles pointed at
you the whole time, and if your father and mother had
walked away without you, you would have flopped down
dead in that nigger cemetery, for God will not be
mocked."

I couldn't tell if he was trying to provoke me or scare
me or what, but either way, it was working.

"The Lord has chosen you for his servant, Mick, just
like he's chosen all of us. The rest of the world doesn't
understand this. But Grandpa Jake saw it. Long ago, back

in 1820, he saw how everybody he hated had a way of dying without him lifting a finger. And for a time he thought that maybe he was like those old witches, who curse people and they wither up and die by the power of the devil. But he was a god-fearing man, and he had no truck with Satan. He was living in rough times, when a man was likely to kill in a quarrel, but Grandpa Jake never killed. Never even struck out with his fists. He was a peaceable man, and he kept his anger inside him, as the Lord commands in the New Testament. So surely he was not a servant of Satan!"

Papa Lem's voice rang through that little village, he was talking so loud, and I noticed there was a bunch of people all around. Not many kids now, all grownups, maybe there to hear Lem, but even more likely they was there to see me. Because it was like the lady in Roanoke said, there wasn't a one of them was half as sparky as me. I didn't know if they could all see that, but I could. Compared to normal folks they was all dusty enough, I suppose, but compared to me, or even to my mama and daddy, they was a pretty dim bunch.

"He studied the scriptures to find out what it meant that his enemies all suffered from tumors and bleeding and coughing and rot, and he came upon the verse of Genesis where the Lord said unto Abraham, 'I will bless them that bless thee, and curse him that curseth thee.' And he knew in his heart that the Lord had chosen him the way he chose Abraham. And when Isaac gave the blessing of God to Jacob, he said, 'Let people serve thee, and nations bow down to thee: cursed be every one that curseth thee, and blessed be he that blesseth thee.' The promises to the patriarchs were fulfilled again in Grandpa Jake, for whoever cursed him was cursed by God."

When he said those words from the Bible, Papa Lem sounded like the voice of God himself, I've got to tell you. I felt exalted, knowing that it was God who gave such power to my family. It was to the whole family, the way Papa Lem told it, because the Lord promised Abraham that his children would be as many as there was stars in the sky, which is a lot more than Abraham knew about seeing how he didn't have no telescope. And that promise now applied to Grandpa Jake, just like the one that said "in thee shall all families of the earth be blessed." So Grandpa Jake set to studying the book of Genesis so he could fulfil those promises just like the patriarchs did. He saw how they went to a lot of trouble to make sure they only married kinfolk—you know how Abraham married his brother's daughter, Sarah, and Isaac married his cousin Rebekah, and Jacob married his cousins Leah and Rachel. So Grandpa Jake left his first wife cause she was unworthy, meaning she probably wasn't particularly sparky, and he took up with his brother's daughter and when his brother threatened to kill him if he laid a hand on the girl, Grandpa Jake run off with her and his own brother died of a curse which is just exactly what happened to Sarah's father in the Bible. I mean Grandpa Jake worked it out just right. And he made sure all his sons married their first cousins, and so all of them had sparkiness twice over, just like breeding pointers with pointers and not mixing them with other breeds, so the strain stays pure.

There was all kinds of other stuff about Lot and his daughters, and if we remained faithful then we would be the meek who inherit the Earth because we were the chosen people and the Lord would strike down everybody who stood in our way, but what it all came down to at the moment was this: You marry whoever the patriarch tells you to marry, and Papa Lem was the patriarch. He had my mama marry my daddy even though they never particularly liked each other, growing up cousins, because he could see that they was both specially chosen, which means to say they was both about the sparkiest there was. And when I was born, they knew it was like a confirmation of Papa Lem's decision, because the Lord had blessed them with a kid who gave off dust thicker than a dump truck on a dirt road.

One thing he asked me real particular was whether I

ever been laid. He says to me, "Have you spilled your seed among the daughters of Ishmael and Esau?"

I knew what spilling seed was, cause we got lectures about that at the Children's Home. I wasn't sure who the daughters of Ishmael and Esau was, but since I never had a hot date, I figured I was pretty safe saying no. Still, I did consider a second, because what came to mind was the lady in Roanoke, stoking me up just by wanting me, and I was thinking about how close I'd come to not being a virgin after all. I wondered if the lady from Roanoke was a daughter of Esau.

Papa Lem picked up on my hesitation, and he wouldn't let it go. "Don't lie to me boy. I can see a lie." Well, since *I* could see a lie, I didn't doubt but what maybe he could too. But then again, I've had plenty of grownups tell me they could spot a lie—but half the time they accused me of lying when I was telling the truth, and the other half they believed me when I was telling whoppers so big it'd take two big men to carry them upstairs. So maybe he could and maybe he couldn't. I figured I'd tell him just as much truth as I wanted. "I was just embarrassed to tell you I never had a girl," I says.

"Ah, the deceptions of the world," he says. "They make promiscuity seem so normal that a boy is ashamed to admit that he is chaste." Then he got a glint in his eye. "I know the children of Esau have been watching you, wanting to steal your birthright. Isn't that so?"

"I don't know who Esau is," says I.

The folks who was gathered around us started muttering about that.

I says, "I mean, I know who he was in the Bible, he was the brother of Jacob, the one who sold him his birthright for split pea soup."

"Jacob was the rightful heir, the true eldest son," says Papa Lem, "and don't you forget it. Esau is the one who went away from his father, out into the wilderness, rejecting the things of God and embracing the lies and sins of the world. Esau is the one who married a strange woman, who was not of the people! Do you understand me?"

I understood pretty good by then. Somewhere along the line somebody got sick of living under the thumb of Papa Lem, or maybe the patriarch before him, and they split.

"Beware," says Papa Lem, "because the children of Esau and Ishmael still covet the blessings of Jacob. They want to corrupt the pure seed of Grandpa Jake. They have enough of the blessing of God to know that you're a remarkable boy, like Joseph who was sold into Egypt, and they will come to you with their whorish plans, the way Potiphar's wife came to Joseph, trying to persuade you to give them your pure and undefiled seed so that they can have the blessing that their fathers rejected."

I got to tell you that I didn't much like having him talk about my seed so much in front of mixed company, but that was nothing compared to what he did next. He waved his hand to a girl standing there in the crowd, and up she came. She wasn't half bad-looking, in a country sort of way. Her hair was mousy and she wasn't altogether clean and she stood with a two-bucket slouch, but her face wasn't bad and she looked to have her teeth. Sweet, but not my type, if you know what I mean.

Papa Lem introduced us. It was his daughter, which I might've guessed, and then he says to her, "Wilt thou go with this man?" And she looks at me and says, "I will go." And then she gave me this big smile, and all of a sudden it was happening again, just like it did with the lady in Roanoke, only twice as much, cause after all the lady in Roanoke wasn't hardly sparky. I was standing there and all I could think about was how I wanted all her clothes off her and to do with her right there in front of everybody and I didn't even care that all those people were watching, that's how strong it was.

And I liked it, I got to tell you. I mean you don't ignore a feeling like that. But another part of me was standing back and it says to me, "Mick Winger you damn fool, that girl's as homely as the bathroom sink, and all

these people are watching her make an idiot out of you,"
and it was that part of me that got mad, because I didn't
like her making me do something, and I didn't like it
happening right out in front of everybody, and I specially
didn't like Papa Lem sitting there looking at his own
daughter and me like we was in a dirty magazine.

Thing is, when I get mad I get all sparky, and the
madder I got, the more I could see how she was doing
it, like she was a magnet, drawing me to her. And as
soon as I thought of it like us being magnets, I took all
the sparkiness from being mad and I used it. Not to hurt
her or nothing, because I didn't put it on her the way I
did with the people I killed. I just kind of turned the
path of her sparks plain upside down. She was spinning
it just as fast as ever, but it went the other way, and the
second that started, why, it was like she disappeared. I
mean, I could see her all right, but I couldn't hardly
notice her. I couldn't focus my eyes on her.

Papa Lem jumped right to his feet, and the other folks
were gasping. Pretty quick that girl stopped sparking at
me, you can bet, and there she was on her knees, throwing up. She must've had a real weak digestion, or else
what I done was stronger than I thought. She was really
pouring on the juice, I guess, and when I flung it back
at her and turned her upside down, well, she couldn't
hardly walk when they got her up. She was pretty hysterical, too, crying about how awful and ugly I was, which
might've hurt my feelings except that I was scared to
death.

Papa Lem was looking like the wrath of God. "You
have rejected the holy sacrament of marriage! You have
spurned the handmaid God prepared for you!"

Now you've got to know that I hadn't put everything
together yet, or I wouldn't have been so afraid of him,
but for all I knew right then he could kill me with a
cancer. And it was a sure thing he could've had those
people beat me to death or whatever he wanted, so
maybe I was right to be scared. Anyway I had to think
of a way to make him not be mad at me, and what I

came up with must not've been too bad because it worked, didn't it?

I says to him, as calm as I can, "Papa Lem, she was not an acceptable handmaiden." I didn't watch all those TV preachers for nothing. I knew how to talk like the Bible. I says, "She was not blessed enough to be my wife. She wasn't even as blessed as my mama. You can't tell me that she's the best the Lord prepared for me."

And sure enough, he calmed right down. "I know that," he says. And he isn't talking like a preacher any more, it's *me* talking like a preacher and him talking all meek. "You think I don't know it? It's those children of Esau, that's what it is, Mick, you got to know that. We had five girls who were a lot dustier than her, but we had to put them out into other families, cause they were like you, so strong they would've killed their own parents without meaning to."

And I says, "Well, you brought me back, didn't you?"

And he says, "Well you were *alive*, Mick, and you got to admit that makes it easier."

"You mean those girls're all dead?" I says.

"The children of Esau," he says. "Shot three of them, strangled one, and we never found the body of the other. They never lived to be ten years old."

And I thought about how the lady in Roanoke told me she had me in her gunsights a few times. But she let me live. Why? For my seed? Those girls would've had seed too, or whatever. But they killed those girls and let me live. I didn't know why. Hell, I still don't, not if you mean to keep me locked up like this for the rest of my life. I mean you might as well have blasted my head off when I was six, and then I can name you a dozen good folks who'd still be alive, so no thanks for the favor if you don't plan to let me go.

Anyway, I says to him, "I didn't know that. I'm sorry."

And he says to me, "Mick, I can see how you'd be disappointed, seeing how you're so blessed by the Lord. But I promise you that my daughter is indeed the best girl of marriageable age that we've got here. I wasn't trying to foist her off on you because she's my daughter—it would be blasphemous for me to try it, and I'm a true servant of the Lord. The people here can testify for me, they can tell you that I'd never give you my own daughter unless she was the best we've got."

If she was the best they got then I had to figure the laws against inbreeding made pretty good sense. But I says to him, "Then maybe we ought to wait and see if there's somebody younger, too young to marry right now." I remembered the story of Jacob from Sunday School, and since they set such store by Jacob I figured it'd work. I says, "Remember that Jacob served seven years before he got to marry Rachel. I'm willing to wait."

That impressed hell out of him, you can bet. He says, "You truly have the prophetic spirit, Mick. I have no doubt that someday you'll be Papa in my place, when the Lord has gathered me unto my fathers. But I hope you'll also remember that Jacob married Rachel, but he first married the older daughter, Leah."

The ugly one, I thought, but I didn't say it. I just smiled and told him how I'd remember that, and there was plenty of time to talk about it tomorrow, because it was dark now and I was tired and a lot of things had happened to me today that I had to think over. I was really getting into the spirit of this Bible thing, and so I says to him, "Remember that before Jacob could dream of the ladder into heaven, he had to sleep."

Everybody laughed, but Papa Lem wasn't satisfied yet. He was willing to let the marriage thing wait for a few days. But there was one thing that couldn't wait. He looks me in the eye and he says, "Mick, you got a choice to make. The Lord says those who aren't for me are against me. Joshua said choose ye this day whom ye will serve. And Moses said, 'I call heaven and earth to record this day against you, that I have set before you life and death, blessing and cursing: therefore choose life, that both thou and thy seed may live.'"

Well I don't think you can put it much plainer than that. I could choose to live there among the chosen people, surrounded by dirty kids and a slimy old man telling me who to marry and whether I could raise my own children, or I could choose to leave and get my brains blasted out or maybe just pick up a stiff dose of cancer—I wasn't altogether sure whether they'd do it quick or slow. I kind of figured they'd do it quick, though, so I'd have no chance to spill my seed among the daughters of Esau.

So I gave him my most solemn and hypocritical promise that I would serve the Lord and live among them all the days of my life. Like I told you, I didn't know whether he could tell if I was lying or not. But he nodded and smiled so it looked like he believed me. Trouble was, I knew *he* was lying, and so that meant he *didn't* believe me, and that meant I was in deep poo, as Mr. Kaiser's boy Greggy always said. In fact, he was pretty angry and pretty scared, too, even though he tried to hide it by smiling and keeping a lid on himself. But I knew that he knew that I had no intention of staying there with those crazy people who knocked up their cousins and stayed about as ignorant as I ever saw. Which meant that he was already planning to kill me, and sooner rather than later.

No, I better tell the truth here, cause I wasn't *that* smart. It wasn't till I was halfway to the house that I really wondered if he believed me, and it wasn't till Mama had me with a nice clean pair of pajamas up in a nice clean room, and she was about to take my jeans and shirt and underwear and make *them* nice and clean that it occurred to me that maybe I was going to wish I had more clothes on than pajamas that night. I really got kind of mad before she finally gave me back my clothes—she was scared that if she didn't do what I said, I'd do something to her. And then I got to thinking that maybe I'd made things even *worse* by not giving her the clothes, because that might make them think that I was planning to skip out, and so maybe they weren't planning to kill me before but now they would, and so I probably just made things worse. Except when it came down to it, I'd rather be wrong about the one thing and at least have my clothes, than be wrong about the other thing and have to gallivant all over the country in pajamas. You don't get much mileage on country roads barefoot in pajamas, even in the summer.

As soon as Mama left and went on downstairs, I got dressed again, including my shoes, and climbed in under the covers. I'd slept out in the open, so I didn't mind sleeping in my clothes. What drove me crazy was getting my shoes on the sheets. They would've yelled at me so bad at the Children's Home.

I laid there in the dark, trying to think what I was going to do. I pretty much knew how to get from this house out to the road, but what good would that do me? I didn't know where I was or where the road led or how far to go, and you don't cut cross country in North Carolina—if you don't trip over something in the dark, you'll bump into some moonshine or marijuana operation and they'll blast your head off, not to mention the danger of getting your throat bit out by some tobacco farmer's mean old dog. So there I'd be running along a road that leads nowhere with them on my tail and if they wanted to run me down, I don't think fear of cancer would slow down your average four-wheeler.

I thought about maybe stealing a car, but I don't have the first idea how to hotwire anything. It wasn't one of the skills you pick up at the Children's Home. I knew the idea of it, somewhat, because I'd done some reading on electricity with the books Mr. Kaiser lent me so I could maybe try getting ready for the GED, but there wasn't a chapter in there on how to get a Lincoln running without a key. Didn't know how to drive, either. All the stuff you pick up from your dad or from your friends at school, I just never picked up at all.

Maybe I dozed off, maybe I didn't. But I suddenly noticed that I could see in the dark. Not *see*, of course. Feel the people moving around. Not far off at first, except like a blur, but I could feel the near ones, the other ones in the house. It was cause they was sparky, of course, but as I laid there feeling them drifting here and there, in the rhythms of sleep and dreams, or walking around, I began to realize that I'd been feeling people all along, only I didn't know it. They wasn't sparky, but I always knew where they were, like shadows drifting in the back of your mind, I didn't even know that I knew it, but they were there. It's like when Diz Riddle got him his glasses when he was ten years old and all of a sudden he just went around whooping and yelling about all the stuff he saw. He always used to see it before, but he didn't rightly know what half the stuff was. Like pictures on coins. He knew the coins was bumpy, but he didn't know they was pictures and writing and stuff. That's how this was.

I laid there and I could make a map in my brain where I could see a whole bunch of different people, and the more I tried, the better I could see. Pretty soon it wasn't just in that house. I could feel them in other houses, dimmer and fainter. But in my mind I didn't see no walls so I didn't know whether somebody was in the kitchen or in the bathroom, I had to think it out, and it was hard, it took all my concentration. The only guide I had was that I could see electric wires when the current was flowing through them, so wherever a light was on or a clock was running or something, I could feel this thin line, really thin, not like the shadows of people. It wasn't much, but it gave me some idea of where some of the walls might be.

If I could've just told who was who I might have made some guesses about what they was doing. Who was asleep and who was awake. But I couldn't even tell who was a kid and who was a grown-up, cause I couldn't see sizes, just brightness. Brightness was the only way I knew who was close and who was far.

I was pure lucky I got so much sleep during the day when that guy was giving me a ride from Roanoke to Eden. Well, that wasn't lucky, I guess, since I wished I hadn't gone to Eden at all, but at least having that long

nap meant that I had a better shot at staying awake until
things quieted down.

There was a clump of them in the next house. It was
hard to sort them out, cause three of them was a lot
brighter, so I thought they was closer, and it took a while
to realize that it was probably Mama and Daddy and
Papa Lem along with some others. Anyway it was a meeting, and it broke up after a while, and all except Papa
Lem came over. I didn't know what the meeting was
about, but I knew they was scared and mad. Mostly
scared. Well, so was I. But I calmed myself down, the
way I'd been practicing, so I didn't accidently kill nobody.
That kind of practice made it so I could keep myself
from getting too lively and sparky, so they'd think I was
asleep. They didn't see as clear as I did, too, so that'd
help. I thought maybe they'd all come up and get me,
but no, they just all waited downstairs while one of them
came up, and he didn't come in and get me, neither. All
he did was go to the other rooms and wake up whoever
was sleeping there and get them downstairs and out of
the house.

Well, that scared me worse than ever. That made it
plain what they had in mind, all right. Didn't want me
giving off sparks and killing somebody close by when they
attacked me. Still, when I thought about it, I realized that
it was also a good sign. They was scared of me, and
rightly so. I could reach farther and strike harder than
any of them. And they saw I could throw off what got
tossed at me, when I flung back what Papa Lem's daughter tried to do to me. They didn't know how much I
could do.

Neither did I.

Finally all the people was out of the house except the
ones downstairs. There was others outside the house,
maybe watching, maybe not, but I figured I better not
try to climb out the window.

Then somebody started walking up the stairs again,
alone. There wasn't nobody else to fetch down, so they
could only be coming after me. It was just one person,

but that didn't do me no good—even one grown man who knows how to use a knife is better off than me. I still don't have my full growth on me, or at least I sure hope I don't, and the only fights I ever got in were slugging matches in the yard. For a minute I wished I'd took kung fu lessons instead of sitting around reading math and science books to make up for dropping out of school so young. A lot of good math and science was going to do me if I was dead.

The worst thing was I couldn't see him. Maybe they just moved all the children out of the house so they wouldn't make noise in the morning and wake me. Maybe they was just being nice. And this guy coming up the stairs might just be checking on me or bringing me clean clothes or something—I couldn't tell. So how could I twist him up, when I didn't know if they was trying to kill me or what? But if he *was* trying to kill me, I'd wish I'd twisted him before he ever came into the room with me.

Well, that was one decision that got made for me. I laid there wondering what to do for so long that he got to the top of the stairs and came to my room and turned the knob and came in.

I tried to breathe slow and regular, like somebody asleep. Tried to keep from getting too sparky. If it was somebody checking on me, they'd go away.

He didn't go away. And he walked soft, too, so as not to wake me up. He was real scared. So scared that I finally knew there was no way he was there to tuck me in and kiss me good night.

So I tried to twist him, to send sparks at him. But I didn't have any sparks to send! I mean I wasn't mad or anything. I'd never tried to kill somebody on purpose before, it was always because I was already mad and I just lost control and it *happened*. Now I'd been calming myself down so much that I couldn't lose control. I had no sparks at all to send, just my normal shining shadow, and he was right there and I didn't have a second to lose so I rolled over. Toward him, which was maybe dumb, cause I might have run into his knife, but I didn't know yet for sure that he had a knife. All I was thinking was that I had to knock him down or push him or something.

The only person I knocked down was me. I bumped him and hit the floor. He also cut my back with the knife. Not much of a cut, he mostly just snagged my shirt, but if I was scared before, I was terrified now cause I knew he had a knife and I knew even more that I didn't. I scrambled back away from him. There was almost no light from the window, it was like being in a big closet, I couldn't see him, he couldn't see me. Except of course that I *could* see him, or at least sense where he was, and now I was giving off sparks like crazy so unless he was weaker than I thought, he could see me too.

Well, he was weaker than I thought. He just kind of drifted, and I could hear him swishing the knife through the air in front of him. He had no idea where I was.

And all the time I was trying to get madder and madder, and it wasn't working. You can't get mad by trying. Maybe an actor can, but I'm no actor. So I was scared and sparking but I couldn't get that pulse to mess him up. The more I thought about it, the calmer I got.

It's like you've been carrying around a machine gun all your life, accidently blasting people you didn't really want to hurt and then the first time you really want to lay into somebody, it jams.

So I stopped trying to get mad. I just sat there realizing I was going to die, that after I finally got myself under control so I didn't kill people all the time anymore, now that I didn't really want to commit suicide, *now* I was going to get wasted. And they didn't even have the guts to come at me openly. Sneaking in the dark to cut my throat while I was asleep. And in the meeting where they decided to do it, my long lost but loving mama and daddy were right there. Heck, my dear sweet daddy was downstairs right now, waiting for this assassin to come down and tell him that I was dead. Would he cry for me then?

Boo hoo my sweet little boy's all gone? Mick is in the cold cold ground?

I was mad. As simple as that. Stop thinking about being mad, and start thinking about the things that if you think about them, they'll make you mad. I was so sparky with fear that when I got mad, too, it was worse than it ever was before, built up worse, you know. Only when I let it fly, it didn't go for the guy up there swishing his knife back and forth in the dark. That pulse of fire in me went right down through the floor and straight to dear old Dad. I could hear him scream. He felt it, just like that. He felt it. And so did I. Because that wasn't what I meant to do. I only met him that day, but he was my *father*, and I did him worse than I ever did anybody before in my life. I didn't plan to do it. You don't plan to kill your father.

All of a sudden I was blinded by light. For a second I thought it was the other kind of light, sparks, them retaliating, twisting me. Then I realized it was my eyes being blinded, and it was the overhead light in the room that was on. The guy with the knife had finally realized that the only reason not to have the light on was so I wouldn't wake up, but now that I was awake he might as well see what he's doing. Lucky for me the light blinded him just as much as it blinded me, or I'd have been poked before I saw what hit me. Instead I had time to scramble on back to the far corner of the room.

I wasn't no hero. But I was seriously thinking about running at him, attacking a guy with a knife. I would have been killed, but I couldn't think of anything else to do.

Then I thought of something else to do. I got the idea from the way I could feel the electric current in the wires running from the lightswitch through the wall. That was electricity, and the lady in Roanoke called my sparkiness bio-electricity. I ought to be able to do something with it, shouldn't I?

I thought first that maybe I could short-circuit something, but I didn't think I had that much electricity in me. I thought of maybe tapping into the house current to add to my own juice, but then I remembered that connecting up your body to house current is the same thing other folks call *electrocution*. I mean, maybe I can tap into house wiring, but if I was wrong, I'd be real dead.

But I could still do something. There was a table lamp right next to me. I pulled off the shade and threw it at the guy, who was still standing by the door, thinking about what the scream downstairs meant. Then I grabbed the lamp and turned it on, and then smashed the lightbulb on the nightstand. Sparks. Then it was out.

I held the lamp in my hand, like a weapon, so he'd think I was going to beat off his knife with the lamp. And if my plan was a bust, I guess that's what I would've done. But while he was looking at me, getting ready to fight me knife against lamp, I kind of let the jagged end of the lamp rest on the bedspread. And then I used my sparkiness, the anger that was still in me. I couldn't fling it at the guy, or well I could have, but it would've been like the bus driver, a six-month case of lung cancer. By the time he died of *that*, I'd be six months worth of dead from multiple stab wounds to the neck and chest.

So I let my sparkiness build up and flow out along my arm, out along the lamp, like I was making my shadow grow. And it worked. The sparks just went right on down the lamp to the tip, and built up and built up, and all the time I was thinking about how Papa Lem was trying to kill me cause I thought his daughter was ugly and how he made me kill my daddy before I even knew him half a day and that charge built *up*.

It built up enough. Sparks started jumping across inside the broken light bulb, right there against the bedspread. Real sparks, the kind I could *see*, not just feel. And in two seconds that bedspread was on fire. Then I yanked the lamp so the cord shot right out of the wall, and I threw it at the guy, and while he was dodging I scooped up the bedspread and ran at him. I wasn't sure whether I'd catch on fire or he would, but I figured he'd

be too panicked and surprised to think of stabbing me
through the bedspread, and sure enough he didn't, he
dropped the knife and tried to beat off the bedspread.
Which he didn't do too good, because I was still pushing
it at him. Then he tried to get through the door, but I
kicked his ankle with my shoe, and he fell down, still
fighting off the blanket.

I got the knife and sliced right across the back of his
thigh with it. Geez it was sharp. Or maybe I was so mad
and scared that I cut him stronger than I ever thought
I could, but it went clear to the bone. He was screaming
from the fire and his leg was gushing blood and the fire
was catching on the wallpaper and it occurred to me that
they couldn't chase me too good if they was trying to put
out a real dandy house fire.

It also occurred to me that I couldn't run away too
good if I was dead inside that house fire. And thinking
of maybe dying in the fire made me realize that the guy
was burning to death and I did it to him, something
every bit as terrible as cancer, and *I didn't care,* because
I'd killed so many people that it was nothing to me now,
when a guy like that was trying to kill me, I wasn't even
sorry for his pain, cause he wasn't feeling nothing worse
than Old Peleg felt, and in fact that even made me feel
pretty good, because it was like getting even for Old
Peleg's death, even though it was me killed them both.
I mean how could I get *even* for Peleg dying by killing
somebody else? Okay, maybe it makes sense in a way,
cause it was their fault I was in the orphanage instead
of growing up here. Or maybe it made sense because
this guy deserved to die, and Peleg didn't, so maybe
somebody who deserved it had to die a death as bad as
Peleg's, or something. I don't know. I sure as hell wasn't
thinking about that then. I just knew that I was hearing
a guy scream himself to death and I didn't even want to
help him or even *try* to help him or nothing. I wasn't
enjoying it, either, I wasn't thinking, Burn you sucker!
or anything like that, but I knew right then that I wasn't
even human, I was just a monster, like I always thought,

like in the slasher movies. This was straight from the slasher movies, somebody burning up and screaming, and there's the monster just standing there in the flames and he *isn't burning.*

And that's the truth. I wasn't burning. There was flames all around me, but it kind of shied back from me, because I was so full of sparks from hating myself so bad that it was like the flames couldn't get through to me. I've thought about that a lot since then. I mean, even that Swedish scientist doesn't know all about this bio-electrical stuff. Maybe when I get real sparky it makes it so other stuff can't hit me. Maybe that's how some generals in the Civil War used to ride around in the open—or maybe that was that general in World War II, I can't remember—and bullets didn't hit them or anything. Maybe if you're charged up enough, things just can't *get* to you. I don't know. I just know that by the time I finally decided to open the door and actually opened it, the whole room was burning and the door was burning and I just opened it and walked through. Course now I got a bandage on my hand to prove that I couldn't grab a hot doorknob without hurting myself a little, but I shouldn't've been able to stay alive in that room and I came out without even my hair singed.

I started down the hall, not knowing who was still in the house. I wasn't used to being able to see people by their sparkiness yet, so I didn't even think of checking, I just ran down the stairs carrying that bloody knife. But it didn't matter. They all ran away before I got there, all except Daddy. He was lying in the middle of the floor in the living room, doubled up, lying with his head in a pool of vomit and his butt in a pool of blood, shaking like he was dying of cold. I really done him. I really tore him up inside. I don't think he even saw me. But he was my daddy, and even a monster don't leave his daddy for the fire to get him. So I grabbed his arms to try to pull him out.

I forgot how sparky I was, worse than ever. The second I touched him the sparkiness just rushed out of me and all over him. It never went that way before, just completely surrounded him like he was a part of me, like he was completely drowning in my light. It wasn't what I meant to do at all. I just forgot. I was trying to save him and instead I gave him a hit like I never gave nobody before, and I couldn't stand it, I just screamed.

Then I dragged him out. He was all limp, but even if I killed him, even if I turned him to jelly inside, he wasn't going to burn, that's all I could think of, that and how I ought to walk back into that house myself and up the stairs and catch myself on fire and die.

But I didn't do it, as you might guess. There was people yelling Fire! and shouting Stay back! and I knew that I better get out of there. Daddy's body was lying on the grass in front of the house, and I took off around the back. I thought maybe I heard some gunshots, but it could've been popping and cracking of timbers in the fire, I don't know. I just ran around the house and along toward the road, and if there was people in my way they just got *out* of my way, because even the most dimwitted inbred pukebrained kid in that whole village would've seen my sparks, I was so hot.

I ran till the asphalt ended and I was running on the dirt road. There was clouds so the moon was hardly any light at all, and I kept stumbling off the road into the weeds. I fell once and when I was getting up I could see the fire behind me. The whole house was burning, and there was flames above it in the trees. Come to think of it there hadn't been all that much rain, and those trees were dry. A lot more than one house was going to burn tonight, I figured, and for a second I even thought maybe nobody'd chase me.

But that was about as stupid an idea as I ever had. I mean, if they wanted to kill me before because I said Papa Lem's girl was ugly, how do you think they felt about me now that I burned down their little hidden town? Once they realized I was gone, they'd be after me and I'd be lucky if they shot me quick.

I even thought about cutting off the road, dangerous

or not, and hiding in the woods. But I decided to get as much distance as I could along the road till I saw headlights.

Just when I decided that, the road ended. Just bushes and trees. I went back, tried to find the road. It must have turned but I didn't know which way. I was tripping along like a blind man in the grass, trying to feel my way to the ruts of the dirt road, and of course that's when I saw headlights away off toward the burning houses—there was at least three houses burning now. They knew the town was a total loss by now, they was probably just leaving enough folks to get all the children out and away to a safe place, while the men came after me. It's what *I* would've done, and to hell with cancer, they knew I couldn't stop them all before they did what they wanted to me. And here I couldn't even find the road to get away from them. By the time their headlights got close enough to show the road, it'd be too late to get away.

I was about to run back into the woods when all of a sudden a pair of headlights went on not twenty feet away, and pointed right at me. I damn near wet my pants. I thought, Mick Winger, you are a dead little boy right this second.

And then I heard her calling to me. "Get on over here, Mick, you idiot, don't stand there in the light, get on over here." It was the lady from Roanoke. I still couldn't see her cause of the lights, but I knew her voice, and I took off. The road didn't end, it just turned a little and she was parked right where the dirt road met up sideways with a gravel road. I got around to the door of the car she was driving, or truck or whatever it was—a four-wheel-drive Blazer maybe, I know it had a four-wheel-drive shift lever in it—anyway the door was locked and she was yelling at me to get *in* and I was yelling back that it was *locked* until finally she unlocked it and I climbed in. She backed up so fast and swung around onto the gravel in a spin that near threw me right out the door, since I hadn't closed it yet. Then she took off

so fast going *forward,* spitting gravel behind her, that the
door closed itself.

"Fasten your seat belt," she says to me.

"Did you follow me here?" I says.

"No, I just happened to be here picnicking," she says.
"Fasten your damn *seat belt.*"

I did, but then I turned around in my seat and looked
out the back. There was five or six sets of headlights,
making the jog to get from the dirt road onto the gravel
road. We didn't have more than a mile on them.

"We've been looking for this place for years," she says.
"We thought it was in Rockingham County, that's how
far off we were."

"Where is it, then?" I says.

"Alamance County," she says.

And then I says, "I don't give a damn what county it
is! I killed my own daddy back there!"

And she says to me, "Don't get mad now, don't get
mad at me, I'm sorry, just calm down." That was all she
could think of, how I might get mad and lose control
and kill her, and I don't blame her, cause it was the
hardest thing I ever did, keeping myself from busting out
right there in the car, and it would've killed her, too.
The pain in my hand was starting to get to me, too, from
where I grabbed the doorknob. It was just building up
and building up.

She was driving a lot faster than the headlights
reached. We'd be going way too fast for a curve before
she even saw it, and then she'd slam on the brakes and
we'd skid and sometimes I couldn't believe we didn't just
roll over and crash. But she always got out of it.

I couldn't face back anymore. I just sat there with my
eyes closed, trying to get calm, and then I'd remember
my daddy who I didn't even *like* but he was my daddy
lying there in his blood and his puke, and I'd remember
that guy who burned to death up in my room and even
though I didn't care at the time, I sure cared now, I was
so angry and scared and I hated myself so bad I couldn't
hold it in, only I also couldn't let it out, and I kept

wishing I could just die. Then I realized that the guys
following us were close enough that I could feel them.
Or no it wasn't that they was close. They was just so *mad*
that I could see their sparks flying like never before. Well
as long as I could see them I could let fly, couldn't I? I
just flung out toward them. I don't know if I hit them.
I don't know if my bio-electricity is something I can
throw like that or what. But at least I shucked it off
myself, and I didn't mess up the lady who was driving.

When we hit asphalt again, I found out that I didn't
know what crazy driving was before. She peeled out and
now she began to look at a curve ahead and then switch
off the headlights until she was halfway through the
curve, it was the craziest thing I ever saw, but it also
made sense. They had to be following our lights, and
when our lights went out they wouldn't know where we
was for a minute. They also wouldn't know that the road
curved ahead, and they might even crash up or at least
they'd have to slow down. Of course, we had a real good
chance of ending up eating trees ourselves, but she drove
like she knew what she was doing.

We came to a straight section with a crossroads about
a mile up. She switched off the lights again, and I
thought maybe she was going to turn, but she didn't. Just
went on and on and on, straight into the pitch black.
Now, that straight section was long, but it didn't go on
forever, and I don't care how good a driver you are, you
can't keep track of how far you've gone in the dark. Just
when I thought for sure we'd smash into something, she
let off the gas and reached her hand out the window
with a flashlight. We was still going pretty fast, but the
flashlight was enough to make a reflector up ahead flash
back at us, so she knew where the curve was, and it was
farther off than I thought. She whipped us around that
curve and then around another, using just a couple of
blinks from the flashlight, before she switched on her
headlights again.

I looked behind us to see if I could see anybody. "You
lost them!" I says.

"Maybe," she says. "You tell *me*."

So I tried to feel where they might be, and sure enough, they was sparky enough that I could just barely tell where they was, away back. Split up, smeared out. "They're going every which way," I says.

"So we lost a few of them," she says. "They aren't going to give up, you know."

"I know," I says.

"You're the hottest thing going," she says.

"And you're a daughter of Esau," I says.

"Like hell I am," she says. "I'm a great-great-great-granddaughter of Jacob Yow, who happened to be bio-electrically talented. Like if you're tall and athletic, you can play basketball. That's all it is, just a natural talent. Only he went crazy and started inbreeding his whole family, and they've got these stupid ideas about being the chosen of God and all the time they're just *murderers*."

"Tell me about it," I says.

"You can't help it," she says. "You didn't have anybody to teach you. I'm not blaming you."

But I was blaming me.

She says, "Ignorant, that's what they are. Well, my grandpa didn't want to just keep reading the Bible and killing any revenuers or sheriffs or whatever who gave us trouble. He wanted to find out what we *are*. He also didn't want to marry the slut they picked out for him because he wasn't particularly dusty. So he left. They hunted him down and tried to kill him, but he got away, and he married. And he also studied and became a doctor and his kids grew up knowing that they had to find out what it *is*, this power. It's like the old stories of witches, women who get mad and suddenly your cows start dying. Maybe they didn't even know they were doing it. Summonings and love spells and come-hithers, everybody can do it a little, just like everybody can throw a ball and sometimes make a basket, but some people can do it better than others. And Papa Lem's people, they do it best of all, better and better, because they're breeding for it. We've got to stop them, don't you see?

We've got to keep them from learning how to control it. Because now we know more about it. It's all tied up with the way the human body heals itself. In Sweden they've been changing the currents around to heal tumors. Cancer. The opposite of what you've been doing, but it's the same principle. Do you know what that means? If they could control it, Lem's people could be healers, not killers. Maybe all it takes is to do it with love, not anger."

"Did you kill them little girls in orphanages with love?" I says.

And she just drives, she doesn't say a thing, just drives. "Damn," she says, "it's raining."

The road was slick in two seconds. She slowed way down. It came down harder and harder. I looked behind us and there was headlights back there again. Way back, but I could still see them. "They're on us again," I says.

"I can't go any faster in the rain," she says.

"It's raining on them too," I says.

"Not with my luck."

And I says, "It'll put the fire out. Back where they live."

And she says, "It doesn't matter. They'll move. They know we found them, because we picked you up. So they'll move."

I apologized for causing trouble, and she says, "We couldn't let you die in there. I had to go there and save you if I could."

"Why?" I ask her. "Why not let me die?"

"Let me put it another way," she says. "If you decided to stay with them, I had to go in there and kill you."

And I says to her, "You're the queen of compassion, you know?" And I thought about it a little. "You're just like they are, you know?" I says. "You wanted to get pregnant just like they did. You wanted to breed me like a stud horse."

"If I wanted to *breed* you," she says, "I would have done it on the hill this morning. Yesterday morning. You would've done it. And I should've made you, because if you went with them, our only hope was to have a child of yours that we could raise to be a decent person. Only it turned out you're a decent person, so we didn't have to kill you. Now we can study you and learn about this from the strongest living example of the phenomenon"— I don't know how to pronounce that, but you know what I mean. Or what she meant, anyway.

And I says to her, "Maybe I don't want you to study me, did you think of that?"

And she says to me, "Maybe what you want don't amount to a goldfish fart." Or anyway that's what she meant.

That's about when they started shooting at us. Rain or no rain, they was pushing it so they got close enough to shoot, and they wasn't half bad at it, seeing as the first bullet we knew about went right through the back window and in between us and smacked a hole in the windshield. Which made all kinds of cracks in the glass so she couldn't see, which made her slow down more, which meant they was even closer.

Just then we whipped around a corner and our headlights lit up a bunch of guys getting out of a car with guns in their hands, and she says, "Finally." So I figured they was some of her people, there to take the heat off. But at that same second Lem's people must have shot out a tire or maybe she just got a little careless for a second cause after all she couldn't see too good through the windshield, but anyway she lost control and we skidded and flipped over, rolled over it felt like five times, all in slow motion, rolling and rolling, the doors popping open and breaking off, the windshield cracking and crumbling away, and there we hung in our seatbelts, not talking or nothing, except maybe I was saying O my God or something and then we smacked into something and just stopped, which jerked us around inside the car and then it was all over.

I heard water rushing. A stream, I thought. We can wash up. Only it wasn't a stream, it was the gasoline pouring out of the tank. And then I heard gunshots from back up by the road. I didn't know who was fighting who, but if the wrong guys won they'd just love to catch us in a nice hot gasoline fire. Getting out wasn't going to be all that hard. The doors were gone so we didn't have to climb out a window or anything.

We were leaned over on the left side, so her door was mashed against the ground. I says to her, "We got to climb out my door." I had brains enough to hook one arm up over the lip of the car before I unbuckled my seat belt, and then I hoisted myself out and stayed perched up there on the side of the car, up in the air, so I could reach down and help her out.

Only she wasn't climbing out. I yelled at her and she didn't answer. I thought for a second she was dead, but then I saw that her sparks was still there. Funny, how I never saw she had any sparkiness before, because I didn't know to look for it, but now, even though it was dim, I could see it. Only it wasn't so dim, it was real busy, like she was trying to heal herself. The gurgling was still going on, and everything smelled like gasoline. There was still shooting going on. And even if nobody came down to start us on fire on purpose, I saw enough car crashes at the movies to know you didn't need a match to start a car on fire. I sure didn't want to be near the car if it caught, and I sure didn't want her *in* it. But I couldn't see how to climb down in and pull her out. I mean I'm not a weakling but I'm not Mr. Universe either.

It felt like I sat there for a whole minute before I realized I didn't have to pull her out my side of the car, I could pull her out the *front* cause the whole windshield was missing and the roof was only mashed down a little, cause there was a rollbar in the car—that was real smart, putting a rollbar in. I jumped off the car. It wasn't raining right here, but it *had* rained, so it was slippery and wet. Or maybe it was slippery from the gasoline, I don't know. I got around the front of the car and up to the windshield, and I scraped the bits of glass off with my shoe. Then I crawled partway in and reached under her and undid her seatbelt, and tried to pull her out, but her legs was hung up under the steering wheel and it took forever, it was terrible, and all the time I kept listening for her to breathe, and she didn't breathe, and so I kept getting more scared and frustrated and all I was thinking about was how she had to live, she couldn't be dead, she just got through saving my life and now she was dead and she couldn't be and I was going to get her out of the car even if I had to break her legs to do it, only I didn't have to break her legs and she finally slid out and I dragged her away from the car. It didn't catch on fire, but I couldn't know it wasn't going to.

And anyway all I cared about then was her, not breathing, lying there limp on the grass with her neck all floppy and I was holding on to her crying and angry and scared and I had us both covered with sparks, like we was the same person, just completely covered, and I was crying and saying, Live! I couldn't even call her by name or nothing because I didn't know her name. I just know that I was shaking like I had the chills and so was she and she was breathing now and whimpering like somebody just stepped on a puppy and the sparks just kept flowing around us both and I felt like somebody sucked everything out of me, like I was a wet towel and somebody wrung me out and flipped me into a corner, and then I don't remember until I woke up here.

What did it feel like? What you did to her?

It felt like when I covered her with light, it was like I was taking over doing what her own body should've done, it was like I was healing her. Maybe I got that idea because she said something about healing when she was driving the car, but she wasn't breathing when I dragged her out, and then she was breathing. So I want to know if I healed her. Because if she got healed when I covered her with my own light, then maybe I didn't kill my daddy either, because it was kind of like that, I *think* it was kind of like that, what happened when I dragged him out of the house.

I been talking a long time now, and you still told me nothing. Even if you think I'm just a killer and you want me dead, you can tell me about her. Is she alive?

Yes.

Well then how come I can't see her? How come she isn't here with the rest of you?

She had some surgery. It takes time to heal.

But did I help her? Or did I twist her? You got to tell me. Cause if I didn't help her then I hope I fail your test and you kill me cause I can't think of a good reason why I should be alive if all I can do is kill people.

You helped her, Mick. That last bullet caught her in the head. That's why she crashed.

But she wasn't bleeding!

It was dark, Mick. You couldn't see. You had her blood all over you. But it doesn't matter now. We have the bullet out. As far as we can tell, there was no brain damage. There should have been. She should have been dead.

So I did help her.

Yes. But we don't know how. All kinds of stories, you know, about faith healing, that sort of thing. Laying on of hands. Maybe it's the kind of thing you did, merging the bio-magnetic field. A lot of things don't make any sense yet. There's no way we can see that the tiny amount of electricity in a human bio-electric system could influence somebody a hundred miles off, but they summoned you, and you came. We need to study you, Mick. We've never had anybody as powerful as you. Tell the truth, maybe there's never been anybody like you. Or maybe all the healings in the New Testament—

I don't want to hear about no testaments. Papa Lem gave me about all the testaments I ever need to hear about.

Will you help us, Mick?

Help you how?

Let us study you.

Go ahead and study.

Maybe it won't be enough just to study how you _heal_ people.

I'm not going to kill nobody for you. If you try to make

me kill somebody I'll kill you first till you have to kill me
just to save your own lives, do you understand me?

**Calm down, Mick. Don't get angry. There's plenty of
time to think about things. Actually we're glad that
you don't want to kill anybody. If you enjoyed it, or
even if you hadn't been able to control it and kept
on indiscriminately killing anyone who enraged you,
you wouldn't have lived to be seventeen. Because
yes, we're scientists, or at least we're finally learning enough that we can start being scientists. But
first we're human beings, and we're in the middle
of a war, and children like you are the weapons. If
they ever got someone like you to stay with them,
work with them, you could seek us out and destroy
us. That's what they wanted you to do.**

That's right, that's one thing Papa Lem said, I don't
know if I mentioned it before, but he said that the children of Israel were supposed to kill every man, woman,
and child in Canaan, cause idolaters had to make way
for the children of God.

**Well, you see, that's why our branch of the family
left. We didn't think it was such a terrific idea, wip-
ing out the entire human race and replacing it with
a bunch of murderous, incestuous religious fanatics.
For the last twenty years, we've been able to keep
them from getting somebody like you, because
we've murdered the children that were so powerful
they had to put them outside to be reared by others.**

Except me.

**It's a war. We didn't like killing children. But it's
like bombing the place where your enemies are
building a secret weapon. The lives of a few children—no, that's a lie. It nearly split us apart ourselves, the arguments over that. Letting you live—
it was a terrible risk. I voted against it every time.
And I don't apologize for that, Mick. Now that you
know what they are, and you chose to leave, I'm
glad I lost. But so many things could have gone
wrong.**

They won't put any more babies out to orphanages now, though. They're not that dumb.

But now we have *you*. Maybe we can learn how to block what they do. Or how to heal the people they attack. Or how to identify sparkiness, as you call it, from a distance. All kinds of possibilities. But sometime in the future, Mick, you may be the only weapon we have. Do you understand that?

I don't want to.

I know.

You wanted to kill me?

I wanted to protect people from you. It was safest. Mick, I really am glad it worked out this way.

I don't know whether to believe you, Mr. Kaiser. You're such a good liar. I thought you were so nice to me all that time because you were just a nice guy.

Oh, he is, Mick. He's a nice guy. Also a damn fine liar. We kind of needed both those attributes in the person we had looking out for you.

Well, anyway, that's over with.

What's over with?

Killing me. Isn't it?

That's up to you, Mick. If you ever start getting crazy on us, or killing people that aren't part of this war of ours—

I won't do that!

But if you did, Mick. It's never too late to kill you.

Can I see her?

See who?

The lady from Roanoke! Isn't it about time you told me her name?

Come on. She can tell you herself.

Buffalo Gals, Won't You Come Out Tonight

by Ursula K. Le Guin

i

"You fell out of the sky," the coyote said.

Still curled up tight, lying on her side, her back pressed against the overhanging rock, the child watched the coyote with one eye. Over the other eye she kept her hand cupped, its back on the dirt.

"There was a burned place in the sky, up there alongside the rimrock, and then you fell out of it," the coyote repeated, patiently, as if the news was getting a bit stale. "Are you hurt?"

She was all right. She was in the plane with Mr. Michaels, and the motor was so loud she couldn't understand what he said even when he shouted, and the way the wind rocked the wings was making her feel sick, but it was all right. They were flying to Canyonville. In the plane.

She looked. The coyote was still sitting there. It yawned. It was a big one, in good condition, its coat silvery and thick. The dark tear-line from its long yellow eye was as clearly marked as a tabby cat's.

She sat up, slowly, still holding her right hand pressed to her right eye.

"Did you lose an eye?" the coyote asked, interested.

305

"I don't know," the child said. She caught her breath and shivered. "I'm cold."

"I'll help you look for it," the coyote said. "Come on! If you move around you won't have to shiver. The sun's up."

Cold lonely brightness lay across the falling land, a hundred miles of sagebrush. The coyote was trotting busily around, nosing under clumps of rabbit-brush and cheatgrass, pawing at a rock. "Aren't you going to look?" it said, suddenly sitting down on its haunches and abandoning the search. "I knew a trick once where I could throw my eyes way up into a tree and see everything from up there, and then whistle, and they'd come back into my head. But that goddam bluejay stole them, and when I whistled nothing came. I had to stick lumps of pine pitch into my head so I could see anything. You could try that. But you've got one eye that's OK, what do you need two for? Are you coming, or are you dying there?"

The child crouched, shivering.

"Well, come if you want to," said the coyote, yawned again, snapped at a flea, stood up, turned, and trotted away among the sparse clumps of rabbit-brush and sage, along the long slope that stretched on down and down into the plain streaked across by long shadows of sagebrush. The slender, grey-yellow animal was hard to keep in sight, vanishing as the child watched.

She struggled to her feet, and without a word, though she kept saying in her mind, "Wait, please wait," she hobbled after the coyote. She could not see it. She kept her hand pressed over the right eyesocket. Seeing with one eye there was no depth; it was like a huge, flat picture. The coyote suddenly sat in the middle of the picture, looking back at her, its mouth open, its eyes narrowed, grinning. Her legs began to steady and her head did not pound so hard, though the deep, black ache was always there. She had nearly caught up to the coyote when it trotted off again. This time she spoke. "Please wait!" she said.

"OK," said the coyote, but it trotted right on. She followed, walking downhill into the flat picture that at each step was deep.

Each step was different underfoot; each sage bush was different, and all the same. Following the coyote she came out from the shadow of the rimrock cliffs, and the sun at eyelevel dazzled her left eye. Its bright warmth soaked into her muscles and bones at once. The air, that all night had been so hard to breathe, came sweet and easy.

The sage bushes were pulling in their shadows and the sun was hot on the child's back when she followed the coyote along the rim of a gully. After a while the coyote slanted down the undercut slope and the child scrambled after, through scrub willows to the thin creek in its wide sandbed. Both drank.

The coyote crossed the creek, not with a careless charge and splashing like a dog, but singlefoot and quiet like a cat; always it carried its tail low. The child hesitated, knowing that wet shoes make blistered feet, and then waded across in as few steps as possible. Her right arm ached with the effort of holding her hand up over her eye. "I need a bandage," she said to the coyote. It cocked its head and said nothing. It stretched out its forelegs and lay watching the water, resting but alert. The child sat down nearby on the hot sand and tried to move her right hand. It was glued to the skin around her eye by dried blood. At the little tearing-away pain, she whimpered; though it was a small pain it frightened her. The coyote came over close and poked its long snout into her face. Its strong, sharp smell was in her nostrils. It began to lick the awful, aching blindness, cleaning and cleaning with its curled, precise, strong, wet tongue, until the child was able to cry a little with relief, being comforted. Her head was bent close to the grey-yellow ribs, and she saw the hard nipples, the whitish belly-fur. She put her arm around the she-coyote, stroking the harsh coat over back and ribs.

"OK," the coyote said, "let's go!" And set off without

a backward glance. The child scrambled to her feet and followed. "Where are we going?" she said, and the coyote, trotting on down along the creek, answered, "On down along the creek . . ."

There must have been a while she was asleep while she walked, because she felt like she was waking up, but she was walking along, only in a different place. She didn't know how she knew it was different. They were still following the creek, though the gully was flattened out to nothing much, and there was still sagebrush range as far as the eye could see. The eye—the good one—felt rested. The other one still ached, but not so sharply, and there was no use thinking about it. But where was the coyote?

She stopped. The pit of cold into which the plane had fallen re-opened and she fell. She stood falling, a thin whimper making itself in her throat.

"Over here!"

The child turned. She saw a coyote gnawing at the half-dried-up carcass of a crow, black feathers sticking to the black lips and narrow jaw.

She saw a tawny-skinned woman kneeling by a campfire, sprinkling something into a conical pot. She heard the water boiling in the pot, though it was propped between rocks, off the fire. The woman's hair was yellow and grey, bound back with a string. Her feet were bare. The upturned soles looked as dark and hard as shoe soles, but the arch of the foot was high, and the toes made two neat curving rows. She wore bluejeans and an old white shirt. She looked over at the girl. "Come on, eat crow!" she said. The child slowly came toward the woman and the fire, and squatted down. She had stopped falling and felt very light and empty; and her tongue was like a piece of wood stuck in her mouth.

Coyote was now blowing into the pot or basket or whatever it was. She reached into it with two fingers, and pulled her hand away shaking it and shouting, "Ow! Shit! Why don't I ever have any spoons?" She broke off a dead twig of sagebrush, dipped it into the pot, and licked it. "Oh, boy," she said. "Come on!"

The child moved a little closer, broke off a twig, dipped. Lumpy pinkish mush clung to the twig. She licked. The taste was rich and delicate.

"What is it?" she asked after a long time of dipping and licking.

"Food. Dried salmon mush," Coyote said. "It's cooling down." She stuck two fingers into the mush again, this time getting a good load, which she ate very neatly. The child, when she tried, got mush all over her chin. It was like chopsticks, it took practice. She practiced. They ate turn and turn until nothing was left in the pot but three rocks. The child did not ask why there were rocks in the mush-pot. They licked the rocks clean. Coyote licked out the inside of the pot-basket, rinsed it once in the creek, and put it onto her head. It fit nicely, making a conical hat. She pulled off her bluejeans. "Piss on the fire!" she cried, and did so, standing straddling it. "Ah, steam between the legs!" she said. The child, embarrassed, thought she was supposed to do the same thing, but did not want to, and did not. Bareassed, Coyote danced around the dampened fire, kicking her long thin legs out and singing,

> "Buffalo gals, won't you come out tonight,
> Come out tonight, come out tonight,
> Buffalo gals, won't you come out tonight,
> And dance by the light of the moon?"

She pulled her jeans back on. The child was burying the remains of the fire in creek-sand, heaping it over, seriously, wanting to do right. Coyote watched her.

"Is that you?" she said. "A Buffalo Gal? What happened to the rest of you?"

"The rest of me?" The child looked at herself, alarmed.

"All your people."

"Oh. Well, Mom took Bobbie, he's my little brother, away with Uncle Norm. He isn't really my uncle, or any-

thing. So Mr. Michaels was going there anyway so he
was going to fly me over to my real father, in Canyonville.
Linda, my stepmother, you know, she said it was OK for
the summer anyhow if I was there, and then we could
see. But the plane."

In the silence the girl's face became dark red, then
greyish white. Coyote watched, fascinated. "Oh," the girl
said, "Oh—Oh—Mr. Michaels—he must be—Did the—"

"Come on!" said Coyote, and set off walking.

The child cried, "I ought to go back—"

"What for?" said Coyote. She stopped to look round
at the child, then went on faster. "Come on, Gal!" She
said it as a name; maybe it was the child's name, Myra,
as spoken by Coyote. The child, confused and despairing,
protested again, but followed her. "Where are we going?
Where *are* we?"

"This is my country," Coyote answered, with dignity,
making a long, slow gesture all round the vast horizon.
"I made it. Every goddam sage bush."

And they went on. Coyote's gait was easy, even a little
shambling, but she covered the ground; the child struggled not to drop behind. Shadows were beginning to pull
themselves out again from under the rocks and shrubs.
Leaving the creek, they went up a long, low, uneven
slope that ended away off against the sky in rimrock.
Dark trees stood one here, another way over there; what
people called a juniper forest, a desert forest, one with
a lot more between the trees than trees. Each juniper
they passed smelled sharply, cat-pee smell the kids at
school called it, but the child liked it; it seemed to go
into her mind and wake her up. She picked off a juniper
berry and held it in her mouth, but after a while spat it
out. The aching was coming back in huge black waves,
and she kept stumbling. She found that she was sitting
down on the ground. When she tried to get up her legs
shook and would not go under her. She felt foolish and
frightened, and began to cry.

"We're home!" Coyote called from way on up the hill.

The child looked with her one weeping eye, and saw

sagebrush, juniper, cheatgrass, rimrock. She heard a coyote yip far off in the dry twilight.

She saw a little town up under the rimrock, board
houses, shacks, all unpainted. She heard Coyote call
again, "Come on, pup! Come on, Gal, we're home!" She
could not get up, so she tried to go on all fours, the long
way up the slope to the houses under the rimrock. Long
before she got there, several people came to meet her.
They were all children, she thought at first, and then
began to understand that most of them were grown people, but all were very short; they were broad-bodied, fat,
with fine, delicate hands and feet. Their eyes were bright.
Some of the women helped her stand up and walk, coaxing her, "It isn't much farther, you're doing fine." In the
late dusk lights shone yellow-bright through doorways
and through unchinked cracks between boards. Wood-
smoke hung sweet in the quiet air. The short people
talked and laughed all the time, softly. "Where's she
going to stay?"—"Put her in with Robin, they're all
asleep already!"—"Oh, she can stay with us."

The child asked hoarsely. "Where's Coyote?"

"Out hunting," the short people said.

A deeper voice spoke: "Somebody new has come into
town?"

"Yes, a new person," one of the short men answered.

Among these people the deep-voiced man bulked
impressive; he was broad and tall, with powerful hands,
a big head, a short neck. They made way for him respect-
fully. He moved very quietly, respectful of them also.
His eyes when he stared down at the child were amazing.
When he blinked, it was like the passing of a hand before
a candle-flame.

"It's only an owlet," he said. "What have you let happen to your eye, new person?"

"I was—We were flying—"

"You're too young to fly," the big man said in his deep,
soft voice. "Who brought you here?"

"Coyote."

And one of the short people confirmed: "She came here with Coyote, Young Owl."

"Then maybe she should stay in Coyote's house tonight," the big man said.

"It's all bones and lonely in there," said a short woman with fat cheeks and a striped shirt. "She can come with us."

That seemed to decide it. The fat-cheeked woman patted the child's arm and took her past several shacks and shanties to a low, windowless house. The doorway was so low even the child had to duck down to enter. There were a lot of people inside, some already there and some crowding in after the fat-cheeked woman. Several babies were fast asleep in cradle-boxes in corners. There was a good fire, and a good smell, like toasted sesame seeds. The child was given food, and ate a little, but her head swam and the blackness in her right eye kept coming across her left eye so she could not see at all for a while. Nobody asked her name or told her what to call them. She heard the children call the fat-cheeked woman Chipmunk. She got up courage finally to say, "Is there somewhere I can go to sleep, Mrs. Chipmunk?"

"Sure, come on," one of the daughters said, "in here," and took the child into a back room, not completely partitioned off from the crowded front room, but dark and uncrowded. Big shelves with mattresses and blankets lined the walls. "Crawl in!" said Chipmunk's daughter, patting the child's arm in the comforting way they had. The child climbed onto a shelf, under a blanket. She laid down her head. She thought, "I didn't brush my teeth."

ii

She woke; she slept again. In Chipmunk's sleeping room it was always stuffy, warm, and half-dark, day and night. People came in and slept and got up and left, night and day. She dozed and slept, got down to drink from the bucket and dipper in the front room, and went back to sleep and doze.

She was sitting up on the shelf, her feet dangling, not feeling bad any more, but dreamy, weak. She felt in her jeans pockets. In the left front one was a pocket comb and a bubblegum wrapper, in the right front, two dollar bills and a quarter and a dime.

Chipmunk and another woman, a very pretty dark-eyed plump one, came in. "So you woke up for your dance!" Chipmunk greeted her, laughing, and sat down by her with an arm around her.

"Jay's giving you a dance," the dark woman said. "He's going to make you all right. Let's get you all ready!"

There was a spring up under the rimrock, that flattened out into a pool with slimy, reedy shores. A flock of noisy children splashing in it ran off and left the child and the two women to bathe. The water was warm on the surface, cold down on the feet and legs. All naked, the two soft-voiced laughing women, their round bellies and breasts, broad hips and buttocks gleaming warm in the late afternoon light, sluiced the child down, washed and stroked her limbs and hands and hair, cleaned around the cheekbone and eyebrow of her right eye with infinite softness, admired her, sudsed her, rinsed her, splashed her out of the water, dried her off, dried each other off, got dressed, dressed her, braided her hair, braided each other's hair, tied feathers on the braid-ends, admired her and each other again, and brought her back down into the little straggling town and to a kind of playing field or dirt parking lot in among the houses. There were no streets, just paths and dirt, no lawns and gardens, just sagebrush and dirt. Quite a few people were gathering or wandering around the open place, looking dressed up, wearing colorful shirts, print dresses, strings of beads, earrings. "Hey there, Chipmunk, Whitefoot!" they greeted the women.

A man in new jeans, with a bright blue velveteen vest over a clean, faded blue workshirt, came forward to meet them, very handsome, tense, and important. "All right,

Gal!" he said in a harsh, loud voice, which startled among all these soft-speaking people. "We're going to get that eye fixed right up tonight! You just sit down here and don't worry about a thing." He took her wrist, gently despite his bossy, brassy manner, and led her to a woven mat that lay on the dirt near the middle of the open place. There, feeling very foolish, she had to sit down, and was told to stay still. She soon got over feeling that everybody was looking at her, since nobody paid her more attention than a checking glance or, from Chipmunk or Whitefoot and their families, a reassuring wink. Every now and then Jay rushed over to her and said something like, "Going to be as good as new!" and went off again to organize people, waving his long blue arms and shouting.

Coming up the hill to the open place, a lean, loose, tawny figure—and the child started to jump up, remembered she was to sit still, and sat still, calling out softly, "Coyote! Coyote!"

Coyote came lounging by. She grinned. She stood looking down at the child. "Don't let that Bluejay fuck you up, Gal," she said, and lounged on.

The child's gaze followed her, yearning.

People were sitting down now over on one side of the open place, making an uneven half-circle that kept getting added to at the ends until there was nearly a circle of people sitting on the dirt around the child, ten or fifteen paces from her. All the people wore the kind of clothes the child was used to, jeans and jeans-jackets, shirts, vests, cotton dresses, but they were all barefoot, and she thought they were more beautiful than the people she knew, each in a different way, as if each one had invented beauty. Yet some of them were also very strange: thin black shining people with whispery voices, a long-legged woman with eyes like jewels. The big man called Young Owl was there, sleepy-looking and dignified, like Judge McCown who owned a sixty-thousand acre ranch; and beside him was a woman the child thought might be his sister, for like him she had a hook nose and big, strong hands; but she was lean and dark, and there was a crazy look in her fierce eyes. Yellow eyes, but round, not long and slanted like Coyote's. There was Coyote sitting yawning, scratching her armpit, bored. Now somebody was entering the circle: a man, wearing only a kind of kilt and a cloak painted or beaded with diamond shapes, dancing to the rhythm of the rattle he carried and shook with a buzzing fast beat. His limbs and body were thick yet supple, his movements smooth and pouring. The child kept her gaze on him as he danced past her, around her, past again. The rattle in his hand shook almost too fast to see, in the other hand was something thin and sharp. People were singing around the circle now, a few notes repeated in time to the rattle, soft and tuneless. It was exciting and boring, strange and familiar. The Rattler wove his dancing closer and closer to her, darting at her. The first time she flinched away, frightened by the lunging movement and by his flat, cold face with narrow eyes, but after that she sat still, knowing her part. The dancing went on, the singing went on, till they carried her past boredom into a floating that could go on forever.

Jay had come strutting into the circle, and was standing beside her. He couldn't sing, but he called out, "Hey! Hey! Hey! Hey!" in his big, harsh voice, and everybody answered from all round, and the echo came down from the rimrock on the second beat. Jay was holding up a stick with a ball on it in one hand, and something like a marble in the other. The stick was a pipe: he got smoke into his mouth from it and blew it in four directions and up and down and then over the marble, a puff each time. Then the rattle stopped suddenly, and everything was silent for several breaths. Jay squatted down and looked intently into the child's face, his head cocked to one side. He reached forward, muttering something in time to the rattle and the singing that had started up again louder than before; he touched the child's right eye in the black center of the pain. She flinched and endured. His touch was not gentle. She saw the marble, a dull yellow ball like beeswax, in his hand; then she shut her seeing eye and set her teeth.

"There!" Jay shouted. "Open up. Come on! Let's see!"

Her jaw clenched like a vise, she opened both eyes. The lid of the right one stuck and dragged with such a searing white pain that she nearly threw up as she sat there in the middle of everybody watching.

"Hey, can you see? How's it work? It looks great!" Jay was shaking her arm, railing at her. "How's it feel? Is it working?"

What she saw was confused, hazy, yellowish. She began to discover, as everybody came crowding around peering at her, smiling, stroking and patting her arms and shoulders, that if she shut the hurting eye and looked with the other, everything was clear and flat; if she used them both, things were blurry and yellowish, but deep.

There, right close, was Coyote's long nose and narrow eyes and grin. "What is it, Jay?" she was asking peering at the new eye. "One of mine you stole that time?"

"It's pine pitch," Jay shouted furiously. "You think I'd use some stupid secondhand coyote eye? I'm a doctor!"

"Ooooh, ooooh, a doctor," Coyote said. "Boy, that is one ugly eye. Why didn't you ask Rabbit for a rabbit-dropping? That eye looks like shit." She put her lean face yet closer, till the child thought she was going to kiss her; instead, the thin, firm tongue once more licked accurate across the pain, cooling, clearing. When the child opened both eyes again the world looked pretty good.

"It works fine," she said.

"Hey!" Jay yelled. "She says it works fine! It works fine, she says so! I told you! What'd I tell you?" He went off waving his arms and yelling. Coyote had disappeared. Everybody was wandering off.

The child stood up, stiff from long sitting. It was nearly dark; only the long west held a great depth of pale radiance. Eastward the plains ran down into night.

Lights were on in some of the shanties. Off at the

edge of town somebody was playing a creaky fiddle, a lonesome chirping tune.

A person came beside her and spoke quietly: "Where will you stay?"

"I don't know," the child said. She was feeling extremely hungry. "Can I stay with Coyote?"

"She isn't home much," the soft-voiced woman said. "You were staying with Chipmunk, weren't you? Or there's Rabbit or Jackrabbit, they have families . . ."

"Do you have a family?" the girl asked, looking at the delicate, soft-eyed woman.

"Two fawns," the woman answered, smiling. "But I just came into town for the dance."

"I'd really like to stay with Coyote," the child said after a little pause, timid, but obstinate.

"OK, that's fine. Her house is over here." Doe walked along beside the child to a ramshackle cabin on the high edge of town. No light shone from inside. A lot of junk was scattered around the front. There was no step up to the half-open door. Over the door a battered pine board, nailed up crooked, said BIDE-A-WEE.

"Hey, Coyote? Visitors," Doe said. Nothing happened.

Doe pushed the door farther open and peered in. "She's out hunting, I guess. I better be getting back to the fawns. You going to be OK? Anybody else here will give you something to eat—you know . . . OK?"

"Yeah. I'm fine. Thank you," the child said.

She watched Doe walk away through the clear twilight, a severely elegant walk, small steps, like a woman in high heels, quick, precise, very light.

Inside Bide-A-Wee it was too dark to see anything and so cluttered that she fell over something at every step. She could not figure out where or how to light a fire. There was something that felt like a bed, but when she lay down on it, it felt more like a dirty-clothes pile, and smelt like one. Things bit her legs, arms, neck, and back. She was terribly hungry. By smell she found her way to what had to be a dead fish hanging from the ceiling in one corner. By feel she broke off a greasy flake and

tasted it. It was smoked dried salmon. She ate one succu-
lent piece after another until she was satisfied, and licked
her fingers clean. Near the open door starlight shone on
water in a pot of some kind; the child smelled it cautiously, tasted it cautiously, and drank just enough to
quench her thirst, for it tasted of mud and was warm
and stale. Then she went back to the bed of dirty clothes
and fleas, and lay down. She could have gone to Chipmunk's house, or other friendly households; she thought
of that as she lay forlorn in Coyote's dirty bed. But she
did not go. She slapped at fleas until she fell asleep.

Along in the deep night somebody said, "Move over,
pup," and was warm beside her.

Breakfast, eaten sitting in the sun in the doorway, was
dried-salmon-powder mush. Coyote hunted, mornings
and evenings, but what they ate was not fresh game but
salmon, and dried stuff, and any berries in season. The
child did not ask about this. It made sense to her. She
was going to ask Coyote why she slept at night and waked
in the day like humans, instead of the other way round
like coyotes, but when she framed the question in her
mind she saw at once that night is when you sleep and
day when you're awake; that made sense too. But one
question she did ask, one hot day when they were lying
around slapping fleas.

"I don't understand why you all look like people," she
said.

"We are people."

"I mean, people like me, humans."

"Resemblance is in the eye," Coyote said. "How is that
lousy eye, by the way?"

"It's fine. But—like you wear clothes—and live in
houses—with fires and stuff—"

"That's what you think ... If that loudmouth Jay
hadn't horned in, I could have done a really good job."

The child was quite used to Coyote's disinclination to
stick to any one subject, and to her boasting. Coyote was

like a lot of kids she knew, in some respects. Not in others.

"You mean what I'm seeing isn't true? Isn't real—like on TV, or something?"

"No," Coyote said. "Hey, that's a tick on your collar." She reached over, flicked the tick off, picked it up on one finger, bit it, and spat out the bits.

"Yecch!" the child said. "So?"

"So, to me you're basically greyish yellow and run on four legs. To that lot—" she waved disdainfully at the warren of little houses next down the hill—"you hop around twitching your nose all the time. To Hawk, you're an egg, or maybe getting pinfeathers. See? It just depends on how you look at things. There are only two kinds of people."

"Humans and animals?"

"No. The kind of people who say. 'There are two kinds of people' and the kind of people who don't.'" Coyote cracked up, pounding her thigh and yelling with delight at her joke. The child didn't get it, and waited.

"OK," Coyote said. "There's the first people, and then the others. That's the two kinds."

"The first people are—?"

"Us, the animals . . . and things. All the old ones. You know. And you pups, kids, fledglings. All first people."

"And the—others?"

"Them," Coyote said. "You know. The others. The new people. The ones who came." Her fine, hard face had gone serious, rather formidable. She glanced directly, as she seldom did, at the child, a brief gold sharpness. "We were here," she said. "We were always here. We are always here. Where we are is here. But it's their country now. They're running it . . . Shit, even I did better!"

The child pondered and offered a word she had used to hear a good deal: "They're illegal immigrants."

"Illegal!" Coyote said, mocking, sneering. "Illegal is a sick bird. What the fuck's illegal mean? You want a code of justice from a coyote? Grow up, kid!"

"I don't want to."

"You don't want to grow up?"

"I'll be the other kind if I do."

"Yeah. So," Coyote said, and shrugged. "That's life." She got up and went around the house, and the child heard her pissing in the back yard.

A lot of things were hard to take about Coyote as a mother. When her boyfriends came to visit, the child learned to go stay with Chipmunk or the Rabbits for the night, because Coyote and her friend wouldn't even wait to get on the bed but would start doing that right on the floor or even out in the yard. A couple of times Coyote came back late from hunting with a friend, and the child had to lie up against the wall in the same bed and hear and feel them doing that right next to her. It was something like fighting and something like dancing, with a beat to it, and she didn't mind too much except that it made it hard to stay asleep.

Once she woke up and one of Coyote's friends was stroking her stomach in a creepy way. She didn't know what to do, but Coyote woke up and realized what he was doing, bit him hard, and kicked him out of bed. He spent the night on the floor, and apologized next morning—"Aw, hell, Ki, I forgot the kid was there, I thought it was you—"

Coyote, unappeased, yelled, "You think I don't got any standards? You think I'd let some coyote rape a kid in my bed?" She kicked him out of the house, and grumbled about him all day. But a while later he spent the night again, and he and Coyote did that three or four times.

Another thing that was embarrassing was the way Coyote peed anywhere, taking her pants down in public. But most people here didn't seem to care. The thing that worried the child most, maybe, was when Coyote did number two anywhere and then turned around and talked to it. That seemed so awful. As if Coyote was— the way she often seemed, but really wasn't—crazy.

The child gathered up all the old dry turds from around the house one day while Coyote was having a

nap, and buried them in a sandy place near where she
and Bobcat and some of the other people generally went
and did and buried their number twos.

Coyote woke up, came lounging out of Bide-A-Wee,
rubbing her hands through her thick, fair, greyish hair
and yawning, looked all around once with those narrow
eyes, and said, "Hey! Where are they?" Then she
shouted, "Where are you? Where are you?"

And a faint, muffled chorus came from over in the
sandy draw, "Mommy! Mommy! We're here!"

Coyote trotted over, squatted down, raked out every
turd, and talked with them for a long time. When she
came back she said nothing, but the child, redfaced and
heart pounding, said, "I'm sorry I did that."

"It's just easier when they're all around close by," Coyote said, washing her hands (despite the filth of her
house, she kept herself quite clean, in her own fashion).

"I kept stepping on them," the child said, trying to
justify her deed.

"Poor little shits," said Coyote, practicing dance-steps.

"Coyote," the child said timidly. "Did you ever have
any children? I mean real pups?"

"Did I? Did I have children? Litters! That one that
tried feeling you up, you know? that was my son. Pick
of the litter . . . Listen, Gal. Have daughters. When you
have anything, have daughters. At least they clear out."

iii

The child thought of herself as Gal, but also sometimes
as Myra. So far as she knew, she was the only person in
town who had two names. She had to think about that,
and about what Coyote had said about the two kinds of
people; she had to think about where she belonged.
Some persons in town made it clear that as far as they
were concerned she didn't and never would belong there.
Hawk's furious stare burned through her; the Skunk chil-

dren made audible remarks about what she smelled like. And though Whitefoot and Chipmunk and their families were kind, it was the generosity of big families, where one more or less simply doesn't count. If one of them, or Cottontail, or Jackrabbit, had come upon her in the desert lying lost and half-blind, would they have stayed with her, like Coyote? That was Coyote's craziness, what they called her craziness. She wasn't afraid. She went between the two kinds of people, she crossed over. Buck and Doe and their beautiful children weren't really afraid, because they lived so constantly in danger. The Rattler wasn't afraid, because he was so dangerous. And yet maybe he was afraid of her, for he never spoke, and never came close to her. None of them treated her the way Coyote did. Even among the children, her only constant playmate was one younger than herself, a preposterous and fearless little boy called Horned Toad Child. They dug and built together, out among the sagebrush, and played at hunting and gathering and keeping house and holding dances, all the great games. A pale, squatty child with fringed eyebrows, he was a self-contained but loyal friend; and he knew a good deal for his age.

"There isn't anybody else like me here," she said, as they sat by the pool in the morning sunlight.

"There isn't anybody much like me anywhere," said Horned Toad Child.

"Well, you know what I mean."

"Yeah . . . There used to be people like you around, I guess."

"What were they called?"

"Oh—people. Like everybody . . ."

"But where do my people live? They have towns. I used to live in one. I don't know where they are, is all. I ought to find out. I don't know where my mother is now, but my daddy's in Canyonville. I was going there when."

"Ask Horse," said Horned Toad Child, sagaciously. He had moved away from the water, which he did not like and never drank, and was plaiting rushes.

"I don't know Horse."

"He hangs around the butte down there a lot of the time. He's waiting till his uncle gets old and he can kick him out and be the big honcho. The old man and the women don't want him around till then. Horses are weird. Anyway, he's the one to ask. He gets around a lot. And his people came here with the new people, that's what they say, anyhow."

Illegal immigrants, the girl thought. She took Horned Toad's advice, and one long day when Coyote was gone on one of her unannounced and unexplained trips, she took a pouchful of dried salmon and salmonberries and went off alone to the flat-topped butte miles away in the southwest.

There was a beautiful spring at the foot of the butte, and a trail to it with a lot of footprints on it. She waited there under willows by the clear pool, and after a while Horse came running, splendid, with copper-red skin and long, strong legs, deep chest, dark eyes, his black hair whipping his back as he ran. He stopped, not at all winded, and gave a snort as he looked at her. "Who are you?"

Nobody in town asked that—ever. She saw it was true: Horse had come here with her people, people who had to ask each other who they were.

"I live with Coyote," she said, cautiously.

"Oh, sure, I heard about you," Horse said. He knelt to drink from the pool, long deep drafts, his hands plunged in the cool water. When he had drunk he wiped his mouth, sat back on his heels, and announced, "I'm going to be king."

"King of the Horses?"

"Right! Pretty soon now. I could lick the old man already, but I can wait. Let him have his day," said Horse, vainglorious, magnanimous. The child gazed at him, in love already, forever.

"I can comb your hair, if you like," she said.

"Great!" said Horse, and sat still while she stood behind him, tugging her pocket comb through his coarse, black, shining, yard-long hair. It took a long time to get it smooth. She tied it in a massive ponytail with willowbark when she was done. Horse bent over the pool to admire himself. "That's great," he said. "That's really beautiful!"

"Do you ever go . . . where the other people are?" she asked in a low voice.

He did not reply for long enough that she thought he wasn't going to; then he said, "You mean the metal places, the glass places? The holes? I go around them. There are all the walls now. There didn't used to be so many. Grandmother said there didn't used to be any walls. Do you know Grandmother?" he asked naively, looking at her with his great dark eyes.

"Your grandmother?"

"Well, yes—Grandmother—You know. Who makes the web. Well, anyhow. I know there's some of my people, horses, there. I've seen them across the walls. They act really crazy. You know, we brought the new people here. They couldn't have got here without us, they only have two legs, and they have those metal shells. I can tell you that whole story. The King has to know the stories."

"I like stories a lot."

"It takes three nights to tell it. What do you want to know about them?"

"I was thinking that maybe I ought to go there. Where they are."

"It's dangerous. Really dangerous. You can't go through—they'd catch you."

"I'd just like to know the way."

"I know the way," Horse said, sounding for the first time entirely adult and reliable; she knew he did know the way. "It's a long run for a colt." He looked at her again. "I've got a cousin with different-color eyes," he said, looking from her right to her left eye. "One brown and one blue. But she's an Appaloosa."

"Bluejay made the yellow one," the child explained. "I

lost my own one. In the . . . when . . . You don't think I
could get to those places?"

"Why do you want to?"

"I sort of feel like I have to."

Horse nodded. He got up. She stood still.

"I could take you, I guess," he said.

"Would you? When?"

"Oh, now, I guess. Once I'm King I won't be able to
leave, you know. Have to protect the women. And I sure
wouldn't let my people get anywhere near those places!"
A shudder ran right down his magnificent body, yet he
said, with a toss of his head, "They couldn't catch me,
of course, but the others can't run like I do . . ."

"How long would it take us?"

Horse thought a while. "Well, the nearest place like
that is over by the red rocks. If we left now we'd be
back here around tomorrow noon. It's just a little hole."

She did not know what he meant by "a hole," but did
not ask.

"You want to go?" Horse said, flipping back his
ponytail.

"OK," the girl said, feeling the ground go out from
under her.

"Can you run?"

She shook her head. "I walked here, though."

Horse laughed, a large, cheerful laugh. "Come on," he
said, and knelt and held his hands backturned like stir-
rups for her to mount to his shoulders. "What do they
call you?" he teased, rising easily, setting right off at a
jogtrot. "Gnat? Fly? Flea?"

"Tick, because I stick!" the child cried, gripping the
willowbark tie of the black mane, laughing with delight
at being suddenly eight feet tall and traveling across the
desert without even trying, like the tumbleweed, as fast
as the wind.

Moon, a night past full, rose to light the plains for
them. Horse jogged easily on and on. Somewhere deep
in the night they stopped at a Pygmy Owl camp, ate a

little, and rested. Most of the owls were out hunting, but an old lady entertained them at her campfire, telling them tales about the ghost of a cricket, about the great invisible people, tales that the child heard interwoven with her own dreams as she dozed and half-woke and dozed again. Then Horse put her up on his shoulders and on they went at a tireless slow lope. Moon went down behind them, and before them the sky paled into rose and gold. The soft nightwind was gone; the air was sharp, cold, still. On it, in it, there was a faint, sour smell of burning. The child felt Horse's gait change, grow tighter, uneasy.

"Hey, Prince!"

A small, slightly scolding voice: the child knew it, and placed it as soon as she saw the person sitting by a juniper tree, neatly dressed, wearing an old black cap.

"Hey, Chickadee!" Horse said, coming round and stopping. The child had observed, back in Coyote's town, that everybody treated Chickadee with respect. She didn't see why. Chickadee seemed an ordinary person, busy and talkative like most of the small birds, nothing like so endearing as Quail or so impressive as Hawk or Great Owl.

"You're going on that way?" Chickadee asked Horse.

"The little one wants to see if her people are living there," Horse said, surprising the child. Was that what she wanted?

Chickadee looked disapproving, as she often did. She whistled a few notes thoughtfully, another of her habits, and then got up. "I'll come along."

"That's great," Horse said, thankfully.

"I'll scout," Chickadee said, and off she went, surprisingly fast, ahead of them, while Horse took up his steady long lope.

The sour smell was stronger in the air.

Chickadee halted, way ahead of them on a slight rise, and stood still. Horse dropped to a walk, and then stopped. "There," he said in a low voice.

The child stared. In the strange light and slight mist before sunrise she could not see clearly, and when she

strained and peered she felt as if her left eye were not
seeing at all. "What is it?" she whispered.

"One of the holes. Across the wall—see?"

It did seem there was a line, a straight, jerky line
drawn across the sagebrush plain, and on the far side of
it—nothing? Was it mist? Something moved there—"It's
cattle!" she said. Horse stood silent, uneasy. Chickadee
was coming back towards them.

"It's a ranch," the child said. "That's a fence. There's
a lot of Herefords." The words tasted like iron, like salt
in her mouth. The things she named wavered in her sight
and faded, leaving nothing—a hole in the world, a
burned place like a cigarette burn. "Go closer!" she
urged Horse. "I want to see."

And as if he owed her obedience, he went forward,
tense but unquestioning.

Chickadee came up to them. "Nobody around," she
said in her small, dry voice, "but there's one of those fast
turtle things coming."

Horse nodded, but kept going forward.

Gripping his broad shoulders, the child stared into the
blank, and as if Chickadee's words had focused her eyes,
she saw again: the scattered whitefaces, a few of them
looking up with bluish, rolling eyes—the fences—over
the rise a chimneyed house-roof and a high barn—and
then in the distance something moving fast, too fast,
burning across the ground straight at them at terrible
speed. "Run!" she yelled to Horse, "run away! Run!" As
if released from bonds he wheeled and ran, flat out, in
great reaching strides, away from sunrise, the fiery burning chariot, the smell of acid, iron, death. And Chickadee
flew before them like a cinder on the air of dawn.

iv

"Horse?" Coyote said. "That prick? Catfood!"

Coyote had been there when the child got home to
Bide-A-Wee, but she clearly hadn't been worrying about

where Gal was, and maybe hadn't even noticed she was gone. She was in a vile mood, and took it all wrong when the child tried to tell her where she had been.

"If you're going to do damn fool things, next time do 'em with me, at least I'm an expert," she said, morose, and slouched out the door. The child saw her squatting down, poking an old, white turd with a stick, trying to get it to answer some question she kept asking it. The turd lay obstinately silent. Later in the day the child saw two coyote men, a young one and a mangy-looking older one, loitering around near the spring, looking over at Bide-A-Wee. She decided it would be a good night to spend somewhere else.

The thought of the crowded rooms of Chipmunk's house was not attractive. It was going to be a warm night again tonight, and moonlit. Maybe she would sleep outside. If she could feel sure some people wouldn't come around, like the Rattler . . . She was standing indecisive halfway through town when a dry voice said, "Hey, Gal."

"Hey, Chickadee."

The trim, black-capped woman was standing on her doorstep shaking out a rug, She kept her house neat, trim like herself. Having come back across the desert with her the child now knew, though she still could not have said, why Chickadee was a respected person.

"I thought maybe I'd sleep out tonight," the child said, tentative.

"Unhealthy," said Chickadee. "What are nests for?"

"Mom's kind of busy," the child said.

"Tsk!" went Chickadee, and snapped the rug with disapproving vigor. "What about your little friend? At least they're decent people."

"Horny-toad? His parents are so shy . . ."

"Well. Come in and have something to eat, anyhow," said Chickadee.

The child helped her cook dinner. She knew now why there were rocks in the mush-pot.

"Chickadee," she said, "I still don't understand, can I ask you? Mom said it depends who's seeing it, but still,

I mean if I see you wearing clothes and everything like humans, then how come you cook this way, in baskets, you know, and there aren't any—any of the things like they have—there where we were with Horse this morning?"

"I don't know," Chickadee said. Her voice indoors was quite soft and pleasant. "I guess we do things the way they always were done. When your people and my people lived together, you know. And together with everything else here. The rocks, you know. The plants and everything." She looked at the basket of willowbark, fernroot and pitch, at the blackened rocks that were heating in the fire. "You see how it all goes together . . . ?"

"But you have fire—That's different—"

"Ah!" said Chickadee, impatient, "you people! Do you think you invented the sun?"

She took up the wooden tongs, plopped the heated rocks into the water-filled basket with a terrific hiss and steam and loud bubblings. The child sprinkled in the pounded seeds, and stirred.

Chickadee brought out a basket of fine blackberries. They sat on the newly-shaken-out rug, and ate. The child's two-finger scoop technique with mush was now highly refined.

"Maybe I didn't cause the world," Chickadee said, "but I'm a better cook than Coyote."

The child nodded, stuffing.

"I don't know why I made Horse go there," she said, after she had stuffed. "I got just as scared as him when I saw it. But now I feel again like I have to go back there. But I want to stay here. With my, with Coyote. I don't understand."

"When we lived together it was all one place," Chickadee said in her slow, soft home-voice. "But now the others, the new people, they live apart. And their places are so heavy. They weigh down on our place, they press on it, draw it, suck it, eat it, eat holes in it, crowd it out . . . Maybe after a while longer there'll only be one place again, their place. And none of us here. I knew Bison, out over the mountains. I knew Antelope right here. I knew Grizzly and Greywolf, up west there. Gone. All gone. And the salmon you eat at Coyote's house, those are the dream salmon, those are the true food; but in the rivers, how many salmon now? The rivers that were red with them in spring? Who dances, now, when the First Salmon offers himself? Who dances by the river? Oh, you should ask Coyote about all this. She knows more than I do! But she forgets . . . She's hopeless, worse than Raven, she has to piss on every post, she's a terrible housekeeper . . ." Chickadee's voice had sharpened. She whistled a note or two, and said no more.

After a while the child asked very softly, "Who is Grandmother?"

"Grandmother," Chickadee said. She looked at the child, and ate several blackberries thoughtfully. She stroked the rug they sat on.

"If I built the fire on the rug, it would burn a hole in it," she said. "Right? So we build the fire on sand, on dirt . . . Things are woven together. So we call the weaver the Grandmother." She whistled four notes, looking up the smokehole. "After all," she added, "maybe all this place, the other places too, maybe they're all only one side of the weaving, I don't know. I can only look with one eye at a time, how can I tell how deep it goes?"

Lying that night rolled up in a blanket in Chickadee's back yard, the child heard the wind soughing and storming in the cottonwoods down in the draw, and then slept deeply, weary from the long night before. Just at sunrise she woke. The eastern mountains were a cloudy dark red as if the level light shone through them as through a hand held before the fire. In the tobacco patch—the only farming anybody in this town did was to raise a little wild tobacco—Lizard and Beetle were singing some kind of growing song or blessing song, soft and desultory, huh-huh-huh-huh, huh-huh-huh-huh, and as she lay warm-curled on the ground the song made her feel rooted in the ground, cradled on it and in it, so where her fingers ended and the dirt began she did not know, as if she were dead, but she was wholly alive, she was the earth's life. She got up dancing, left the blanket folded neatly on Chickadee's neat and already empty bed, and danced up the hill to Bide-A-Wee. At the half-open door she sang,

> *"Danced with a gal with a hole in her stocking*
> *And her knees kept a knocking and her toes*
> *kept a rocking,*
> *Danced with a gal with a hole in her stocking,*
> *Danced by the light of the moon!"*

Coyote emerged, tousled and lurching, and eyed her narrowly. "Sheeeoot," she said. She sucked her teeth and then went to splash water all over her head from the gourd by the door. She shook her head and the waterdrops flew. "Let's get out of here," she said. "I have had it. I don't know what got into me. If I'm pregnant again, at my age, oh, shit. Let's get out of town. I need a change of air."

In the foggy dark of the house, the child could see at least two coyote men sprawled snoring away on the bed and floor. Coyote walked over to the old white turd and kicked it. "Why didn't you stop me?" she shouted.

"I *told* you," the turd muttered sulkily.

"Dumb shit," Coyote said. "Come on, Gal. Let's go. Where to?" She didn't wait for an answer. "I know. Come on!"

And she set off through town at that lazy-looking rangy walk that was so hard to keep up with. But the child was full of pep, and came dancing, so that Coyote began dancing too, skipping and pirouetting and fooling around all the way down the long slope to the level plains. There she slanted their way off north-eastward. Horse Butte was at their backs, getting smaller in the distance.

Along near noon the child said, "I didn't bring anything to eat."

"Something will turn up," Coyote said, "sure to." And pretty soon she turned aside, going straight to a tiny grey shack hidden by a couple of half-dead junipers and a stand of rabbit-brush. The place smelled terrible. A sign on the door said: FOX. PRIVATE. NO TRESPASSING!—but Coyote pushed it open, and trotted right back out with half a small smoked salmon. "Nobody home but us chickens," she said, grinning sweetly.

"Isn't that stealing?" the child asked, worried.

"Yes," Coyote answered, trotting on.

They ate the fox-scented salmon by a dried-up creek, slept a while, and went on.

Before long the child smelled the sour burning smell, and stopped. It was as if a huge, heavy hand had begun pushing her chest, pushing her away, and yet at the same time as if she had stepped into a strong current that drew her forward, helpless.

"Hey, getting close!" Coyote said, and stopped to piss by a juniper stump.

"Close to what?"

"Their town. See?" She pointed to a pair of sage-spotted hills. Between them was an area of greyish blank.

"I don't want to go there."

"We won't go all the way in. No way! We'll just get a little closer and look. It's fun," Coyote said, putting her head on one side, coaxing. "They do all these weird things in the air."

The child hung back.

Coyote became business-like, responsible. "We're going to be very careful," she announced. "And look out for big dogs, OK? Little dogs I can handle. Make a good lunch. Big dogs, it goes the other way. Right? Let's go, then."

Seemingly as casual and lounging as ever, but with a tense alertness in the carriage of her head and the yellow glance of her eyes, Coyote led off again, not looking back; and the child followed.

All around them the pressures increased. It was if the air itself was pressing on them, as if time was going too fast, too hard, not flowing but pounding, pounding, pounding, faster and harder till it buzzed like Rattler's rattle. Hurry, you have to hurry! everything said, there isn't time! everything said. Things rushed past screaming and shuddering. Things turned, flashed, roared, stank, vanished. There was a boy—he came into focus all at once, but not on the ground: he was going along a couple of inches above the ground, moving very fast, bending his legs from side to side in a kind of frenzied swaying dance, and was gone. Twenty children sat in rows in the air all singing shrilly and then the walls closed over them. A basket no a pot no a can, a garbage can, full of salmon smelling wonderful no full of stinking deerhides and rotten cabbage stalks, keep out of it, Coyote! Where was she?

"Mom!" the child called. "Mother!"—standing a moment at the end of an ordinary small-town street near the gas station, and the next moment in a terror of blanknesses, invisible walls, terrible smells and pressures and the overwhelming rush of Time straight forward rolling her helpless as a twig in the race above a waterfall. She clung, held on trying not to fall—"Mother!"

Coyote was over by the big basket of salmon, approaching it, wary, but out in the open, in the full sunlight, in the full current. And a boy and a man borne by the same current were coming down the long, sage-spotted hill behind the gas station, each with a gun, red hats, hunters, it was killing season. "Hell, will you look at that damn coyote in broad daylight big as my wife's ass," the man said, and cocked aimed shot all as Myra screamed and ran against the enormous drowning torrent. Coyote fled past her yelling, "Get out of here!" She turned and was borne away.

Far out of sight of that place, in a little draw among low hills, they sat and breathed air in searing gasps until after a long time it came easy again.

"Mom, that was *stupid*," the child said furiously.

"Sure was," Coyote said. "But did you see all that food!"

"I'm not hungry," the child said sullenly. "Not till we get all the way away from here."

"But they're your folks," Coyote said. "All yours. Your

kith and kin and cousins and kind. Bang! Pow! There's
Coyote! Bang! There's my wife's ass! Pow! There's anything—BOOOOM! Blow it away, man! BOOOOOOM!"

"I want to go home," the child said.

"Not yet," said Coyote. "I got to take a shit." She did
so, then turned to the fresh turd, leaning over it. "It says
I have to stay," she reported, smiling.

"It didn't say anything! I was listening!"

"You know how to understand? You hear everything,
Miss Big Ears? Hears all—Sees all with her crummy
gummy eye—"

"You have pine-pitch eyes too! You told me so!"

"That's a story," Coyote snarled. "You don't even know
a story when you hear one! Look, do what you like, it's
a free country. I'm hanging around here tonight. I like
the action." She sat down and began patting her hands
on the dirt in a soft four-four rhythm and singing under
her breath, one of the endless tuneless songs that kept
time from running too fast, that wove the roots of trees
and bushes and ferns and grass in the web that held the
stream in the streambed and the rock in the rock's place
and the earth together. And the child lay listening.

"I love you," she said.

Coyote went on singing.

Sun went down the last slope of the west and left a
pale green clarity over the desert hills.

Coyote had stopped singing. She sniffed. "Hey," she
said. "Dinner." She got up and moseyed along the little
draw. "Yeah," she called back softly. "Come on!"

Stiffly, for the fear-crystals had not yet melted out of
her joints, the child got up and went to Coyote. Off to
one side along the hill was one of the lines, a fence. She
didn't look at it. It was OK. They were outside it.

"Look at that!"

A smoked salmon, a whole chinook, lay on a little
cedarbark mat. "An offering! Well, I'll be darned!" Coyote was so impressed she didn't even swear. "I haven't
seen one of these for years! I thought they'd forgotten!"

"Offering to who?"

"Me! Who else? Boy, *look* at that!"

The child looked dubiously at the salmon.

"It smells funny."

"How funny?"

"Like burned."

"It's smoked, stupid! Come on."

"I'm not hungry."

"OK. It's not your salmon anyhow. It's mine. My offering, for me. Hey, you people! You people over there! Coyote thanks you! Keep it up like this and maybe I'll do some things for you too!"

"Don't, don't yell, Mom! They're not that far away—"

"They're all my people," said Coyote with a great gesture, and then sat down cross-legged, broke off a big piece of salmon, and ate.

Evening Star burned like a deep, bright pool of water in the clear sky. Down over the twin hills was a dim suffusion of light, like a fog. The child looked away from it, back at the star.

"Oh," Coyote said. "Oh, shit."

"What's wrong?"

"That wasn't so smart, eating that," Coyote said, and then held herself and began to shiver, to scream, to choke—her eyes rolled up, her long arms and legs flew out jerking and dancing, foam spurted out between her clenched teeth. Her body arched tremendously backwards, and the child, trying to hold her, was thrown violently off by the spasms of her limbs. The child scrambled back and held the body as it spasmed again, twitched, quivered, went still.

By moonrise Coyote was cold. Till then there had been so much warmth under the tawny coat that the child kept thinking maybe she was alive, maybe if she just kept holding her, keeping her warm, she would recover, she would be all right. She held her close, not looking at the black lips drawn back from the teeth, the white balls of the eyes. But when the cold came through the fur as the presence of death, the child let the slight, stiff corpse lie down on the dirt.

She went nearby and dug a hole in the stony sand of the draw, a shallow pit. Coyote's people did not bury their dead, she knew that. But her people did. She carried the small corpse to the pit, laid it down, and covered it with her blue and white bandanna. It was not large enough; the four stiff paws stuck out. The child heaped the body over with sand and rocks and a scurf of sagebrush and tumbleweed held down with more rocks. She also went to where the salmon had lain on the cedar mat, and finding the carcass of a lamb heaped dirt and rocks over the poisoned thing. Then she stood up and walked away without looking back.

At the top of the hill she stood and looked across the draw toward the misty glow of the lights of the town lying in the pass between the twin hills.

"I hope you all die in pain," she said aloud. She turned away and walked down into the desert.

v

It was Chickadee who met her, on the second evening, north of Horse Butte.

"I didn't cry," the child said.

"None of us do," said Chickadee. "Come with me this way now. Come into Grandmother's house."

It was underground, but very large, dark and large, and the Grandmother was there at the center, at her loom. She was making a rug or blanket of the hills and the black rain and the white rain, weaving in the lightning. As they spoke she wove.

"Hello, Chickadee. Hello, New Person."

"Grandmother," Chickadee greeted her.

The child said, "I'm not one of them."

Grandmother's eyes were small and dim. She smiled and wove. The shuttle thrummed through the warp.

"Old Person, then," said Grandmother. "You'd better go back there now, Granddaughter. That's where you live."

"I lived with Coyote. She's dead. They killed her."

"Oh, don't worry about Coyote!" Grandmother said, with a little huff of laughter. "She gets killed all the time."

The child stood still. She saw the endless weaving.

"Then I—Could I go back home—to her house?"

"I don't think it would work," Grandmother said. "Do you, Chickadee?"

Chickadee shook her head once, silent.

"It would be dark there now, and empty, and fleas . . . You got outside your people's time, into our place; but I think that Coyote was taking you back, see. Her way. If you go back now, you can still live with them. Isn't your father there?"

The child nodded.

"They've been looking for you."

"They have?"

"Oh, yes, ever since you fell out of the sky. The man was dead, but you weren't there—they kept looking."

"Serves him right. Serves them all right," the child said. She put her hands up over her face and began to cry terribly, without tears.

"Go on, little one, Granddaughter," Spider said. "Don't be afraid. You can live well there. I'll be there too, you know. In your dreams, in your ideas, in dark corners in the basement. Don't kill me, or I'll make it rain . . ."

"I'll come around," Chickadee said. "Make gardens for me."

The child held her breath and clenched her hands until her sobs stopped and let her speak.

"Will I ever see Coyote?"

"I don't know," the Grandmother replied.

The child accepted this. She said, after another silence, "Can I keep my eye?"

"Yes. You can keep your eye."

"Thank you, Grandmother," the child said. She turned away then and started up the night slope towards the next day. Ahead of her in the air of dawn for a long way a little bird flew, black-capped, light-winged.

Why I Left Harry's All-Night Hamburgers

by Lawrence Watt-Evans

Harry's was a nice place—probably still is. I haven't been back lately. It's a couple of miles off I-79, a few exits north of Charleston, near a place called Sutton. Used to do a pretty fair business until they finished building the Interstate out from Charleston and made it worthwhile for some fast-food joints to move in right next to the cloverleaf; nobody wanted to drive the extra miles to Harry's after that. Folks used to wonder how old Harry stayed in business, as a matter of fact, but he did all right even without the Interstate trade. I found out when I worked there.

Why did I work there, instead of at one of the fast-food joints? Because my folks lived in a little house just around the corner from Harry's, out in the middle of nowhere—not in Sutton itself, just out there on the road. Wasn't anything around except our house and Harry's place. He lived out back of his restaurant. That was about the only thing I could walk to in under an hour, and I didn't have a car.

This was when I was sixteen. I needed a job, because my dad was out of work again and if I was gonna do anything I needed my own money. Mom didn't mind my using her car—so long as it came back with a full tank of gas and I didn't keep it too long. That was the rule. So I needed some work, and Harry's All-Night Hamburgers was the only thing within walking distance. Harry said he had all the help he needed—two cooks and two people working the counter, besides himself. The others worked days, two to a shift, and Harry did the late night stretch all by himself. I hung out there a little, since I didn't have anywhere else, and it looked like pretty easy work—there was hardly any business, and those guys mostly sat around telling dirty jokes. So I figured it was perfect.

Harry, though, said that he didn't need any help.

I figured that was probably true, but I wasn't going to let logic keep me out of driving my mother's car. I did some serious begging, and after I'd made his life miserable for a week or two, Harry said he'd take a chance and give me a shot, working the graveyard shift, midnight to eight A.M., as his counterman, busboy, and janitor all in one.

I talked him down to 7:30, so I could still get to school, and we had us a deal. I didn't care about school so much myself, but my parents wanted me to go, and it was a good place to see my friends, y'know? Meet girls and so on.

So I started working at Harry's nights. I showed up at midnight the first night, and Harry gave me an apron and a little hat, like something from a diner in an old movie, same as he wore himself. I was supposed to wait tables and clean up, not cook, so I don't know why he wanted me to wear them, but he gave them to me, and I needed the bucks, so I put them on and pretended I didn't notice that the apron was all stiff with grease and smelled like something nasty had died on it a few weeks back. And Harry—he's a funny old guy, always looked fifty-ish, as far back as I can remember. Never young, but never getting really old, either, you know? Some people do that, they just seem to go on forever. Anyway, he showed me where everything was in the kitchen and back room, told me to keep busy cleaning up whatever looked like it wanted cleaning, and told me, over and over again, like he was really worried that I was going to cause trouble, "Don't bother the customers. Just take their orders, bring them their food, and don't bother them. You got that?"

"Sure," I said, "I got it."

"Good," he said. "We get some funny guys in here at night, but they're good customers, most of them, so don't you screw up with anyone. One customer complains, one customer stiffs you for the check, and you're out of work, you got that?"

"Sure," I said, though I've gotta admit I was wondering what to do if some cheapskate skipped without paying. I tried to figure how much of a meal would be worth paying for in order to keep the job, but with taxes and all it got too tricky for me to work out, and I decided to wait until the time came, if it ever did.

Then Harry went back in the kitchen, and I got a broom and swept up out front a little until a couple of truckers came in and ordered burgers and coffee.

I was pretty awkward at first, but I got the hang of it after a little bit. Guys would come in, women, too, one or two at a time, and they'd order something, and Harry'd have it ready faster than you can say "cheese," practically, and they'd eat it, and wipe their mouths, and go use the john, and drive off, and none of them said a damn thing to me except their orders, and I didn't say anything back except "Yes, sir," or "Yes, ma'am," or "Thank you, come again." I figured they were all just truckers who didn't like the fast-food places.

That was what it was like at first, anyway, from midnight to about one, one-thirty, but then things would slow down. Even the truckers were off the roads by then, I guess, or they didn't want to get that far off the Interstate, or they'd all had lunch, or something. Anyway, by about two that first night I was thinking it was pretty clear why Harry didn't think he needed help on this shift, when the door opened and the little bell rang.

I jumped a bit; that bell startled me, and I turned around, but then I turned back to look at Harry, 'cause I'd seen him out of the corner of my eye, you know, and he'd got this worried look on his face, and *he* was watching *me*; he wasn't looking at the customer at all.

About then I realized that the reason the bell had startled me was that I hadn't heard anyone drive up, and who the hell was going to be out walking to Harry's place at two in the morning in the West Virginia mountains? The way Harry was looking at me, I knew this must be one of those special customers he didn't want me to scare away.

So I turned around, and there was this short little guy in a really heavy coat, all zipped up, made of that shiny silver fabric you see race-car drivers wear in the cigarette ads, you know? And he had on padded ski pants of the same stuff, with pockets all over the place, and he was just putting down a hood, and he had on big thick goggles like he'd been out in a blizzard, but it was April and there hadn't been any snow in weeks and it was about fifty, sixty degrees out.

Well, I didn't want to blow it, so I pretended I didn't notice, I just said, "Hello, sir; may I take your order?"

He looked at me funny and said, "I suppose so."

"Would you like to see a menu?" I said, trying to be on my best behavior—hell, I was probably overdoing it; I'd let the truckers find their own menus.

"I suppose so," he said again, and I handed him the menu.

He looked it over, pointed to a picture of a cheeseburger that looked about as much like anything from Harry's grill as Sly Stallone looks like me, and I wrote it down and passed the slip back to Harry, and he hissed at me, "Don't bother the guy!"

I took the hint, and went back to sweeping until the burger was up, and as I was handing the plate to the guy there was a sound out front like a shotgun going off, and this green light flashed in through the window, so I nearly dropped the thing, but I couldn't go look because the customer was digging through his pockets for money, to pay for the burger.

"You can pay after you've eaten, sir," I said.

"I will pay first," he said, real formal. "I may need to depart quickly. My money may not be good here."

The guy hadn't got any accent, but with that about the money I figured he was a foreigner, so I waited, and he hauled out a handful of weird coins, and I told him, "I'll need to check with the manager." He gave me the coins, and while I was taking them back to Harry and trying to see out the window, through the curtain, to see where that green light came from, the door opened and these three women came in, and where the first guy was all wrapped up like an Eskimo, these people weren't wearing anything but jeans. Women, remember, and it was only April.

Hey, I was just sixteen, so I tried real hard not to stare and I went running back to the kitchen and tried to tell Harry what was going on, but the money and the green light and the half-naked women all got tangled up and I didn't make much sense.

"I *told* you I get some strange customers, kid," he said. "Let's see the money." So I gave him the coins, and he said, "Yeah, we'll take these," and made change—I don't know how, because the writing on the coins looked like Russian to me, and I couldn't figure out what any of them were. He gave me the change, and then looked me in the eye and said, "Can you handle those women, boy? It's part of the job; I wasn't expecting them tonight, but we get strange people in here, I told you that. You think you can handle it without losing me any customers, or do you want to call it a night and find another job?"

I really wanted that paycheck; I gritted my teeth and said, "No problem!"

When you were sixteen, did you ever try to wait tables with six bare boobs right there in front of you? Those three were laughing and joking in some foreign language I'd never heard before, and I think only one of them spoke English, because she did all the ordering. I managed somehow, and by the time they left Harry was almost smiling at me.

Around four things slowed down again, and around

four-thirty or five the breakfast crowd began to trickle in, but between two and four there were about half a dozen customers, I guess; I don't remember who they all were any more, most of them weren't that strange, but that first little guy and the three women, them I remember. Maybe some of the others were pretty strange, too, maybe stranger than the first guy, but he was the *first*, which makes a difference, and then those women—well, that's gonna really make an impression on a sixteen-year-old, y'know? It's not that they were particularly beautiful or anything, because they weren't, they were just women, and I wasn't used to seeing women with no shirts.

When I got off at seven-thirty, I was all mixed up; I didn't know what the hell was going on. I was beginning to think maybe I imagined it all.

I went home and changed clothes and caught the bus to school, and what with not really having adjusted to working nights, and being tired, and having to think about schoolwork, I was pretty much convinced that the whole thing had been some weird dream. So I came home, slept through until about eleven, then got up and went to work again.

And damn, it was almost the same, except that there weren't any half-naked women this time. The normal truckers and the rest came in first, then they faded out, and the weirdos starting turning up.

At sixteen, you know, you think you can cope with anything. At least, I did. So I didn't let the customers bother me, not even the ones who didn't look like they were exactly human beings to begin with. Harry got used to me being there, and I did make it a lot easier on him, so after the first couple of weeks it was pretty much settled that I could stay on for as long as I liked.

And I liked it fine, really, once I got used to the weird hours. I didn't have much of a social life during the week, but I never had, living where I did, and I could afford to do the weekends up in style with what Harry paid me and the tips I got. Some of those tips I had to take to the jewelers in Charleston, different ones so nobody would notice that one guy was bringing in all these weird coins and trinkets, but Harry gave me some pointers—he'd been doing the same thing for years, except that he'd gone through every jeweler in Charleston and Huntington and Wheeling and Washington, PA., and was halfway through Pittsburgh.

It was fun, really, seeing just what would turn up there and order a burger. I think my favorite was the guy who walked in, no car, no lights, no nothing, wearing this electric blue hunter's vest with wires all over it, and these medieval tights with what Harry called a codpiece, with snow and some kind of sticky goop all over his vest and in his hair, shivering like it was the Arctic out there, when it was the middle of July. He had some kind of little animal crawling around under that vest, but he wouldn't let me get a look at it; from the shape of the bulge it made it might have been a weasel or something. He had the strangest damn accent you ever heard, but he acted right at home and ordered without looking at the menu.

Harry admitted, when I'd been there awhile, that he figured anyone else would mess things up for him somehow. I might have thought I was going nuts, or I might have called the cops, or I might have spread a lot of strange stories around, but I didn't, and Harry appreciated that.

Hey, that was easy. If these people didn't bother Harry, I figured, why should they bother me? And it wasn't anybody else's business, either. When people asked, I used to tell them that sure, we got weirdos in the place late at night—but I never said just how weird.

And I never got as cool about it as Harry was; I mean, a flying saucer in the parking lot wouldn't make Harry blink. *I* blinked, when we got 'em—we did, but not very often, and I had to really work not to stare at them. Most of the customers had more sense; if they came in something strange they hid it in the woods or something. But there were always a few who couldn't be bothered.

If any state cops ever cruised past there and saw those things, I guess they didn't dare report them. No one would've believed them anyway.

I asked Harry once if all these guys came from the same place.

"Damned if I know," he said. He'd never asked, and he didn't want me to, either.

Except he was wrong about thinking that would scare them away. Sometimes you can tell when someone wants to talk, and some of these people did. So I talked to them.

I think I was seventeen by the time someone told me what was really going on, though.

Before you ask any stupid questions, no, they weren't any of them Martians or monsters from outer space or anything like that. Some of them were from West Virginia, in fact. Just not *our* West Virginia. Lots of different West Virginias, instead. What the science fiction writers called "parallel worlds." That's one name, anyway. Other dimensions, alternate realities, they had lots of different names for it.

It all makes sense, really. A couple of them explained it to me. See, everything that ever could possibly have happened, in the entire history of the universe right from the Big Bang up until now, *did* happen—somewhere. And *every* possible difference means a different universe. Not just if Napoleon lost at Waterloo, or won, or whatever he didn't do here; what does Napoleon matter to the *universe*, anyway? Betelgeuse doesn't give a flying damn for all of Europe, past, present, or future. But every single atom or particle or whatever, whenever it had a chance to do something—break up or stay together, or move one direction instead of another, whatever—it did *all* of them, but all in different universes. They didn't branch off, either—all the universes were always there, there just wasn't any difference between them until this particular event came along. And that means that there are millions and millions of identical universes, too, where the differences haven't happened yet. There's an infinite number of universes—more than that, an infinity of infinities. I mean, you can't really comprehend it; if you think you're close, then multiply that a few zillion times. *Everything* is out there.

And that means that in a lot of those universes, people figured out how to travel from one to another. Apparently it's not that hard; there are lots of different ways to do it, too, which is why we got everything from guys in street clothes to people in spacesuits and flying saucers.

But there's one thing about it—with an infinite number of universes, I mean really infinite, how can you find just one? Particularly the first time out? Fact is, you can't. It's just not possible. So the explorers go out, but they don't come back. Maybe if some *did* come back, they could look at what they did and where it took them and figure out how to measure and aim and all that, but so far as any of the ones I've talked to know, nobody has ever done it. When you go out, that's it, you're out there. You can go on hopping from one world to the next, or you can settle down in one forever, but like the books say, you *really* can't go home again. You can get close, maybe—one way I found out a lot of this was in exchange for telling this poor old geezer a lot about the world outside Harry's. He was pretty happy about it when I was talking about what I'd seen on TV, and naming all the presidents I could think of, but then he asked me something about some religion I'd never heard of that he said he belonged to, and when I said I'd never heard of it he almost broke down. I guess he was looking for a world like his own, and ours was, you know, close, but not close enough. He said something about what he called a "random walk principle"—if you go wandering around at random you keep coming back close to where you started, but you'll never have your feet in *exactly* the original place, they'll always be a little bit off to one side or the other.

So there are millions of these people out there drifting from world to world, looking for whatever they're looking for, sometimes millions of them identical to each other, too, and they run into each other. They know what to look for, see. So they trade information, and some of them tell me they're working on figuring out how to *really* navigate whatever it is they do, and they've figured out some of it already, so they can steer a little.

I wondered out loud why so many of them turn up at Harry's, and this woman with blue-grey skin—from some kind of medication, she told me—tried to explain it. West Virginia is one of the best places to travel between worlds, particularly up in the mountains around Sutton, because it's a pretty central location for eastern North America, but there isn't anything there. I mean, there aren't any big cities, or big military bases, or anything, so that if there's an atomic war or something—and apparently there have been a *lot* of atomic wars, or wars with even worse weapons, in different worlds—nobody's very likely to heave any missiles at Sutton, West Virginia. Even in the realities where the Europeans never found America and it's the Chinese or somebody building the cities, there just isn't any reason to build anything near Sutton. And there's something in particular that makes it an easy place to travel between worlds, too; I didn't follow the explanation. She said something about the Earth's magnetic field, but I didn't catch whether that was part of the explanation or just a comparison of some kind.

The mountains and forests make it easy to hide, too, which is why our area is better than out in the desert someplace.

Anyway, right around Sutton it's pretty safe and easy to travel between worlds, so lots of people do.

The strange thing, though, is that for some reason that nobody really seemed very clear on, Harry's, or something like it, is in just about the same place in millions of different realities. More than millions; infinities, really. It's not always exactly Harry's All-Night Hamburgers; one customer kept calling Harry Sal, for instance. It's *there*, though, or something like it, and one thing that doesn't seem to change much is that travelers can eat there without causing trouble. Word gets around that Harry's is a nice, quiet place, with decent burgers, where nobody's going to hassle them about anything, and they can pay in gold or silver if they haven't got the local money, or in trade goods or whatever they've got that Harry can use. It's easy to find, because it's in a lot of universes, relatively—as I said, this little area isn't one that varies a whole lot from universe to universe, unless you start moving long distances. Or maybe not *easy* to find, but it can be found. One guy told me that Harry's seems to be in more universes than Washington, D.C. He'd even seen one of my doubles before, last time he stopped in, and he thought he might have actually gotten back to the same place until I swore I'd never seen him before. He had these really funny eyes, so I was sure I'd have remembered him.

We never actually got repeat business from other worlds, y'know, not once, not ever; nobody could ever find the way back to exactly our world. What we got were people who had heard about Harry's from other people, in some other reality. Oh, maybe it wasn't exactly the same Harry's they'd heard about, but they'd heard that there was usually a good place to eat and swap stories in about that spot.

That's a weird thought, you know, that every time I served someone a burger a zillion of me were serving burgers to a zillion others—not all of them the same, either.

So they come to Harry's to eat, and they trade information with each other there, or in the parking lot, and they take a break from whatever they're doing.

They came there, and they talked to me about all those other universes, and I was seventeen years old, man. It was like those Navy recruiting ads on TV, see the world—except it was see the *worlds*, all of them, not just one. I listened to everything those guys said. I heard them talk about the worlds where zeppelins strafed Cincinnati in a Third World War, about places the dinosaurs never died out and mammals never evolved any higher than rats, about cities built of colored glass or dug miles underground, about worlds where all the men were dead, or all the women, or both, from biological warfare. Any story you ever heard, anything you ever read, those guys could top it. Worlds where speaking aloud could get you the death penalty—not what you said, just saying *anything* out loud. Worlds with spaceships fighting a war against Arcturus. Beautiful women, strange places, everything you could ever want, out there *somewhere*, but it might take forever to find it.

I listened to those stories for months. I graduated from high school, but there wasn't any way I could go to college, so I just stayed on with Harry—it paid enough to live on, anyway. I talked to those people from other worlds, even got inside some of their ships, or time machines, or whatever you want to call them, and I thought about how great it would be to just go roaming from world to world. Any time you don't like the way things are going, just pop! And the whole world is different! I could be a white god to the Indians in a world where the Europeans and Asians never reached America, I figured, or find a world where machines do all the work and people just relax and party.

When my eighteenth birthday came and went without any sign I'd ever get out of West Virginia, I began to really think about it, you know? I started asking customers about it. A lot of them told me not to be stupid; a lot just wouldn't talk about it. Some, though, some of them thought it was a great idea.

There was one guy, this one night—well, first, it was September, but it was still hot as the middle of summer, even in the middle of the night. Most of my friends were gone—they'd gone off to college, or gotten jobs somewhere, or gotten married, or maybe two out of the three. My dad was drinking a lot. The other kids were back in school. I'd started sleeping days, from eight in the morning until about four P.M., instead of evenings. Harry's air conditioner was busted, and I really wanted to just leave it all behind and go find myself a better world. So when I heard these two guys talking at one table about whether one of them had extra room in his machine, I sort of listened, when I could, when I wasn't fetching burgers and Cokes.

Now, one of these two I'd seen before—he'd been coming in every so often ever since I started working at Harry's. He looked like an ordinary guy, but he came in about three in the morning and talked to the weirdos like they were all old buddies, so I figured he had to be from some other world originally himself, even if he stayed put in ours now. He'd come in about every night for a week or two, then disappear for months, then start turning up again, and I had sort of wondered whether he might have licked the navigation problem all those other people had talked about. But then I figured, probably not, either he'd stopped jumping from one world to the next, or else it was just a bunch of parallel people coming in, and it probably wasn't ever the same guy at all, really. Usually, when that happened, we'd get two or three at a time, looking like identical twins or something, but there was only just one of this guy, every time, so I figured, like I said, either he hadn't been changing worlds at all, or he'd figured out how to navigate better than anyone else, or something.

The guy he was talking to was new; I'd never seen him before. He was big, maybe six-four and heavy. He'd come in shaking snow and soot off a plastic coverall of some kind, given me a big grin, and ordered two of Harry's biggest burgers, with everything. Five minutes later the regular customer sat down across the table from him, and now he was telling the regular that he had plenty of room in his ship for anything anyone might want him to haul cross-time.

I figured this was my chance, so when I brought the burgers I said something real polite, like, "Excuse me, sir, but I couldn't help overhearing; d'you think you'd have room for a passenger?"

The big guy laughed and said, "Sure, kid! I was just telling Joe here that I could haul him and all his freight, and there'd be room for you, too, if you make it worth my trouble!"

I said, "I've got money; I've been saving up. What'll it take?"

The big guy gave me a big grin again, but before he could say anything Joe interrupted.

"Sid," he said, "could you excuse me for a minute? I want to talk to this young fellow for a minute, before he makes a big mistake."

The big guy, Sid, said, "Sure, sure, I don't mind." So Joe got up, and he yelled to Harry, "Okay if I borrow your counterman for a few minutes?"

Harry yelled back that it was okay. I didn't know what the hell was going on, but I went along, and the two of us went out to this guy's car to talk.

And it really was a car, too—an old Ford van. It was customized, with velvet and bubble windows and stuff, and there was a lot of stuff piled in the back, camping gear and clothes and things, but no sign of machinery or anything. I still wasn't sure, you know, because some of these guys did a really good job of disguising their ships, or time machines, or whatever, but it sure *looked* like an ordinary van, and that's what Joe said it was. He got into the driver's seat, and I got into the passenger seat, and we swiveled around to face each other.

"So," he said. "Do you know who all these people are? I mean people like Sid?"

"Sure," I said. "They're from other dimensions, parallel worlds and like that."

He leaned back and looked at me hard, and said, "You know that, huh? Did you know that none of them can ever get home?"

"Yes, I knew that," I told him, acting pretty cocky.

"And you still want to go with Sid to other universes? Even when you know you'll never come home to this universe again?"

"That's right, Mister," I told him. "I'm sick of this one. I don't have anything here but a nothing job in a diner;

I want to *see* some of the stuff these people talk about, instead of just hearing about it."

"You want to see wonders and marvels, huh?"

"Yes!"

"You want to see buildings a hundred stories high? Cities of strange temples? Oceans thousands of miles wide? Mountains miles high? Prairies, and cities, and strange animals and stranger people?"

Well, that was just exactly what I wanted, better than I could have said it myself. "Yes," I said. "You got it, Mister."

"You lived here all your life?"

"You mean this world? Of course I have."

"No, I meant here in Sutton. You lived here all your life?"

"Well, yeah," I admitted. "Just about."

He sat forward and put his hands together, and his voice got intense, like he wanted to impress me with how serious he was. "Kid," he said, "I don't blame you a bit for wanting something different; I sure as hell wouldn't want to spend my entire life in these hills. But you're going about it the wrong way. You don't want to hitch with Sid."

"Oh, yeah?" I said. "Why not? Am I supposed to build my own machine? Hell, I can't even fix my mother's carburetor."

"No, that's not what I meant. But kid, you can see those buildings a thousand feet high in New York, or in Chicago. You've got oceans here in your own world as good as anything you'll find anywhere. You've got the mountains, and the seas, and the prairies, and all the rest of it. I've been in your world for eight years now, checking back here at Harry's every so often to see if anyone's figured out how to steer in no-space and get me home, and it's one hell of a big, interesting place."

"But," I said, "what about the spaceships, and . . ."

He interrupted me, and said, "You want to see spaceships? You go to Florida and watch a shuttle launch. Man, that's a spaceship. It may not go to other worlds, but that *is* a spaceship. You want strange animals? You go to Australia or Brazil. You want strange people? Go to New York or Los Angeles, or almost anywhere. You want a city carved out of a mountain top? It's called Machu Picchu, in Peru, I think. You want ancient, mysterious ruins? They're all over Greece and Italy and North Africa. Strange temples? Visit India; there are supposed to be over a thousand temples in Benares alone. See Angkor Wat, or the pyramids—not just the Egyptian ones, but the Mayan ones, too. And the great thing about all of these places, kid, is that afterwards, if you want to, you can come home. You don't *have* to, but you *can*. Who knows? You might get homesick some day. Most people do. *I* did. I wish to hell I'd seen more of my own world before I volunteered to try any others."

I kind of stared at him for a while. "I don't know," I said. I mean, it seemed so easy to just hop in Sid's machine and be gone forever, I thought, but New York was five hundred miles away—and then I realized how stupid that was.

"Hey," he said, "don't forget, if you decide I was wrong, you can always come back to Harry's and bum a ride with someone. It won't be Sid, he'll be gone forever, but you'll find someone. Most world-hoppers are lonely, kid; they've left behind everyone they ever knew. You won't have any trouble getting a lift."

Well, that decided it, because, you know, he was obviously right about that, as soon as I thought about it. I told him so.

"Well, good!" he said. "Now, you go pack your stuff and apologize to Harry and all that, and I'll give you a lift to Pittsburgh. You've got money to travel with from there, right? These idiots still haven't figured out how to steer, so I'm going back home—not my *real* home, but where I live in your world—and I wouldn't mind a passenger." And he smiled at me, and I smiled back, and we had to wait until the bank opened the next morning, but he didn't really mind. All the way to Pittsburgh he was singing these hymns and war-songs from his home world, where there was a second civil war in the nineteen-twenties because of some fundamentalist preacher trying to overthrow the Constitution and set up a church government; he hadn't had anyone he could sing them to in years, he said.

That was six years ago, and I haven't gone back to Harry's since.

So that was what got me started traveling. What brings *you* to Benares?

APPENDIX
THE HUGO AWARDS

1991: **Novel:** *The Vor Game* by Lois McMaster Bujold
Novella: "The Hemingway Hoax" by Joe Haldeman
Novelette: "The Manamouki" by Mike Resnick
Short Story: "Bears Discover Fire" by Terry Bisson
Non-Fiction Book: *How to Write Science Fiction & Fantasy* by Orson Scott Card
Dramatic Presentation: *Edward Scissorhands*
Professional Editor: Gardner Dozois
Professional Artist: Michael Whelan
Semi-prozine: *Locus* (Charles N. Brown, ed.)
Fanzine: *Lan's Lantern* (George Laskowski, ed.)
Fan Writer: Dave Langford
Fan Artist: Teddy Harvia
Campbell Award: Julia Ecklar
Special Award: Andrew Porter for *Science Fiction Chronicle*

1990: **Novel:** *Hyperion*, by Dan Simmons
Novella: "The Mountains of Mourning" by Lois McMaster Bujold
Novelette: "Enter a Soldier. Later: Enter Another" by Robert Silverberg
Short Story: "Lost Boys" by Orson Scott Card
Non-Fiction Book: *The World Beyond the Hill* by Alexei and Cory Panshin
Dramatic Presentation: *Indiana Jones and the Last Crusade*
Professional Editor: Gardner Dozois
Professional Artist: Don Maitz
Semi-prozine: *Locus* (Charles N. Brown, ed.)
Fanzine: *The Mad 3 Party* (Leslie Turek, ed.)
Fan Writer: Dave Langford
Fan Artist: Stu Shiffman
Campbell Award: Kristine Kathryn Rusch

1989: **Novel:** *Cyteen*, by C. J. Cherryh
Novella: "The Last of the Winnebagos" by Connie Willis

Novelette: "Schrödinger's Kitten" by George Alec Effinger
Short Story: "Kirinyaga" by Mike Resnick
Non-Fiction Book: *The Motion of Light in Water* by Samuel R. Delany
Dramatic Presentation: *Who Framed Roger Rabbit?*
Professional Editor: Gardner Dozois
Professional Artist: Michael Whelan
Semi-prozine: *Locus* (Charles N. Brown, ed.)
Fanzine: *File 770* (Mike Glyer, ed.)
Fan Writer: David Langford
Fan Artist: Brad Foster, Diana Gallagher Wu (tie)
Campbell Award: Michaela Roessner

1988: **Novel:** *The Uplift War* by David Brin
Novella: "Eye for Eye" by Orson Scott Card
Novelette: "Buffalo Gals, Won't You Come Out Tonight" by Ursula K. Le Guin
Short Story: "Why I Left Harry's All-Night Hamburgers" by Lawrence Watt-Evans
Non-Fiction Book: *Michael Whelan's Works of Wonder* by Michael Whelan
Dramatic Presentation: *The Princess Bride*
Professional Editor: Gardner Dozois
Professional Artist: Michael Whelan
Semi-prozine: *Locus* (Charles N. Brown, ed.)
Fanzine: *Texas SF Inquirer* (Pat Mueller, ed.)
Fan Writer: Mike Glyer
Fan Artist: Brad Foster
Campbell Award: Judith Moffett

1987: **Novel:** *Speaker for the Dead* by Orson Scott Card
Novella: "Gilgamesh in the Outback" by Robert Silverberg
Novelette: "Permafrost" by Roger Zelazny
Short Story: "Tangents" by Greg Bear
Non-Fiction Book: *Trillion Year Spree* by Brian Aldiss with David Wingrove
Dramatic Presentation: *Aliens*
Professional Editor: Terry Carr
Professional Artist: Jim Burns
Semi-prozine: *Locus* (Charles N. Brown, ed.)
Fanzine: *Ansible* (Dave Langford, ed.)
Fan Writer: Dave Langford

Fan Artist: Brad Foster
Campbell Award: Karen Joy Fowler

1986: **Novel:** *Ender's Game* by Orson Scott Card
Novella: "24 Views of Mount Fuji, by Hokusai" by Roger Zelazny
Novelette: "Paladin of the Lost Hour" by Harlan Ellison
Short Story: "Fermi and Frost" by Frederik Pohl
Non-Fiction Book: *Science Made Stupid* by Tom Weller
Dramatic Presentation: *Back to the Future*
Professional Editor: Judy-Lynn del Rey
Professional Artist: Michael Whelan
Semi-prozine: *Locus* (Charles N. Brown, ed.)
Fanzine: *Lan's Lantern* (George Laskowski, ed.)
Fan Writer: Mike Glyer
Fan Artist: joan hanke-woods
Campbell Award: Melissa Scott

1985: **Novel:** *Neuromancer* by William Gibson
Novella: "Press Enter ■" by John Varley
Novelette: "Bloodchild" by Octavia Butler
Short Story: "The Crystal Spheres" by David Brin
Non-Fiction Book: *Wonder's Child: My Life in Science Fiction* by Jack Williamson
Dramatic Presentation: *2010*
Professional Editor: Terry Carr
Professional Artist: Michael Whelan
Semi-prozine: *Locus* (Charles N. Brown, ed.)
Fanzine: *File 770* (Mike Glyer, ed.)
Fan Writer: Dave Langford
Fan Artist: Alexis Gilliland
Campbell Award: Lucius Shepard

1984: **Novel:** *Startide Rising* by David Brin
Novella: "Cascade Point" by Timothy Zahn
Novelette: "Blood Music" by Greg Bear
Short Story: "Speech Sounds" by Octavia Butler
Non-Fiction Book: *Encyclopedia of Science Fiction and Fantasy*, vol. III, by Donald Tuck
Dramatic Presentation: *Return of the Jedi*
Professional Editor: Shawna McCarthy
Professional Artist: Michael Whelan

Semi-prozine: *Locus* (Charles N. Brown, ed.)
Fanzine: *File 770* (Mike Glyer, ed.)
Fan Writer: Mike Glyer
Fan Artist: Alexis Gilliland
Campbell Award: R. A. MacAvoy

1983: **Novel:** *Foundation's Edge* by Isaac Asimov
Novella: "Souls" by Joanna Russ
Novelette: "Fire Watch" by Connie Willis
Short Story: "Melancholy Elephants" by Spider Robinson
Non-Fiction Book: *Isaac Asimov: The Foundations of Science Fiction* by James Gunn
Dramatic Presentation: *Blade Runner*
Professional Editor: Edward L. Ferman
Professional Artist: Michael Whelan
Fanzine: *Locus* (Charles N. Brown, ed.)
Fan Writer: Richard E. Geis
Fan Artist: Alexis Gilliland
Campbell Award: Paul O. Williams

1982: **Novel:** *Downbelow Station* by C. J. Cherryh
Novella: "The Saturn Game" by Poul Anderson
Novelette: "Unicorn Variation" by Roger Zelazny
Short Story: "The Pusher" by John Varley
Non-Fiction Book: *Danse Macabre* by Stephen King
Dramatic Presentation: *Raiders of the Lost Ark*
Professional Editor: Edward L. Ferman
Professional Artist: Michael Whelan
Fanzine: *Locus* (Charles N. Brown, ed.)
Fan Writer: Richard E. Geis
Fan Artist: Victoria Poyser
Campbell Award: Alexis Gilliland

1981: **Novel:** *The Snow Queen* by Joan D. Vinge
Novella: "Lost Dorsai" by Gordon R. Dickson
Novelette: "The Cloak and the Staff" by Gordon R. Dickson
Short Story: "Grotto of the Dancing Deer" by Clifford D. Simak
Non-Fiction Book: *Cosmos* by Carl Sagan
Dramatic Presentation: *The Empire Strikes Back*
Professional Editor: Edward L. Ferman
Professional Artist: Michael Whelan

Fanzine: *Locus* (Charles N. Brown, ed.)
Fan Writer: Susan Wood
Fan Artist: Victoria Poyser
Campbell Award: Somtow Sucharitkul

1980: **Novel:** *The Fountains of Paradise* by Arthur C. Clarke
Novella: "Enemy Mine" by Barry B. Longyear
Novelette: "Sandkings" by George R. R. Martin
Short Story: "The Way of Cross and Dragon" by
George R. R. Martin
Non-Fiction Book: *The Science Fiction Encyclopedia*
(Peter Nicholls, ed.)
Dramatic Presentation: *Alien*
Professional Editor: George H. Scithers
Professional Artist: Michael Whelan
Fanzine: *Locus* (Charles N. Brown, ed.)
Fan Writer: Bob Shaw
Fan Artist: Alexis Gilliland
Campbell Award: Barry B. Longyear
Gandalf Award (Grand Master): Ray Bradbury

1979: **Novel:** *Dreamsnake* by Vonda McIntyre
Novella: "The Persistence of Vision" by John Varley
Novelette: "Hunter's Moon" by Poul Anderson
Short Story: "Cassandra" by C. J. Cherryh
Dramatic Presentation: *Superman*
Professional Editor: Ben Bova
Professional Artist: Vincent DiFate
Fanzine: *Science Fiction Review* (Richard E. Geis, ed.)
Fan Writer: Bob Shaw
Fan Artist: Bill Rotsler
Campbell Award: Stephen R. Donaldson
Gandalf Award (Grand Master): Ursula K. Le Guin
Gandalf Award (Book-Length Fantasy): *The White Dragon*
by Anne McCaffrey

1978: **Novel:** *Gateway* by Frederik Pohl
Novella: "Stardance" by Spider and Jeanne Robinson
Novelette: "Eyes of Amber" by Joan D. Vinge
Short Story: "Jeffty Is Five" by Harlan Ellison
Dramatic Presentation: *Star Wars*
Professional Editor: George H. Scithers
Professional Artist: Rick Sternbach

Amateur Magazine: *Locus* (Charles and Dena Brown, eds.)
Fan Writer: Richard E. Geis
Fan Artist: Phil Foglio
Campbell Award: Orson Scott Card
Gandalf Award (Grand Master): Poul Anderson
Gandalf Award (Book-Length Fantasy): *The Silmarillion* by J. R. R. Tolkein

1977: **Novel:** *Where Late the Sweet Birds Sang* by Kate Wilhelm
Novella: "By Any Other Name" by Spider Robinson, and
   "Houston, Houston, Do You Read?" by James Tiptree, Jr. (tie)
Novelette: "The Bicentennial Man" by Isaac Asimov
Short Story: "Tricentennial" by Joe Haldeman
Dramatic Presentation: (No Award)
Professional Editor: Ben Bova
Professional Artist: Rick Sternbach
Amateur Magazine: *Science Fiction Review* (Richard E. Geis, ed.)
Fan Writer: Susan Wood and
   Richard E. Geis (tie)
Fan Artist: Phil Foglio
Campbell Award: C. J. Cherryh
Special Award: George Lucas for *Star Wars*
Gandalf Award (Grand Master): Andre Norton

1976: **Novel:** *The Forever War* by Joe Haldeman
Novella: "Home is the Hangman" by Roger Zelazny
Novelette: "The Borderland of Sol" by Larry Niven
Short Story: "Catch That Zeppelin!" by Fritz Leiber
Dramatic Presentation: *A Boy and His Dog*
Professional Editor: Ben Bova
Professional Artist: Frank Kelly Freas
Fanzine: *Locus* (Charles and Dena Brown, eds.)
Fan Writer: Richard E. Geis
Fan Artist: Tim Kirk
Campbell Award: Tom Reamy

1975: **Novel:** *The Dispossessed* by Ursula K. Le Guin
Novella: "A Song for Lya" by George R. R. Martin

Novelette: "Adrift Just Off the Islets of Langerhans" by Harlan Ellison
Short Story: "The Hole Man" by Larry Niven
Dramatic Presentation: *Young Frankenstein*
Professional Editor: Ben Bova
Professional Artist: Frank Kelly Freas
Amateur Magazine: *The Alien Critic* (Richard E. Geis, ed.)
Fan Writer: Richard E. Geis
Fan Artist: Bill Rotsler
Campbell Award: P. J. Plauger
Gandalf Award (Grand Master): Fritz Leiber

1974: Novel: *Rendezvous with Rama* by Arthur C. Clarke
Novella: "The Girl Who Was Plugged In" by James Tiptree, Jr.
Novelette: "The Deathbird" by Harlan Ellison
Short Story: "The Ones Who Walk Away from Omelas" by Ursula K. Le Guin
Dramatic Presentation: *Sleeper*
Professional Editor: Ben Bova
Professional Artist: Frank Kelly Freas
Amateur Magazine: *Algol* (Andy Porter, ed.) and *The Alien Critic* (Richard E. Geis, ed.) (tie)
Fan Writer: Susan Wood
Fan Artist: Tim Kirk
Campbell Award: Spider Robinson and Lisa Tuttle (tie)
Gandalf Award (Grand Master): J. R. R. Tolkein

1973: Novel: *The Gods Themselves* by Isaac Asimov
Novella: "The Word for World is Forest" by Ursula K. Le Guin
Novelette: "Goat Song" by Poul Anderson
Short Story: "Eurema's Dam" by R. A. Lafferty and "The Meeting" by Frederik Pohl and C. M. Kornbluth (tie)
Dramatic Presentation: *Slaughterhouse-Five*
Professional Editor: Ben Bova
Professional Artist: Frank Kelly Freas
Amateur Magazine: *Energumen* (Mike Glicksohn and Susan Wood Glicksohn, eds.)
Fan Writer: Terry Carr

Fan Artist: Tim Kirk
Campbell Award: Jerry Pournelle

1972: **Novel:** *To Your Scattered Bodies Go* by Philip José Farmer
Novella: "The Queen of Air and Darkness" by Poul Anderson
Short Story: "Inconstant Moon" by Larry Niven
Dramatic Presentation: *A Clockwork Orange*
Professional Magazine: *Fantasy and Science Fiction*
Professional Artist: Frank Kelly Freas
Amateur Magazine: *Locus* (Charles and Dena Brown, eds.)
Fan Writer: Harry Warner, Jr.
Fan Artist: Tim Kirk

1971: **Novel:** *Ringworld* by Larry Niven
Novella: "Ill Met in Lankhmar" by Fritz Leiber
Short Story: "Slow Sculpture" by Theodore Sturgeon
Dramatic Presentation: (No award)
Professional Magazine: *Fantasy and Science Fiction*
Professional Artist: Leo and Diane Dillon
Fanzine: *Locus* (Charles and Dena Brown, eds.)
Fan Writer: Richard E. Geis
Fan Artist: Alicia Austin

1970: **Novel:** *The Left Hand of Darkness* by Ursula K. Le Guin
Novella: "Ship of Shadows" by Fritz Leiber
Short Story: "Time Considered as a Helix of Semi-Precious Stones" by Samuel R. Delany
Dramatic Presentation: News coverage of Apollo XI
Professional Magazine: *Fantasy and Science Fiction*
Professional Artist: Frank Kelly Freas
Fanzine: *Science Fiction Review* (Richard E. Geis, ed.)
Fan Writer: Bob Tucker
Fan Artist: Tim Kirk

1969: **Novel:** *Stand on Zanzibar* by John Brunner
Novella: "Nightwings" by Robert Silverberg
Novelette: "The Sharing of Flesh" by Poul Anderson
Short Story: "The Beast That Shouted Love at the Heart of the World" by Harlan Ellison
Dramatic Presentation: *2001: A Space Odyssey*

Professional Magazine: *Fantasy and Science Fiction*
Professional Artist: Jack Gaughan
Fanzine: *Science Fiction Review* (Richard E. Geis, ed.)
Fan Writer: Harry Warner, Jr.
Fan Artist: George Barr

1968: **Novel:** *Lord of Light* by Roger Zelazny
    Novella: "Weyr Search" by Anne McCaffrey and
        "Riders of the Purple Wage" by Phillip José Farmer
    (tie)
    Novelette: "Gonna Roll Them Bones" by Fritz Leiber
    Short Story: "I Have No Mouth, and I Must Scream"
    by Harlan Ellison
    Dramatic Presentation: "City on the Edge of Forever"
    (Star Trek)
    Professional Magazine: *If*
    Professional Artist: Jack Gaughan
    Fanzine: *Amra* (George Scithers, ed.)
    Fan Writer: Ted White
    Fan Artist: George Barr

1967: **Novel:** *The Moon is a Harsh Mistress* by Robert A.
    Heinlein
    Novelette: "The Last Castle" by Jack Vance
    Short Story: "Neutron Star" by Larry Niven
    Dramatic Presentation: "The Menagerie" *(Star Trek)*
    Professional Magazine: *If*
    Professional Artist: Jack Gaughan
    Fanzine: *Niekas* (Ed Meskys and Felice Rolfe, eds.)
    Fan Writer: Alexei Panshin
    Fan Artist: Jack Gaughan

1966: **Novel:** . . . *And Call Me Conrad* by Roger Zelazny and
        Dune by Frank Herbert (tie)
    Short Fiction: " 'Repent, Harlequin!' Said the Ticktock-
    man" by Harlan Ellison
    Professional Magazine: *If*
    Professional Artist: Frank Frazetta
    Amateur Magazine: *ERB-dom* (Camille Cazedessus,
    Jr., ed.)
    Best All-Time Series: the "Foundation" series by Isaac
    Asimov

1965: **Novel:** *The Wanderer* by Fritz Leiber
Short Story: "Soldier, Ask Not" by Gordon R. Dickson
Special Drama: *Dr. Strangelove*
Magazine: *Analog*
Artist: John Schoenherr
Publisher: Ballantine
Fanzine: *Yandro* (Robert and Juanita Coulson, eds.)

1964: **Novel:** *Way Station* by Clifford D. Simak
Short Fiction: "No Truce with Kings" by Poul Anderson
Professional Magazine: *Analog*
Professional Artist: Ed Emshwiller
SF Book Publisher: Ace Books
Amateur Magazine: *Amra* (George Scithers, ed.)

1963: **Novel:** *The Man in the High Castle* by Philip K. Dick
Short Fiction: "The Dragon Masters" by Jack Vance
Dramatic Presentation: (No Award)
Professional Magazine: *Fantasy & Science Fiction*
Professional Artist: Roy G. Krenkel
Amateur Magazine: *Xero* (Richard and Pat Lupoff, eds.)

1962: **Novel:** *Stranger in a Strange Land* by Robert A. Heinlein
Short Fiction: the "Hothouse" series by Brian W. Aldiss
Dramatic Presentation: *The Twilight Zone*
Professional Magazine: *Analog*
Professional Artist: Ed Emshwiller
Fanzine: *Warhoon* (Richard Bergeron, ed.)

1961: **Novel:** *A Canticle for Leibowitz* by Walter M. Miller, Jr.
Short Fiction: "The Longest Voyage" by Poul Anderson
Dramatic Presentation: *The Twilight Zone*
Professional Magazine: *Astounding/Analog*
Professional Artist: Ed Emshwiller
Fanzine: *Who Killed Science Fiction?* (Earl Kemp, ed.)

1960: **Novel:** *Starship Troopers* by Robert A. Heinlein
Short Fiction: "Flowers for Algernon" by Daniel Keyes
Dramatic Presentation: *The Twilight Zone*

Professional Magazine: *Fantasy & Science Fiction*
Professional Artist: Ed Emshwiller
Fanzine: *Cry of the Nameless* (F. M. and Elinor Busby, Burnett Toskey, and Wally Weber, eds.)

1959: **Novel:** *A Case of Conscience* by James Blish
Novelette: "The Big Front Yard" by Clifford D. Simak
Short Story: "That Hell-Bound Train" by Robert Bloch
SF or Fantasy Movie: (No Award)
Professional Magazine: *Fantasy & Science Fiction*
Professional Artist: Frank Kelly Freas
Amateur Magazine: *Fanac* (Ron Ellik and Terry Carr, eds.)
New Author of 1958: (No Award, but Brian W. Aldiss received a plaque as runner-up)

1958: **Novel or Novelette:** *The Big Time* by Fritz Leiber
Short Story: "Or All the Seas With Oysters" by Avram Davidson
Outstanding Movie: *The Incredible Shrinking Man*
Magazine: *Fantasy & Science Fiction*
Outstanding Artist: Frank Kelly Freas
Outstanding Actifan: Walter A. Willis

1957: **American Professional Magazine:** *Astounding*
British Professional Magazine: *New Worlds*
Fan Magazine: *Science-Fiction Times* (James V. Taurasi, Sr., Ray Van Houten, and Frank Prieto, eds.)

1956: **Novel:** *Double Star* by Robert A. Heinlein
Novelette: "Exploration Team" by Murray Leinster
Short Story: "The Star" by Arthur C. Clarke
Feature Writer: Willy Ley
Magazine: *Astounding*
Artist: Frank Kelly Freas
Fan Magazine: *Inside & Science Fiction Advertiser* (Ron Smith ed.)
Most Promising New Author: Robert Silverberg
Book Reviewer: Damon Knight

1955: **Novel:** *They'd Rather Be Right* by Mark Clifton and Frank Riley
Novelette: "The Darfsteller" by Walter M. Miller, Jr.

Short Story: "Allamagoosa" by Eric Frank Russell
Magazine: *Astounding*
Artist: Frank Kelly Freas
Fan Magazine: *Fantasy Times* (James V. Taurasi, Sr.
and Ray Van Houten, eds.)

1954: (No awards given)

1953: **Novel:** *The Demolished Man* by Alfred Bester
Professional Magazine: *Galaxy* and
   Astounding (tie)
Excellence in Fact Articles: Willy Ley
Cover Artist: Ed Emshwiller and Hannes Bok (tie)
Interior Illustrator: Virgil Finlay
New SF Author or Artist: Philip José Farmer
Number 1 Fan Personality: Forrest J Ackerman

An excerpt from MAN-KZIN WARS II, created by *Larry Niven*:

The Children's Hour

Chuut-Riit always enjoyed visiting the quarters of his male offspring.

"What will it be this time?" he wondered, as he passed the outer guards.

The household troopers drew claws before their eyes in salute, faceless in impact-armor and goggled helmets, the beam-rifles ready in their hands. He paced past the surveillance cameras, the detector pods, the death-casters and the mines; then past the inner guards at their consoles, humans raised in the household under the supervision of his personal retainers.

The retainers were males grown old in the Riit family's service. There had always been those willing to exchange the uncertain rewards of competition for a secure place, maintenance, and the odd female. Ordinary kzin were not to be trusted in so sensitive a position, of course, but these were families which had served the Riit clan for generation after generation. There was a natural culling effect; those too ambitious left for the Patriarchy's military and the slim chance of advancement, those too timid were not given opportunity to breed.

Perhaps a pity that such cannot be used outside the household, Chuut-Riit thought. Competition for rank was far too intense and personal for that, of course.

He walked past the modern sections, and into an area that was pure Old Kzin; maze-walls of reddish sandstone with twisted spines of wrought-iron on their tops, the tips glistening razor-edged. Fortress-architecture from a world older than this, more massive, colder and drier; from a planet harsh enough that a plains carnivore had changed its ways, put to different use an upright posture designed to place its head above savanna grass, grasping paws evolved to climb rock. Here the modern features were reclusive, hidden in wall and buttress. The door was a hammered slab graven with the faces of night-hunting beasts, between towers five times the height of a kzin. The air smelled of wet rock and the raked sand of the gardens.

Chuut-Riit put his hand on the black metal of the outer portal, stopped. His ears pivoted, and he blinked; out of the corner of his eye he saw a pair of tufted eyebrows glancing through the thick twisted metal on the rim of the ten-meter battlement. *Why, the little sthondats,* he thought affectionately. *They managed to put it together out of reach of the holo pickups.*

The adult put his hand to the door again, keying the locking sequence, then bounded backward four times his own length from a standing start. Even under the lighter gravity of Wunderland, it was a creditable feat. And necessary, for the massive panels rang and toppled as the rope-swung boulder slammed forward. The children had hung two cables from either tower, with the rock at the point of the V and a third rope to draw it back. As the doors bounced wide he saw the blade they had driven into the apex of the egg-shaped granite rock, long and barbed and polished to a wicked point.

Kittens, he thought. *Always going for the dramatic.* If that thing had struck him, or the doors under its impetus had, there would have been no need of a blade. *Watching too many historical adventure holos. "Errorowwww!"* he shrieked in mock-rage bounding through the shattered portal and into the interior court, halting atop the kzin-high boulder. A round dozen of his older sons were grouped behind the rock, standing in a defensive clump and glaring at him, the crackly scent of their excitement and fear made the fur bristle along his spine. He glared until they dropped their eyes, continued it until they went down on their stomachs, rubbed their chins along the ground and then rolled over for a symbolic exposure of the stomach.

"Congratulations," he said. "That was the closest you've gotten. Who was in charge?"

More guilty sidelong glances among the adolescent males crouching among their discarded pull-rope, and then a lanky youngster with platter-sized feet and hands came squatting-erect. His fur was in the proper flat posture, but the naked pink of his tail still twitched stiffly.

"I was," he said keeping his eyes formally down. "Honored Sire Chuut-Riit," he added, at the adult's warning rumble.

"Now, youngling, What did you learn from your first attempt?"

"That no one among us is your match, Honored Sire Chuut-Riit," the kitten said. Uneasy ripples went over the black-striped orange of his pelt.

"And what have you learned from this attempt?"

"That all of us together are no match for you, Honored Sire Chuut-Riit," the striped youth said.

"That we didn't locate all of the cameras," another muttered. "You idiot, Spotty." That to one of his siblings; they snarled at each other from their crouches, hissing past barred fangs and making striking motions with unsheathed claws.

"No, you did locate them all, cubs," Chuut-Riit said. "I presume you stole the ropes and tools from the workshop, prepared the boulder in the ravine in the next courtyard, then rushed to set it all up between the time I cleared the last gatehouse and my arrival?"

Uneasy nods. He held his ears and tail stiffly, letting his whiskers quiver slightly and holding in the rush of love and pride he felt, more delicious than milk heated with bourbon. *Look at them!* he thought. At the age when most young kzin were helpless prisoners of instinct and hormone, wasting their strength ripping each other up or making fruitless direct attacks on their sires, or demanding to be allowed to join the Patriarchy's service *at once* to win a Name and household of their own . . . *His* get had learned to *cooperate* and use their minds!

"Ah, Honored Sire Chuut-Riit, we set the ropes up beforehand, but made it look as if we were using them for tumbling practice," the one the others called Spotty said. Some of them glared at him, and the adult raised his hand again.

"No, no, I am *moderately* pleased." A pause. "You did not hope to take over my official position if you had disposed of me?"

"No, Honored Sire Chuut-Riit," the tall leader said. There had been a time when any kzin's holdings were the prize of the victor in a duel, and the dueling rules were interpreted more leniently for a young subadult. Everyone had a sentimental streak for a successful youngster; every male kzin remembered the intolerable stress of being physically mature but remaining under dominance as a child.

Still, these days affairs were handled in a more civilized manner. Only the Patriarchy could award military and political office. And this mass assassination attempt was . . . unorthodox, to say the least. Outside the rules more because of its rarity than because of formal disapproval. . . .

A vigorous toss of the head. "Oh, no, Honored Sire Chuut-Riit. We had an agreement to divide the private possessions. The lands and the, ah, females." Passing their own mothers to half-siblings, of course. "Then we wouldn't each have so much we'd get too many challenges, and we'd agreed to help each other against outsiders," the leader of the plot finished virtuously.

"Fatuous young scoundrels," Chuut-Riit said. His eyes narrowed dangerously. "You haven't been communicating outside the household, have you?" he snarled.

"Oh, *no*, Honored Sire Chuut-Riit!"

"Word of honor! May we die nameless if we should do such a thing!"

The adult nodded, satisfied that good family feeling had prevailed. "Well as I said, I am somewhat pleased. If you have been keeping up with your lessons. Is there anything you wish?"

"Fresh meat, Honored Sire Chuut-Riit," the spotted one said. The adult could have told him by the scent, of course, a kzin never forgot another's personal odor, that was one reason why names were less necessary among their species. "The reconstituted stuff from the dispensers is always . . . so . . . *quiet*."

Chuut-Riit hid his amusement. Young Heroes-to-be were always kept on an inadequate diet, to increase their aggressiveness. A matter for careful gauging, since too much hunger would drive them into mindless cannibalistic frenzy.

"And couldn't we have the human servants back? They were nice." Vigorous gestures of assent. Another added: "They told good stories. I miss my Clothilda-human."

"Silence!" Chuut-Riit roared. The youngsters flattened stomach and chin to the ground again. "Not until you can be trusted not to injure them; how many times do I have to tell you, it's dishonorable to attack household servants! Until you learn self-control, you will have to make do with machines."

This time all of them turned and glared at a mottled youngster in the rear of their group; there were half-healed scars over his head and shoulders. "It bared its *teeth* at me," he said sulkily. "All I did was swipe at it, how was I supposed to know it would die?" A chorus of rumbles, and this time several of the covert kicks and clawstrikes landed.

"Enough," Chuut-Riit said after a moment. *Good, they have even learned how to discipline each other as a unit.* "I will consider it, when all of you can pass a test on the interpretation of human expressions and body-language." He drew himself up. "In the meantime, within the next two eight-days, there will be a formal hunt and meeting in the Patriarch's Preserve; kzinti homeworld game, the best Earth animals, and even some feral-human outlaws, perhaps!"

He could smell their excitement increase, a mane-crinkling musky odor not unmixed with the sour whiff of fear. Such a hunt was not without danger for adolescents, being a good opportunity for hostile adults to cull a few of a hated rival's offspring with no possibility of blame. *They will be in less danger than most,* Chuut-Riit thought judiciously. *In fact, they may run across a few of my subordinates' get and mob them. Good.*

"And if we do well, afterwards a feast and a visit to the Sterile Ones." That had them all quiveringly alert, their tails held rigid and tongues lolling; nonbearing females were kept as a rare privilege for Heroes whose accomplishments were not *quite* deserving of a mate of their own. Very rare for kits still in the household to be granted such, but Chuut-Riit thought it past time to admit that modern society demanded a prolonged adolescence. The day when a male kit could be given a spear, a knife, a rope and a bag of salt and kicked out the front gate at puberty were long gone. Those were the wild, wandering years in the old days, when survival challenges used up the superabundant energies. Now they must be spent learning history, technology, xenology, none of which burned off the gland-juices saturating flesh and brain.

He jumped down amid his sons, and they pressed around him, purring throatily with adoration and fear and respect;

his presence and the failure of their plot had reestablished his personal dominance unambiguously, and there was no danger from them for now. Chuut-Riit basked in their worship, feeling the rough caress of their tongues on his fur and scratching behind his ears. *Together*, he thought. *Together we will do wonders.*

From "The Children's Hour" by Jerry Pournelle & S.M. Stirling

_____

A SIMPLE SEER

In a display he had never before witnessed, the Stone threw off rays of red and purple light, erupting like gobbets of liquid rock and sparks from the vent of a volcano. Amnet felt the heat against his face. At the focus of the rays was something bright and golden, like a ladle of molten metal held up to him. Without moving, he felt himself pitching forward, drawn down by a pull that was separate from gravity, separate from distance, space, and time. The heat grew more intense. The light more blinding. The angle of his upper body slid from the perpendicular. He was burning. He was falling. . . .

Amnet shook himself.

The Stone, still nestled in the sand, was an inch from his face. Its surface was dark and opaque. The fire among the twigs had burned out. The alembic was clear of smoke, with a puddle of blackened gum at its bottom.

Amnet shook himself again.

What did a vision of the end of the world portend?

And what could a simple aromancer do about it?

HOW TO IMPROVE SCIENCE FICTION

Want to improve SF? Want to make sure you always have a good selection of SF to choose from? Then do the thing that has made SF great from the very beginning—talk about SF. Communicate with those who make it happen. Tell your bookstore when you like a book. If you can't find something you want, let the manager know. But money speaks louder than mere words—so *order* the book from the bookstore, special. Tell your friends about good books. Encourage *them* to special order the good ones. A special order is worth a thousand words. If you can prove to your bookstore that there's a market for what you like, they'll probably start to cater to it. And that means better SF in your neighborhood.

Tell 'Em What You Want

We, the publishers, want to know what you want more of—and if you can't get it. But the people who order the books—they need to know first. So, before you buy a book directly from the publisher, talk to your bookstore; don't be shy. It doesn't matter if it's a chain bookstore or a specialty shop, or something in between—all businesses need to know what their customers like. Tell them: and the state of SF in your community is sure to improve.

And Get a Free Poster!

To encourage your feedback: A free poster to the first 100 readers who send us a list of their 5 best SF reads in the last year, and their 5 worst.

Write to: Baen Books, Dept. FP, P.O. Box 1403, Riverdale, NY 10471. And thanks!

Name:_____

Address:_____

Best Reads	Worst Reads
1)	1)
2)	2)
3)	3)
4)	4)
5)	5)